大学英语水平测试系列 **710分**

大学英语六级水平测试试题集

（710分版）

College English Practice Tests (Band 6)

编者 张雪波 黄 莺
毛伟芬

上海外语教育出版社
外教社 SHANGHAI FOREIGN LANGUAGE EDUCATION PRESS

图书在版编目(CIP)数据

大学英语六级水平测试试题集(710分版)/张雪波,黄莺,毛伟芬编.
—上海：上海外语教育出版社，2008
(大学英语水平测试系列 710 分)
ISBN 978-7-5446-1024-7

Ⅰ.大…　Ⅱ.①张…②黄…③毛…　Ⅲ.英语—高等学校—水平
考试—习题 Ⅳ.H319.6

中国版本图书馆 CIP 数据核字(2008)第 128769 号

出版发行：**上海外语教育出版社**
　　　　　　(上海外国语大学内)　邮编：**200083**
电　　话：021-65425300 (总机)
电子邮箱：bookinfo@sflep.com.cn
网　　址：http://www.sflep.com.cn　http://www.sflep.com
责任编辑：曹　娟

印　　刷：上海长阳印刷厂
经　　销：新华书店上海发行所
开　　本：787×1092　1/16　印张 19.25　字数 465 千字
版　　次：2008 年 12 月第 1 版　2008 年 12 月第 1 次印刷
印　　数：5 000 册

书　　号：ISBN 978-7-5446-1024-7 / G · 0489
定　　价：39.00 元

本版图书如有印装质量问题，可向本社调换

前　言

　　本书共收大学英语六级水平测试练习题十套,试题后附答案及简要的提示或解释,包括词汇结构释义、写作范文、篇章结构的理解和语篇深层含义的分析,另附听力部分的录音文字材料。

　　为使试题集适合文、理、工各类院校的学生使用,我们根据《大学英语课程教学要求(试行)》(2004 年)以及《全国大学英语四、六级考试改革方案(试行)》的要求编写了这套试题集。在结构和体例上,完全参照全国大学英语四、六级考试委员会发布的满分为 710分的六极样卷,测试题的题型、题目数、计分方法和考试时间均与六级考试相同,在难度和内容上,和样卷相当,主要考核学生运用语言的能力,同时也考核学生对词语用法和语法结构的掌握程度。测试题的材料大多摘选自国内外权威的各种图书、报刊、词典,选材广泛、新颖。学生在考前熟悉试题形式,进行及时、有效的复习,对考试成绩的提高一定会有促进作用。这是我们修订本书的基本出发点。

　　根据《全国大学英语四、六级考试改革方案(试行)》的要求,六级考试加大了听力理解部分的题量和比例,增加快速阅读理解测试,提高非选择性试题的比例。听力理解部分的比例提高到 35%,其中听力对话占 15%,听力短文占 20%。听力对话部分包括短对话和长对话的听力理解;听力短文部分包括短文听写和选择题型的短文理解。阅读理解部分比例调整为 35%,其中深入阅读部分占 25%,快速阅读部分占 10%。深入阅读部分除测试篇章阅读理解外,还包括对篇章语境中的词汇理解的测试;快速阅读部分测试各种快速阅读技能。综合测试比例为 15%,由两部分构成。第一部分为改错,占 10%;第二部分为翻译,占 5%。写作能力测试部分比例为 15%,体裁一般为议论文。除了作为大学英语六级考试的必备测试题外,本书同样适用于 TOEFL, GRE, GMAT 及硕士和博士研究生(包括在职人员)学位考试等各类高级英语水平考试者使用。

　　本试题集的编审工作得到了复旦大学大学英语部余建中教授的大力支持和帮助,余教授为本书的编写提出了合理化的建议,并担任了本书的顾问。在此,谨向余教授表示衷心的感谢。曾在复旦大学大学英语部任教的英国语言专家 Bill Marcus 和美国语言专家 Ken Nealy 担任了本试题集的审阅工作,在此表示衷心的感谢。

编　者

2008 年 2 月于复旦大学

CONTENTS

Part One   Practice Tests 1

PRACTICE TEST 1 3

PRACTICE TEST 2 23

PRACTICE TEST 3 41

PRACTICE TEST 4 59

PRACTICE TEST 5 77

PRACTICE TEST 6 95

PRACTICE TEST 7 113

PRACTICE TEST 8 131

PRACTICE TEST 9 149

PRACTICE TEST 10 167

Part Two   Key and Notes 183

Part Three   Tapescripts 241

PART ONE

PRACTICE TESTS

PART ONE

PRACTICE TESTS

PRACTICE TEST 1

Part I Writing

(30 minutes)

注意：此部分试题在**答题卡** 1 上。

Part II Reading Comprehension (Skimming and Scanning)

(15 minutes)

Directions: *In this part, you will have 15 minutes to go over the passage quickly and answer the questions on **Answer Sheet 1**.*

For questions 1 – 4, mark

Y *(for YES)*   *if the statement agrees with the information given in the passage;*

N *(for NO)*   *if the statement contradicts the information given in the passage;*

NG *(for NOT GIVEN)*   *if the information is not given in the passage.*

For questions 5 – 10, complete the sentences with the information given in the passage.

I Gave Him Up at 16. Could We Try Again?

The call came in May. "Hello," the woman said. "My name is Ann Hurd. I work with the New Hampshire courts. I want you to sit down. Your son is looking for you."

I had been hoping for this call for 21 years, and it came like a dream into an ordinary spring day.

"We will take this very slowly," she said. "This can cause enormous problems for both the child and the birth mother."

"But I'm ready now. I've been waiting for years."

"First you will write letters for a while, through me. It is devastating to the child to experience a second abandonment." "I could never abandon him again."

"But it happens a lot," she said. "Where is he?"

"I can't tell you that yet." "Can you tell me his name?" I felt myself separate from my voice.

"His name," she said, "is Ron."

This sound was electric. My son had a name!

"Your son," Ann told me, "is extraordinary. Ron is a spectacular young man."

Three weeks later, a letter finally came through Ann. There was a picture enclosed, my first sight of my lost child. It was blurred and gray, but here was Ron — serious, a strong jaw, intelligent eyes.

Dear Meredith, he wrote. *I don't know what to say. I don't know how to do this. Ron.*

His handwriting was slanted along the page, hurried. I carried his note in my pocket, reading it again and again as I stared at his photograph.

Ann called and said, "Write back to him right away. He is very scared. Ask him some questions."

Dear Ron. My name is Meredith Hall. I live in East Boothbay on the coast of Maine. I have a son, Morgan, who is 10. And a son named Zachary, who is 7. We keep sheep and chickens and big gardens. Tell me about your family. Tell me about your room. Tell me about what you like to do. I want you to know that I have always loved you.

Ann edited our letters for revealing details. They came to us blacked out:

My name is Meredith. I live in ... on the coast of ...

My name is Ron. I grew up on a farm in ... in southern ... My mother and father, ... and ..., are very loving and supportive.

Our ghost lives slowly took shape. Five months later, Ann arranged for us to meet.

It was 10 a.m., Oct. 18. Ron drove slowly along my dirt road. He glanced at me quickly as I stood waiting on the porch steps. I could see blond hair, curls. He turned off the car, got out, looked at me, and our eyes locked. He was thin, athletic, and handsome. My son. He was not a child. He was a young man, wearing jeans, a striped sweater and soft old loafers. He came toward me, crunching on the stone path. His teeth were brilliant white, with a space in the front. My father had a space like that. I moved toward him. Every day, for 21 years, I had played this scene. I had never known what to do, and I did not know now. I was breaking with joy, and with grief too, because here he was a grown man, here I was nearly 40, all those years lost forever. I reached for him, held him in to me, a stranger, my son, this beautiful, radiant, terrified, smiling son.

We did not hold each other long because we were shy, strangers to each other. We walked to the railing of the porch and stood, three feet between us, facing the river, looking out over the coast of Maine. I could not find the question that would start our

PART ONE

PRACTICE TESTS

PART ONE

PRACTICE TESTS

PRACTICE TEST 1

Part I   Writing   (30 minutes)

注意：此部分试题在答题卡 1 上。

Part II   Reading Comprehension (Skimming and Scanning)
                                                      (15 minutes)

Directions: *In this part, you will have 15 minutes to go over the passage quickly and answer the questions on* **Answer Sheet 1.**

    For questions 1 – 4, mark

Y *(for YES)*	*if the statement agrees with the information given in the passage;*
N *(for NO)*	*if the statement contradicts the information given in the passage;*
NG *(for NOT GIVEN)*	*if the information is not given in the passage.*

    For questions 5 – 10, complete the sentences with the information given in the passage.

I Gave Him Up at 16. Could We Try Again?

    The call came in May. "Hello," the woman said. "My name is Ann Hurd. I work with the New Hampshire courts. I want you to sit down. Your son is looking for you."

    I had been hoping for this call for 21 years, and it came like a dream into an ordinary spring day.

    "We will take this very slowly," she said. "This can cause enormous problems for both the child and the birth mother."

    "But I'm ready now. I've been waiting for years."

    "First you will write letters for a while, through me. It is devastating to the child to experience a second abandonment." "I could never abandon him again."

    "But it happens a lot," she said. "Where is he?"

    "I can't tell you that yet." "Can you tell me his name?" I felt myself separate from my voice.

"His name," she said, "is Ron."

This sound was electric. My son had a name!

"Your son," Ann told me, "is extraordinary. Ron is a spectacular young man."

Three weeks later, a letter finally came through Ann. There was a picture enclosed, my first sight of my lost child. It was blurred and gray, but here was Ron — serious, a strong jaw, intelligent eyes.

Dear Meredith, he wrote. *I don't know what to say. I don't know how to do this. Ron.*

His handwriting was slanted along the page, hurried. I carried his note in my pocket, reading it again and again as I stared at his photograph.

Ann called and said, "Write back to him right away. He is very scared. Ask him some questions."

Dear Ron. My name is Meredith Hall. I live in East Boothbay on the coast of Maine. I have a son, Morgan, who is 10. And a son named Zachary, who is 7. We keep sheep and chickens and big gardens. Tell me about your family. Tell me about your room. Tell me about what you like to do. I want you to know that I have always loved you.

Ann edited our letters for revealing details. They came to us blacked out:

My name is Meredith. I live in ... on the coast of ...

My name is Ron. I grew up on a farm in ... in southern ... My mother and father, ... and ..., are very loving and supportive.

Our ghost lives slowly took shape. Five months later, Ann arranged for us to meet.

It was 10 a.m., Oct. 18. Ron drove slowly along my dirt road. He glanced at me quickly as I stood waiting on the porch steps. I could see blond hair, curls. He turned off the car, got out, looked at me, and our eyes locked. He was thin, athletic, and handsome. My son. He was not a child. He was a young man, wearing jeans, a striped sweater and soft old loafers. He came toward me, crunching on the stone path. His teeth were brilliant white, with a space in the front. My father had a space like that. I moved toward him. Every day, for 21 years, I had played this scene. I had never known what to do, and I did not know now. I was breaking with joy, and with grief too, because here he was a grown man, here I was nearly 40, all those years lost forever. I reached for him, held him in to me, a stranger, my son, this beautiful, radiant, terrified, smiling son.

We did not hold each other long because we were shy, strangers to each other. We walked to the railing of the porch and stood, three feet between us, facing the river, looking out over the coast of Maine. I could not find the question that would start our life together. What I wanted to ask was: Have you felt my love each day? Have you felt me missing you? Have you known how sorry I am? Have you been loved? Have you been happy? Will you forgive me?

All I could come up with was, "Do you like U. N. H. ?"

"Yes." His first word to me. His voice was soft and deep.

"What year are you?"

"Well, I'm working my way through so I have another two years."

His body was taut, as if he were ready to fight something off. His face was open, his eyes enormous, blue, set wide apart. He had a scar across his chin. He was very serious. He turned to me and smiled suddenly. He had deep dimples. My brother had those dimples. We smiled, then turned to the ocean again in overwhelmed silence.

"Do you want to go for a walk?" I asked. I felt deep happiness.

We walked down the dirt road to the river, blurting out every thought that came, our conversation leaping as we tried to reconstruct the lost years.

"This is the owl tree," I said. "Morgan and Zachary are my sons. Your brothers." I saw Ron tense for just a moment, then slip back into the rhythm of our walking. "They find owl pellets? Here and we dissect them."

Ron said, "My mother let me play hooky to go fishing with her."

My mother. I breathed. Of course. We were two mothers.

We sat on an old bench above the undulating seaweed, talking fast. I knew he would drive away that afternoon, and I didn't know if he would ever come again. He must have wondered if I would want him to come again. Sometimes, we found ourselves laughing. Twice, Ron said, "I've never told anyone this before."

We climbed back up the hill, and I showed him the downstairs of our homey little Cape.

"Do you want to see your brothers' rooms?" I asked.

"Yes," he said quietly.

He glanced quickly into their sunny rooms, at their toys and books, at his brothers' lives here with me where they've been loved, safe, not given away. We went back down to the kitchen. Eating tuna sandwiches, we returned to our stories.

"Would you like me to tell you about your father?"

His hands stopped midair, a picture of our first day I will never forget.

"You look like him," I said.

"He lives in Massachusetts. I was 16, and he was a sophomore at Villanova University. We met at the beach. He came to see me after you were born, for five or six years, showing up, never asking any questions."

I watched him struggle to integrate this information into his 21-year-old identity.

"It doesn't matter anyway," was all he could say.

He let me hug him goodbye at his car. He called on Wednesday and said he was coming on Sunday.

"Can the boys be there?" he asked.

I was overcome by his courage. It was the beginning of our new family.

I ached with guilt about my two young sons, understanding that I was asking them to take in stride the effects of my own enormous history. They never balked. When I told them they had a big brother, they immediately embraced him. They stood in front of Ron at that first meeting and grinned. They climbed on him, giggling. Like monkeys, they studied every inch of him, probing and touching, pulling off his socks and shoes, studying his toes and hands and back, comparing their own. They peered inside his mouth. Morgan draped his arm over his shoulder while they sat on the couch; Zachary got in under Ron's arm. Ron came every Sunday, then for weekends, then for the summer. I was stunned by my sons' capacity to include Ron, to give him part of me.

And Ron took me to his family, too. "This is my mother, Rose," he joked. "This is my other mother, Meredith." He did not call me Mom, or Mum, or Mumma, like Morgan and Zachary. He had a mother. He had a sister, Tammy, adopted when she was 2. He had a father, Hank. Astonishingly, Rose and Hank welcomed me as if they were happy I had come into Ron's life. I felt as if I had stolen their son.

Those months were confusing, upheaving, yet laughter often filled the house. And we cried. We rested in our deep love for each other, then we would fly apart in despair or hurt. Some days we needed to be reassured that this was forever. Other days, we fought for our lives, the lives that had worked pretty well before. Sometimes we couldn't contain everything that had been lost.

I had never told my friends about this child. The grief and shame of losing him at 16 had stayed with me all my life as a fiercely private sorrow. Now they argued with me, telling me that Morgan and Zachary should not have to pay the price of my history. "Are you telling me I should send this child away again?" I asked. "Yes," they said. "This isn't fair to your children." But an older friend disagreed, telling me, "This is your son. Don't listen to them. This is a miracle. It is a fairy tale with a happy ending."

Then it was Oct. 18 again, our first anniversary. Our days had found rhythm. The upheaving emotions were quieting. My friend was right: this was a miracle, a fairy tale, though each day felt fragile, as if it all might disappear if we turned our backs. Still, our old lives receded, and our new family held together. I had my son. He had his mother.

To mark the day, I gave him my small clay owl, the only thing I had from those devastating years after he was born. "This is to remind you every day that this place in my life is forever," I said.

He gave me an acorn. "My renaissance," he said, his voice soft and hopeful.

There were no patterns for how to do this, how to hold each other safely and fully after a lifetime apart. We could not plot out the future. We were a family. We loved each other. We needed each other. That was our only map.

注意：此部分试题请在**答题卡**1上作答。

1. Ann corrected their letters to show both of them more details.
2. For 21 years the mother worked as an actress and played the same scene on the stage.
3. When the mother met her lost son for the first time, she was both happy and sorrowful.
4. One year after their first meet, both the mother and her lost son adjusted themselves to the new life and new family.
5. According to the writer, "our ghost lives" means _____.
6. When the mother first met her lost son, they went for a walk and _____.
7. The mother ached with guilt and some of her friends felt it unfair _____.
8. The lost son _____ when the mother told him about his father.
9. Rose and Hank happily welcomed the mother while she _____.
10. They were confident that they would hold each other safely and fully in the future after a lifetime apart because _____.

Part III Listening Comprehension   (35 minutes)

Section A

Directions: *In this section, you will hear 8 short conversations and 2 long conversations. At the end of each conversation, one or more questions will be asked about what was said. Both the conversation and the questions will be spoken only once. After each question there will be a pause. During the pause, you must read the four choices marked A), B), C) and D), and decide which is the best answer. Then mark the corresponding letter on **Answer Sheet 2** with a single line through the center.*

注意：此部分试题请在**答题卡**2上作答。

11. A) She wasn't used to playing in rain.

B) Her boyfriend gave her bad advice.

C) She tried to show off before her boyfriend.

D) Her boyfriend didn't appreciate her playing tennis.

12. A) The man is occupied in writing to the woman.

    B) The man hasn't received any letter from the woman for two months.

    C) The man hasn't written to the woman for two months.

    D) The man has been writing frequently to the woman.

13. A) She will accompany the boss to attend the conference next month.

    B) She is writing a report for the conference.

    C) She is not sure if the boss would allow her to leave.

    D) She doesn't want to go on holiday with the man.

14. A) Every one of us likes her.   C) Not all of us like her.

    B) No one likes her.   D) She likes no one.

15. A) In a police station.   C) In a department store.

    B) In an airplane.   D) In a customs house.

16. A) 50 dollars.   C) 20 dollars.

    B) 45 dollars.   D) 180 dollars.

17. A) She thinks the man is very careful.

    B) She thinks the man should be more careful.

    C) She doesn't think it necessary to be so careful.

    D) She is never so careful as the man.

18. A) In the office.   C) At a restaurant.

    B) On a bus.   D) At the library.

Questions 19 to 21 are based on the conversation you have just heard.

19. A) Tibet.   C) Paris.

    B) New York.   D) Berlin.

20. A) Success means that you should let other people know you're successful.

    B) It is so important to have learning experiences.

    C) People can make a lot of money if they do stock analysis.

    D) To travel and see the world is important.

21. A) The man thinks that one should have enough money to do what she/he cares about.

    B) The man will go to Europe next month to take part in a big conference.

C) The woman got precious experiences when she spent her vacation in Tibet last summer.

D) The woman is showy because she wants others to know she's successful.

Questions 22 to 25 are based on the conversation you have just heard.

22. A) In the morning.
    B) At noon.
    C) In the afternoon.
    D) In the evening.

23. A) Customer and shop assistant.
    B) Teacher and student.
    C) Female boss and male secretary.
    D) Tourist and customs officer.

24. A) The saucepan should come back in daylight.
    B) The saucepan is not what the woman is looking for.
    C) The man-made lights make the saucepan look a bit different.
    D) The woman should come back tomorrow and she will be shown the right one.

25. A) The saucepans were in a sale in this shop last week.
    B) One quarter of the saucepans' original price was reduced in a sale last week.
    C) The woman said one of her neighbors saw the saucepans in the shop yesterday.
    D) The man was a bit impatient because the shop would close in five minutes.

Section B

Directions: *In this section, you will hear 3 short passages. At the end of each passage, you will hear some questions. Both the passage and the questions will be spoken only once. After you hear a question, you must choose the best answer from the four choices marked A), B), C) and D). Then mark the corresponding letter on the Answer Sheet 2 with a single line through the center.*

注意：此部分试题请在**答题卡**2上作答。

Passage One

Questions 26 to 29 are based on the passage you have just heard.

26. A) For each computer sold that contained and could run Microsoft software.
    B) For each computer sold that contained Microsoft software.
    C) For each computer sold that ran Microsoft software.

D) For each computer sold that could run Microsoft software.

27. A) Because Microsoft tries to defeat its competitors unfairly.
    B) Because Microsoft nearly dominates the software market.
    C) Because Microsoft manipulates design decisions.
    D) Because Microsoft uses competitive pricing.

28. A) He objects to the government reaching an agreement with Microsoft.
    B) He is indifferent to the agreement.
    C) He disapproves of the agreement.
    D) He thinks he should perform a more important role than the government.

29. A) Iron.   C) Steel.
    B) Oil.   D) Power.

Passage Two

Questions 30 to 32 are based on the passage you have just heard.

30. A) Because it produces a protein that appears green under yellow light.
    B) Because it produces a protein that appears blue under green light.
    C) Because it produces a protein that appears green under blue light.
    D) Because it produces a protein that appears yellow under blue light.

31. A) Because it helps fertilize the eggs.
    B) Because it can be put into the eggs of the monkeys.
    C) Because it prevents infection.
    D) Because it can hold the particular gene.

32. A) The monkey has developed some human diseases.
    B) It is the first time that the method has been used to genetically engineer animals.
    C) Human genetic diseases are caused by a missing, added, or abnormal gene.
    D) The research may have little practical application in medicine.

Passage Three

Questions 33 to 35 are based on the passage you have just heard.

33. A) Wolves.   C) Foxes.
    B) Mice.   D) Fish.

34. A) They give medical care for animals.

B) They adopt abused animals.

C) They bury pets in cemetery after death.

D) They provide health insurance for pets.

35. A) Pets can help young couples take care of their children.

B) Pets can foster interpersonal relationships.

C) Pets can rid the home of some pests.

D) Pets can relax one's mood and lower his blood pressure.

Section C

Directions: *In this section, you will hear a passage three times. When the passage is read for the first time, you should listen carefully for its general idea. When the passage is read for the second time, you are required to fill in the blanks numbered from 36 to 43 with the exact words you have just heard. For blanks numbered from 44 to 46 you are required to fill in the missing information. For these blanks, you can either use the exact words you have just heard or write down the main points in your own words. Finally, when the passage is read for the third time, you should check what you have written.*

注意：此部分试题在答题卡 2 上；请在答题卡 2 上作答。

Part IV Reading Comprehension (Reading in Depth)

(25 minutes)

Section A

Directions: *In this section, there is a short passage with 5 questions or incomplete statements. Read the passage carefully. Then answer the questions or complete the statements in the fewest possible words on Answer Sheet 2.*

Questions 47 to 51 are based on the following passage.

Why should the jelly mould served at the end of English meals be shaped like a cathedral? Why are Americans still hungry after eating a Chinese dinner? Cross-cultural studies show that meals are designed to follow strict progression of cues based on shape, colour, temperature, odour, or specific taste sensation.

Fox never appears on our dinner tables, nor dog. But at one time, fox was reckoned a delicacy in Russia, as was dog in China. Sometimes we admit that our strong rejection of certain meats is not founded in physiology but in aesthetics. We shrink from the thought of eating insects or singing birds, but we know that grubs and grass-hoppers, blackbirds and larks, are served elsewhere.

In recent years, some anthropologists who study eating habits in different societies have argued that it is never useful to ask questions about one item lifted out of its cultural context. To question only why fox is rejected from the diet encourages a single cause-and-effect chain of reasoning that leads incorrectly to biological explanations. If biology were the basis for the selection of human foods, diets around the world would be quite similar. In fact, no human activity more puzzlingly crosses the divide between nature and culture than the selection of food. It is part of the nurture of the body, but it is also very much a social matter.

In most cultures, certain meals have some consistent structure that makes people know what to expect. One kind of the structure depends on spatial layout, as in Indian meals, where the foods are arranged on the right, left, and middle of the dish. Meals can also be served chronologically, with a beginning, a middle, and a steady progression toward an anticipated end. When the English see tea, or Americans coffee, they know dinner is over. When we cross cultural barriers in dining, we may miss our accustomed stop signals and end up feeling either hungry or overstuffed. I suspect that the well-known complaint about Chinese food may be based on such cultural confusion. "An hour after a Chinese meal," people say, "I'm hungry again." While American Chinese food may have been adapted to American tastes, it hasn't been adapted to American form. Individuals who are accustomed to a main course with clearly defined portions of meat, vegetables, and so on, topped of by a big dessert, miss the same sense of crescendo（高潮）when they eat certain foreign foods. Nothing signals them that the meal is over.

注意：此部分试题请在**答题卡**2 上作答。

47. Why does fox never appear on dinner tables?

48. Why can't the selection of human foods be explained biologically?

49. What are the two consistent structures of meals?

50. What might happen if people from one culture have dinner of another culture?

51. Why do Americans still feel hungry after eating a Chinese dinner?

Section B

Directions: *There are 2 passages in this section. Each passage is followed by some* *questions or unfinished statements. For each of them there are four choices marked A), B), C) and D). You should decide on the best choice and mark the corresponding letter on **Answer Sheet 2** with a single line through the center.*

Passage One

Questions 52 to 56 are based on the following passage.

A blind baby is doubly handicapped. Not only is it unable to see, but is likely to be slow in intellectual development. Now a ten-month-old baby is the subject of an unusual psychological experiment designed to prevent a lag in the learning process. With the aid of a sonar-type electronic device that he wears on his head, infant Dennis is learning to identify the people and objects in the world around him by means of echoes.

Dennis was born almost three months too early and developed an eye disorder usually caused by overexposure to oxygen in an incubator. He went blind, but his parents were contacted by psychologist Bower who wanted to see how a blind infant might respond if given an echo-sounding device to help him cope with his surroundings.

By the time the child was six weeks old, his parents noticed that he continuously uttered sharp clicking sounds with his tongue. Bower explained that blind people often use echoes to orient themselves, and that the clicking sounds were the boy's way of creating echoes. This, Bower believed, made the child an ideal subject for testing with an electronic echo-sounding device.

The device used in the study is a refinement of an instrument used by blind adults in addition to a cane or guiding dog. As adapted for Dennis, it consists of a battery-powered system (including a transmitter and two receivers) about the size of a half dollar that is worn on a headgear. The transmitter emits an ultrasonic pulse that creates an 80-degree cone (圆锥体) of sound at 6 feet. Echoes from objects within the cone are changed by two receivers into audible signals fed into each ear. The signals are perceived as sounds that vary in pitch and volume with the size and distance of the object.

The closer an object is, the lower the pitch, and the larger the object, the louder the signal. Hard surfaces produce a sharp ping, while soft ones send back signals with a slightly fuzzy quality. An object slightly to the right of Denny's head sends back a louder sound to his right ear than to the left. Thus, by simply moving his head, he can not only locate an object but also get some notion of its shape and size. Dennis likes to use the device to play a kind of peek-a-boo with his mother. Standing on her knee and facing her directly, he receives a strong signal in both ears. By turning his head away, he makes her seem to disappear. The boy has learned to identify many objects.

So far, the study has shown that a normal blind baby can employ echoes as well as, or even better than, an unsighted adult can. What remains to be determined is how well the device will help Dennis cope with his surroundings as he begins to walk and venture further into his environment.

注意：此部分试题请在**答题卡2**上作答。

52. What makes Dennis an ideal subject for testing with an electronic echo-sounding device?
    A) His blindness at birth.
    B) His still being an infant.
    C) The cause of his blindness: overexposure to oxygen.
    D) His utterance of sharp clicking sounds with his tongue.

53. Which of the following statements is TRUE according to the passage?
    A) Dennis doesn't hear the sound made by the transmitter.
    B) With the headgear on, Dennis can identify objects behind him.
    C) Dennis can identify anything closer than 6 feet from him.
    D) Dennis has a wider range of "vision" 6 feet from his eyes than 2 feet from them.

54. We can infer from the passage that _____.
    A) visual stimuli are more important to intellectual development than audible stimuli
    B) when Dennis grows up, he will not need to use a guiding dog or a cane like other blind people
    C) Dennis has learned the relationship between the echoes he hears and the shape, size, distance and color of an object in front of him
    D) Dennis is the first blind person to use a sonar-type electronic device to identify objects

55. How could Dennis distinguish between a small ball and a large one from a distance of 3 feet? The small ball could produce _____.
    A) a sharper sound   C) a softer sound
    B) a lower-pitched sound   D) a louder sound

56. If someone holds a book 6 feet directly in front of Dennis and then moves it to only 1 foot directly in front of him, what change in sound does Dennis hear?
    A) The sound becomes sharper.
    B) The sound becomes lower-pitched.

C) The sound becomes softer.
D) The sound becomes louder.

Passage Two

Questions 57 to 61 are based on the following passage.

The bridegroom, dressed in a blue blazer and brown suede Adidas sneakers, nervously cleared his throat when his bride, in traditional white, walked down the classroom aisle. As the mock minister led the students — and ten other couples in the room — through the familiar marriage ceremony, the giggles almost drowned him out. But it was no laughing matter. In the next semester, each "couple" would buy a house, have a baby — and get a divorce.

In a most unusual course at Parkrose Senior High School, social science teacher Allen leads his students through the trials and tribulations of married life. Instead of the traditional course, which dwells on the psychological and sexual adjustments young marrieds must face, Allen exposes his students to the nitty-gritty problems of housing, insurance and child care. "No one tells kids about financial problems," says Allen, 36. "It's like sex — you don't talk about it in front of them."

Students act out in nine weeks what normally takes couples ten years to accomplish. In the first week, one member of each couple is required to get an after-school job — a real one. During the semester, the salary, computed on a full-time basis with yearly increases factored in, serves as the guideline for their life-style. The third week, the couples must locate an apartment they can afford and study the terms of the lease.

In the fifth week, the couples "have a baby" and then compute the cost by totaling hospital and doctor bills, prenatal and postnatal care, baby clothes and furniture. In week eight, disaster strikes: the marriages are strained to the breaking point by such calamities as a mother-in-law moving in, death, or imprisonment. It's all over by week nine (the tenth year after marriage). After lectures by marriage counselors and divorce lawyers and computations of child support, the students get divorced.

Allen's course, which has "married" 1,200 students since its inception five years ago, is widely endorsed by parents and students. Some of the participants have found the experience chastening to their real-life marital plans. "Bride" Valerie Payne, 16, and her "groom", David Cooper, 19, still plan to marry in July, but, said Cooper, the course pointed out "the troubles you can have". The course was more unsettling to Marianne Baldrica, 17, who tried "marriage" last term with her boyfriend Eric Zook, 18. "Eric and I used to get along pretty well before we took the course together,"

Marianne said. "But I wanted to live in the city, he wanted the country. He wanted lots of kids, I wanted no kids. It's been four weeks since the course ended and Eric and I are just starting to talk to each other again!"

注意：此部分试题请在**答题卡 2**上作答。

57. What does Allen think is the biggest problem students should face in marriage?
    A) Sexual adjustment.
    B) Financial problem.
    C) Divorce.
    D) Child care.

58. The word "mock" (Line 3, Para. 1) most probably means "_____".
    A) religious
    B) strange
    C) imitative
    D) solemn

59. What's the students' response to the marriage preparation course?
    A) Doubtful.
    B) Credulous.
    C) Cautious.
    D) Approving.

60. Which of the following statements is NOT true according to the passage?
    A) Some students give up the idea of marriage after the course.
    B) Allen believes that traditional courses do not adequately prepare young people for married life.
    C) A couple is most likely to split in the tenth year after marriage.
    D) The course requires students to marry, buy a house and get a divorce.

61. How does the course affect the students?
    A) They change their minds about marriage.
    B) They become doubtful about marriage.
    C) They are awakened to the marital problems.
    D) They stand firm in the determination to marriage.

Part V Error Correction   (15 minutes)

Directions: *This part consists of a short passage. In this passage, there are altogether 10 mistakes, one in each numbered line. You may have to change a word, add a word or delete a word. Mark out the mistakes and put the corrections in the blanks provided. If you change a word, cross it out and write the correct word in the corresponding blank. If you add a word, put an insertion mark (∧) in the right place and write the missing word in the blank. If you delete a word, cross it out and put a slash (/) in the blank.*

注意：此部分试题在**答题卡**2上；请在**答题卡**2上作答。

Part VI   Translation   (5 minutes)

Directions: *Complete the following sentences on **Answer Sheet 2** by translating into English the Chinese given in brackets.*

注意：此部分试题请在**答题卡**2上作答，只需写出译文部分。

72. I was defeated in the table tennis match _____ (部分原因应该归咎于紧身的衣服，在某种程度上，它阻碍了我的行动).

73. In spite of the lack of the scientists' support, many local residents _____ _____ (声称他们所看见的是个真正的不明飞行物)，not their imagination.

74. The migratory habits of some fish _____ (使科学家很难精确定位它们产卵的地方).

75. _____ (基于人人生来平等的前提)，the constitution forbids the rich to challenge the right of the impoverished.

76. Money was to be provided for the playground _____ (只要镇政务会委员一致同意该方案).

答题卡 1 (Answer Sheet 1)

Part I   **Writing**   **(30 minutes)**

Directions: *For this part, you are allowed 30 minutes to write a short essay entitled Should China OK Euthanasia? You should write at least 150 words following the outline given below:*

1. 有些人认为安乐死在中国应该实行
2. 有些人认为安乐死在中国应该缓行
3. 我的看法

Should China OK Euthanasia?

_____

_____

_____

_____

_____

_____

_____

_____

_____

_____

_____

_____

答题卡 1 (Answer Sheet 1)

Part II　Reading Comprehension (Skimming and Scanning) (15 minutes)

1. [Y] [N] [NG]　　5. _____　　8. _____
2. [Y] [N] [NG]
3. [Y] [N] [NG]　　6. _____　　9. _____
4. [Y] [N] [NG]　　7. _____　　10. _____

答题卡 2 (Answer Sheet 2)

Part III   Section A   Section B

11. [A] [B] [C] [D]   16. [A] [B] [C] [D]   21. [A] [B] [C] [D]   26. [A] [B] [C] [D]   31. [A] [B] [C] [D]
12. [A] [B] [C] [D]   17. [A] [B] [C] [D]   22. [A] [B] [C] [D]   27. [A] [B] [C] [D]   32. [A] [B] [C] [D]
13. [A] [B] [C] [D]   18. [A] [B] [C] [D]   23. [A] [B] [C] [D]   28. [A] [B] [C] [D]   33. [A] [B] [C] [D]
14. [A] [B] [C] [D]   19. [A] [B] [C] [D]   24. [A] [B] [C] [D]   29. [A] [B] [C] [D]   34. [A] [B] [C] [D]
15. [A] [B] [C] [D]   20. [A] [B] [C] [D]   25. [A] [B] [C] [D]   30. [A] [B] [C] [D]   35. [A] [B] [C] [D]

Part III   Section C

Latin America has (36) _____ sheer economic troubles. The debt crisis of the 1980s led to what many observers called the lost (37) _____, a period when most countries in the region experienced little economic (38) _____. Just as many countries were beginning to (39) _____ from the lost period, they faced a second major crisis, brought on by the (40) _____ of the Mexico Peso（比索）in 1994. By last year, most countries in Latin America were experiencing growth rates nearly (41) _____ to growth rates in Asia before the region (42) _____ into its current crisis. As a result, prices for some (43) _____, such as copper and oil, dropped dramatically, forcing government to cut spending. (44) _____

_____.

But Latin bankers are expected to be in better shape than their colleagues in Asia. (45) _____

_____.

So there is little chance that Latin America's economy will suffer the same type of problems that Asian economies went through. (46) _____

_____.

答题卡 2 (Answer Sheet 2)

Part IV   Section A   Part V   Error Correction   (15 minutes)

47. _____

_____

48. _____

_____

49. _____

_____

50. _____

_____

51. _____

_____

Part IV   Section B

52. [A][B][C][D]
53. [A][B][C][D]
54. [A][B][C][D]
55. [A][B][C][D]
56. [A][B][C][D]
57. [A][B][C][D]
58. [A][B][C][D]
59. [A][B][C][D]
60. [A][B][C][D]
61. [A][B][C][D]

More than a third of all students are women. Although
many woman who have received high education do not   62. _____
spend the whole of their lives following careers which their   63. _____
education has prepared them, this is accepted that the   64. _____
benefits of a university career are useless even for those who 65. _____
do not work in the ordinary sense. Many women work as
teachers, particularly in junior school; but only minority of   66. _____
university teachers are women, and very few women are
heads of departments or in other very senior position.   67. _____

With such great a proportion of the young people   68. _____
entering universities, there is a problem of maintaining
academic standards. Half of those who embark on higher
studies fail to graduate. Though there is no evidence that   69. _____
even incomplete university study gives a person better career
prospects than none at all, the number who drop out after
one or two years is disturbing large. On the other hand, one 70. _____
in five of who receive bachelor's degrees go on to take   71. _____
higher degrees, so the number of people receiving higher
degrees each year is by now over 100,000.

Part VI   Translation   (5 minutes)

72. _____

73. _____

74. _____

75. _____

76. _____

PRACTICE TEST 2

Part I Writing

(30 minutes)

注意：此部分试题在答题卡 1 上。

Part II Reading Comprehension (Skimming and Scanning)

(15 minutes)

Directions: *In this part, you will have 15 minutes to go over the passage quickly and answer the questions on* **Answer Sheet 1**.
For questions 1 − 4, mark

Y *(for YES)*   *if the statement agrees with the information given in the passage;*

N *(for NO)*   *if the statement contradicts the information given in the passage;*

NG *(for NOT GIVEN)*   *if the information is not given in the passage.*

For questions 5 − 10, complete the sentences with the information given in the passage.

My Friend Luke

I have a friend who must be the sweetest, shyest person in the world. He is forty years old, rather short and skinny, and has a thin moustache and even thinner hair on his head. Since his vision is not perfect, he wears glasses: they are small, round and frameless.

In order not to inconvenience anyone, he always walks sideways. Instead of saying "Excuse me", he prefers to glide by one side. If the gap is so narrow that it will not allow him to pass, Luke waits patiently until the obstruction — be it animate or inanimate, rational or irrational — moves by itself. Stray dogs and cats panic him, and in order to avoid them he constantly crosses from one side of the road to the other.

He speaks in a very thin, subtle voice, so inaudible that it is hard to tell if he is speaking at all. He has never interrupted anybody. On the other hand, he can never manage more than two words without somebody interrupting him. This does not seem to irritate him; in fact, he actually appears happy to have been able to utter those two words.

My friend Luke has been married for years. His wife is a thin, choleric, nervous woman who, as well as having an unbearably shrill voice, a viperous tongue and the personality of a lion tamer. Luke — you have to wonder how — has succeeded in producing a child named (by his mother) Juan Manuel. He is tall, blond, intelligent, distrustful and sarcastic. It is not entirely true that he only obeys his mother. However, the two of them have always agreed that Luke has little to offer the world and therefore choose to ignore his scarce and rarely expressed opinions.

Luke is the oldest and the least important employee of a dismal company that imports cloth. It operates out of a very dark building with black-stained wooden floors. The owner — I know him personally — is called Don Aquerontido. He has a ferocious moustache, is bald and has a thunderous voice. He is also violent and greedy. My friend Luke goes to work dressed all in black, wearing a very old suit that shines from age. He only owns one shirt — the one he wore for the first time on the day of his marriage. He also only owns one tie, so frayed and greasy that it looks more like a shoelace. Unable to bear the disapproving looks of Don Aquerontido, Luke, unlike his colleagues, does not dare work without his jacket on and in order to keep this jacket in good condition he wears a pair of grey sleeve-protectors. His salary is ludicrously low, but he still stays behind in the office every day and works for another three or four hours: the tasks Don Aquerontido gives him are so huge that he has no chance of accomplishing them within normal hours. Now, just after Don Aquerontido cut his salary yet again, his wife has decided that Juan Manuel must not do his secondary studies in a state school. She has chosen to put his name down for a very costly institution. In view of the extortionate outlay this involves, Luke has stopped buying his newspaper and (an even greater sacrifice) the *Reader's Digest*, his two favourite publications. The last article he managed to read in the *Reader's Digest* explained how husbands should repress their own overwhelming personality in order to make room for the actualisation of the rest of the family group.

There is, however, one remarkable aspect to Luke: his behaviour as soon as he steps on a bus. Generally, this is what happens:

He requests a ticket and begins to look for his money, slowly. He holds up one hand to ensure that the driver keeps waiting. Luke does not hurry. In fact, I would say that the driver's impatience gives him a certain amount of pleasure. Then he pays with the largest possible number of small coins. For some reason, this disturbs the driver, who, apart from having to pay attention to other cars, the traffic lights, other passengers getting on or off, and having to drive the bus, is forced to perform complicated arithmetic. Luke aggravates the problem by including in his payment an old Paraguayan coin that he keeps for the purpose and which is invariably returned to him. This way, mistakes are usually made in the accounts and an argument ensues. Then, in a serene but firm manner, Luke begins to defend his rights, employing arguments so contradictory that it is impossible to understand what point he is actually trying to make. Finally, the driver, at the end of the last tether of his sanity and in an act of final resignation, chooses to throw out the coins — perhaps as a means of repressing his wish to throw out Luke or, indeed, himself.

When winter comes, Luke always travels with the windows wide open. The first to suffer as a result of this is Luke himself: he has developed a chronic cough that often forces him to stay awake entire nights. During the summer, he closes his window and will not allow anyone to lower the shade that would protect him from the sun. More than once he has ended up with first-degree burns.

Because of his weak lungs, Luke is not allowed to smoke and, in fact, he hates smoking. In spite of this, once inside the bus he cannot resist the temptation to light up a cheap, heavy cigar that clogs up his windpipe and makes him cough. After he gets off, he puts away his cigar in preparation for his next journey.

Luke is a tiny, sedentary, squalid person and has never been interested in sports. But on Saturday evenings, he switches on his portable radio and turns the volume up full in order to follow the boxing match. Sundays he dedicates to football and tortures the rest of the passengers with the noisy broadcasts.

The back seat is for five passengers. In spite of his very small size, Luke sits so as to allow room for only four or even three people on the seat. If four are already seated and Luke is standing up, he demands permission, in an indignant and reproachful tone, to sit down — which he then does, managing to take up an excessive amount of space. To this end, he puts his hands in his pockets so that his elbows will remain firmly embedded in his neighbours' ribs.

Luke's resources are plentiful and diverse.

When he has to travel standing up, he always keeps his jacket unbuttoned, carefully adjusting his posture so that the lower edge of his jacket hits the face or the eyes of those sitting down.

If anyone is reading, they are easy prey for Luke. Watching him or her closely, Luke places his head near the light so as to throw a shadow on the victim's book. Every now and then he withdraws his head as if by chance. The reader will anxiously devour one or two words before Luke moves back into position.

My friend Luke knows the times when the bus will be fully packed. On those occasions, he consumes a salami sandwich and a glass of red wine. Then, with breadcrumbs and threads of salami still between his teeth and pointing his mouth towards the other passenger's noses, he walks along the vehicle shouting loudly, "Excuse me".

If he manages to take the front seat, he never gives it up to anyone. But should he find himself in one of the last rows, the moment he sees a woman with a child in her arms or a weak, elderly person climb on board he immediately stands up and calls very loudly to the front passenger to offer them his seat. Later he usually makes some reproachful remark against those that kept their seats. His eloquence is always effective, and some mortally ashamed passenger gets off at the next stop. Instantly, Luke takes his place.

My friend Luke gets off the bus in a very good mood. Timidly, he walks home, staying out of the way of anyone he meets. He is not allowed a key, so he has to ring the bell. If anyone is home, they rarely refuse to open the door to him. But if neither his wife nor his son is to be found, Luke sits on the doorstep until someone arrives.

注意：此部分试题请在**答题卡** 1 上作答。

1. Luke wears small, round and frameless glasses because he thinks other glasses are not good enough.
2. Juan Manuel, Luke's son, only obeys his mother and ignores Luke's opinions.
3. Because of the heavy tasks the boss gives him, Luke has to work over-time but is poorly paid.
4. Luke has developed a chronic cough and hates smoking, so he never smokes.
5. After his wife has chosen to put their son's name down for a very costly institution, Luke has _____.
6. On Saturday evenings and Sundays, Luke tortures the rest of the passengers in a bus by _____.
7. If four have already been sitting at the back seat, Luke will sit down and take up an excessive amount of space by _____.
8. When Luke finds anyone reading in a bus, he _____.
9. If the bus is very crowded, Luke will _____ and then point his mouth towards the others' noses, shouting "Excuse me" loudly.
10. Luke calls very loudly to offer others his seat when _____.

Part III   Listening Comprehension   (35 minutes)

Section A

Directions: *In this section, you will hear 8 short conversations and 2 long* *conversations. At the end of each conversation, one or more questions will be asked about what was said. Both the conversation and the questions will be spoken only once. After each question there will be a pause. During the pause, you must read the four choices marked A), B), C) and D), and decide which is the best answer. Then mark the corresponding letter on Answer Sheet 2 with a single line through the center.*

注意：此部分试题请在**答题卡** 2 上作答。

11. A) In a museum.
    B) In a theatre.
    C) In Chicago.
    D) On a plane.

12. A) He will see her at the tennis club meeting.
    B) He has not completed the assignment.
    C) He has no time to tell her the assignment now.
    D) He didn't attend class today either.

13. A) She spent just 75 dollars on a newer model.
    B) She could have saved 75 dollars.
    C) She should have paid 75 dollars more for the model she bought.
    D) She bought a less expensive model.

14. A) Bill surpasses John in math.
    B) John scores higher than Bill in math.
    C) John always does Bill's math for him.
    D) Bill and John make the same grades in math.

15. A) He wants to get a check.
    B) He wants to get money.
    C) He wants to get a valid driver's license.
    D) He wants to get a photo.

16. A) Her suggestion is reasonable.
    B) Her suggestion is not feasible.
    C) Her suggestion is off the point.
    D) She can ask any question.

17. A) He will wash the dishes himself.
    B) He will repair the dishwasher himself.
    C) He will call the service center to repair the dishwasher.
    D) He will throw the dishwasher away.

18. A) The dryer breaks down.
    B) She is working at the electric company.
    C) She doesn't like the electric company.

大学英语六级水平测试试题集 **710**分

D) She wants to save money.

Questions 19 to 21 are based on the conversation you have just heard.

19. A) Watching television.   C) Knitting socks.
    B) Button collection.   D) Making Turkish cakes.

20. A) Relaxation is to have a change.
    B) Relaxation is to watch educational programmes on TV.
    C) Relaxation is to watch TV.
    D) Relaxation is to go to sleep.

21. A) At home.   C) In a restaurant.
    B) In the school.   D) In a gym.

Questions 22 to 25 are based on the conversation you have just heard.

22. A) He started when he was eighteen.
    B) He started when he was sixteen.
    C) He started when he was a freshman.
    D) He started when he finished school.

23. A) Both her family and her friends smoked.
    B) When school was over, she and her friends went to the park and smoked.
    C) Her friends around her at the university all smoked.
    D) Her family smoked and that made her want to.

24. A) Now she thinks that smoking will lead to cancer.
    B) Now she thinks that smoking makes one look like a grown-up.
    C) Now she thinks that smoking is a good way to be sociable.
    D) Now she thinks that smoking is not worth the time and money.

25. A) When they first started they didn't know how to draw cigarettes.
    B) Both of them think that it was not pleasant when they first started smoking.
    C) They started smoking because they thought that smoking drew a line between children and adults and they wanted to be adults.
    D) They felt embarrassed to give up when they just started and as time went by both of them were so hooked that they couldn't give up.

Section B

Directions: *In this section, you will hear 3 short passages. At the end of each passage,* *you will hear some questions. Both the passage and the questions will be spoken only once. After you hear a question, you must choose the best answer from the four choices marked A）, B）, C) and D). Then mark the corresponding letter on **Answer Sheet 2** with a single line through the center.*

注意：此部分试题请在**答题卡**2上作答。

Passage One

Questions 26 to 29 are based on the passage you have just heard.

26. A）Little knowledge of reading, writing and arithmetic.
    B）The negative influence of television.
    C）Lack of strict discipline.
    D）High dropout rates.

27. A）Overcrowding and lack of discipline.
    B）Overemphasis on practical subjects.
    C）Overemphasis on art and drama.
    D）Rising expectations of parents.

28. A）Smaller classes and emphasis on practical subjects.
    B）Stricter discipline and emphasis on practical subjects.
    C）Smaller classes and stricter discipline.
    D）Smaller classes, emphasis on practical subjects and stricter discipline.

29. A）27 percent.   C）13 percent.
    B）15 percent.   D）50 percent.

Passage Two

Questions 30 to 32 are based on the passage you have just heard.

30. A）Water shortage.   C）Food shortage.
    B）Flooding.   D）Lack of medicine.

31. A）Trucks broke down.   C）Diseases spread.
    B）Roads were washed away.   D）Food supplies were damaged.

32. A）To urge people to donate money.
    B）To draw world attention to the sufferings of people in Somalia.
    C）To call on wealthy nations to help the poor people.

D) To report the problems threatening the lives of the poor people.

Passage Three

Questions 33 to 35 are based on the passage you have just heard.

33. A) What elements sea water contains.
    B) How heat and moisture are exchanged between the ocean and the air.
    C) How to bring sea water to deserts.
    D) How water and heat affect sound travel.

34. A) Camera.   C) Submarine.
    B) Weighted-rope.   D) Sound.

35. A) About thirty miles off the coast.
    B) Around the edges of the continents.
    C) In the middle of the ocean.
    D) In the part of the ocean where water is not deep.

Section C

Directions: *In this section, you will hear a passage three times. When the passage is read for the first time, you should listen carefully for its general idea. When the passage is read for the second time, you are required to fill in the blanks numbered from 36 to 43 with the exact words you have just heard. For blanks numbered from 44 to 46 you are required to fill in the missing information. For these blanks, you can either use the exact words you have just heard or write down the main points in your own words. Finally, when the passage is read for the third time, you should check what you have written.*

注意：此部分试题在**答题卡2**上；请在**答题卡2**上作答。

Part IV Reading Comprehension (Reading in Depth)

(25 minutes)

Section A

Directions: *In this section，there is a short passage with 5 questions or incomplete statements. Read the passage carefully. Then answer the questions or complete the statements in the fewest possible words on **Answer Sheet 2**.*

Questions 47 to 51 are based on the following passage.

With the all-purpose response, "I know, mom, but everyone's doing it", millions of teenagers have sought to explain to their parents why they experiment with drugs or alcohol, color their hair purple, or wear multiple pierced earrings. Their desire to conform to the fashions of their fellows is more a hope to gain approval from their peers than an excuse.

Teenage fashions touchingly reflect the social environment. During the roaring twenties, for example, rapid industrial growth and expanding capitalism generated intense competition for scarce economic resources. How did the "flaming youth" of the decade respond? With contests of skill and endurance: cross-country races, pie-eating contests, kissing and dancing marathons, gum-chewing and peanut-pushing contests.

Conventional values influence adolescent fashions in yet another way. They set the limits as to just how far those fads are permitted to go before they are sanctioned by adult society. In 1974, undergraduates began to engage in "streaking". Society's tolerance for streaking was a result of the sexual revolution of the 1960s. Any student who had dared run naked through a college campus in the 1950s would, in all likelihood, have been quickly locked as a sexual menace to society.

Even the most absurd practices can become the basis for an adolescent fashion, given the right social climate. During the Great Depression of the 1930s, at a time when many Americans were having trouble putting food on the table, parents lost their appetites. From Massachusetts to Missouri, students took to swallowing goldfish.

Teenagers in the 1990s trip over their own feet by wearing their sneakers unlaced, increase their chances of illness by refusing to wear winter hats or raincoats, and ruin their feet with pointy-toed shoes, all because these are in fashion. In general, they are seen as doing things that aren't very good for them.

注意：此部分试题请在**答题卡** 2 上作答。

47. Why do young people follow fashions?

48. The fashion "streaking" refers to _____.

49. Why did parents lose their appetites?

50. Adolescent fashions are largely affected by _____.

51. What does the writer think of the teenage fashions in the 1990s?

Section B

Directions: *There are 2 passages in this section. Each passage is followed by some questions or unfinished statements. For each of them there are four choices marked A), B), C) and D). You should decide on the best choice and mark the corresponding letter on **Answer Sheet 2** with a single line through the center.*

Passage One

Questions 52 to 56 are based on the following passage.

The tendency to look for some outside group to blame for our misfortunes is certainly common and it is often sustained by social pressures. There seems to be little doubt that one of the principal causes of prejudice is fear: in particular the fear that the interests of our own group are going to be endangered by the actions of another. This is less likely to be the case in a stable, relatively unchanging society in which the members of different social and occupational groups know what to expect of each other, and know what to expect for themselves. In times of rapid social and economic change, however, new occupations and new social roles appear, and people start looking jealously at each other to see whether their own group is being left behind.

When a community begins to feel unsure of its future, it becomes especially liable to turn in upon itself, to imagine that surrounding groups are threatening and hostile. At a time like this, distorted ideas about another community are readily believed and are passed on as statements of fact. One of the tragic things about intercommunal strife is that both parties quickly find themselves believing the worst about each other. And, at the same time, by a process which we might call "moral rationalisation", each of the antagonists insists — and believes — that its own actions are inspired by lofty ideals, even when they are really acting out of pure self-interest. To a third party neutral to the dispute, it may seem obvious that both are behaving unreasonably; but when one's emotions are involved, and especially the emotion of fear, it is extremely difficult to remain rational.

Once prejudice develops, it is hard to stop, because there are often social forces at work which actively encourage unfounded attitudes of hostility and fear towards other groups. One such force is education: we all know that children can be taught history in such a way as to perpetuate old feuds and old prejudices between racial and political groups. Another social influence that has to be reckoned with is the pressure of public opinion. People often think and act differently in groups from the way they would do as individuals. It takes a considerable effort of will, and often calls for great courage to stand out against one's fellows and insist that they are wrong.

Why is it that we hear so much more about the failures of relationships between communities than we do about the success? I am afraid it is partly due to the increase in communications which radio, television and the popular press have brought about. In those countries where the media of mass communication are commercial enterprises, they tend to measure success by the size of their audience; and people are more likely to buy a newspaper, for instance, if their attention is caught by something dramatic, something sensational, or something that arouses their anxiety. The popular press flourishes on "scare headlines", and popular orators, especially if they are politicians addressing a relatively unsophisticated audience, know that the best way to arouse such an audience is to frighten them.

Where there is a real or imaginary threat to economic security, this is especially likely to inflame group prejudice. It is important to remember economic factors if we wish to lessen prejudice between groups, because unless they are dealt with squarely it will be little use simply exhorting people not to be prejudiced against other groups whom they see as their rivals, if not their enemies.

注意：此部分试题请在**答题卡**2 上作答。

52. The writer holds that people in a stable society are _____ than people in a rapidly changing society.
    A) more jealous   C) less rational
    B) less prejudiced   D) more contented with their lives

53. Judging by the context, the word "strife" (Line 4, Para. 2) most probably means _____.
    A) accord   C) hatred
    B) harmony   D) conflict

54. Which of the following statements is NOT true according to the passage?
    A) Communities feeling unsure of themselves will try to communicate with the outside world.
    B) History education makes children prejudiced.
    C) Communities are more antagonistic to each other if they are in constant change.
    D) Economic security plays a role in reducing social prejudice.

55. The writer thinks that the failures of relationships between communities are brought about by all the following EXCEPT _____.
    A) the mass media   C) the communities' self-interests
    B) the communities' neutrality   D) the communities' antagonism

56. The passage is mainly about _____ .

A) how to eliminate social prejudice　　C) what a rational society is like

B) what causes social prejudice　　D) how to build a rational society

Passage Two

Questions 57 to 61 are based on the following passage.

From the time they were first proposed, the 1962 Amendments to the Food, Drug and Cosmetic Act have been the subject to controversy among some elements of the health community and the pharmaceutical industry. The Amendments add a new requirement for Food and Drug Administration approval of any new drug: the drug must be demonstrated to be effective by substantial evidence consisting of adequate and well-controlled investigations. To meet this effectiveness requirement, a pharmaceutical company must spend considerable time and effort on clinical research before it can market a new product in the United States. Only then can it begin to recoup its investment. Critics of the requirement argue that the added expense of the research to establish effectiveness is reflected in higher drug costs, decreased profits, or both, and that this has resulted in a "drug lag".

The term "drug lag" has been used in several different ways. It has been argued that the research required to prove effectiveness creates a lag between the time when a drug could theoretically be marketed without proving effectiveness and the time when it is actually marketed. Drug lag has also been used to refer to the difference between the number of new drugs introduced annually before 1962 and the number of new drugs introduced each year after that date. It's also argued that the Amendments resulted in a lag between the time when new drugs are available in other countries and the time when the same drugs are available in the United States. And drug lag has also been used to refer to a difference in the number of new drugs introduced per year in other advanced nations and the number introduced in the same year in the United States.

Some critics have used drug lag arguments in an attempt to prove that the 1962 Amendments have actually reduced the quality of health care in the United States and that, on balance, they have done more harm than good. These critics recommend that the effectiveness requirement be drastically modified or even abandoned. Most of the specific claims of the drug lag theoreticians, however, have been refuted. The drop in new drugs approved annually, for example, began at least as early as 1959, perhaps five years before the new law was fully effective. In most instances, when a new drug was available in a foreign country but not in the United States, other effective drugs for the condition were available in this country and sometimes not available in the foreign country used for comparison. Further, although the number of new chemical entities introduced annually dropped from more than 50 in 1959 to about 12 to 18 in the 1960s and 1970s, the number of these that can be termed important — some of them of "breakthrough" caliber — has remained reasonably close to 5 to 6 per year. Few, if any, specific examples have actually been offered to show how the effectiveness requirement have done significant harm to the health of Americans. The requirement does ensure that a patient exposed to a drug has the likelihood of benefiting from it, an assessment that is most important, considering the possibility, always present, that adverse effects will be discovered later.

注意：此部分试题请在**答题卡2**上作答。

57. It can be concluded from the first paragraph that before 1962, when a new drug was marketed, its effectiveness _____.
    A) had been demonstrated by abundant evidence
    B) was seldom taken into account by the pharmaceutical industry
    C) had not been fully demonstrated by ample evidence
    D) was paid great attention to by doctors

58. Which of the following does NOT the term "drug lag" mean?
    A) The difference in time between the invention and the marketing of a new drug.
    B) The difference between the time when new drugs are marketed in other countries and the time when the same drugs are marketed in the United States.
    C) The difference in the number of new drugs invented annually in other developed countries and the number invented in the United States.
    D) The difference in the number of new drugs approved annually before 1962 and the number approved each year after that.

59. Judging by the context the word "entities" (Line 11, Para. 3) most probably means _____.
    A) companies   C) amendments
    B) breakthroughs   D) drugs

60. What does "the possibility" in the last sentence most probably refer to?
    A) The adverse effects discovered later.
    B) The likelihood of a patient benefiting from it.
    C) The availability of a new drug in a foreign country but not in the United States.
    D) The harm the effectiveness requirement may do to the health of Americans.

61. The writer's attitude toward the effectiveness requirement is _____.

A) approving
    C) indifferent

B) suspicious
    D) unclear

Part V Error Correction   (15 minutes)

Directions: *This part consists of a short passage. In this passage, there are altogether 10 mistakes, one in each numbered line. You may have to change a word, add a word or delete a word. Mark out the mistakes and put the corrections in the blanks provided. If you change a word, cross it out and write the correct word in the corresponding blank. If you add a word, put an insertion mark (∧) in the right place and write the missing word in the blank. If you delete a word, cross it out and put a slash (/) in the blank.*

注意：此部分试题在**答题卡2**上；请在**答题卡2**上作答。

Part VI Translation   (5 minutes)

Directions: *Complete the following sentences on **Answer Sheet 2** by translating into English the Chinese given in brackets.*

注意：此部分试题请在**答题卡2**上作答，只需写出译文部分。

72. _____（从听众的厌烦状态中就能明白）
that his lengthy explanations were superfluous.

73. The information we have received has _____
（确认了我们对他勾结敌方的怀疑）.

74. If you _____
（在适合用较简单的单词的地方使用了太多的大字眼）, you may sound pretentious
as if you're showing off.

75. The criminal was told _____
（他将被免除惩罚）, if he said what he knew of the murder.

76. My dog seems to have _____
（一种直觉,告诉它去相信谁）.

答题卡 1 (Answer Sheet 1)

学校:		准 考 证 号															

姓名:

划线要求	

[0] [0] [0] [0] [0] [0] [0] [0] [0] [0] [0] [0] [0] [0] [0]
[1] [1] [1] [1] [1] [1] [1] [1] [1] [1] [1] [1] [1] [1] [1]
[2] [2] [2] [2] [2] [2] [2] [2] [2] [2] [2] [2] [2] [2] [2]
[3] [3] [3] [3] [3] [3] [3] [3] [3] [3] [3] [3] [3] [3] [3]
[4] [4] [4] [4] [4] [4] [4] [4] [4] [4] [4] [4] [4] [4] [4]
[5] [5] [5] [5] [5] [5] [5] [5] [5] [5] [5] [5] [5] [5] [5]
[6] [6] [6] [6] [6] [6] [6] [6] [6] [6] [6] [6] [6] [6] [6]
[7] [7] [7] [7] [7] [7] [7] [7] [7] [7] [7] [7] [7] [7] [7]
[8] [8] [8] [8] [8] [8] [8] [8] [8] [8] [8] [8] [8] [8] [8]
[9] [9] [9] [9] [9] [9] [9] [9] [9] [9] [9] [9] [9] [9] [9]

Part I   **Writing**   **(30 minutes)**

Directions: *For this part, you are allowed 30 minutes to write a short essay entitled **On Cloning**. You should write at least **150** words following the outline given below:*

1. 克隆技术将造福人类,因为……
2. 克隆技术将给人类带来灾难,因为……
3. 我的观点

On Cloning

答题卡 1 (Answer Sheet 1)

Part II   Reading Comprehension (Skimming and Scanning) (15 minutes)

1. [Y] [N] [NG]

2. [Y] [N] [NG]

3. [Y] [N] [NG]

4. [Y] [N] [NG]

5. _____

6. _____

7. _____

8. _____

9. _____

10. _____

答题卡 2 (Answer Sheet 2)

学校：		准 考 证 号

姓名：

划线要求	

准 考 证 号

[0]	[0]	[0]	[0]	[0]	[0]	[0]	[0]	[0]	[0]	[0]	[0]	[0]	[0]	[0]
[1]	[1]	[1]	[1]	[1]	[1]	[1]	[1]	[1]	[1]	[1]	[1]	[1]	[1]	[1]
[2]	[2]	[2]	[2]	[2]	[2]	[2]	[2]	[2]	[2]	[2]	[2]	[2]	[2]	[2]
[3]	[3]	[3]	[3]	[3]	[3]	[3]	[3]	[3]	[3]	[3]	[3]	[3]	[3]	[3]
[4]	[4]	[4]	[4]	[4]	[4]	[4]	[4]	[4]	[4]	[4]	[4]	[4]	[4]	[4]
[5]	[5]	[5]	[5]	[5]	[5]	[5]	[5]	[5]	[5]	[5]	[5]	[5]	[5]	[5]
[6]	[6]	[6]	[6]	[6]	[6]	[6]	[6]	[6]	[6]	[6]	[6]	[6]	[6]	[6]
[7]	[7]	[7]	[7]	[7]	[7]	[7]	[7]	[7]	[7]	[7]	[7]	[7]	[7]	[7]
[8]	[8]	[8]	[8]	[8]	[8]	[8]	[8]	[8]	[8]	[8]	[8]	[8]	[8]	[8]
[9]	[9]	[9]	[9]	[9]	[9]	[9]	[9]	[9]	[9]	[9]	[9]	[9]	[9]	[9]

Part III   Section A   **Section B**

11. [A] [B] [C] [D]   16. [A] [B] [C] [D]   21. [A] [B] [C] [D]   26. [A] [B] [C] [D]   31. [A] [B] [C] [D]
12. [A] [B] [C] [D]   17. [A] [B] [C] [D]   22. [A] [B] [C] [D]   27. [A] [B] [C] [D]   32. [A] [B] [C] [D]
13. [A] [B] [C] [D]   18. [A] [B] [C] [D]   23. [A] [B] [C] [D]   28. [A] [B] [C] [D]   33. [A] [B] [C] [D]
14. [A] [B] [C] [D]   19. [A] [B] [C] [D]   24. [A] [B] [C] [D]   29. [A] [B] [C] [D]   34. [A] [B] [C] [D]
15. [A] [B] [C] [D]   20. [A] [B] [C] [D]   25. [A] [B] [C] [D]   30. [A] [B] [C] [D]   35. [A] [B] [C] [D]

Part III   Section C

For many young people, the late 1960s was a period of revolt against the (36) _____ values that had been the (37) _____ and pride of the past generation. They didn't want to be hardworking and (38) _____, as their ancestors had been. They rejected all forms of (39) _____ and the idea that individuals must make (40) _____ when it is necessary for the good of their children or of their community. All these (41) _____ ideas, they declared, were things of the past and had always been wrong anyway. It was a (42) _____ time for their elders. Previously happy parents found themselves (43) _____ by the young, (44) _____

_____.

More parents found it hard to accept their children's attitude. (45) _____

_____.

However, the young people claimed that true success is not a matter of money or position. It's a matter of self-fulfillment. (46) _____

_____.

答题卡 2 (Answer Sheet 2)

Part IV   Section A   Part V   Error Correction   (15 minutes)

47. _____

_____

48. _____

_____

49. _____

_____

50. _____

51. _____

_____

Today most people who bother with this matter at all would admit that English language is in a bad way, but it is generally assumed that we can by conscious action do anything about it. Our civilization is decaying and our language must inevitably share in the general collapse. It follows that any struggle for the abuse of language must be in vain. Underneath these arguments lie the sub-conscious belief that a language is not an instrument which we shape our own purposes, but something natural.

62. _____

63. _____

64. _____

65. _____

66. _____

Part IV   Section B

52. [A][B][C][D]
53. [A][B][C][D]
54. [A][B][C][D]
55. [A][B][C][D]
56. [A][B][C][D]
57. [A][B][C][D]
58. [A][B][C][D]
59. [A][B][C][D]
60. [A][B][C][D]
61. [A][B][C][D]

Now it is clear that the decline of a language must ultimately have had social causes: it is not due simply to the bad influence on this or that individual writer. It becomes ugly and inaccurate because our thoughts are foolish; but the decadence of language makes easier for us to have foolish thoughts. The point is that the process is not reversible. Modern English, especially written English, is full of bad habits which spread by imitation and which can be avoided if one is willing to take the necessary trouble. If one gets rid of the habits one can think less clearly. This is the necessary first step in the fight against bad English.

67. _____

68. _____

69. _____

70. _____

71. _____

Part VI   Translation   (5 minutes)

72. _____

73. _____

74. _____

75. _____

76. _____

PRACTICE TEST 3

Part I Writing   (30 minutes)

注意：此部分试题在**答题卡** 1 上。

Part II Reading Comprehension (Skimming and Scanning)
(15 minutes)

Directions: *In this part, you will have 15 minutes to go over the passage quickly and answer the questions on **Answer Sheet 1**.*

For questions 1 – 4, mark

Y *(for YES)*   *if the statement agrees with the information given in the passage;*

N *(for NO)*   *if the statement contradicts the information given in the passage;*

NG *(for NOT GIVEN)*   *if the information is not given in the passage.*

For questions 5 – 10, complete the sentences with the information given in the passage.

Folk Games

The folk games all people play, whether children, adolescents, or adults, may be based on the movements of the body (stepping, running, hopping, jumping, etc.), on simple social activities (chasing, hiding, fighting, dramatizing, etc.), on chance (the fall of dices, cards, bones, coins, etc.), or on elementary mathematics or mechanics (counting, sorting, balancing, throwing, handling equipment, etc.). These common foundation blocks may explain the similarity of certain games through long periods of time and in widespread cultures, or diffusion of folklore may better account for some similar forms. (It is the question once again of polygenesis versus diffusion from a single origin.) Only detailed studies of many versions of different games can begin to suggest answers to such questions.

By their very nature as voluntary recreations with rules fixed only by custom and tradition, folk games reveal much about the societies in which they are played and about the individuals who play them. Game preferences, the forms of games, local variations, attitudes toward play, and play behavior are all valuable cultural, sociological, and psychological data to be documented and analyzed. In such research, the non-verbal elements of games are significant along with such verbal ones as traditional sayings, rhymes, or songs associated with games.

The problem of classifying games, basic to further research, has not been completely solved. The singing or non-singing dichotomy suggested by Newell's and Brewster's works is no better than other proposed systems that separate games of boys from those of girls, or indoor from outdoor games, or games of different age groups. One writer suggests grouping games into four classes depending upon the elements of competition, chance, mimicry, or vertigo (motion alone, i. e., teeter-tottering). But these categories are too broad for classification purposes, and it is not clear that the last two represent games at all. A better grouping made by anthropologists classifies games according to their requirements for either physical skill, strategy, or chance. This has proved meaningful for studying the relationship of games to cultural and environmental factors. But for folklore purposes — especially folklore archiving — a more workable classification might be made on the basis of the primary kind of play activity involved — whether physical action, manipulation of objects, or mental activity.

First, **pastimes** (or "amusements") must be distinguished from true games. A pastime, as the name suggests, is a traditional recreation performed simply to pass the time away. It lacks what true games have — the element of competition, the possibility of winning or losing, and a measure of organization with some kind of controlling rules. Most pastimes are solo activities such as bouncing a ball, juggling, balancing oneself on an object, swinging, walking on stilts, spinning a top, operating a yo-yo, and making "Cat's Cradles" (string patterns on one's fingers). When two or more individuals toss a ball about, they are engaging in a mere pastime as long as they introduce on rules and on way of distinguishing a winner. Yo-yoing, top-spinning, rope-jumping, or other such activities may lead to a contest of skill or of endurance and thus turn into true games. Two people balance on a teetertotter more commonly than just one (in the middle of the board), and sometimes two may swing together with one seated and the other standing and "pumping"; these activities, however, remain pastimes.

A solo recreation, on the other hand, may be a game — "Solitare", for instance, is played against an imaginary opponent, and the player may win, or (more commonly) lose. Puzzle solving is something of a game if one thinks of "winning" by finishing the picture or word pattern in a specified time with no outside help. We even bribe ourselves to finish unpleasant or tiresome tasks by "making a game of it" or by promising ourselves a reward upon completion.

Games of physical action may be subdivided by the principal action involved. There are hopping games ("Hopscotch"), chasing games, hiding games, battle games, and dramatic games. At their simplest level, such games are merely outlets for high spirits and a means of getting lively exercise. They provide healthy competitions in strength and skill between individuals or teams. Games like running races, "Leap Frog", "Tag", "Johnny on the Pony", "King on the Hill" satisfy these needs.

Most of the active games involve a certain amount of mimicry of life situations, although it is only the most complex of these recreations that are usually called "dramatic games". Little children play a game that begins with all but one player in a "Jampile" — everyone falls down in a heap with limbs tangled. Then they cry "Doctor, doctor, we need help!" and the remaining child hurries to untangle them. The game is a simple, playful enactment of a horrible scene that might occur in accidents. The game of "Fox Hunt" (or "Hare and Hounds") imitates hunting, with bits of scattered paper instead of a scent as the trail. The city child's counterpart game, "Arrow Chase", is an adaptation for sidewalk playing with detective-like overtones.

Games of mental activity are characterized by guessing, figuring, choosing, and the like, although, of course, they usually also involve some physical action as well, and often manipulation of objects. It is difficult to classify a game like "Lemonade" that involves dialogue, acting, guessing, and chasing. But the heart of the game, is the procedure of one team acting out a kind of work and the other team guessing what it is. When the correct trade is named, the guesser chase the actors, and the game continues with different trades being imitated until all players have been caught. The game of "Statues" is a similar active-mental combination game. A leader whirls and release each player who must then "freeze" in whatever posture the motion leaves him in. Then the leader selects the best "statue," or the funniest, to be next leader.

A few other games of mental activity are played outdoors — "Stone School" on the front steps of a house, for instance, with each child advancing up a grade (i. e., a step) as he guesses which of "teacher's" hands holds a stone. But most are indoor games, frequently what are called parlor games or party games. "Charades" and "Twenty Questions" are two of these which eventually found their way into television "game shows", but a more complex one in folk tradition is "Botticelli", often played by college students or faculty. It requires a leader to give the initials only of a personality, recent or past — real or fictional, in art, music, literature, history, etc. The group guesses at his identification by listing credentials that fit such figures with the same initials. Each time the leader cannot come up with the name that another player has in mind，he must answer truthfully a direct "yes or no" question.

注意：此部分试题请在**答题卡1**上作答。

1. Both the verbal and non-verbal elements of games are important in some researches.
2. Newell's and Brewster's works suggest that games can be divided into singing and non-singing，which is worse than other proposed systems.
3. It is a game when two people swing together with one seated and the other standing and "pumping".
4. An unpleasant or tiresome task might be turned into a game if we promise ourselves a reward upon finishing it.
5. _____ has proved meaningful for studying the relationship of games to cultural and environmental factors.
6. For the purpose of folklore archiving, _____ might be the basis of a more workable classification.
7. Games like "Leap Frog"，"Tag"，and "King on the Hill" satisfy the needs of _____.
8. Games，such as "Jampile"，"Fox Hunt" and "Arrow Chase"，involve _____.
9. In television game shows we can find two folk games. They are _____.
10. When playing the folk game，"Botticelli"，people should ask the leader _____ question.

Part III Listening Comprehension　　　　　(35 minutes)

Section A

Directions: *In this section, you will hear 8 short conversations and 2 long conversations. At the end of each conversation, one or more questions will be asked about what was said. Both the conversation and the questions will be spoken only once. After each question there will be a pause. During the pause, you must read the four choices marked A), B), C) and D), and decide which is the best answer. Then mark the corresponding letter on **Answer Sheet 2** with a single line through the center.*

注意：此部分试题请在**答题卡2**上作答。

11. A) 185 cents.　　　　　　　　　　C) 85 cents.

B) 45 cents.   D) 145 cents.

12. A) Plan C is more comprehensive than plan B.
    B) Plan B is less complete than plan A.
    C) Plan C is the least comprehensive.
    D) Plan A is the most comprehensive.

13. A) She was bored to death by the lecture.
    B) The lecture was not given yesterday after all.
    C) She didn't go to all of yesterday's lectures.
    D) The lecture was rather interesting.

14. A) The camera needs new batteries.
    B) The batteries are not correctly positioned.
    C) There are no batteries inside the camera.
    D) The man should change a new camera.

15. A) The computer isn't working, so we can't get the data this time.
    B) We will have the data shortly if the computer doesn't stop working.
    C) The data is not available from the computer.
    D) We won't get the data until the computer is repaired.

16. A) Professor Smith's success is hard to understand.
    B) Professor Smith is extremely successful.
    C) Professor Smith is less successful this year than he was last year.
    D) Professor Smith's success is due to his good luck.

17. A) She should bring her brother to the party.
    B) The party is going to be very crowded.
    C) He is sorry she can't come to the party.
    D) His brother is coming to the party.

18. A) He hopes to see John after everyone else does.
    B) John was the last person the man saw.
    C) He hasn't seen John for a long time either.
    D) He doesn't want to see John at all.

Questions 19 to 21 are based on the conversation you have just heard.

19. A) Husband and wife.   C) Students.
    B) Co-workers.   D) Brother and sister.

20. A) To hire a home health care worker.   C) To take care of her by himself.

B) To put her into a home.   D) To leave her alone.

21. A) That involves coming home after working a full day and caring not only for your own family but for an elderly woman who needs special things.

B) It will be difficult for other family members to preserve their privacy and other rights.

C) They may not know if grandma will get the care she needs and she will be lonely.

D) If grandma is put into a home, she can't take care of the family.

Questions 22 to 25 are based on the conversation you have just heard.

22. A) His wife doesn't cook him delicious meals.

B) He has a good job and he earns too much money.

C) He never has enough time for exercise.

D) He is worried that he may make a mistake because he has taken a hard job recently.

23. A) For 2 hours.   C) For 7 hours.

B) For 5 hours.   D) For 3 hours.

24. A) The doctor gives him some medicine to help him sleep.

B) The doctor gives him some advice to keep healthy.

C) The doctor is angry with him.

D) The doctor finds something very wrong with him.

25. A) Try to find a different job.

B) Go to see a different doctor.

C) Go back home and have a good sleep.

D) Go to work again in a month's time.

Section B

Directions: *In this section, you will hear 3 short passages. At the end of each passage, you will hear some questions. Both the passage and the questions will be spoken only once. After you hear a question, you must choose the best answer from the four choices marked A), B), C) and D). Then mark the corresponding letter on* **Answer Sheet 2** *with a single line through the center.*

注意：此部分试题请在**答题卡 2** 上作答。

Passage One

Questions 26 to 29 are based on the passage you have just heard.

26. A) Less than one year.   C) More than one year.
    B) One year.   D) Five years.

27. A) Unemployment benefits.   C) Pension.
    B) Free medical treatment.   D) Sickness benefits.

28. A) A 68-year-old man working.   C) A 63-year-old man retired.
    B) A 55-year-old woman retired.   D) A 66-year-old woman working.

29. A) They are willing to pay the high taxes.
    B) They complain of the high taxes.
    C) They don't agree on whether to pay the high taxes or let fellow citizens starve.
    D) They don't think taxes very high.

Passage Two

Questions 30 to 32 are based on the passage you have just heard.

30. A) Britain.   C) France.
    B) Spain.   D) Italy.

31. A) Conservative.   C) Scientific.
    B) Practical.   D) Literary.

32. A) Newspapers.   C) Travel.
    B) Radio and television.   D) Books.

Passage Three

Questions 33 to 35 are based on the passage you have just heard.

33. A) Violating school admission policy.
    B) Rejecting other children attending the school.
    C) Receiving special treatment in school admission.
    D) All the above.

34. A) The newspaper distorts the truth.
    B) The media is biased against children of prominent public figures.
    C) Their privacy has been invaded by the newspaper.

D) Not enough protection is given to children of prominent public figures.

35. A) There's no other school nearby.
    B) The school has good faculty.
    C) The school is located in London.
    D) It is a girls school.

Section C

Directions: *In this section, you will hear a passage three times. When the passage is read for the first time, you should listen carefully for its general idea. When the passage is read for the second time, you are required to fill in the blanks numbered from 36 to 43 with the exact words you have just heard. For blanks numbered from 44 to 46 you are required to fill in the missing information. For these blanks, you can either use the exact words you have just heard or write down the main points in your own words. Finally, when the passage is read for the third time, you should check what you have written.*

注意：此部分试题在**答题卡 2**上；请在**答题卡 2**上作答。

Part IV   Reading Comprehension (Reading in Depth)
(25 minutes)

Section A

Directions: *In this section，there is a short passage with 5 questions or incomplete statements．Read the passage carefully．Then answer the questions or complete the statements in the fewest possible words on **Answer Sheet 2**.*

Questions 47 to 51 are based on the following passage.

Throwing criminals in jail is an ancient and widespread method of punishment，but is it a wise one? It does seem reasonable to keep wrongdoers in a place where they find fewer opportunities to hurt innocent people. The system has long been considered fair and sound by those who want to see the guilty punished and society protected. Yet the value of this form of justice is now being questioned by the very men who have to apply it：the judges.

Does it really help society，or the victim，or the victim's family，to put in jail a man who，while drunk at the wheel of his car，has injured or killed another person? It would be more helpful to make the man pay for his victim's medical bills and compensate him for the bad experience，the loss of working time，and any other problems arising from the accident. If the victim is dead, in most cases his family could use some financial assistance.

And a young thief who spends time in jail receives there a thorough education in crime from his fellow prisoners. Willingly or not, he has to associate with tough criminals who will drag him into more serious offenses and more prison terms.

Such considerations have caused a number of English and American judges to try some new forms of punishment for light criminals, unpleasant enough to discourage the offenders from repeating their offenses, but safe for them because they are not exposed to dangerous company. They pay for their crime by helping their victims, financially or otherwise, or doing unpaid labor for their community; or perhaps they take a job and repay their victim out of their salary. This sort of punishment is applied only to nonviolent criminals who are not likely to be dangerous to the public, such as forgers（伪造者）, shoplifters, and drivers who have caused traffic accidents. The sentenced criminal has the right to refuse the new type of punishment if he prefers a prison term.

注意：此部分试题请在**答题卡**2 上作答。

47. Why is throwing criminals in jail a reasonable method of punishment?

48. Why do the judges doubt the value of throwing criminals in jail as a form of justice?

49. The judges try punishing the light criminals by _____.

50. How do the new forms of punishment benefit the light criminals?

51. What if a criminal refuses the new form of punishment?

Section B

Directions: *There are 2 passages in this section. Each passage is followed by some questions or unfinished statements. For each of them there are four choices marked A), B), C) and D). You should decide on the best choice and mark the corresponding letter on Answer Sheet 2 with a single line through the center.*

Passage One

Questions 52 to 56 are based on the following passage.

In reading the pages of *American Scientist*, I have been struck by the stunning progress being made in science and engineering, new phenomena discovered, new materials synthesized, new methods developed. What I see behind many of these exciting stories is the widespread and even evolutionary use of distributed intelligence that is made possible by the "wiring" of the scientific community. It is more than a time saver or a communication enhance; it is enabling us to think in new ways and its impact on society may be monumental.

The term "information age" probably does not do justice to the possibilities of this emerging era. This is an age of "knowledge and distributed intelligence", in which knowledge is available to anyone, located anywhere, at any time; and in which power, information, and control are moving from centralized systems to individuals. This era calls for a new form of leadership and vision from the academic science and engineering community. Academic science and engineering have enabled our society to make the most of new technologies. We wouldn't have today's advanced computer graphics systems if mathematicians hadn't been able to solve problems related to surface geometry. We wouldn't have networks capable of handling massive amounts of data if physicists and astronomers hadn't continuously forged tools to look more deeply into subatomic structures and the cosmos. And the information made available by the sequencing of the human genome（基因组）has caused us to rethink how to store, manipulate, and retrieve data most effectively. It will take new insights from studies of human cognition, linguistics, neurobiology, computing, and more to develop systems that truly augment our capacity to learn and create. The best may be yet to come.

Despite brutally tight constraints on federal discretionary spending, President Clinton has stepped forward to champion a 3 percent increase in the national 1998 budget. The President's request is only the first step in the congressional budget process ahead. Given that the priorities of Congress will almost certainly differ from those of the President, it will take an unprecedented level of input and commitment from the research community to ensure the investments in science and engineering.

注意：此部分试题请在**答题卡 2** 上作答。

52. The word "wiring" (Line 5, Para. 1) most probably means _____.
   A) competition   C) advancement
   B) cooperation   D) expansion

53. By mentioning "advanced computer graphics systems" and mathematicians' solutions to "problems related to surface geometry", the writer means _____.
   A) we have entered an age of "knowledge and distributed intelligence"

B) stunning progress has been made in science and engineering

C) academic science and engineering have enabled our society to make the most of new technologies

D) distributed intelligence is a time saver and a communication enhance

54. By saying "It will take new insights from studies of human cognition, linguistics, neurobiology, computing, and more to develop systems that truly augment our capacity to learn and create", the writer suggests _____.

A) applying academic studies to practical use

B) making knowledge accessible to anyone, anywhere, at any time

C) moving power, information and control from centralized systems to individuals

D) thinking of new ways to store, manipulate and retrieve data most effectively

55. It can be inferred from the last paragraph that _____.

A) President Clinton does not give priority to the research community

B) Congress is not very satisfied with the research community and thus unwilling to invest in science and engineering

C) the research community should work hard to get more federal spending in science and engineering

D) Congress will not grant President Clinton's request

56. The main purpose of this passage is to _____.

A) inform the public of the stunning progress being made in science and engineering

B) encourage scientists to make more breakthroughs in academic studies

C) urge the application of academic science and engineering to produce new technologies

D) secure the financial support from Congress

Passage Two

Questions 57 to 61 are based on the following passage.

Much of the American anxiety about old age is a flight from the reality of death. One of the striking qualities of the American character is the unwillingness to face either the fact or meaning of death. In the more somber tradition of American literature — from Hawthorne and Melville and Poe to Faulkner and Hemingway — one finds a tragic depth that belies the surface thinness of the ordinary American death attitudes. By an effort of the imagination, the great writers faced problems which the culture in action is reluctant to face — the fact of death, its mystery, and its place in the back-and-forth shuttling of the eternal recurrence. The unblinking confrontation of death in Greek times, the elaborate patterns woven around it in the Middle Ages, the ritual celebration of it in the rich peasant cultures of Latin and Slavic Europe and in primitive cultures; these are difficult to find in American life.

Whether through fear of the emotional depths, or because of a drying up of the sluices of religious intensity, the American avoids dwelling on death or even coming to terms with it; he finds it morbid and recoils from it, surrounding it with word avoidance (Americans never die; they "pass away") and various taboos of speech and practice. A "funeral parlor" is decorated to look like a bank; everything in a funeral ceremony is done in hushed tones, as if it were something furtive, to be concealed from the world; there is so much emphasis on being dignified that the ceremony often loses its quality of dignity. In some of the primitive cultures, there is difficulty in understanding the causes of death; it seems puzzling and even unintelligible. Living in a scientific culture, Americans have a ready enough explanation of how it comes, yet they show little capacity to come to terms with the fact of death itself and with the grief that accompanies it. "We jubilate over birth and dance at weddings," writes Margaret Mead, "but more and more hustle the dead off the scene without ceremony, without an opportunity for young and old to realize that death is as much a fact of life as is birth." And, one may add, even in its hurry and brevity, the last stage of an American's life — the last occasion of his relation to his society — is as standardized as the rest.

注意：此部分试题请在**答题卡** 2 上作答。

57. Which of the following best describes the American attitude toward death?
    A) Indifference.   C) Hatred.
    B) Grief.   D) Disgust.
58. In the literature by great American writers, one will find _____.
    A) the ordinary American attitude toward death
    B) a willingness to accept death as a fact of life
    C) an imaginary introduction to other cultures' attitudes toward death
    D) the foundation of modern American beliefs about death
59. The phrase "pass away" suggests _____.
    A) the religious overtones of death
    B) indifference with which most Americans regard death
    C) American reluctance to face the reality of death
    D) the average American belief in immortality

60. Margaret Mead suggests that _____ .

A) we should not rejoice at birth and marriage

B) death should be accepted in the same spirit as marriage and birth

C) we should grieve over death just as we rejoice at birth and marriage

D) dignity should be emphasized at death as well as birth and marriage

61. In one respect, an American's burial is much like the rest of his life because it is

_____ .

A) morbid   C) in a hurry

B) full of anxiety   D) standardized

Part V Error Correction   (15 minutes)

Directions: *This part consists of a short passage. In this passage, there are altogether 10 mistakes, one in each numbered line. You may have to change a word, add a word or delete a word. Mark out the mistakes and put the corrections in the blanks provided. If you change a word, cross it out and write the correct word in the corresponding blank. If you add a word, put an insertion mark (∧) in the right place and write the missing word in the blank. If you delete a word, cross it out and put a slash (/) in the blank.*

注意：此部分试题在**答题卡** 2 上；请在**答题卡** 2 上作答。

Part VI Translation   (5 minutes)

Directions: *Complete the following sentences on **Answer Sheet 2** by translating into English the Chinese given in brackets.*

注意：此部分试题请在**答题卡** 2 上作答,只需写出译文部分。

72. The government was corrupt because of _____
（一些受贿事件和官员们的贪婪）.

73. They have pledged that they will _____
（在任何情况下严格保守这个秘密）.

74. At least one newspaper contended that _____

（如果保安的数量没有减少的话，这个灾难是可以被避免的）.

75. The reason why the Hiltons are having problems with their son is that they were
_____（在他小的时候对他太宽容，他要什么给什么）.

76. The government will _____
（把那五个被怀疑是间谍的人驱逐出境）.

答题卡 1 (Answer Sheet 1)

	准		考		证		号							
[0]	[0]	[0]	[0]	[0]	[0]	[0]	[0]	[0]	[0]	[0]	[0]	[0]	[0]	[0]
[1]	[1]	[1]	[1]	[1]	[1]	[1]	[1]	[1]	[1]	[1]	[1]	[1]	[1]	[1]
[2]	[2]	[2]	[2]	[2]	[2]	[2]	[2]	[2]	[2]	[2]	[2]	[2]	[2]	[2]
[3]	[3]	[3]	[3]	[3]	[3]	[3]	[3]	[3]	[3]	[3]	[3]	[3]	[3]	[3]
[4]	[4]	[4]	[4]	[4]	[4]	[4]	[4]	[4]	[4]	[4]	[4]	[4]	[4]	[4]
[5]	[5]	[5]	[5]	[5]	[5]	[5]	[5]	[5]	[5]	[5]	[5]	[5]	[5]	[5]
[6]	[6]	[6]	[6]	[6]	[6]	[6]	[6]	[6]	[6]	[6]	[6]	[6]	[6]	[6]
[7]	[7]	[7]	[7]	[7]	[7]	[7]	[7]	[7]	[7]	[7]	[7]	[7]	[7]	[7]
[8]	[8]	[8]	[8]	[8]	[8]	[8]	[8]	[8]	[8]	[8]	[8]	[8]	[8]	[8]
[9]	[9]	[9]	[9]	[9]	[9]	[9]	[9]	[9]	[9]	[9]	[9]	[9]	[9]	[9]

学校:

姓名:

划线要求

Part I　　　　　　　　　　**Writing**　　　　　　　　**(30 minutes)**

Directions: *For this part, you are allowed 30 minutes to write a short essay entitled* **DINK** *Family. You should write at least* **150** *words following the outline given below:*

1. 丁克家庭的出现
2. 人们选择丁克家庭的原因
3. 我的观点

DINK Family

答题卡 1 (Answer Sheet 1)

Part II   Reading Comprehension (Skimming and Scanning) (15 minutes)

1. [Y] [N] [NG]   5. _____   8. _____
2. [Y] [N] [NG]
3. [Y] [N] [NG]   6. _____   9. _____
4. [Y] [N] [NG]
                       7. _____   10. _____

答题卡 2 (Answer Sheet 2)

学校:	准　　考　　证　　号

学校:

姓名:

划线要求

准　考　证　号

[0] [0] [0] [0] [0] [0] [0] [0] [0] [0] [0] [0] [0] [0] [0]
[1] [1] [1] [1] [1] [1] [1] [1] [1] [1] [1] [1] [1] [1] [1]
[2] [2] [2] [2] [2] [2] [2] [2] [2] [2] [2] [2] [2] [2] [2]
[3] [3] [3] [3] [3] [3] [3] [3] [3] [3] [3] [3] [3] [3] [3]
[4] [4] [4] [4] [4] [4] [4] [4] [4] [4] [4] [4] [4] [4] [4]
[5] [5] [5] [5] [5] [5] [5] [5] [5] [5] [5] [5] [5] [5] [5]
[6] [6] [6] [6] [6] [6] [6] [6] [6] [6] [6] [6] [6] [6] [6]
[7] [7] [7] [7] [7] [7] [7] [7] [7] [7] [7] [7] [7] [7] [7]
[8] [8] [8] [8] [8] [8] [8] [8] [8] [8] [8] [8] [8] [8] [8]
[9] [9] [9] [9] [9] [9] [9] [9] [9] [9] [9] [9] [9] [9] [9]

Part III　Section A

11. [A] [B] [C] [D]
12. [A] [B] [C] [D]
13. [A] [B] [C] [D]
14. [A] [B] [C] [D]
15. [A] [B] [C] [D]
16. [A] [B] [C] [D]
17. [A] [B] [C] [D]
18. [A] [B] [C] [D]
19. [A] [B] [C] [D]
20. [A] [B] [C] [D]
21. [A] [B] [C] [D]
22. [A] [B] [C] [D]
23. [A] [B] [C] [D]
24. [A] [B] [C] [D]
25. [A] [B] [C] [D]

Section B

26. [A] [B] [C] [D]
27. [A] [B] [C] [D]
28. [A] [B] [C] [D]
29. [A] [B] [C] [D]
30. [A] [B] [C] [D]
31. [A] [B] [C] [D]
32. [A] [B] [C] [D]
33. [A] [B] [C] [D]
34. [A] [B] [C] [D]
35. [A] [B] [C] [D]

Part III　Section C

The supporters of traditional education have always (36) _____ that maturity of thought could only be gained by the study of past thinkers and past events. In their view only a thorough (37) _____ training can give a person the ability to look at (38) _____ problems from above in a (39) _____ way. They remind the students that the purpose of a college education is to (40) _____ the mind; it has never been to help graduates get a (41) _____ job. And, they add, this broad education was (42) _____ because it was never limited to a narrow (43) _____. However, a majority of students complain that (44) _____
_____.

Since sciences and techniques have changed a great deal in the latter half of the century, they think, (45) _____
_____.

There is much more to know in every field to get prepared for a career, a job. Moreover, (46) _____
_____.

答题卡 2 (Answer Sheet 2)

Part IV   Section A   Part V   Error Correction   (15 minutes)

47. _____

_____

48. _____

_____

49. _____

_____

50. _____

_____

51. _____

_____

Part IV   Section B

52. [A][B][C][D]
53. [A][B][C][D]
54. [A][B][C][D]
55. [A][B][C][D]
56. [A][B][C][D]
57. [A][B][C][D]
58. [A][B][C][D]
59. [A][B][C][D]
60. [A][B][C][D]
61. [A][B][C][D]

For centuries keeping apart the sick and the supposedly
sick was the chief defense of nations for infectious diseases.   62. _____
Quarantine (检疫) was particularly hard on travelers entering a
country from an infecting area — which recently meant most of   63. _____
the world. In holding such persons for a fixed time, it was   64. _____
believed that enough time would be given for any undeveloped
disease to show itself.

Although it was started with goodwill, the good name of
quarantine was ruined by the bad uses in which it was put.   65. _____
Traders, being angered by constant delays, finally turned against   66. _____
it. By the middle of the nineteenth century the feeling has   67. _____
become so great that the first international meeting on
Quarantine was held. Twelve countries took part. After half a
year of talk an agreement was arrived, dealing with the control   68. _____
of three major infectious diseases. Only three countries signed
the agreement, and two of which later insisted on getting out of   69. _____
it.

Still, it was a start. Ten international meetings in the next
half century showed more agreement on the part of nations to
talk about health problems. Once it was known that caused   70. _____
outbreaks it was much easier to take measures to stop it.   71. _____

Part VI   Translation   (5 minutes)

72. _____

73. _____

74. _____

75. _____

76. _____

PRACTICE TEST 4

Part I   Writing   (30 minutes)

注意：此部分试题在答题卡 1 上。

Part II   Reading Comprehension (Skimming and Scanning)
(15 minutes)

Directions: *In this part, you will have 15 minutes to go over the passage quickly and answer the questions on* **Answer Sheet 1**.

For questions 1 – 4, mark

Y *(for YES)*   *if the statement agrees with the information given in the passage;*

N *(for NO)*   *if the statement contradicts the information given in the passage;*

NG *(for NOT GIVEN)*   *if the information is not given in the passage.*

For questions 5 – 10, complete the sentences with the information given in the passage.

The Industrial Revolution

There is a tendency in many histories to confuse together what we have called the *mechanical revolution*, which was an entirely new thing in human experience arising out of the development of organised science, a new step like the invention of agriculture or the discovery of metals, with something else, quite different in its origins, something for which there was already an historical precedent, the social and financial development which is called the *industrial revolution*. The two processes were going on together, they were constantly reacting upon each other, but they were in root and essence different. There would have been an industrial revolution of sorts if there had been no coal, no steam, no machinery; but in that case it would probably have followed far more closely upon the lines of the social and financial developments of the later years of the Roman republic. It would have repeated the story of dispossessed free cultivators, gang labour, great estates, great financial fortunes, and a socially destructive financial process. Even the factory method came before power and machinery. Factories were the product not of machinery, but of the "division of labour". Drilled and sweated workers were making such things as millinery, cardboard boxes and furniture, and colouring maps and book illustrations and so forth, before even water-wheels had been used for industrial purposes. There were factories in Rome in the days of Augustus. New books, for instance, were dictated to rows of copyists in the factories of the book-sellers. The attentive students of Defoe and of the political pamphlets of Fielding will realise that the idea of herding poor people · into establishments to work collectively for their living was already current in Britain before the close of the seventeenth century. There are intimations of it even as early as More's *Utopia* (1516). It was a social and not a mechanical development.

Up to past the middle of the eighteenth century the social and economic history of western Europe was in fact retreading the path along which the Roman state had gone in the last three centuries B. C. But the political disunions of Europe, the political convulsions against monarchy, the recalcitrance of the common folk and perhaps also the great accessibility of the western European intelligence to mechanical ideas and inventions, turned the process into quite novel directions. Ideas of human solidarity, thanks to Christianity, were far more widely diffused in the newer European world, political power was not so concentrated, and the man of energy anxious to get rich turned his mind, therefore, very willingly from the ideas of the slave and of gang labour to the idea of mechanical power and the machine.

The mechanical revolution, the process of mechanical invention and discovery, was a new thing in human experience, and it went on regardless of the social, political, economic and industrial consequences it might produce. The industrial revolution, on the other hand, like most other human affairs, was and is more and more profoundly changed and deflected by the constant variation in human conditions caused by the mechanical revolution. And the essential difference between the amassing of riches, the extinction of small farmers and small business men, and the phase of big finance in the latter centuries of the Roman republic on the one hand, and the very similar concentration of capital in the eighteenth and nineteenth centuries on the other, lies in the profound difference in the character of labour that the mechanical revolution was bringing about. The power of the Old World was human power; everything depended ultimately upon the driving power of human muscle, the muscle of ignorant and subjugated men. A little animal muscle, supplied by draft oxen, horse traction, and the like, contributed. Where a weight had to be lifted, men lifted it; where a rock had to be quarried, men chipped it out; where a field had to be ploughed, men and oxen ploughed it; the Roman equivalent of the steamship was the galley with its banks of sweating rowers. A vast proportion of mankind in the early civilisations were employed in purely mechanical drudgery. At its onset, power-driven machinery did not seem to promise any release from such unintelligent toil. Great gangs of men were employed in excavating canals, in making railway cuttings and embankments, and the like. The number of miners increased enormously. But the extension of facilities and the output of commodities increased much more. And as the nineteenth century went on, the plain logic of the new situation asserted itself more clearly. Human beings were no longer wanted as a source of mere indiscriminated power. What could be done mechanically by a human being could be done faster and better by a machine. The human being was needed now only where choice and intelligence had to be exercised. Human beings were wanted only as human beings. The *drudge*, on whom all the previous civilisation had rested, the creature of mere obedience, the man whose brains were superfluous, had become unnecessary to the welfare of mankind.

This was as true of such ancient industries as agriculture and mining as it was of the newest metallurgical processes. For ploughing, sowing, and harvesting, swift machines came forward to do the work of scores of men. The Roman civilization was built upon cheap and degraded human beings; modern civilization is being rebuilt upon cheap mechanical power. For a hundred years power has been getting cheaper and labour dearer. If for a generation or so machinery has had to wait its turn in the mine, it is simply because for a time men were cheaper than machinery.

Now here was a change-over of quite primary importance in human affairs. The chief solicitude of the rich and of the ruler in the old civilization had been to keep up a supply of drudges. As the nineteenth century went on, it became more and more plain to the intelligent people that the common man had now to be something better than a drudge. He had to be educated — if only to secure "industrial efficiency." He had to understand what he was about. From the days of the first Christian propaganda, popular education had been smouldering in Europe, just as it had smouldered in Asia wherever Islam has set its food, because of the necessity of making the believer understand a little of the belief by which he is saved, and of enabling him to read a little in the sacred books by which his belief is conveyed. Christian controversies, with their competition for adherents, ploughed the ground for the harvest of popular education. In England, for instance, by the thirties and forties of the nineteenth century, the disputes of the sects and the necessity of catching adherents young had produced a series of competing educational organisations for children, the church "National" schools, the dissenting "British" schools, and even Roman Catholic elementary schools. The second half of the nineteenth century was a period of rapid advance in popular education throughout all the westernised world. There was no parallel advance in the education of the upper class — some advance, no doubt, but nothing to correspond — and so the great gulf that had divided that world hitherto into the readers and the non-reading mass became little more than a slightly perceptible difference in educational level. At the back of this process was the mechanical revolution, apparently regardless of social conditions, but really insisting inexorably upon the complete abolition of a totally illiterate class throughout the world.

The economic revolution of the Roman republic had never been clearly apprehended by the common people of Rome. The ordinary Roman citizen never saw the changes through which he lived, clearly and comprehensively as we see them. But the industrial revolution, as it went on towards the end of the nineteenth century, was more and more distinctly *seen* as one whole process by the common people it was affecting, because presently they could read and discuss and communicate, and because they went about and saw things as no commonly had ever done before.

注意：此部分试题请在**答题卡** 1 上作答。

1. The mechanical revolution and the industrial revolution are two processes going on together and reacting upon each other, but were different in root and essence.

2. For the social and financial development called the mechanical revolution there was already an historical precedent.

3. Factories were the result of division of labour and they came before there were power and machinery.

4. Up to past the middle of the eighteenth century the man of energy turned his mind very willingly to the idea of mechanical power and the machine.

5. As early as the close of the seventeenth century, _____ was already current in Britain.

6. The concentration of capital in the 18th and 19th centuries lies in _____.

7. In the Old World obedient men whose brains were superfluous were needed while in the 19th century _____ were in need.

8. Before mechanical revolution _____ was cheaper than _____ _____.

9. _____ was a period of rapid advance in popular education throughout all the westernised world.

10. The common people, affected by the industrial revolution, could clearly see it as one whole process because they could _____.

Part III Listening Comprehension   (35 minutes)

Section A

Directions: *In this section, you will hear 8 short conversations and 2 long conversations. At the end of each conversation, one or more questions will be asked about what was said. Both the conversation and the questions will be spoken only once. After each question there will be a pause. During the pause, you must read the four choices marked A), B), C) and D), and decide which is the best answer. Then mark the corresponding letter on the **Answer Sheet 2** with a single line through the center.*

注意：此部分试题请在**答题卡** 2 上作答。

11. A) She will put on makeup for the exam.
    B) She failed the exam.
    C) She did very well in the exam.
    D) She hopes to take another exam.

12. A) Tom won a close game.
    B) Tom didn't get a single point.
    C) It is too bad Tom didn't score another point.
    D) Tom is the best one by far.

13. A) She is sorting the mails.
    B) She is going through the procedures for a visa.
    C) She is sending a registered letter.
    D) She is applying to a university.

14. A) Four.   C) Eleven.
    B) Seven.   D) Twelve.

15. A) At 6:30.   C) At 8:30.
    B) At 7:30.   D) At 10:30.

16. A) He thinks they should walk home.
    B) He doesn't agree with the woman.
    C) He thinks it is better to wait.
    D) He prefers to take a bus.

17. A) He feels better now.   C) He feels rather angry.

B) He feels still sick.   D) He feels pretty fine.

18. A) The man used Frank's car without his permission.

 B) Louise borrowed a car from Frank and the man didn't give it back.

 C) Louise lent Frank's car to the man without his knowledge.

 D) The man lent Louise Frank's car.

Questions 19 to 21 are based on the conversation you have just heard.

19. A) In a school.   C) In a shop.

 B) At a work place.   D) In a post office.

20. A) He will show little enthusiasm.

 B) He will not buy a car or a house to start a family.

 C) He will try to find a job in another company.

 D) He will not make the office run efficiently.

21. A) Bob didn't work in that company long enough.

 B) Bob didn't do his work adequately.

 C) Bob's expenses were too much to be covered.

 D) Bob's merit didn't deserve a raise at that time.

Questions 22 to 25 are based on the conversation you have just heard.

22. A) Forty million people.   C) Eight million people.

 B) Twenty million people.   D) Seven million people.

23. A) He has never seen real food in his life.

 B) He sees that rich people eat only tomato, lettuce and beef.

 C) He is hungry and homeless.

 D) He can eat soylent, which people eat like crackers.

24. A) At that time, half of the people there are unemployed.

 B) It is much hotter than it is today all year round.

 C) Most people have no real food to eat and no apartment to live in.

 D) People see the sun every day and it is hot all year round.

25. A) It isn't far from the reality because the greenhouse effect is beginning.

 B) He is scared because it might happen.

 C) The movie is a wrong prediction of the future.

 D) It is disgusting to avoid New York in 2022.

Section B

Directions: *In this section, you will hear 3 short passages. At the end of each passage, you will hear some questions. Both the passage and the questions will be spoken only once. After you hear a question, you must choose the best answer from the four choices marked A), B), C) and D). Then mark the corresponding letter on Answer Sheet 2 with a single line through the center.*

注意：此部分试题请在**答题卡**2上作答。

Passage One

Questions 26 to 29 are based on the passage you have just heard.

26. A) Juvenile crime.
    B) Theft.
    C) Robbery.
    D) Murder.

27. A) New York.
    B) Chicago.
    C) Washington.
    D) Los Angeles.

28. A) One in ten.
    B) One in twenty.
    C) One in thirty.
    D) One in forty.

29. A) Because he broke traffic rules.
    B) Because he murdered a gas station owner.
    C) Because he committed robbery.
    D) Because he was identified as the killer by witnesses.

Passage Two

Questions 30 to 32 are based on the passage you have just heard.

30. A) Problems of world energy.
    B) Third world affairs.
    C) U.S. relationship with Canada and Mexico.
    D) Recent conflicts in the Middle East.

31. A) Women's different ideas.
    B) A couple dealing with middle age.
    C) American foreign policy.
    D) Music.

32. A) At 6:00.
    B) At 8:00.
    C) At 10:30.
    D) At 12:30.

Passage Three

Questions 33 to 35 are based on the passage you have just heard.

33. A) There are fewer young smokers than adult smokers.
    B) Young smokers smoke more on special social occasions.
    C) Young smokers smoke less than adult smokers.
    D) The progression through the three stages varies with the age at which one starts smoking.

34. A) The first stage.   C) The third stage.
    B) The second stage.   D) All the three stages.

35. A) Smokers tend to associate with each other.
    B) Smokers tend to be more independent than non-smokers.
    C) Children whose family members smoke are more likely to smoke.
    D) Poor students are more likely to smoke than good ones.

Section C

Directions: *In this section, you will hear a passage three times. When the passage is read for the first time, you should listen carefully for its general idea. When the passage is read for the second time, you are required to fill in the blanks numbered from 36 to 43 with the exact words you have just heard. For blanks numbered from 44 to 46 you are required to fill in the missing information. For these blanks, you can either use the exact words you have just heard or write down the main points in your own words. Finally, when the passage is read for the third time, you should check what you have written.*

注意：此部分试题在**答题卡**2上；请在**答题卡**2上作答。

Part IV   Reading Comprehension (Reading in Depth)
(25 minutes)

Section A

Directions: *In this section, there is a short passage with 5 questions or incomplete statements. Read the passage carefully. Then answer the questions or complete the statements in the fewest possible words on **Answer Sheet 2**.*

Questions 47 to 51 are based on the following passage.

Since World War II, there has been a clearly discernible trend, especially among the growing group of college students, toward early marriage. Many youths begin dating in the first stages of adolescence, "go steady" through high school, and marry before their formal education has been completed. However, emotional maturity is no respecter of birthdays; it does not arrive automatically at twenty-one or twenty-five. Some achieve it surprisingly early, while others never do, even in three score years and ten.

Many students are marrying as an escape from their own personal problems of isolation and loneliness. However any marriage entered into as an escape cannot prove entirely successful. The sad fact is that marriage seldom solves one's problems; more often, it merely intensifies them. Furthermore, it is doubtful whether the home as an institution is capable of carrying all that the young are seeking to put into it. Young people correctly understand that their parents are wrong in believing that success is the ultimate good, but they erroneously believe that they themselves have found the true center of life's meaning. Their expectations of marriage are essentially utopian or unrealistic, and therefore incapable of fulfilment. They want too much, and tragic disillusionment is often bound to follow.

Shall we, then, join chorus of misery over early marriages? One cannot generalize: all early marriages are not bad any more than all later ones are good. Satisfactory marriages are determined not by chronological age, but by the emotional maturity of the partners. Therefore, each case must be judged on its own merits. If the early marriage is not an escape, if it is entered into with relatively few illusions or false expectations, and if it is economically feasible, why not? Good marriages can be made from sixteen to sixty, and so can bad ones.

注意：此部分试题请在**答题卡 2** 上作答。

47. Why do young people marry at an early age?

48. What do people who marry early believe?

49. Youthful expectations of marriage can be described as _____.

50. What is the result of the high expectations of marriage?

51. What plays a decisive role in a happy marriage?

Section B

Directions: *There are 2 passages in this section. Each passage is followed by some questions or unfinished statements. For each of them there are four choices marked A), B), C) and D). You should decide on the best choice and mark the corresponding letter on **Answer Sheet 2** with a single line through the center.*

Passage One

Questions 52 to 56 are based on the following passage.

In a recent survey, researchers concluded that the average half-hour children's television show contains 47 violent acts. When asked about the survey, network television executive Jean Pater responded, "I sure as heck don't think that Bugs Bunny's pouring a glass of milk over a chipmunk's head is violence." The real issue is whether children view such acts as violence.

The violence programming aimed at children always appears in the context of fantasy. Cartoon violence generally includes animation, humor and a remote setting; make-believe violence generally uses only the first two cues; realistic, acted violence, which is not used in programming for children, depends entirely on the viewer's knowledge that the portrayal is fictional. Most children as young as four years can distinguish these three contexts, though there is no support for the idea that children, especially young children, can differentiate types of violence on a cognitive or rational basis — for example, by justification of the motives for the violent behavior.

There is no evidence of direct imitation of television violence by children, though there is evidence that fantasy violence can energize previously learned aggressive responses, such as a physical attack on another child during play. It is by no means clear, however, that the violence in a portrayal is solely responsible for this energizing effect. Rather, the evidence suggests that any exciting material can trigger subsequent aggressive behavior and that it is the excitation rather than the portrayal of violence that instigates or energizes any subsequent violent behavior. "Cold" imitation by children is extremely rare, and the very occasional evidence of direct association between television violence and aggressive behavior has been limited to extremely novel and violent acts by teenagers or adults with already established patterns of deviant behavior. The instigational effect means, in the short term, that exposure to violent portrayals could be dangerous if shortly after the exposure (within 15 to 20 minutes), the child happens to be in a situation that calls for interpersonal aggression as an appropriate response — for example, an argument between siblings or among peers. This same instigational effect, however, could be produced by other exciting but nonviolent television content or by any other excitational source, including, ironically, a parent's turning off the set.

So there is no convincing causal evidence of any cumulative instigational effects such as more aggressive or violent dispositions in children. The evidence does not warrant the strong conclusions advanced by many critics who tend to use television violence as a scapegoat to draw public attention away from the real causes and parents and a culture that celebrates violence generally.

注意：此部分试题请在**答题卡 2** 上作答。

52. According to the passage, children can NOT distinguish between _____.
    A) violent and nonviolent acts   C) different types of violence
    B) underlying motives for violence   D) realistic and fantasy violence

53. Which of the following does NOT belong to the three contexts of violence?
    A) Acted violence.   C) Cartoon violence.
    B) Fictional violence.   D) Make-believe violence.

54. "Cold imitation" (Line 7, Para. 3) refers to _____.
    A) violent behavior as a result of exposure to exciting but nonviolent television content
    B) violent behavior as a result of exposure to violent portrayals only
    C) established patterns of deviant behavior
    D) aggressive personality formed by imitation of television violence

55. According to the passage, the instigational effect can _____.
    A) energize previously learned aggressive responses
    B) make the exposure to violent portrayals more dangerous
    C) trigger subsequent violent behavior
    D) form more violent dispositions in children

56. We can conclude from the passage that _____.
    A) children's view of violence is different from that of adults
    B) the culture helps foster violent behavior in children
    C) the public do not pay adequate attention to the causes of violence in children
    D) heavy viewing of television violence will make people aggressive by nature

Passage Two

Questions 57 to 61 are based on the following passage.

In the United States and other developed countries, the numbers of new AIDS diagnoses and deaths have fallen substantially during the past three years. The age-adjusted death rate from AIDS declined 48 percent from 1996 to 1997. These trends are due to several factors, including improved prophylaxis against opportunistic infections and improved treatment, the growing experience among health professionals in caring for HIV-infected patients, improved access to health care, and the decrease in the number of new HIV infections due to prevention efforts and to the fact that a substantial proportion of persons with high-risk behavior are already infected.

However, the most influential factor has clearly been the increased use of potent anti-HIV drugs, generally administered in combinations of three or more agents. Such combinations are known as highly active antiretroviral therapy (抗逆转录酶病毒疗法). The development of therapies for HIV infection has been remarkably successful, reflecting an effective synergy among government, industry, and academia. Sixteen anti-HIV drugs are now licensed by the U. S. Food and Drug Administration. These drugs have had dramatic effects in reversing the extent of illness in many patients with advanced disease, as well as in preventing the progression of disease in those who are relatively healthy.

Consensus guidelines have been developed for the use of highly active anti-retroviral therapy in adults and adolescents, as well as in children and in HIV-infected pregnant women. These guidelines, when appropriately applied, have greatly improved the prognosis for HIV-infected people and have markedly reduced the risk of HIV transmission from mother to baby.

Despite the enormous beneficial effects of highly active antiretroviral therapy, many HIV-infected people have unfortunately not had adequate responses to the regimens, cannot tolerate the toxic effects, or have difficulty complying with treatment that involves large numbers of pills, myriad interactions with other drugs, and complicated dosing schedules in which intake of food and liquids must be taken into account. In addition, the emergence of strains of HIV that are resistant to currently available drugs is a widespread and growing problem.

Although there is evidence of improvement in immune-system function in most patients who receive combination antiretroviral therapy, complete normalization of the immune system and complete eradication of the virus from the body appear unlikely with currently available therapies. The persistence of latent HIV despite therapy that successfully suppresses detectable levels of HIV in plasma (血浆) is particularly problematic and suggests that lifelong treatment may be necessary with drugs that are currently expensive. In patients in whom plasma HIV had been suppressed by highly active antiretroviral therapy to be below detectable levels for a median of 390 days, levels invariably rebounded within three weeks after the cessation of therapy.

注意：此部分试题请在**答题卡2**上作答。

57. The following factors have contributed to the decrease of the new AIDS diagnoses and death toll in the developed countries EXCEPT _____.
    A) the improved prophylaxis against opportunistic infections
    B) the improved professional caring for HIV-infected patients
    C) the modification of people's high-risk behaviors
    D) the increased use of potent anti-HIV drugs

58. Which of the following statements is NOT true about anti-HIV drugs?
    A) They reflect the effective cooperation among government，industry and academia.
    B) They can relieve the illness in patients and prevent the healthy from HIV.
    C) They cannot improve immune-system functions once for all.
    D) They can prevent new-born babies from being infected.

59. The word "prognosis"（Line 4，Para. 3）most probably means _____.
    A) the diagnosis of AIDS
    B) the effect of the treatment
    C) the development of the therapy
    D) the normalization of the immune system

60. The antiretroviral therapy has the following problems EXCEPT _____.
    A) the side effects
    B) the growing resistance of HIV to currently available drugs
    C) the complicated interactions with other drugs
    D) the complicated schedules of intake of food and liquids

61. The antiretroviral therapy can _____.
    A) lead to complete normalization of the immune system
    B) suppress detectable levels of HIV and latent HIV
    C) not be suspended for more than three weeks
    D) not be used with other drugs

Part V Error Correction   (15 minutes)

Directions： *This part consists of a short passage. In this passage, there are altogether 10 mistakes, one in each numbered line. You may have to change a word, add a word or* *delete a word. Mark out the mistakes and put the corrections in the blanks provided. If you change a word, cross it out and write the correct word in the corresponding blank. If you add a word, put an insertion mark (∧) in the right place and write the missing word in the blank. If you delete a word, cross it out and put a slash (/) in the blank.*

注意：此部分试题在**答题卡 2** 上；请在**答题卡 2** 上作答。

Part VI Translation (5 minutes)

Directions: *Complete the following sentences on* **Answer Sheet 2** *by translating into English the Chinese given in brackets.*

注意：此部分试题请在**答题卡 2** 上作答，只需写出译文部分。

72. As they entered the village, the old lady behind the counter _____ (向他们亲切微笑以示欢迎).

73. My fingernails are so brittle that _____ (它们还没长到足够去抛光的长度就断裂了).

74. _____ (总统没有公开指责邻国的政策) alienated his supporters and jeopardized his position.

75. _____ (以丑闻为威胁，他胁迫该公司支付) him a large sum of money for keeping quiet.

76. A dialogue _____ (迎合学生们的好奇心的) has an inherent interest for him.

答题卡 1 (Answer Sheet 1)

| 学校: |
| 姓名: |
| 划线要求 |

准	考	证	号

[0]	[0]	[0]	[0]	[0]	[0]	[0]	[0]	[0]	[0]	[0]	[0]	[0]	[0]	[0]
[1]	[1]	[1]	[1]	[1]	[1]	[1]	[1]	[1]	[1]	[1]	[1]	[1]	[1]	[1]
[2]	[2]	[2]	[2]	[2]	[2]	[2]	[2]	[2]	[2]	[2]	[2]	[2]	[2]	[2]
[3]	[3]	[3]	[3]	[3]	[3]	[3]	[3]	[3]	[3]	[3]	[3]	[3]	[3]	[3]
[4]	[4]	[4]	[4]	[4]	[4]	[4]	[4]	[4]	[4]	[4]	[4]	[4]	[4]	[4]
[5]	[5]	[5]	[5]	[5]	[5]	[5]	[5]	[5]	[5]	[5]	[5]	[5]	[5]	[5]
[6]	[6]	[6]	[6]	[6]	[6]	[6]	[6]	[6]	[6]	[6]	[6]	[6]	[6]	[6]
[7]	[7]	[7]	[7]	[7]	[7]	[7]	[7]	[7]	[7]	[7]	[7]	[7]	[7]	[7]
[8]	[8]	[8]	[8]	[8]	[8]	[8]	[8]	[8]	[8]	[8]	[8]	[8]	[8]	[8]
[9]	[9]	[9]	[9]	[9]	[9]	[9]	[9]	[9]	[9]	[9]	[9]	[9]	[9]	[9]

Part I   **Writing**   **(30 minutes)**

Directions: *For this part, you are allowed 30 minutes to write a short essay entitled* **Should the Exam System Be Abolished?** *You should write at least* **150** *words following the outline given below:*

1. 有人认为考试制度应该被取消,因为……
2. 取消考试制度是否可行

Should the Exam System Be Abolished?

答题卡 1 (Answer Sheet 1)

Part II Reading Comprehension (Skimming and Scanning) (15 minutes)

1. [Y] [N] [NG]   5. _____   8. _____

2. [Y] [N] [NG]

3. [Y] [N] [NG]   6. _____   9. _____

4. [Y] [N] [NG]   7. _____   10. _____

答题卡 2 (Answer Sheet 2)

学校:	准 考 证 号
姓名:	
划线要求	

准 考 证 号

[0]	[0]	[0]	[0]	[0]	[0]	[0]	[0]	[0]	[0]	[0]	[0]	[0]	[0]	[0]
[1]	[1]	[1]	[1]	[1]	[1]	[1]	[1]	[1]	[1]	[1]	[1]	[1]	[1]	[1]
[2]	[2]	[2]	[2]	[2]	[2]	[2]	[2]	[2]	[2]	[2]	[2]	[2]	[2]	[2]
[3]	[3]	[3]	[3]	[3]	[3]	[3]	[3]	[3]	[3]	[3]	[3]	[3]	[3]	[3]
[4]	[4]	[4]	[4]	[4]	[4]	[4]	[4]	[4]	[4]	[4]	[4]	[4]	[4]	[4]
[5]	[5]	[5]	[5]	[5]	[5]	[5]	[5]	[5]	[5]	[5]	[5]	[5]	[5]	[5]
[6]	[6]	[6]	[6]	[6]	[6]	[6]	[6]	[6]	[6]	[6]	[6]	[6]	[6]	[6]
[7]	[7]	[7]	[7]	[7]	[7]	[7]	[7]	[7]	[7]	[7]	[7]	[7]	[7]	[7]
[8]	[8]	[8]	[8]	[8]	[8]	[8]	[8]	[8]	[8]	[8]	[8]	[8]	[8]	[8]
[9]	[9]	[9]	[9]	[9]	[9]	[9]	[9]	[9]	[9]	[9]	[9]	[9]	[9]	[9]

Part III Section A   Section B

11. [A] [B] [C] [D]   16. [A] [B] [C] [D]   21. [A] [B] [C] [D]   26. [A] [B] [C] [D]   31. [A] [B] [C] [D]
12. [A] [B] [C] [D]   17. [A] [B] [C] [D]   22. [A] [B] [C] [D]   27. [A] [B] [C] [D]   32. [A] [B] [C] [D]
13. [A] [B] [C] [D]   18. [A] [B] [C] [D]   23. [A] [B] [C] [D]   28. [A] [B] [C] [D]   33. [A] [B] [C] [D]
14. [A] [B] [C] [D]   19. [A] [B] [C] [D]   24. [A] [B] [C] [D]   29. [A] [B] [C] [D]   34. [A] [B] [C] [D]
15. [A] [B] [C] [D]   20. [A] [B] [C] [D]   25. [A] [B] [C] [D]   30. [A] [B] [C] [D]   35. [A] [B] [C] [D]

Part III   Section C

A study of facts and figures on development (36) _____ that China has made remarkable social (37) _____ in a range of significant areas. China (38) _____ 22 percent of the world's population with only 7 percent of the world's farmland. (39) _____ has improved greatly for both urban and (40) _____ residents. The Chinese government has taken a series of measures to (41) _____ or reduce poverty. Educational developments have liberated millions of Chinese people from (42) _____ and illiteracy. In 1986，China instituted 9 years of (43) _____ schooling with the result that by 1993，school enrolment had reached 97.7 percent. (44) _____

_____ .

Ecological methods of farming are promoted and forest coverage has increased. (45) _____

_____ .

China is also working toward the goal of health care for everyone. (46) _____

_____ .

答题卡 2 (Answer Sheet 2)

Part IV　Section A　Part V　Error Correction　(15 minutes)

47. _____

　　_____

48. _____

　　_____

49. _____

　　_____

50. _____

　　_____

51. _____

　　_____

Part IV　Section B

52. [A][B][C][D]
53. [A][B][C][D]
54. [A][B][C][D]
55. [A][B][C][D]
56. [A][B][C][D]
57. [A][B][C][D]
58. [A][B][C][D]
59. [A][B][C][D]
60. [A][B][C][D]
61. [A][B][C][D]

In American society children have watched approximately 18,000 television commercials at the time that they have reached their middle teens. My friend Jolie learned this fact a few weeks ago and decided to do something about it. She thinks the number of commercials children see influence the way which they view the world. That is, Jolie believes that children who watch so many ads will grow up to believe that the most important thing in life is to buy! This, says Jolie, is wrong. A little child cannot understand advertisements for which they are and so believes totally in what he or she hears. I had been thinking about what Jolie told me. I suppose that she is right. I know that it is easy to manipulate the minds of children because they don't see things carefully, as adults are. But I wonder myself that the advertisers can control a child's outlook on the world. I think I should join with Jolie in her efforts to change advertising tactics when she comes to advertisements for children. I really have a responsibility to make it sure that the younger generations are given every chance to develop their minds without the interference of mass media.

62. _____

63. _____

64. _____

65. _____

66. _____

67. _____

68. _____

69. _____

70. _____

71. _____

Part VI　Translation　(5 minutes)

72. _____

73. _____

74. _____

75. _____

76. _____

PRACTICE TEST 5

Part I Writing
(30 minutes)

注意：此部分试题在**答题卡**1上。

Part II Reading Comprehension (Skimming and Scanning)
(15 minutes)

Directions: *In this part, you will have 15 minutes to go over the passage quickly and answer the questions on **Answer Sheet 1**.*

For questions 1 – 4, mark

Y *(for YES)*   *if the statement agrees with the information given in the passage;*

N *(for NO)*   *if the statement contradicts the information given in the passage;*

NG *(for NOT GIVEN)*   *if the information is not given in the passage.*

For questions 5 – 10, complete the sentences with the information given in the passage.

Cow Tongue and Colombian Coffee

They don't really sound pleasant, do they? I didn't think so. I shuddered at the thought of having a pair of legs for lunch or a nice floppy cow tongue for dinner. What about armadillo or cubes of blood? No, this seemed to be more of a freak show or an episode of *Fear Factor*, a reality TV show that prides on having contestants confront their worst fear (i.e. eating a blended drink of maggots, bugs, liver, etc.).

But we were standing in the meat section of an Asian supermarket. My parents and I were used to seeing such odds and ends because we went to these stores often to buy food. My dad and I would constantly poke fun at the weird food items. When I was a kid, I used to watch the frogs pile on top of each other in the glass container. For a while, I thought that people bought them for pets and not for eating. I wasn't very bright. Once, one old lady told the person behind the counter to fry the creature.

The frog returned gold and crisp. I cried and ran away.

A past hobby was fondling the blue crabs. I taunted and poke them. I hit them on their shell and swung them around when their claws clung to my tong. I had the intelligence to put my finger in front of one. It nearly took my right index finger off. Again, I cried and ran away with a bleeding finger. The crab had its glory for a minute. I bet my money that he had a smirk on its crabby face. Well, not for long though. We had that one for dinner. I ate my opponent.

I was a shopaholic. But unlike most shopaholic people who did shopping sprees on cute scarves and matching pink pumps, I shopped food. Trout. Curry sauce. Italian cucumbers. Capers. Strings of garlic. While other people my age thought bonfires at the beach was fun, I considered roaming supermarket aisles fun. My parents thought it was just a phase. I never actually grew out of that "phase". I still love to go investigate the rainbow of supermarket types. My hypothesis to this obsession is: Because I love eating, my love and curiosity melted into my love for grocery shopping.

At the end of the day, I placed supermarkets in two categories: the Asian supermarket and the European supermarket. They were significantly different in style, in atmosphere, and in products.

I took my friend, Nick, to an Asian supermarket just a few weekends ago. At Stanford, we both lived in the same dorm. He was on the third floor and I was on the second. We became pretty good friends in the beginning of the school year. His mother was born in England and his father was born in New Zealand. His ancestry seemed to hop on all predominantly white cultures: England, New Zealand, Scotland, and Australia.

His whiteness stood out in the yellow sea of consumers. And standing at almost 6 feet, he had a good height advantage, too. The Asian supermarket choked of fish smells and pungent spices. I noticed that the "smell", the particular "Asian" smell, dominated all of the Asian-oriented supermarkets. Even in Korean markets, the smell still thrived. It wasn't a good smell. It was pickled eggs and stewing cabbage. I couldn't put my finger on it. And I didn't want to either.

"What is that smell?" Nick crinkled his nose.

"Ah, the smell of years and years of history." I breathed in the air and pushed my shopping cart like a kid breaking into a candy store. My left arm and right arm were busy picking and loading. It was the shopping dance. Lift. Grab. Load. Wiggle.

The meat, poultry, and seafood counter was in the back of the supermarket. The people behind the counter picked up orders with a fast pace. "You wanted 5 pounds of ground beef?" "Two racks of lamb?" "King crab?" It was the raw world where blood was the flag of commerce. I loved this world. Nick, on the other hand, was not as loving. He stared at the blood cubes. His face turned a bit purple. Americans were always shell-shocked when I brought them to these places. It was like entering a whole new dimension. "People eat this stuff? Wait, how do you eat pig brains?" That was the usual reaction. "Is it legal to eat armadillo?" "Oh my god, that chicken is black. I didn't know there were black chickens. Shoot, that wasn't a racial slur. I swear."

Everything was unpredictable at an Asian supermarket. Everything was familiar, at least to me. Old people wandered the aisles. Little people scattered the grounds, some playing with plastic bags and others sword-fighting with cucumbers. The mothers picked out fresh bean sprouts and the fathers stood by like side-kicks. And everyone was talking — Mandarin, Cantonese, Korean, Japanese, and all types of Asian dialects. Behind the noise, there was usually some old, 1950s Asian song playing on repeat. Every once in a while, depending on location, there were a few foreigners scouting the food. To foreigners, this was considered exotic. To the average Asian, it was routine. Before long, Nick started playing with the blue crabs.

At a European supermarket or grocery store, the first thing you would notice is the noise level. No one really talked. They played elevator music in the background. I could grimace at the sound of the shopping cart wheel. However, the European supermarket was sparkling clean, fancy, classy, and expensive. Stepping into a Jonathans or a Ralphs or a Trader Joes was stepping into a high middle-class family's life: Customers bought the trademark and not the good. At these stores, it was also comfortable. But it was a different type of comfortable. This was the comfortable you could associate with the image: a glass of aged red wine in front of a toasty fire. Everything there was kosher. The staff spoke to you with a grin and a recommendation. And unlike Asian supermarkets, European supermarkets had absolutely no flies. "Whatever. Flies contain protein," said some woman in 99 Ranch Market, a Chinese supermarket, once. While I agree with this woman, I happened to like my food bug-free.

Their food was also exotic. There were a lot of products imported from the Caribbean, Thailand, Jamaica, Italy, Venice, Madrid, etc. There were all kinds of boxes and bottles of different attractive shapes and colors. Yet, the products were also pricey. A box of biscotti could cost up to six dollars.

But shopping was shopping. It gave me the same wonderful feeling of warmth and comfortableness. At Stanford, I had dreams about walking down a white tiled supermarket aisle with rows and rows and rows of food. And wait, wait, wait. There is a point here. People are like these food products. It doesn't take much to see a difference. But there's always a similarity. So, whether or not if we like cow tongues or Colombian coffee, we all enjoy the comfort of food and the comfort of family.

注意：此部分试题请在**答题卡**1上作答。

1. I didn't like the idea of *Fear Factor*, a TV show that prides on having contestants confront their worst fear.

2. I was a shopaholic for grocery shopping because I love eating very much.

3. My friend, Nick, who has grown up in white culture, stood in the yellow sea with me a few weeks ago.

4. In the back of the Asian supermarket, where raw food was sold, Americans were always astonished at the blood and products as if they had entered a new dimension.

5. My parents and I often went to _____ to buy food.

6. After the blue crab hurt me, it was _____.

7. Everything at an Asian supermarket was familiar to me, but to foreigners, it was _____.

8. _____ was clean, fancy, classy and expensive.

9. At the European supermarket customers bought the goods according to _____.

10. In spite of the difference between the Asian and the European supermarket, there's always a similarity, that is to say, _____.

Part III   Listening Comprehension   (35 minutes)

Section A

Directions: *In this section, you will hear 8 short conversations and 2 long conversations. At the end of each conversation, one or more questions will be asked about what was said. Both the conversation and the questions will be spoken only once. After each question there will be a pause. During the pause, you must read the four choices marked A), B), C) and D), and decide which is the best answer. Then mark the corresponding letter on Answer Sheet 2 with a single line through the center.*

注意：此部分试题请在**答题卡**2上作答。

11. A) The professor missed the bus stop because he lost his way.
    B) The professor was so absorbed in thinking that he lost his car.
    C) The professor thought he was lost, so he stopped driving.
    D) The professor passed his stop because he wasn't paying attention.

12. A) The man hadn't planned to take a bus.
    B) The man couldn't find a place to park.

C) The man parked his car illegally.

D) The man didn't know the way.

13. A) In a police station.   C) In a restaurant.

    B) In a lawyer's office.   D) In a doctor's office.

14. A) Mary couldn't go to the conference because her employer wouldn't pay her while she was away.

B) Mary was able to attend the conference at her employer's expense.

C) Although Mary's employer had offered to cover her expenses for the conference, she didn't go.

D) Mary's employer refused to give her money to attend the conference, but she went anyway.

15. A) Jeff was convicted guilty.

B) Jeff shouldn't have been set free.

C) Jeff should have been imprisoned.

D) Jeff shouldn't have been sent to imprisonment for the crime he committed.

16. A) The woman couldn't pass the exam.

B) It is impossible for the woman not to pass the exam.

C) The man doesn't like serious talk.

D) The woman has already passed the exam.

17. A) Fix the slot machine.

B) Make a phone call.

C) Have a cup of coffee.

D) Get some coins from the slot machine.

18. A) At 6.   C) At 10.

    B) At 8.   D) At 12.

Questions 19 to 21 are based on the conversation you have just heard.

19. A) A congressional aide.   C) A senator.

    B) A young journalist.   D) A police woman.

20. A) They had a wonderful working relationship.

B) They broke up during filming.

C) They are working through a difficult time right now and the film has something to do with it.

D) They have a hard time now, but the film has nothing to do with it.

21. A) Phyllis thinks that her son, Jarrad, is very sensitive.

  B) Phyllis thinks that it is hard being a son of a well-known mother.

  C) Phyllis strongly feels it is high time to protect her son from being interviewed by the police.

  D) Phyllis strongly feels it is high time to protect her son's well-being.

Questions 22 to 25 are based on the conversation you have just heard.

22. A) At Pacific College in Canada French is used as instruction language.

  B) At the College of the Adriatic Italian is used as instruction language.

  C) Spanish is the main language of instruction in all the colleges.

  D) English is mainly used as the language of instruction in all the colleges.

23. A) They should be very rich.

  B) They should pay all the tuition fee.

  C) They are asked to pay as much as they can afford.

  D) They should not pay anything because there are scholarships.

24. A) His or her academic ability.

  B) Where he or she comes from.

  C) Whether he or she is mature enough.

  D) His or her ability to get on well with people from different countries.

25. A) Each college's teachers.   C) The environment of the college.

  B) The student's other interests.   D) Students' application.

Section B

Directions: *In this section, you will hear 3 short passages. At the end of each passage, you will hear some questions. Both the passage and the questions will be spoken only once. After you hear a question, you must choose the best answer from the four choices marked A), B), C) and D). Then mark the corresponding letter on* **Answer Sheet 2** *with a single line through the center.*

注意：此部分试题请在**答题卡 2** 上作答。

Passage One

Questions 26 to 29 are based on the passage you have just heard.

26. A) Japan.   C) Canada.

B) Britain.   D) Spain.

27. A) Showing a license to own weapons.
    B) Taking an examination in the presence of a police officer.
    C) Proving experience or training in using guns.
    D) Proving a specific need for guns.

28. A) Sociologists think there is a direct relationship between lower figures for violent crimes and laws controlling guns.
    B) Canada has much lower violent crime rate.
    C) Protection of property is a reason to apply for a gun in Britain.
    D) Japan places control on the possession of some swords.

29. A) 1 year.   C) 5 years.
    B) 3 years.   D) 6 years.

Passage Two

Questions 30 to 32 are based on the passage you have just heard.

30. A) The most active and heavy-weighted man.
    B) The most active and light-weighted man.
    C) The least active and heavy-weighted man.
    D) The least active and light-weighted man.

31. A) Compared with non-smokers, the risk of suffering a first heart attack doubles for smokers.
    B) Heavier men have a 50 percent greater risk of suffering a first heart attack.
    C) Women who gain much weight since age 25 have an increased risk of heart attacks.
    D) Jewish men have a lower rate of heart attacks than Christians.

32. A) Exercise habits.   C) Sex.
    B) Smoking.   D) Race.

Passage Three

Questions 33 to 35 are based on the passage you have just heard.

33. A) She was shocked.
    B) She felt it was not all her husband's fault.
    C) She covered up the truth.
    D) She asked for a divorce.

34. A) Sleeping problems.
    B) Low achievements at school.
    C) Violent behaviors.
    D) Lack of friends.

35. A) 60 percent.   C) 30 percent.
    B) 16 percent.   D) 13 percent.

Section C

Directions: *In this section, you will hear a passage three times. When the passage is read for the first time, you should listen carefully for its general idea. When the passage is read for the second time, you are required to fill in the blanks numbered from 36 to 43 with the exact words you have just heard. For blanks numbered from 44 to 46 you are required to fill in the missing information. For these blanks, you can either use the exact words you have just heard or write down the main points in your own words. Finally, when the passage is read for the third time, you should check what you have written.*

注意：此部分试题在**答题卡 2** 上；请在**答题卡 2** 上作答。

Part IV   Reading Comprehension (Reading in Depth)
(25 minutes)

Section A

Directions: *In this section, there is a short passage with 5 questions or incomplete statements. Read the passage carefully. Then answer the questions or complete the statements in the fewest possible words on **Answer Sheet 2**.*

Questions 47 to 51 are based on the following passage.

Few modern works of social science have aroused so wide an interest as David Riesman's *The Lonely Croud*. Published in 1950 by a university press, it soon transcended the limited audience for which it was intended. When the book was brought out in a paper-bound edition, it sold so widely that it became a prodigy of the publishing world. The terminology of the work, especially the phrases "inner directed" and "other directed", has become part of the American vocabulary.

The Lonely Croud presents the hypothesis that there has been a significant change in the character and ideals of the American people over the past few decades. This change is described as a movement from "inner direction" to "other direction". It is not possible in this space to do justice to the meaning of the two concepts. In general, it may be said that the trend away from inner direction toward other direction implies that the ambitious and competitive character is becoming less typical of the American culture and is conforming to the requirements of the group and taking direction from the ideals and demands of others.

Mr. Riesman wishes not to totally support either form of "direction", although he is aware that most of his readers will find that inner direction is more attractive than other direction. He accepts neither as an ideal form of motivation. But as an objective observer of American life, he can note the advantages as well as the dangers of the new tendency. He sees the diminishing of inner direction as implying a lessening of individualism and energy. But he is no less aware that the increase of other direction implies an increase of cooperativeness and of friendliness, if not of friendship.

注意：此部分试题请在**答题卡 2** 上作答。

47. What category does the book *The Lonely Croud* fall into?

48. In general, the inner directed man can be described as _____.

49. What does Mr. Riesman think is more representative of present American people?

50. What is the advantage of the change in the character of the American people?

51. What is the disadvantage of the change in the character of the American people?

Section B

Directions: *There are 2 passages in this section. Each passage is followed by some questions or unfinished statements. For each of them there are four choices marked A), B), C) and D). You should decide on the best choice and mark the corresponding letter on Answer Sheet 2 with a single line through the center.*

Passage One

Questions 52 to 56 are based on the following passage.

African art could have been observed and collected by Europeans no earlier than the fifteenth century. Unfortunately, until the latter years of the nineteenth century Europe was little interested in the arts of Africa except as curiosities and souvenirs of exotic peoples. Indeed, with the growth of the colonial exploitation and Christian missionizing the arts were presented as evidence of the low state of savagery of the African, justifying both exploitation and missionary zeal.

In recent years the development of critical studies of oral traditions, of the descriptions of the coast by early European travelers, and — above all — of the concept of cultural relativism, has led to a far more realistic assessment of the African, his culture, history, and arts.

Cultural relativism is, in essence, the attitude whereby cultures other than one's own are viewed in their terms and on their merits. As an alternative to the prejudgment of missionaries and colonials it allows us to view the cultures and arts of the African without the necessity of judging his beliefs and actions against a Christian moralistic base.

Curiously, the "discovery" and enthusiasm for African art early in this century was not based on an objective, scientific assessment but rather resulted from an excess of romantic rebellion at the end of the last century against the Classical and Naturalist roots of Western art. Unfortunately this uncritical adulation swept aside many rational concerns to focus upon African sculpture as if it were the product of a romantic, rebellious European movement. Obviously, African art is neither anti-classical nor anti-naturalistic: to be either it would have had to have had its roots in Classicism or in Naturalism, both European in origin. Nor was the concept of rebellion a part of the heritage of African art, rather, as we shall see, it was an art conservative in impulse and stable in concept.

We may admire these sculptures from a purely twentieth century esthetic, but if we so limit our admiration we will most certainly fail to understand them in the context of their appearance as documents of African thought and action.

In sharp contrast to the arts of the recent past in the Western world, by far the greatest part, in fact nearly all of the art of the history of the world, including traditional Africa, was positive in its orientation; that is, it conformed in style and meaning to the expectations — the norms — of its patrons and audience. Those norms were shaped by nearly all members of the society; thus, the arts were conservative and conformist. However, it must be stressed that they were not merely passive reflections, for they contributed actively to the sense of well-being of the parent culture. Indeed, the perishable nature of wood — the dominant medium for sculpture — ensured that each generation reaffirmed its faith by recreating its arts.

注意：此部分试题请在**答题卡 2** 上作答。

52. Which of the following is the result of the concept of cultural relativism?

A) The prejudgment of missionaries and colonials.

B) The biased assumption of African art.

C) The objective assessment of African art.

D) The judgment of the beliefs and actions of the African against a Christian moralistic base.

53. What leads to the European passion for African art?

A) The realistic assessment of African art.

B) Cultural relativism.

C) Colonial exploitation and Christian mission.

D) The romantic rebellion against the roots of Western art.

54. The phrase "this uncritical adulation" (Line 4, Para. 4) is based on _____.

A) enthusiasm for African art

B) an objective, scientific assessment of African art

C) an excess of romantic rebellion

D) the Classical and Naturalist roots of Western art

55. Which of the following statements is NOT true about African art?

A) It has no element of rebellion.

B) It is conservative in impulse and stable in concept.

C) It was first introduced into Europe before the fifteenth century.

D) It has neither roots in Classicism nor in Naturalism.

56. From the passage, we can infer that _____.

A) the art of the recent past in the Western world was not positive in its orientation

B) colonials and missionaries helped improve African art from the low state of savagery

C) African art cannot be appreciated from a purely twentieth century esthetic

D) wood was chosen as the dominant medium for sculpture although it couldn't last long

Passage Two

Questions 57 to 61 are based on the following passage.

As far as technology is concerned there is no indication of an end or, on a certain level, even of a saturation. One reason is that in technology one essentially moves toward constructive complexity in the development of the world, a complexity for which there is no plausible limit. In addition the technical potential of scientific knowledge is by no means exhausted. On the contrary, some qualitative leaps may be expected from the solution of the remaining fundamental questions. There is no reasonable foresight in technology, only science fiction. To my mind there is only one possible end to technological growth — which may be illustrated by the story of Babel's tower. The technical transformation of the world is indeed akin to the building of the tower. The construction of the tower, the Bible tells us, was brought to a standstill by a confusion of languages. However, paintings such as Altdorfer's suggest another interpretation: namely, that one day the construction of the tower could not proceed any further because all of the manpower was already needed for repair. Our present second nature, the technical environment in which we live, is for the most part a heritage of our ancestors. This second nature in our time already consumes so much manpower and other resources for its reconstruction that one may imagine that some day in the future enlargement will no longer be possible. However — and at this point technical imagination again comes into play — it might be possible to develop self-reproducing technical systems. Biotechnology, the best clue to technology to come, might be a step in this direction.

If there are any doubts concerning progress in technology or in the whole complex of science and technology, these doubts do not concern the possibility of some further development; rather, they question whether technological progress has produced human progress. Although the actual enhancement of human life through science and technology must not be contested, doubts nevertheless arise when we observe the enhancements have meant deteriorations at the same time — that gains have been connected with losses. The fascinating improvement in control over nature at the same time has brought a frightening increase in man's power to destroy. Looking more closely, we must even say that the type of domination of nature which is provided by science and technology is more akin to destruction than conservation. Its manner of thinking — causal, linear, elementary — is much more capable of destroying a system than of keeping it alive.

注意：此部分试题请在**答题卡**2上作答。

57. Which of the following is NOT the reason why there is no indication of an end to technology?

A) Some qualitative achievements may be expected from the solution of the remaining fundamental questions.

B) The technical potential of scientific knowledge is never exhausted.

C) There is no reasonable foresight in technology.

D) Technology is getting increasingly complicated.

58. The writer thinks that the construction of Babel's tower stopped because _____.

    A) there was a confusion of languages

    B) no people were left for the construction

    C) no one could repair the tower

    D) the tower was too huge to repair so people gave up the construction

59. The writer mentions Babel's tower to illustrate that _____.

    A) technological development has consumed a lot of manpower and other resources

    B) technological development has no end

    C) the ultimate solution to technological development is to develop self-reproducing technical systems

    D) further development of technology will be impossible

60. Which of the following statements does the writer most probably agree with?

    A) Technological development has increased man's power to dominate nature.

    B) Technological development has produced human progress.

    C) Technology is getting too complicated to handle.

    D) The enhancements brought by technological development can offset the deterioration.

61. The writer's attitude toward technological development can be best described as _____.

    A) negative   C) appreciative

    B) unconcerned   D) objective

Part V Error Correction

(15 minutes)

Directions: *This part consists of a short passage. In this passage, there are altogether 10 mistakes, one in each numbered line. You may have to change a word, add a word or delete a word. Mark out the mistakes and put the corrections in the blanks provided. If you change a word, cross it out and write the correct word in the corresponding blank. If you add a word, put an insertion mark (∧) in the right place and write the missing word in the blank. If you delete a word, cross it out and put a slash (/) in the blank.*

注意：此部分试题在**答题卡**2上；请在**答题卡**2上作答。

Part VI   Translation   (5 minutes)

Directions: *Complete the following sentences on **Answer Sheet 2** by translating into English the Chinese given in brackets.*

注意：此部分试题请在**答题卡**2上作答，只需写出译文部分。

72. _____
(你必须向校长递交一份报告) on the meeting because your expenses were paid by the school.

73. _____
(当比较温和的措施没有产生任何改变) in the rules, the students resorted to violence.

74. This material was exposed to the sunshine too often，_____
(结果，仅仅半年时间里它就褪色了，从深蓝色变成灰色).

75. Father says _____ (必须省出一些钱来备用) in emergency.

76. My husband tried to _____
(逗我笑来缓和他同我的争论)，but I didn't buy it.

答题卡 1 (Answer Sheet 1)

学校:
姓名:
划线要求

准		考		证		号	

[0] [0] [0] [0] [0] [0] [0] [0] [0] [0] [0] [0] [0] [0] [0]
[1] [1] [1] [1] [1] [1] [1] [1] [1] [1] [1] [1] [1] [1] [1]
[2] [2] [2] [2] [2] [2] [2] [2] [2] [2] [2] [2] [2] [2] [2]
[3] [3] [3] [3] [3] [3] [3] [3] [3] [3] [3] [3] [3] [3] [3]
[4] [4] [4] [4] [4] [4] [4] [4] [4] [4] [4] [4] [4] [4] [4]
[5] [5] [5] [5] [5] [5] [5] [5] [5] [5] [5] [5] [5] [5] [5]
[6] [6] [6] [6] [6] [6] [6] [6] [6] [6] [6] [6] [6] [6] [6]
[7] [7] [7] [7] [7] [7] [7] [7] [7] [7] [7] [7] [7] [7] [7]
[8] [8] [8] [8] [8] [8] [8] [8] [8] [8] [8] [8] [8] [8] [8]
[9] [9] [9] [9] [9] [9] [9] [9] [9] [9] [9] [9] [9] [9] [9]

Part I   **Writing**   **(30 minutes)**

Directions: *For this part, you are allowed 30 minutes to write a short essay entitled **Should High School Students Study Abroad**? You should write at least **150** words following the outline given below:*

1. 高中生留学的好处
2. 高中生留学的弊端
3. 我的观点

Should High School Students Study Abroad?

答题卡 1 (Answer Sheet 1)

Part II **Reading Comprehension (Skimming and Scanning) (15 minutes)**

1. [Y] [N] [NG]
2. [Y] [N] [NG]
3. [Y] [N] [NG]
4. [Y] [N] [NG]

5. _____

6. _____

7. _____

8. _____

9. _____

10. _____

答题卡 2 (Answer Sheet 2)

Part III Section A

Section B

11. [A] [B] [C] [D]　16. [A] [B] [C] [D]　21. [A] [B] [C] [D]　26. [A] [B] [C] [D]　31. [A] [B] [C] [D]
12. [A] [B] [C] [D]　17. [A] [B] [C] [D]　22. [A] [B] [C] [D]　27. [A] [B] [C] [D]　32. [A] [B] [C] [D]
13. [A] [B] [C] [D]　18. [A] [B] [C] [D]　23. [A] [B] [C] [D]　28. [A] [B] [C] [D]　33. [A] [B] [C] [D]
14. [A] [B] [C] [D]　19. [A] [B] [C] [D]　24. [A] [B] [C] [D]　29. [A] [B] [C] [D]　34. [A] [B] [C] [D]
15. [A] [B] [C] [D]　20. [A] [B] [C] [D]　25. [A] [B] [C] [D]　30. [A] [B] [C] [D]　35. [A] [B] [C] [D]

Part III Section C

Western attitudes towards the societies of East Asia are a sad reflection of an (36) _____ to appreciate the economic achievements and (37) _____ of Japan, South Korea, Singapore, and, more recently, China. No (38) _____ observer can deny that Asian models of economic and political development are proving successful. (39) _____ rates of economic growth have been achieved in at least some East Asian (40) _____. The resulting standard of health care and education is (41) _____ to that of many western countries. In addition, social (42) _____ is frequently (43) _____ with these East Asian economic success stories. Asian models of political and economic development draw on their cultural tradition. However, there is still a widespread belief that (44) _____

_____.

For many people in the West, their Western ideals and practices have universal authority. (45) _____

_____.

Crimes against poverty in Britain are very common. Over 1 million U.S. citizens are currently being kept in prison. (46) _____

_____.

答题卡 2 (Answer Sheet 2)

Part IV   Section A   Part V   Error Correction   (15 minutes)

47. _____

48. _____

49. _____

50. _____

51. _____

Many changes are taking place in the way in which men and women look at their roles in society. We see these changes most dramatically in job and business situations. It is not longer unusual to find a male nurse or a female construction worker. How dramatic these changes, they are not as important as the changes that have taken place between men and women's roles in family life.

62. _____

63. _____

64. _____

The fact that so many women today have entered the job market and building independent careers has altered the traditional family structure in many ways. Men have discovered at last that they too are capable of preparing for the family dinner, rather than thinking that they are only capable of taking out the garbage.

65. _____

66. _____

Part IV   Section B

52. [A][B][C][D]
53. [A][B][C][D]
54. [A][B][C][D]
55. [A][B][C][D]
56. [A][B][C][D]
57. [A][B][C][D]
58. [A][B][C][D]
59. [A][B][C][D]
60. [A][B][C][D]
61. [A][B][C][D]

Perhaps the greatest change that has taken place in the family is in parents' new attitudes toward bringing up children. When it is true that only mothers can breastfeed infants, nowhere has it written that fathers cannot bathe their own babies. These days, a full-time parent is a job that fathers and mothers both share. Many men no longer feel that they must be the only bread earner in the family and many women no longer feel that they should be obedient. Changes like this do not occur overnight and even in a few years because they involve fundamental changes in attitudes and behaviors.

67. _____

68. _____

69. _____

70. _____

71. _____

Part VI   Translation   (5 minutes)

72. _____

73. _____

74. _____

75. _____

76. _____

PRACTICE TEST 6

Part I   Writing   (30 minutes)

注意：此部分试题在**答题卡** 1 上。

Part II   Reading Comprehension (Skimming and Scanning)
(15 minutes)

Directions: *In this part, you will have 15 minutes to go over the passage quickly and answer the questions on **Answer Sheet 1**.*

For questions 1 − 4, mark

Y *(for YES)*   *if the statement agrees with the information given in the passage;*

N *(for NO)*   *if the statement contradicts the information given in the passage;*

NG *(for NOT GIVEN)*   *if the information is not given in the passage.*

For questions 5 − 10, complete the sentences with the information given in the passage.

Taking Play Seriously

On a drizzly Tuesday night in late January, 200 people came out to hear a psychiatrist talk rhapsodically about play — not just the intense, joyous play of children, but play for all people, at all ages, at all times. (All species too; the lecture featured touching photos of a polar bear and a husky engaging playfully at a snowy outpost in northern Canada.) Stuart Brown, president of the National Institute for Play, was speaking at the New York Public Library's main branch on 42nd Street. He created the institute in 1996, after more than 20 years of psychiatric practice and research persuaded him of the dangerous long-term consequences of play deprivation. In a sold-out talk at the library, he and Krista Tippett, host of the public-radio program "Speaking of Faith", discussed the biological and spiritual underpinnings of play. Brown called play part of the "developmental sequencing of becoming a human primate. If you look at what produces learning and memory and well-being, play is as fundamental as any other aspect of life, including sleep and dreams."

The message seemed to resonate with audience members, who asked anxious questions about what seemed to be the loss of play in their children's lives. Their concern came, no doubt, from the recent deluge of eulogies to play. Educators fret that school officials are hacking away at recess to make room for an increasingly crammed curriculum. Psychologists complain that overscheduled kids have no time left for the real business of childhood: idle, creative, unstructured free play. Public health officials link insufficient playtime to a rise in childhood obesity. Parents bemoan the fact that kids don't play the way they themselves did — or think they did. And everyone seems to worry that without the chance to play stickball or hopscotch out on the street, to play with dolls on the kitchen floor or climb trees in the woods, today's children are missing out on something essential.

The success of *The Dangerous Book for Boys* — which has been on the best-seller list for the last nine months — and its step-by-step instructions for activities like folding paper airplanes is testament to the generalized longing for play's good old days. So were the questions after Stuart Brown's library talk; one woman asked how her children will learn trust, empathy and social skills when their most frequent playing is done online. Brown told her that while video games do have some play value, a true sense of "interpersonal nuance" can be achieved only by a child who is engaging all five senses by playing in the three-dimensional world.

Discussions about play force us to reckon with our underlying ideas about childhood, sex differences, creativity and success. Do boys play differently than girls? Are children being damaged by staring at computer screens and video games? Are they missing something when fantasy play is populated with characters from Hollywood's imagination and not their own? Most of these issues are too vast to be addressed by a single field of study (let alone a magazine article). But the growing science of play does have much to add to the conversation. Armed with research grounded in evolutionary biology and experimental neuroscience, some scientists have shown themselves eager — at times perhaps a little too eager — to promote a scientific argument for play. They have spent the past few decades learning how and why play evolved in animals, generating insights that can inform our understanding of its evolution in humans too. They are studying, from an evolutionary perspective, to what extent play is a luxury that can be dispensed with when there are too many other competing claims on the growing brain, and to what extent it is central to how that brain grows in the first place.

注意：此部分试题请在**答题卡**1上作答。

1. People who listened to the lecture agree that play is the right of children. When they grow up, this right will be deprived.

2. Play too much will lead to kids' obesity.

3. Stuart Brown regarded video games as complete trash.

4. Researchers are beginning to learn more about play from evolutionary perspective.

5. What produces learning and memory and well-being at least include _____ _____, _____ and _____.

6. According to psychologists, the real business of childhood are _____ _____.

7. Parents complain that _____.

8. Brown holds that a true sense of "interpersonal nuance" can be achieved only if _____.

9. Some scientists armed themselves with research grounded in evolutionary biology in order to _____.

10. Most of these issues researchers are doing with are such big topics that _____.

Part III   Listening Comprehension   (35 minutes)

Section A

Directions: *In this section, you will hear 8 short conversations and 2 long conversations. At the end of each conversation, one or more questions will be asked about what was said. Both the conversation and the questions will be spoken only once. After each question there will be a pause. During the pause, you must read the four choices marked A), B), C) and D), and decide which is the best answer. Then mark the corresponding letter on Answer Sheet 2 with a single line through the center.*

注意：此部分试题请在**答题卡**2 上作答。

11. A) The woman should not talk to Paul.
    B) The woman should not take Paul's words too seriously.
    C) The woman should take some salt to Paul.
    D) The woman should take some grain to Paul.

12. A) He will help the woman with the project.
    B) He will turn the radio on.
    C) He will turn the radio up.

D) He will turn the radio down.

13. A) The man has run into problems in his project.
    B) The project being undertaken is new to the man.
    C) The man hasn't started the project.
    D) Somebody is against the project.

14. A) He will do the washing.
    B) He will repair the machine.
    C) The woman can wash the clothes later.
    D) The clothes can be washed by somebody else.

15. A) His wife doesn't like Australia.
    B) His wife was too busy.
    C) They would go to Australia soon.
    D) They have already been to Australia.

16. A) He doesn't know where the stadium is.
    B) He tends to be forgetful.
    C) The stadium is hard to find.
    D) He doesn't want to go to the stadium.

17. A) Tell Jane about the speech contest at lunch.
    B) Ask Jane to come to the contest after lunch.
    C) Tell Jane the sports meeting has been cancelled.
    D) Ask Jane to come to her for lunch.

18. A) He won't have a reading course that afternoon.
    B) He is happy to have a reading course.
    C) He doesn't need a dictionary that afternoon.
    D) He forgets his dictionary when leaving home.

Questions 19 to 21 are based on the conversation you have just heard.

19. A) He is given the wrong box of paper which wrote A3 on the box.
    B) He is declined of the requirement of getting refund.
    C) He wants a box of paper smaller than A4.
    D) He gets his money back at last.

20. A) The woman shop assistant is pretty rude to the customer.
    B) The woman is so careless to give the man the wrong box with A4 paper.
    C) The man is not quite upset though he doesn't get paper at last.

D) The woman reluctantly agrees to refund the man.

21. A) The man gets all his money back, which is totally 11.95.
    B) The man needs to pay 11.95 more for paper of bigger size.
    C) The woman gives 11.95 to the man to pay for the price gap between A4 and paper of smaller size.
    D) The woman gives the man 11.95 extra as a compensation for the inconvenience.

Questions 22 to 25 are based on the conversation you have just heard.

22. A) Both of them like it.
    B) Neither of them likes it.
    C) The woman likes it while the man doesn't.
    D) The man likes it while the woman doesn't.

23. A) Michelin restaurant.
    B) Three products: hotel and restaurant guides, guide books of places to see and maps.
    C) guides to Michelin restaurant.
    D) Tourist maps.

24. A) Newly-weds.   C) Advertisers.
    B) Families looking for fun.   D) Motorists and tourists.

25. A) Beautiful scenery.   C) Adventurous journey.
    B) Delicious food.   D) It's different for each product.

Section B

Directions: *In this section, you will hear 3 short passages. At the end of each passage, you will hear some questions. Both the passage and the questions will be spoken only once. After you hear a question, you must choose the best answer from the four choices marked A), B), C) and D). Then mark the corresponding letter on Answer Sheet 2 with a single line through the center.*

注意：此部分试题请在**答题卡 2** 上作答。

Passage One

Questions 26 to 28 are based on the passage you have just heard.

26. A) To point out the reasons for numerous children's death.

    B) To point out the progress and shortcomings of the current situation of global children's welfare.

    C) To call for more attention to AIDS effect on children's welfare.

    D) To call for more attention to the bad effect of war on children's welfare.

27. A) The effect of ethnic conflicts.   C) HIV-AIDS effect.

    B) The effect of civil wars.   D) Childhood malnutrition.

28. A) Millions of children nowadays still die each year from easily preventable causes.

    B) HIV-AIDS is now an African issue as to what Ms. Bellamy has said.

    C) Many children have become direct targets or collateral victims in recent years.

    D) The problems relating to HIV-AIDS and children will be a major topic on a special session by U. N. General Assembly soon.

Passage Two

Questions 29 to 31 are based on the passage you have just heard.

29. A) AIDS.   C) Malaria.

    B) Pneumonia.   D) Heart disease.

30. A) Warfare.   C) Poverty.

    B) Famine.   D) Diseases.

31. A) North Korea's health care system is now near collapse as to WHO report.

    B) Tuberculosis has struck tens of thousands of people in North Korea.

    C) Dr. Brundtland will open the WHO's first permanent office in Pyongyang.

    D) As to what Dr. Brundtland said, the health care crisis can be solved by North Korea only.

Passage Three

Questions 32 to 35 are based on the passage you have just heard.

32. A) U. S. astronauts install an exterior passageway on the International Space Station.

    B) U. S. shuttle Atlantis visited the International Space Station.

    C) Two shuttle crewmen stayed outside in the vacuum of space.

    D) The new arm of the station will go to work for the first time.

33. A) It can give the station a portal to space.

B) It will enable the following assembling of the outpost.

C) It will enable the following maintaining of the outpost.

D) It can help people on the station communicate with the earth more easily.

34. A) Disconnect and reconnect cables and other hardware on the passageway.

B) Lift the passageway out of the shuttle's cargo bay.

C) Move the passageway to the outpost.

D) Communicate with the people on U.S. shuttle Atlantis.

35. A) Two weeks later.　　　　C) Later this week.

B) Next week.　　　　　　　D) Unknown.

Section C

Directions: *In this section, you will hear a passage three times. When the passage is read for the first time, you should listen carefully for its general idea. When the passage is read for the second time, you are required to fill in the blanks numbered from 36 to 43 with the exact words you have just heard. For blanks numbered from 44 to 46 you are required to fill in the missing information. For these blanks, you can either use the exact words you have just heard or write down the main points in your own words. Finally, when the passage is read for the third time, you should check what you have written.*

注意：此部分试题在**答题卡** 2 上；请在**答题卡** 2 上作答。

Part IV　Reading Comprehension (Reading in Depth)

(25 minutes)

Section A

Directions: *In this section, there is a short passage with 5 questions or incomplete statements. Read the passage carefully. Then answer the questions or complete the statements in the fewest possible words on **Answer Sheet 2**.*

Questions 47 to 51 are based on the following passage.

Computers and connecting to the Internet computer system have become important in recent years. Information and communication technologies make this happen.

Many organizations believe that everyone, even poor people, should be able to use information and communication technologies. However, people must know how to read and write in order to use computers. In many countries, more than half the adult population cannot read or write. Now a United Nations agency has an idea about how to bring information from the Internet to people who cannot read or write. The agency is UNESCO — the United Nations Educational, Scientific and Cultural Organization. UNESCO has projects that combine two information and communication technologies. One technology is community broadcast radio. The radio station you are listening to now has big powerful transmitters set up around the world. But it is also possible to use small transmitters operating at low power. Broadcasts from these stations reach only a few square kilometers. But many people can listen to the radio within this area.

Community broadcast radio is combined with computers and the Internet at a multi-media community center. For example, farmers can go to the center and ask a question about a farming problem. Then workers at the center search the Internet for an answer. They broadcast the answer to the whole community over the radio station. Many groups are experimenting with this idea. One is Radio Kothmale in Sri Lanka. People from community radio stations all over the world met in Kothmale at a meeting supported by UNESCO. They learned what has made Radio Kothmale a success. And they learned how to use the Internet in their own programs to help people who cannot read or write.

注意：此部分试题请在**答题卡** 2 上作答。

47. What technologies have UNESCO used to help people?

48. According to this passage, what is a disadvantage for some people to use information technologies?

49. How can people listen to the broadcast radio in a remote area?

50. How can people get information from a multi-media community center?

51. Why did people go to Kothmale from all over the world?

Section B

Directions: *There are 2 passages in this section. Each passage is followed by some questions or unfinished statements. For each of them there are four choices marked A), B), C) and D). You should decide on the best choice and mark the corresponding letter on Answer Sheet 2 with a single line through the center.*

Passage One

Questions 52 to 56 are based on the following passage.

"I'm feeling a bit under the weather" is a common complaint in Britain, especially on Monday mornings, and it seems that weather really can be responsible for moods. Studies have shown that changeable weather can make it hard to concentrate, cloudy skies slow down reflexes, and high humidity with hot, dry winds makes many people irritable and snappy.

If you live in a place like Britain, where the weather seems to change daily if not hourly, you could be forgiven for thinking that the weather is random. In fact the weather is controlled by systems which move around areas of the globe. In the UK the weather depends on depressions, often called "lows", and anticyclones, also known as "highs". These systems start in the Atlantic Ocean, and make their way across the British Isles from the west to the east. Highs bring sunny weather, while lows bring rain and wind.

The human race has always tried to guess the weather, especially in areas of the world where there are frequent changes. Traditional rhymes point to early attempts to identify weather patterns and popular poems include: Red sky at night, shepherds delight; Red sky in the morning, shepherds warning. Flies will swarm before a storm. Rain before seven, clear by eleven. Two other popular traditional ways of forecasting the weather used pine cones and seaweed. When the air has a high level of humidity there is a higher chance of rain, when the humidity is slow, there is more chance of fine weather. Pine cones and seaweed react to changes in humidity — pine cones open, and seaweed feels dry when the humidity is low, while high humidity has the opposite effect.

A recent study by an Australian psychologist suggests that certain people may have a special gift for predicting the weather. However it is possible that these people would use their talent in another way, since the same group had considerable success in forecasting changes in another chaotic system — the stock market.

It appears that a study of weather patterns may also enable scientists to predict the outbreak of a disease. An Ebola epidemic in Uganda in the year 2000 came after the same rare weather conditions that had been present before an outbreak six years earlier. Efforts to limit the spread of airborne diseases such as foot and mouth, are also strongly dependent on favorable wind conditions.

52. What does "I am feeling a bit under the weather" in Para. 1 mean?
    A) I am feeling a bit depressed.

B) I am feeling a bit uncomfortable.

C) I am feeling a bit stressed.

D) I don't like such weather.

53. What is true about British weather?

A) It's changeable but can be controlled.

B) It's controlled by depressions from the Atlantic Ocean.

C) It's completely random and unpredictable.

D) It is controlled by the alternation of highs and lows.

54. which of the following suggests the traditional ways of forecasting the weather?

A) Using ships and balloons with monitoring equipment.

B) Open pine cones and observing.

C) Reciting traditional poems about weather.

D) Observing pine cones and seaweed.

55. The word "chaotic" (Line 4, Para. 4) most probably means _____.

A) random   C) unpredictable

B) disordered   D) out of order

56. Which of the following statements is true?

A) People with a special gift for predicting the weather must be successful in the stock market.

B) Modern technology helps people with a special gift succeed in the stock market.

C) The epidemic in Uganda was caused by rare weather conditions.

D) Favorable wind conditions help to control diseases.

Passage Two

Questions 57 to 61 are based on the following passage.

The traditional image of the British policeman as a jolly and friendly neighborhood character may have changed over the years as society has become more violent. But one thing about the British policeman had, until recently, not been tampered with: the dark blue conical helmet worn by the British policeman (the policewoman wears a different cap). It's as familiar to tourists to Britain as London taxis and the red London bus, and you can buy imitation helmets, policeman costume dolls, and posters and postcards depicting the British policeman, from virtually every London souvenir stall.

However, it looks as if the traditional helmet — like the red telephone box — is on its way out. In February of this year, in a radical redesign of the police uniform, the police force of the city of Manchester, in the northwest of England, replaced the traditional helmet with a flat peaked cap, thus becoming the first force in England and Wales to do so. (Scottish police forces replaced the conical helmet with a flat cap back in the 1950s.) Other police forces throughout England and Wales are now reviewing their uniforms. Recommendations for changes will be made later in the year by the Association of Chief Police Officers, although any decision to change will be up to individual forces (they are all autonomous).

The Greater Manchester police force only decided to abandon the conical hat after examining the results of a nationwide study and carrying out a three-year trial period of their new outfit. The study, which was undertaken to design the ideal police uniform, indicated that the majority of officers found the traditional helmet unpractical: it was uncomfortable (too heavy and too hot in summer); it was easily knocked off (often by hooligans); it fell off immediately as officers gave chase; and it was too easily seen from afar, thereby inadvertently warning criminals that the law was approaching.

However, not everyone within police ranks agrees. Mike Bennett of the Metropolitan Police believes that the traditional helmet's shape, solidity and heaviness are an advantage, for they help deflect blows to the head. It is an important symbol of police presence and thereby reassures the law-abiding public. Others are worried that, with flat caps, it will become difficult to distinguish policemen and women from security guards. Another argument for keeping the traditional helmet is that it lends an air of authority. Says a former policeman, "I not only looked six inches taller. I felt six inches taller."

57. What is the phrase "tamper with" (Line 3, Para. 1) most likely to mean?
   A) Tolerate.   C) Neglect.
   B) Change.   D) Deal with.

58. The conical helmet was first replaced in _____.
   A) England   C) Scotland
   B) Wales   D) Ireland

59. All of the following except _____ are advantages of the conical helmet.
   A) that it makes the policeman look authoritative
   B) that it diminishes the force of blows to the head
   C) that it is warm in winter
   D) that its presence makes citizens feel safe

60. All of the following except _____ are traditional tourist sights in Britain.
   A) London taxis   C) the conical helmet

B) red double-decker buses   D) red telephone boxes

61. All of the following except _____ are arguments for abandoning the conical helmet.

A) that it is too heavy and too hot in summer

B) that it is the first thing to come off when an officer is attacked or chases a suspect

C) that it is sentimentally connected with old traditions

D) that it is conspicuous

Part V Error Correction   (15 minutes)

Directions: *This part consists of a short passage. In this passage, there are altogether 10 mistakes, one in each numbered line. You may have to change a word, add a word or delete a word. Mark out the mistakes and put the corrections in the blanks provided. If you change a word, cross it out and write the correct word in the corresponding blank. If you add a word, put an insertion mark (∧) in the right place and write the missing word in the blank. If you delete a word, cross it out and put a slash (/) in the blank.*

注意：此部分试题在答题卡2上；请在答题卡2上作答。

Part VI Translation   (5 minutes)

Directions: *Complete the following sentences on **Answer Sheet 2** by translating into English the Chinese given in brackets.*

注意：此部分试题请在答题卡2上作答，只需写出译文部分。

72. He won the first prize in spoken English contest, _____

_____

（这在很大程度上归功于他的勤奋和努力，因为他几乎将所有的空余时间都用在了坚持练习上）.

73. It is a common phenomenon that _____

_____（老年人发现很难阻止年轻人的改变）.

74. Some parents fail to know that _____

_____（把自己的观点强加在孩子身上是错误的）.

75. _____

（我宁愿他当初没有出国留学）, though it is too late now.

76. _____

（和谐社会要求每个人都遵守道德准则）, which is known to all.

答题卡 1 (Answer Sheet 1)

学校：	准 考 证 号

姓名：	[0]	[0]	[0]	[0]	[0]	[0]	[0]	[0]	[0]	[0]	[0]	[0]	[0]	[0]
	[1]	[1]	[1]	[1]	[1]	[1]	[1]	[1]	[1]	[1]	[1]	[1]	[1]	[1]
	[2]	[2]	[2]	[2]	[2]	[2]	[2]	[2]	[2]	[2]	[2]	[2]	[2]	[2]
划线要求	[3]	[3]	[3]	[3]	[3]	[3]	[3]	[3]	[3]	[3]	[3]	[3]	[3]	[3]
	[4]	[4]	[4]	[4]	[4]	[4]	[4]	[4]	[4]	[4]	[4]	[4]	[4]	[4]
	[5]	[5]	[5]	[5]	[5]	[5]	[5]	[5]	[5]	[5]	[5]	[5]	[5]	[5]
	[6]	[6]	[6]	[6]	[6]	[6]	[6]	[6]	[6]	[6]	[6]	[6]	[6]	[6]
	[7]	[7]	[7]	[7]	[7]	[7]	[7]	[7]	[7]	[7]	[7]	[7]	[7]	[7]
	[8]	[8]	[8]	[8]	[8]	[8]	[8]	[8]	[8]	[8]	[8]	[8]	[8]	[8]
	[9]	[9]	[9]	[9]	[9]	[9]	[9]	[9]	[9]	[9]	[9]	[9]	[9]	[9]

Part I   **Writing**   **(30 minutes)**

Directions: *For this part, you are allowed 30 minutes to write a short essay entitled My View on Choosing the Right Career. You should write at least 150 words following the outline given below.*

1. 选择适合自己的职业的重要性
2. 如何选择适合自己的职业？
3. 我的看法

My View on Choosing the Right Career

答题卡 1 (Answer Sheet 1)

Part II   Reading Comprehension (Skimming and Scanning) (15 minutes)

1. [Y] [N] [NG]   5. _____   8. _____
2. [Y] [N] [NG]
3. [Y] [N] [NG]   6. _____   9. _____
4. [Y] [N] [NG]
                      7. _____   10. _____

答题卡 2 (Answer Sheet 2)

Part III   Section A   Section B

11. [A] [B] [C] [D]   16. [A] [B] [C] [D]   21. [A] [B] [C] [D]   26. [A] [B] [C] [D]   31. [A] [B] [C] [D]
12. [A] [B] [C] [D]   17. [A] [B] [C] [D]   22. [A] [B] [C] [D]   27. [A] [B] [C] [D]   32. [A] [B] [C] [D]
13. [A] [B] [C] [D]   18. [A] [B] [C] [D]   23. [A] [B] [C] [D]   28. [A] [B] [C] [D]   33. [A] [B] [C] [D]
14. [A] [B] [C] [D]   19. [A] [B] [C] [D]   24. [A] [B] [C] [D]   29. [A] [B] [C] [D]   34. [A] [B] [C] [D]
15. [A] [B] [C] [D]   20. [A] [B] [C] [D]   25. [A] [B] [C] [D]   30. [A] [B] [C] [D]   35. [A] [B] [C] [D]

Part III   Section C

Israeli and Palestinian security officials met Friday to discuss a (36)_____ U. S. brokered cease-fire. Both sides are accusing each other of not (37)_____ the terms of truce.

The (38)_____ of the Israeli and Palestinian security services met to discuss the first 48 hours of the cease-fire, and plans to (39)_____ requirements of the agreement.

In a statement, Israeli Prime Minister Ariel Sharon said violence and acts of terrorism have not stopped, and he accused the Palestinians of failing to arrest Islamic militants. Mr. Sharon said Israel will continue to uphold the cease-fire, but adds it will "(40)_____ between quiet areas and those where violence is continuing."

The prime minister added if (41)_____ continue, Israel will have no alternative but to "foil the attacks and strike at the attackers." Israeli Defense Minister Binyamin Ben Eliezer, speaking during a trip to Paris, said Israel will (42)_____ with the terms of the agreement. "We will increase the support and we will see," he said. "We have enough time to (43)_____ in a different way. We don't want to use that. (44)_____

_____."

Israeli tanks have pulled back in several parts of the occupied territories, (45)_____

_____ and the use of coastal waters off the Gaza Strip. (46)_____

_____ the Palestinian territories with Egypt and Jordan.

答题卡 2 (Answer Sheet 2)

Part IV   Section A   Part V   Error Correction   (15 minutes)

47. _____

48. _____

49. _____

50. _____

51. _____

Part IV   Section B

52. [A][B][C][D]
53. [A][B][C][D]
54. [A][B][C][D]
55. [A][B][C][D]
56. [A][B][C][D]
57. [A][B][C][D]
58. [A][B][C][D]
59. [A][B][C][D]
60. [A][B][C][D]
61. [A][B][C][D]

The World Bank says air pollution is one of the worse environmental problems in large cities around the world. Air pollution causes breathing problems. Which also threatens crop production in farm areas near huge cities. The United Nations Environment Program says that air pollution increases the amount of crops produced. It also reduces the nutrient level of crops.

The UN tells dirty air is a major source of metal in crops. These metals include lead, zinc and copper. These metals can build up to dangerous high levels in the parts of plants that people eat. The German Appropriate Technology Exchange, GATE, reports that eating these metals can cause developmental problems and low intelligence levels within children. Some kinds of cancers and kidney damage have also linked to metals in crops. GATE says air pollution can also reduce the nutritional quality of crops. It can even cause observe damage to the part of the crop that is eaten. This increases the chances of insects or diseases after the crop harvested. The GATE report says air pollution also reduces the length of time that crops can be sold before they are no more fresh.

62. _____

63. _____

64. _____

65. _____

66. _____

67. _____

68. _____

69. _____

70. _____

71. _____

Part VI   Translation   (5 minutes)

72. _____

73. _____

74. _____

75. _____

76. _____

PRACTICE TEST 7

Part I   Writing

(30 minutes)

注意：此部分试题在**答题卡**1上。

Part II   Reading Comprehension (Skimming and Scanning)

(15 minutes)

Directions: *In this part, you will have 15 minutes to go over the passage quickly and answer the questions on **Answer Sheet 1**.*

For questions 1 – 4, mark

Y *(for YES)*   *if the statement agrees with the information given in the passage;*

N *(for NO)*   *if the statement contradicts the information given in the passage;*

NG *(for NOT GIVEN)*   *if the information is not given in the passage.*

For questions 5 – 10, complete the sentences with the information given in the passage.

Dumb and Dumber: Are Americans Hostile to Knowledge?

Popular video on YouTube shows Kellie Pickler, the adorable platinum blonde from "American Idol", appearing on the Fox game show "Are You Smarter Than a 5th Grader?" during celebrity week. Selected from a third-grade geography curriculum, the $25,000 question asked: "Budapest is the capital of what European country?" Ms. Pickler threw up both hands and looked at the large blackboard perplexed. "I thought Europe was a country," she said. Playing it safe, she chose to copy the answer offered by one of the genuine fifth graders: Hungary. "Hungry?" she said, eyes widening in disbelief. "That's a country? I've heard of Turkey. But Hungry? I've never heard of it."

Such, uh, lack of global awareness is the kind of thing that drives Susan Jacoby, author of *The Age of American Unreason*, up a wall. Ms. Jacoby is one of a number of writers with new books that bemoan the state of American culture.

Joining the circle of curmudgeons this season is Eric G. Wilson, whose *Against Happiness* warns that the "American obsession with happiness" could "well lead to a sudden extinction of the creative impulse, that could result in an extermination as horrible as those foreshadowed by global warming and environmental crisis and nuclear proliferation."

Then there is Lee Siegel's *Against the Machine: Being Human in the Age of the Electronic Mob,* which inveighs against the Internet for encouraging solipsism, debased discourse and arrant commercialization. Mr. Siegel, one might remember, was suspended by *The New Republic* for using a fake online persona in order to trash critics of his blog ("you couldn't tie Siegel's shoelaces") and to praise himself ("brave, brilliant").

Ms. Jacoby, whose book came out on Tuesday, doesn't zero in on a particular technology or emotion, but rather on what she feels is a generalized hostility to knowledge. She is well aware that some may tag her a crank. "I expect to get bashed," said Ms. Jacoby, 62, either as an older person who upbraids the young for plummeting standards and values, or as a secularist whose defense of scientific rationalism is a way to disparage religion.

Ms. Jacoby, however, is quick to point out that her indictment is not limited by age or ideology. Yes, she knows that eggheads, nerds, bookworms, longhairs, pointy-heads, highbrows and know-it-alls have been mocked and dismissed throughout American history. And liberal and conservative writers, from Richard Hofstadter to Allan Bloom, have regularly analyzed the phenomenon and offered advice.

But now, Ms. Jacoby said, something different is happening: anti-intellectualism (the attitude that "too much learning can be a dangerous thing") and anti-rationalism (the idea that "there is no such things as evidence or fact, just opinion") have fused in a particularly insidious way.

Not only are citizens ignorant about essential scientific, civic and cultural knowledge, she said, but they also don't think it matters.

She pointed to a 2006 National Geographic poll that found nearly half of 18- to 24-year-olds don't think it is necessary or important to know where countries in the news are located. So more than three years into the Iraq war, only 23 percent of those with some college could locate Iraq, Iran, Saudi Arabia and Israel on a map.

Ms. Jacoby, dressed in a bright red turtleneck with lipstick to match, was sitting, appropriately, in that temple of knowledge, the New York Public Library's majestic Beaux Arts building on Fifth Avenue. The author of seven other books, she was a fellow at the library when she first got the idea for this book back in 2001, on 9/11.

Ms. Jacoby doesn't expect to revolutionize the nation's educational system or cause millions of Americans to switch off "American Idol" and pick up Schopenhauer. But she would like to start a conversation about why the United States seems particularly vulnerable to such a virulent strain of anti-intellectualism. After all, "the empire of infotainment doesn't stop at the American border," she said, yet students in many other countries consistently outperform American students in science, math and reading on comparative tests.

In part, she lays the blame on a failing educational system. "Although people are going to school more and more years, there's no evidence that they know more," she said.

Ms. Jacoby also blames religious fundamentalism's antipathy toward science, as she grieves over surveys that show that nearly two thirds of Americans want creationism to be taught along with evolution.

Ms. Jacoby doesn't leave liberals out of her analysis, mentioning the New Left's attacks on universities in the 1960s, the decision to consign African-American and women's studies to an "academic ghetto" instead of integrating them into the core curriculum, ponderous musings on rock music and pop culture courses on everything from sitcoms to fat that trivialize college-level learning.

Avoiding the liberal or conservative label in this particular argument, she prefers to call herself a "cultural conservationist".

For all her scholarly interests, though, Ms. Jacoby said she recognized just how hard it is to tune out the 24/7 entertainment culture. A few years ago she participated in the annual campaign to turn off the television for a week. "I was stunned at how difficult it was for me," she said.

注意：此部分试题请在**答题卡**1上作答。

1. According to the passage, platinum blondes from "American Idol" tend to be ignorant of geographical knowledge.
2. Mr. Siegel was suspended by *The New Republic* because he used fake persona for his own sake.
3. It is Ms. Jacoby's dream to revolutionize the nation's educational system and resist trash TV program like "American Idol".
4. Ms. Jacoby calls herself a cultural radical people, because she wants to do something to change current situation.
5. _____ drives Susan Jacoby to write her book *The Age of American Unreason*.
6. Jacoby's book focuses on _____ rather than on a particular technology.

7. According to Jacoby, something different is happening, which is _____.

8. Jacoby put major blame on _____.

9. Jacoby's attitude toward religious fundamentalism's antipathy to science is _____.

10. According to the surveys mentioned in the passage, two thirds of Americans want _____.

Part III   Listening Comprehension   (35 minutes)

Section A

Directions: *In this section, you will hear 8 short conversations and 2 long conversations. At the end of each conversation, one or more questions will be asked about what was said. Both the conversation and the questions will be spoken only once. After each question there will be a pause. During the pause, you must read the four choices marked A), B), C) and D), and decide which is the best answer. Then mark the corresponding letter on Answer Sheet 2 with a single line through the center.*

注意：此部分试题请在**答题卡2**上作答。

11. A) He complains that the children are too much burdened.
    B) He complains that the school is a dangerous place.
    C) He complains that children go to school too early.
    D) He thinks that fishing will be more suitable for children than going to school.

12. A) The woman can watch the sports game at a later date free of charge.
    B) The woman has to buy another ticket for the later date.
    C) It won't rain on the sports day.
    D) The woman will be returned the money she has paid for the sports game.

13. A) The woman suggests the man collect books.
    B) The man has no time to collect more rare books now.
    C) The woman has no time to classify more rare stamps.
    D) The man frequently groups his stamps.

14. A) She can't speak clearly to Mary.
    B) She wants the man to turn off the radio.
    C) She wants the man to hang on the phone.

D) She wants to continue her talk with Mary.

15. A) The man thinks the woman is overreacting.
    B) The woman speaks highly of that linguistic lecture.
    C) The man doesn't expect a good lecture from the beginning.
    D) The man feels disappointed with the woman's reaction.

16. A) The man got robbed when buying the bag.
    B) The man got a real bargain for the woman.
    C) The woman thought the man had paid too much for the bag.
    D) The woman was satisfied with the bag.

17. A) Being too careful is not a good thing for a driver sometimes.
    B) A driver should always be careful.
    C) He always feels nervous during driving.
    D) Being nervous only happens to new drivers.

18. A) The advertisement he makes is awful.
    B) He gets on well with his advertisement.
    C) He is unsatisfied with the payment.
    D) His job is free of charge.

Questions 19 to 21 are based on the conversation you have just heard.

19. A) Professor and student.   C) Colleagues.
    B) Interviewer and interviewee.   D) Teacher and parent.

20. A) Possibly, but he hates to do that.
    B) Hopefully, and he is looking forward to that.
    C) There is little chance for him to do that.
    D) Surely he will be there.

21. A) Casual.   C) Business-like.
    B) Formal.   D) serious.

Questions 22 to 25 are based on the conversation you have just heard.

22. A) accountant.   C) director.
    B) sales manager.   D) receptionist.

23. A) Irresponsibility of the employee.   C) Financial problem of J. L.
    B) Carelessness of the boss.   D) Lack of communication.

24. A) He is an employee of the company.
    B) He made a financial mistake in his last trip.
    C) He is a self-employed man in the company.
    D) He complained about the high charges of traveling fee.

25. A) Give J. L. a company credit card.
    B) Cover all his expenses while he is travelling.
    C) Give him some money in advance and cover his ticket fare.
    D) Ask J. L. to pay the money from his own pocket.

Section B

Directions: *In this section, you will hear 3 short passages. At the end of each passage, you will hear some questions. Both the passage and the questions will be spoken only once. After you hear a question, you must choose the best answer from the four choices marked A), B), C) and D). Then mark the corresponding letter on **Answer Sheet 2** with a single line through the center.*

注意：此部分试题请在**答题卡**2上作答。

Passage One

Questions 26 to 28 are based on the passage you have just heard.

26. A) Their mother.   C) Their father.
    B) Their environment.   D) Other humans.

27. A) It is given to prove that babies are born mentally healthy.
    B) It is given to prove that babies are able to understand the story before they were born.
    C) It is given to prove that babies don't understand the story even after their birth.
    D) It is given to prove that the ability to learn exists in babies even before their birth.

28. A) Babies who are breast-fed develop greater intelligence than those who are fed other kinds of milk.
    B) Babies who are formula-fed develop better than those who are fed other kinds of milk.
    C) There is no solid evidence to show what kind of milk is best for children.
    D) There is completely no relationship between milk and children's intelligence.

Passage Two

Questions 29 to 31 are based on the passage you have just heard.

29. A) It is to make AIDS drugs cheaper and more easily available.
    B) It will allow Kenya's government to suspend the patents on essential drugs of AIDS.
    C) It will allow Kenya to get cheaper generic versions of AIDS medication from many countries.
    D) It has successfully led to the drop of prices of AIDS-fighting drugs in large British pharmaceutical companies and thus has attained its goal.

30. A) Sub-Saharan Africa.   C) India and Brazil.
    B) Britain.   D) North America.

31. A) The prices of Anti-retroviral drugs now are well beyond the reach of those infected in developing countries.
    B) The pharmaceutical companies have undergone increasing pressure to tighten drug patents in the developing world.
    C) Many Kenyans are infected with HIV virus that causes AIDS and die from AIDS every day.
    D) Kenya is one of the earliest African countries to move to change its laws to help prolong the lives of people living with AIDS.

Passage Three

Questions 32 to 35 are based on the passage you have just heard.

32. A) To tell some stories behind this song.
    B) To give a brief review of the life of its author.
    C) To argue the time when the song was written.
    D) To give some impression of the song from the author's friends.

33. A) Just before World War Ⅱ.
    B) At the end of World War Ⅰ.
    C) After the Pearl Harbor.
    D) Before 9.11 disaster.

34. A) It inspires people to work together and help one another after the horrible accident happened as it did before.
    B) Some famous American bands have now sung it.
    C) It meets the taste of American people nowadays.

D) It is simple and easy to remember.

35. A) It was not so popular when it was written.
    B) It has never been revised before.
    C) It has inspired American people for many times.
    D) It is simple, to the point and not war-mongering.

Section C

Directions: *In this section, you will hear a passage three times. When the passage is read for the first time, you should listen carefully for its general idea. When the passage is read for the second time, you are required to fill in the blanks numbered from 36 to 43 with the exact words you have just heard. For blanks numbered from 44 to 46 you are required to fill in the missing information. For these blanks, you can either use the exact words you have just heard or write down the main points in your own words. Finally, when the passage is read for the third time, you should check what you have written.*

注意：此部分试题在**答题卡 2** 上；请在**答题卡 2** 上作答。

Part IV Reading Comprehension (Reading in Depth)

(25 minutes)

Section A

Directions: *In this section, there is a short passage with 5 questions or incomplete statements. Read the passage carefully. Then answer the questions or complete the statements in the fewest possible words on **Answer Sheet 2**.*

Questions 47 to 51 are based on the following passage.

Engineers are celebrating the completion of repairs to the Leaning Tower of Pisa. Italian officials closed the Leaning Tower for safety reasons eleven years ago. Experts now say the repairs will make the building safe for at least a few more centuries. The Leaning Tower is leaning because it was built on soft sandy soil. The soil cannot support its weight. The tower weighs about 14,500 metric tons. The ground under the tower first started to sink soon after workers began building the structure in the year 1173. An international team of building experts began a project to make sure the Leaning Tower does not fall down. First, engineers placed 870 metric tons of lead weights on the north side of the tower. This helped stop additional movement. Also, workers tied strong steel cables around the structure. These wires were connected to large weights in the area. Next, engineers slowly removed tons of soil from under the tower. They used special drills to remove small amounts of soil over several months. Slowly the tower moved back to where it stood hundreds of years ago. It still leans, but not as much as before the repairs.

注意：此部分试题请在**答题卡**2 上作答。

47. Why was the Leaning Tower closed?

48. Why is the tower leaning?

49. When was the Leaning tower first built?

50. How can the engineers remove the soil under the tower?

51. Which goal has this repair work achieved?

Section B

Directions: *There are 2 passages in this section. Each passage is followed by some questions or unfinished statements. For each of them there are four choices marked A), B), C) and D). You should decide on the best choice and mark the corresponding letter on **Answer Sheet 2** with a single line through the center.*

Passage One

Questions 52 to 56 are based on the following passage.

Successful international marketing doesn't stop with good translations — other aspects of culture must be researched and understood if marketers are to avoid blunders. When marketers do not understand and appreciate the values, tastes, geography, climate, superstitions, level of literacy, religion, or economic development of a culture, they fail to capture their target market. For example, when a popular American designer tried to introduce a new perfume in the Latin American market, the product aroused little interest and the company lost a lot of money. Ads for the new fragrance highlighted its fresh camellia scent. What marketers had failed to realize was that camellias are traditionally used for funerals in many South American countries.

Procter and Gamble has been successful in marketing its products internationally for many years. Today, overseas markets account for over one third of its sales. However, the company's success in this area didn't happen overnight. Procter and Gamble initially experienced huge losses because marketing managers did not recognize important cultural differences. For instance, when P & G first entered the Japanese market with its popular Cheer laundry detergents, most Japanese housewives weren't interested. The promotional campaign that emphasized Cheer as an effective "all temperature" detergent was lost on the Japanese who usually wash clothes in cold water. Although the ad had been quite successful in the United States where clothes are washed in all temperatures, it fell flat in Japan. All of this could have been avoided if P & G marketers had done more preliminary research before launching the campaign. Once P & G changed its strategy and promised superior cleaning in cold water, sales for Cheer picked up dramatically.

The use of numbers can also be a source of problems for international marketers. The company couldn't figure out why the golf balls weren't selling well until it realized that in Japanese the word for the number four also means death. In Japan four and nine are very unlucky numbers which should be avoided by marketers.

Even illustrations need to be carefully examined. McDonnell Douglas Corporation made an unfortunate error in an aircraft brochure for potential customers in India. It included a picture of men wearing turbans, which was not appreciated by the Indians. A company spokesman reported, "It was politely pointed out to us that turbans were distinctly Pakistani Moslem."

52. Why is the new fragrance not popular in Latin countries?
   A) People are not interested in such fragrance.
   B) The fragrance suggests funerals in Latin countries.
   C) People refuse to accept products made in the USA.
   D) A terrible mistake was made in translation.

53. What does the phrase "pick up" (Last line, Para. 2) mean here?
   A) To take hold of.   C) To become better.
   B) To choose.   D) To become worse.

54. Which of the following statements is NOT true according to the passage?
   A) The word for number four is unlucky in Japan.
   B) One third of P & G sales are in overseas markets.
   C) Cheer is not so effective in cold water.
   D) The picture McDonnell Douglas Corp. used is culturally offensive.

55. The passage is mainly about _____.
   A) the importance of researching and understanding the cultural differences

B) the importance of being familiar with the conventions of a country

C) the value of understanding the language of a nation

D) the value of knowing the set of lucky and unlucky numbers of every culture

56. What is the main topic of the passage?

A) Cultural oversights can be disastrous.

B) The lesson that Procter and Gamble learned.

C) Superstition about numbers.

D) What illustrations show.

Passage Two

Questions 57 to 61 are based on the following passage.

Daydreaming is a healthy and natural act of the human psyche, according to *American Health* magazine.

It is at its peak from noon to 2 pm, when body temperature is at its highest. The phenomenon also reveals a great deal about us. Some people use their fantasies to help them make decisions, while others "escape" to enhance their sense of well-being and creativity, says Pam L. Blondin, a clinical social worker and director of programs and services at the Child and Family Service of Sagisaw County, Michigan.

"Daydreaming can be an escape that feels good in the midst of a hectic day," Blondin explained. "It's a good stress reducer at the desk. Getting away from it all for a while, so to speak, isn't something that is going to hurt anyone. Sometimes it helps people tap into creativity that is not always conscious."

Daydreaming helps people cope with a wide range of problems, partly providing insight into our emotional needs, as well as unmet needs and goals, experts say. By some estimates, approximately half of our waking thoughts consist of daydreams and fantasies. "Daydreaming keeps our personal agendas in front of us," says psychologist Eric Klinger.

Daydreaming plays an important role in organizing our lives, he says. "We can actually learn something by paying attention to the whimsical interludes that occasionally interrupt our more structured thoughts."

Active, imaginative lives are vital to children's development, *American Health* reports. Most children start fantasizing between the ages of 2 and 5. "Children struggle to understand life's complexities, from jet planes to the TV images flashed into their living rooms," says Yale University psychologist Jerome L. Singer. He believes that make believe helps youngsters break down elements to a level they can understand. "Unless a child's daydreaming is interfering with progress in school or hampering his/her social skills, there is no need to discourage it," Singer says.

57. Daydreaming does all of the following except _____.
    A) helping people make decisions
    B) reducing stress
    C) making people think unrealistically
    D) improving people's creativity

58. What is the word "hectic" (Line 1, Para. 3) most likely to mean?
    A) Bad.   C) Extraordinary.
    B) Imaginative.   D) Busy.

59. Children may start to daydream as early as they are _____ years old.
    A) 2   C) 5
    B) 3   D) 6

60. It can be inferred that _____.
    A) daydreaming is most active at noon
    B) daydreaming helps people realize what needs they want to meet
    C) daydreaming helps us forget our agendas
    D) we'd better prevent children from daydreaming

61. Which of the following statements is NOT true according to the passage?
    A) Daydreaming is most active when our body temperature is at its highest.
    B) Daydreams are consistent with our structured thoughts.
    C) Children's daydreaming should not be discouraged unless it results in problems.
    D) There are different definitions of daydreaming.

Part V   Error Correction   (15 minutes)

Directions: *This part consists of a short passage. In this passage, there are altogether 10 mistakes, one in each numbered line. You may have to change a word, add a word or delete a word. Mark out the mistakes and put the corrections in the blanks provided. If you change a word, cross it out and write the correct word in the corresponding blank. If you add a word, put an insertion mark (∧) in the right place and write the missing word in the blank. If you delete a word, cross it out and put a slash (/) in the blank.*

注意：此部分试题在**答题卡**2上；请在**答题卡**2上作答。

Part VI Translation

(5 minutes)

Directions: *Complete the following sentences on **Answer Sheet 2** by translating into English the Chinese given in brackets.*

注意：此部分试题请在**答题卡** 2 上作答，只需写出译文部分。

72. According to the report，_____
    （警察正在试图阻止因吸毒而引起的犯罪）.

73. Only when there is a certain need，_____
    （才有可能有某种发明）.

74. Having dinner at such a fancy hotel _____
    （超出了我们的承受能力）.

75. He took it for granted that _____
    （老板会根据他的实际能力给他加工资）.

76. _____
    （无论他如何努力，他都无法摆脱目前的困境），which makes him quite upset.

答题卡 1 (Answer Sheet 1)

学校:		准　考　证　号															
		[0]	[0]	[0]	[0]	[0]	[0]	[0]	[0]	[0]	[0]	[0]	[0]	[0]	[0]	[0]	[0]
姓名:		[1]	[1]	[1]	[1]	[1]	[1]	[1]	[1]	[1]	[1]	[1]	[1]	[1]	[1]	[1]	[1]
		[2]	[2]	[2]	[2]	[2]	[2]	[2]	[2]	[2]	[2]	[2]	[2]	[2]	[2]	[2]	[2]
		[3]	[3]	[3]	[3]	[3]	[3]	[3]	[3]	[3]	[3]	[3]	[3]	[3]	[3]	[3]	[3]
划		[4]	[4]	[4]	[4]	[4]	[4]	[4]	[4]	[4]	[4]	[4]	[4]	[4]	[4]	[4]	[4]
线		[5]	[5]	[5]	[5]	[5]	[5]	[5]	[5]	[5]	[5]	[5]	[5]	[5]	[5]	[5]	[5]
要		[6]	[6]	[6]	[6]	[6]	[6]	[6]	[6]	[6]	[6]	[6]	[6]	[6]	[6]	[6]	[6]
求		[7]	[7]	[7]	[7]	[7]	[7]	[7]	[7]	[7]	[7]	[7]	[7]	[7]	[7]	[7]	[7]
		[8]	[8]	[8]	[8]	[8]	[8]	[8]	[8]	[8]	[8]	[8]	[8]	[8]	[8]	[8]	[8]
		[9]	[9]	[9]	[9]	[9]	[9]	[9]	[9]	[9]	[9]	[9]	[9]	[9]	[9]	[9]	[9]

Part I   **Writing**   **(30 minutes)**

Directions: *For this part, you are allowed 30 minutes to write a short essay entitled* **The Importance of Environmental Protection***. You should write at least* **150** *words following the outline given below.*

1. 环境保护的现状
2. 环境保护的重要性
3. 我们应该采取的措施

The Importance of Environmental Protection

答题卡 1 (Answer Sheet 1)

Part II   Reading Comprehension (Skimming and Scanning) (15 minutes)

1. [Y] [N] [NG]
2. [Y] [N] [NG]
3. [Y] [N] [NG]
4. [Y] [N] [NG]

5. _____

6. _____

7. _____

8. _____

9. _____

10. _____

答题卡 2 (Answer Sheet 2)

准　　考　　证　　号

[0]	[0]	[0]	[0]	[0]	[0]	[0]	[0]	[0]	[0]	[0]	[0]	[0]	[0]	[0]
[1]	[1]	[1]	[1]	[1]	[1]	[1]	[1]	[1]	[1]	[1]	[1]	[1]	[1]	[1]
[2]	[2]	[2]	[2]	[2]	[2]	[2]	[2]	[2]	[2]	[2]	[2]	[2]	[2]	[2]
[3]	[3]	[3]	[3]	[3]	[3]	[3]	[3]	[3]	[3]	[3]	[3]	[3]	[3]	[3]
[4]	[4]	[4]	[4]	[4]	[4]	[4]	[4]	[4]	[4]	[4]	[4]	[4]	[4]	[4]
[5]	[5]	[5]	[5]	[5]	[5]	[5]	[5]	[5]	[5]	[5]	[5]	[5]	[5]	[5]
[6]	[6]	[6]	[6]	[6]	[6]	[6]	[6]	[6]	[6]	[6]	[6]	[6]	[6]	[6]
[7]	[7]	[7]	[7]	[7]	[7]	[7]	[7]	[7]	[7]	[7]	[7]	[7]	[7]	[7]
[8]	[8]	[8]	[8]	[8]	[8]	[8]	[8]	[8]	[8]	[8]	[8]	[8]	[8]	[8]
[9]	[9]	[9]	[9]	[9]	[9]	[9]	[9]	[9]	[9]	[9]	[9]	[9]	[9]	[9]

Part III　Section A　　　　　　　　Section B

11. [A] [B] [C] [D]　16. [A] [B] [C] [D]　21. [A] [B] [C] [D]　26. [A] [B] [C] [D]　31. [A] [B] [C] [D]
12. [A] [B] [C] [D]　17. [A] [B] [C] [D]　22. [A] [B] [C] [D]　27. [A] [B] [C] [D]　32. [A] [B] [C] [D]
13. [A] [B] [C] [D]　18. [A] [B] [C] [D]　23. [A] [B] [C] [D]　28. [A] [B] [C] [D]　33. [A] [B] [C] [D]
14. [A] [B] [C] [D]　19. [A] [B] [C] [D]　24. [A] [B] [C] [D]　29. [A] [B] [C] [D]　34. [A] [B] [C] [D]
15. [A] [B] [C] [D]　20. [A] [B] [C] [D]　25. [A] [B] [C] [D]　30. [A] [B] [C] [D]　35. [A] [B] [C] [D]

Part III　Section C

In northern Asia, one of the worst (36)＿＿＿＿＿＿ in recent memory is (37)＿＿＿＿＿＿ crops, (38)＿＿＿＿＿＿ and economies. A severe drought in North Korea is raising fresh fears of a serious food crisis in the already (39)＿＿＿＿＿＿ communist country.

A vast area from northwestern China, across Mongolia to the Korean (40)＿＿＿＿＿＿ has had little or no rain for the past three months with little (41)＿＿＿＿＿＿ in sight. In South Korea, the current drought is the worst in almost nine (42)＿＿＿＿＿＿. Serious water shortages have shut down some factories in several cities and rice farmers in the (43)＿＿＿＿＿＿ areas say they may not be able to plant any crops at all. Earlier this week, the government sent more than 110,000 soldiers to the countryside to (44)＿＿＿＿＿＿

＿＿＿＿＿＿＿＿＿＿＿＿＿＿＿ their parched rice paddies.
The situation is even more dire in North Korea. (45)＿＿＿＿＿＿

＿＿＿＿＿＿＿＿＿＿＿＿＿＿＿.

Kathy Zellweger is an aid worker for Caritas in Hong Kong. "The winter wheat, barley, and early potatoes have been badly affected," she said. "Even if it rains within the next few days, (46)＿＿＿＿＿＿

＿＿＿＿＿＿＿＿＿＿＿＿＿＿＿."

答题卡 2 (Answer Sheet 2)

Part IV   Section A   **Part V   Error Correction**   **(15 minutes)**

47. _____

        _____

48. _____

        _____

49. _____

        _____

50. _____

        _____

51. _____

        _____

A new report says people are harming the Wolong
Nature Reserve, China's largest protect area for giant
pandas. The report says the environment in the nature
preserve is being destroyed more quickly than in other parts
of China that not protected. Now only about one thousand
giant panda live in the mountains of southwestern China.
Giant pandas live in mountain areas that there are plenty of
forests. They eat mainly bamboo plants. The researchers
compared the rates of change in Wolong's forests with
environment before and after the reserve opened. The
researchers found that humans have not taken control of
large parts of Wolong. Jianguo Liu of Michigan State
University led the study. He said human settlements have
grown in the reserve, mainly for it has so many visitors.

The human population has increased to seventy percent
since the reserve was created. The people are cutting more
trees for fuel and other uses. Which has destroyed areas
where pandas live.

62. _____

63. _____

64. _____

65. _____

66. _____

67. _____

68. _____

69. _____

70. _____

71. _____

Part IV   Section B

52. [A][B][C][D]
53. [A][B][C][D]
54. [A][B][C][D]
55. [A][B][C][D]
56. [A][B][C][D]
57. [A][B][C][D]
58. [A][B][C][D]
59. [A][B][C][D]
60. [A][B][C][D]
61. [A][B][C][D]

Part VI   **Translation**   **(5 minutes)**

72. _____

73. _____

74. _____

75. _____

76. _____

PRACTICE TEST 8

Part I　Writing

(30 minutes)

注意：此部分试题在**答题卡**1上。

Part II　Reading Comprehension (Skimming and Scanning)

(15 minutes)

Directions: *In this part, you will have 15 minutes to go over the passage quickly and answer the questions on **Answer Sheet 1**.*

For questions 1 – 4, mark

Y *(for YES)*　　　　*if the statement agrees with the information given in the passage;*

N *(for NO)*　　　　*if the statement contradicts the information given in the passage;*

NG *(for NOT GIVEN)*　　*if the information is not given in the passage.*

For questions 5 – 10, complete the sentences with the information given in the passage.

Poverty Is Poison

"Poverty in early childhood poisons the brain." That was the opening of an article in Saturday's *Financial Times*, summarizing research presented last week at the American Association for the Advancement of Science.

As the article explained, neuroscientists have found that "many children growing up in very poor families with low social status experience unhealthy levels of stress hormones, which impair their neural development." The effect is to impair language development and memory — and hence the ability to escape poverty — for the rest of the child's life. So now we have another, even more compelling reason to be ashamed about America's record of failing to fight poverty.

L. B. J. declared his "War on Poverty" 44 years ago. Contrary to cynical legend, there actually was a large reduction in poverty over the next few years, especially among children, who saw their poverty rate fall from 23 percent in 1963 to 14 percent in 1969. But progress stalled thereafter: American politics shifted to the right, attention shifted from the suffering of the poor to the alleged abuses of welfare queens driving Cadillacs, and the fight against poverty was largely abandoned.

In 2006, 17.4 percent of children in America lived below the poverty line, substantially more than in 1969. And even this measure probably understates the true depth of many children's misery.

Living in or near poverty has always been a form of exile, of being cut off from the larger society. But the distance between the poor and the rest of us is much greater than it was 40 years ago, because most American incomes have risen in real terms while the official poverty line has not. To be poor in America today, even more than in the past, is to be an outcast in your own country. And that, the neuroscientists tell us, is what poisons a child's brain.

America's failure to make progress in reducing poverty, especially among children, should provoke a lot of soul-searching. Unfortunately, what it often seems to provoke instead is great creativity in making excuses.

Some of these excuses take the form of assertions that America's poor really aren't all that poor — a claim that always has me wondering whether those making it watched any TV during Hurricane Katrina, or for that matter have ever looked around them while visiting a major American city.

Mainly, however, excuses for poverty involve the assertion that the United States is a land of opportunity, a place where people can start out poor, work hard and become rich. But the fact of the matter is that Horatio Alger stories are rare, and stories of people trapped by their parents' poverty are all too common. According to one recent estimate, American children born to parents in the bottom fourth of the income distribution have almost a 50 percent chance of staying there — and almost a two-thirds chance of remaining stuck if they're black.

That's not surprising. Growing up in poverty puts you at a disadvantage at every step.

I'd bracket those new studies on brain development in early childhood with a study from the National Center for Education Statistics, which tracked a group of students who were in eighth grade in 1988. The study found, roughly speaking, that in modern America parental status trumps ability: students who did very well on a standardized test but came from low-status families were slightly less likely to get through college than students who tested poorly but had well-off parents. None of this is inevitable.

Poverty rates are much lower in most European countries than in the United States, mainly because of government programs that help the poor and unlucky.

And governments that set their minds to it can reduce poverty. In Britain, the

Labor government that came into office in 1997 made reducing poverty a priority — and despite some setbacks, its program of income subsidies and other aid has achieved a great deal. Child poverty, in particular, has been cut in half by the measure that corresponds most closely to the U.S. definition.

At the moment it's hard to imagine anything comparable happening in this country. To their credit — and to the credit of John Edwards, who goaded them into it — both Hillary Clinton and Barack Obama are proposing new initiatives against poverty. But their proposals are modest in scope and far from central to their campaigns.

I'm not blaming them for that; if a progressive wins this election, it will be by promising to ease the anxiety of the middle class rather than aiding the poor. And for a variety of reasons, health care, not poverty, should be the first priority of a Democratic administration. But ultimately, let's hope that the nation turns back to the task it abandoned — that of ending the poverty that still poisons so many American lives.

注意：此部分试题请在**答题卡 1** 上作答。

1. It is said about 20% of children in America lived below the poverty line, substantially more than in 1969. The author thinks it exaggerates the truth.

2. According to the article, the distance between the poor and the rest of us is much greater than it was 40 years ago.

3. A new study on brain development concludes that students from poor family have less chance to get through college.

4. Barack Obama are proposing new initiatives against poverty and have achieved a lot already.

5. Neuroscientists have found that "many children growing up in very poor families with low social status experience _____, which impair their _____."

6. After 1969, attention upon poverty issue shifted from _____ to _____.

7. The neuroscientists tell us _____ poisons a child's brain.

8. America's failure to make progress in reducing poverty unfortunately often seems to provoke _____.

9. Poverty rates are much lower in most European countries than in the United States, which is mainly attributed to _____.

10. The author advocates us to turn back to the task of _____.

Part III   Listening Comprehension   (35 minutes)

Section A

Directions: *In this section, you will hear 8 short conversations and 2 long conversations. At the end of each conversation, one or more questions will be asked about what was said. Both the conversation and the questions will be spoken only once. After each question there will be a pause. During the pause, you must read the four choices marked A), B), C) and D), and decide which is the best answer. Then mark the corresponding letter on **Answer Sheet 2** with a single line through the center.*

注意：此部分试题请在**答题卡** 2 上作答。

11. A) At home.   C) In a phone booth.
    B) In his office.   D) In his neighbor's house.

12. A) The woman expects too much of professors.
    B) The woman overestimates professors.
    C) The man thinks good professors are rare.
    D) The man thinks competent professors are rare.

13. A) In a hospital.   C) In a travel agency.
    B) In a hotel.   D) In a restaurant.

14. A) He doesn't know where his daughter won the championship.
    B) He thinks he can play better than his daughter.
    C) He doesn't play as well himself.
    D) He is still not satisfied with his daughter's performance.

15. A) He doesn't have a sense of humor.
    B) He must learn to understand John's humor better.
    C) He doesn't appreciate John's humor.
    D) He doesn't think John is funny enough.

16. A) 160.   C) 40.
    B) 144.   D) 36.

17. A) He thinks it is a pity.
    B) He is unsympathetic towards John.
    C) He thinks it is unfair for John.
    D) He thinks John deserves the scholarship.

18. A) He is happy to hear that.
    B) He feels a little bit disappointed.
    C) He is indifferent to the news.
    D) He can't believe the news is true.

Questions 19 to 21 are based on the conversation you have just heard.

19. A) The man Mr. Wong is looking for.   C) Mr. Wong's boss.
    B) Mr. Cox's assistant.   D) Mr. Wong's colleague.

20. A) To look for Mrs. Cox for some business issue.
    B) To look for Mrs. Box for some help.
    C) To inform Mrs. Cox of his arriving time in Melbourne.
    D) To check when Mrs. Cox will be in Melbourne.

21. A) Receptionist.   C) Mr. Box's assistant.
    B) Mrs. Cox's assistant.   D) The man's colleague.

Questions 22 to 25 are based on the conversation you have just heard.

22. A) A boss of his own private business.
    B) A general manager of a big company.
    C) A CEO of two factories.
    D) An executive in charge of two factories.

23. A) Australia and Singapore.   C) India and Australia.
    B) America and Singapore.   D) India and Germany.

24. A) They are completely independent.
    B) They are closely related to each other.
    C) They are under the charge of the same CEO.
    D) They are fairly independent，but sometimes there are cooperations.

25. A) They are far from involving in factory management.
    B) They are at the top. But some of them act as directors.
    C) They do a lot to involve in actual management.
    D) Philip never meets them and doesn't say anything about them.

Section B

Directions: *In this section, you will hear 3 short passages. At the end of each passage, you will hear some questions. Both the passage and the questions will be spoken only* *once. After you hear a question, you must choose the best answer from the four choices marked A), B), C) and D). Then mark the corresponding letter on Answer Sheet 2 with a single line through the center.*

注意：此部分试题请在**答题卡**2上作答。

Passage One

Questions 26 to 28 are based on the passage you have just heard.

26. A) U.S. computer experts have successfully installed a patch for military Internet systems.
    B) Some websites of the Pentagon have been temporarily closed.
    C) A new computer virus has been found recently.
    D) Some Internet websites of the Pentagon have been shut down.

27. A) Some Internet websites of the Pentagon have been affected by it.
    B) Some Pentagon experts have got the source of it.
    C) Defense Department websites will soon reopen.
    D) It has not caused serious harm yet.

28. A) It defaces websites.
    B) It instructs infected computers to flood the White House website.
    C) It shuts down the military business accessible to the public.
    D) It has done no serious harm but is inconvenient.

Passage Two

Questions 29 to 31 are based on the passage you have just heard.

29. A) A meeting between U.S. and Mexican Presidents.
    B) The White House.
    C) The Mexican President.
    D) The appeal from Mexican immigrants.

30. A) No decision about it has been made.
    B) It has been passed by U.S. Congress.
    C) It has gained support from normal U.S. residents.
    D) No option about it has been brought out.

31. A) The attitude of Mexican President.
    B) The objection from U.S. Congress.

C) The short time left before the meeting between U. S. and Mexican Presidents.

D) A violation of federal law.

Passage Three

Questions 32 to 35 are based on the passage you have just heard.

32. A) Decide on the place for next year's meeting.

B) Curb emissions of greenhouse gases.

C) Bridge the gap on the Kyoto treaty.

D) Support a new round of world trade talks.

33. A) Italy.   C) USA.

B) Canada.   D) Japan.

34. A) Japan disagrees with the treaty on global warming.

B) A celebration has been held by the local government.

C) Bloodshed has occurred in the streets.

D) The local port has been blocked.

35. A) The access there can be easily controlled.

B) It is small and in Canada.

C) Canada is one of the eight countries.

D) The air pollution problem there is very slight.

Section C

Directions: *In this section, you will hear a passage three times. When the passage is read for the first time, you should listen carefully for its general idea. When the passage is read for the second time, you are required to fill in the blanks numbered from 36 to 43 with the exact words you have just heard. For blanks numbered from 44 to 46 you are required to fill in the missing information. For these blanks, you can either use the exact words you have just heard or write down the main points in your own words. Finally, when the passage is read for the third time, you should check what you have written.*

注意：此部分试题在**答题卡**2上；请在**答题卡**2上作答。

Part IV　Reading Comprehension (Reading in Depth)

(25 minutes)

Section A

Directions: *In this section, there is a short passage with 5 questions or incomplete statements. Read the passage carefully. Then answer the questions or complete the statements in the fewest possible words on **Answer Sheet 2**.*

Questions 47 to 51 are based on the following passage.

Volunteers are people who do things to help others without being paid. Some groups are called Private Voluntary Organizations or PVOs. One such PVO is Volunteers in Technical Assistance or VITA.

VITA is an incorporated, non-profit organization of vendors and users having a common market interest in real-time, modular embedded computing systems. Accredited as an American National Standards Institute (ANSI) developer and a submitter of Industry Trade Agreements to the IEC, the VITA Standards Organization provides its members with the ability to develop and to promote open technology standards.

VITA was established in 1959. It was started by a group of engineers and scientists. They believed information and technology are important for improving the lives of people in developing countries. VITA uses people with important skills and experience, such as engineers, businessmen and farmers. These people volunteer to solve technical problems in developing countries, especially those in Latin America, Africa and Asia. By using volunteers, VITA is able to do more work than it could if it had to pay everyone. VITA's volunteers are happy to do this work during their extra time. They usually work at home on weekends or evenings to answer questions from people who have technical problems. In the past, people asked questions in letters mailed to VITA. Now many people use computers to send questions by electronic mail over the Internet. VITA has produced publications from the answers to the most popular questions.

注意：此部分试题请在**答题卡2**上作答。

47. Who first started the VITA program?

48. What kind of people are used in VITA?

49. What will volunteers do in VITA?

50. When do volunteers usually work in VITA?

51. According to this passage, how to get help from VITA?

Section B

Directions: *There are 2 passages in this section. Each passage is followed by some questions or unfinished statements. For each of them there are four choices marked A), B), C) and D). You should decide on the best choice and mark the corresponding letter on Answer Sheet 2 with a single line through the center.*

Passage One

Questions 52 to 56 are based on the following passage.

If you believe the macroeconomists, Europe's new common currency will bring either economic chaos or the dawn of a new era of growth, restructuring, and prosperity. But for those who will be dealing with the euro on a daily basis, the new currency leads to a much more pragmatic dilemma: just how to put a price on everything from butter to Big Macs.

There's little doubt that consumer demand will lead to some pricing changes, especially after pricing in euros begins in Europe. In France they cost about 2.50, while in the Netherlands they cost 1.00. Priced in guilders and francs, the difference isn't so noticeable. But when pricing in euros begins next year, French ice cream lovers will soon figure out that they're paying 2 times what the Dutch are paying. The same is true for a vast number of products. "Currently we have different prices in different countries, which isn't so visible with different currencies," says Gunther Moissl of German mail order house Quelle Schickendanz. "The moment you price in euros, you can see it."

Of course, nobody is going to drive across borders just to buy cheaper ice cream. But they already do so for big-ticket items such as cars. Moreover, says Jan Harrs, Unilever treasurer, "The attitude of the consumer toward your product may change if he feels ice cream is twice as expensive at home as it is somewhere else." Thus, most people think the euro will force prices to converge. Volkswagen, which has been slapped with fines by the European Commission for trying to keep Germans from buying its cars at lower prices in Italy, says it has already narrowed price differentials to 10 percent. Wolfgang Hartung, head of the euro project at Daimler-Benz, warns that anyone who thinks they can maintain vastly different prices in the era of the euro is engaged in wishful thinking. "People are too well-informed," says Hartung. Quelle says it is thinking about raising prices in less expensive countries to prevent middlemen from buying, say, in Spain and then selling in Germany.

Companies that don't set their own prices have a more difficult problem. Unilever says one reason Magnum bars cost more in France is that French retailers make a larger profit on them. Only half of the 1.50 price difference is accounted for by higher taxes, distribution, and labor costs. If French and Dutch retail margins were equal, Magnum bars would cost only 1.75 in France.

Unilever is trying to persuade retailers to cut margins in order to keep customers. "If retailers don't drop margins, they will go out of business," claims Harrs.

Unilever figures it has a few years to sort out these issues because most people buy groceries with cash. McDonald's, which serves 4.6 million people a day in its 2,300 euro-zone restaurants, also says it won't address price differentials until people can pay with euros. That means Big Mac fans in Finland will keep paying 53 percent more for their burgers than fastfood lovers in Portugal. As one industry executive observes, "You can only take a hamburger across borders in your stomach."

52. What is the word "pragmatic" (Line 4, Para. 1) most likely to mean?
   A) Prompt.　　　　　　　　　　　　C) Primary.
   B) Practical.　　　　　　　　　　　D) Probable.

53. The adoption of the euro causes _____ a more difficult problem.
   A) Unilever　　　　　　　　　　　　C) Volkswagen
   B) Quelle　　　　　　　　　　　　　D) McDonald's

54. French retailers earn _____ more than Dutch retailers for each Magnum ice cream bar sold.
   A) 1.50　　　　　　　　　　　　　　C) 1
   B) 1.75　　　　　　　　　　　　　　D) 0.75

55. It can be inferred that _____.
   A) macroeconomists agree on what the euro will bring about
   B) Volkswagen was fined because it tried to keep Germans from buying cheaper Italian cars
   C) Europeans will not use the euro to buy groceries in a few years
   D) Middlemen can buy hamburgers in Spain and then sell in Germany

56. According to the passage, if people see that the prices of the same item differ a lot in different countries, they will _____.
   A) refuse to buy the item in their own country

B）take the trouble of going to the place where the price of the item is the lowest

C）have different attitudes toward the product

D）not care very much

Passage Two

Questions 57 to 61 are based on the following passage.

There is no better story than history. The cast of characters in the human race gives us plenty of sex, violence and knavery, with occasional acts of genius and nobility that propel the race forward in spite of itself. In fiction, who could come up with people as intrinsically good as Jesus, Moses, Muhammad and the Buddha? Who do we find today as noble as Socrates, Abraham Lincoln, Chief Joseph, Clara Barton or Frederick Douglass? Who has the complexities of nature that King David or Thomas Jefferson had? How can we contemplate through the imagination the horrors that befell the 14th and the 20th centuries? No doubt history has to include rational analysis to strengthen one's ability to make logical conclusions, create intellectual order out of the material and to develop a healthy skepticism. However, history is also the intuitive, the visceral, the imaginative. Otherwise it becomes just another subject geared toward inputs and outputs. No wonder we lose students.

I want a story. I want to know how Themistocles outsmarted the Persian navy at Salamis. I want to know about Henry V and his longbowmen at Agincourt. Tell me about the terror one felt in looking over the one-mile field before Pickett's Charge, or being thrown out of a landing craft on a Normandy beach. Don't make it easy on me — make me feel the guilt and shame of owning slaves in the plantation South or exploiting immigrant workers in late 19th century America. Inspire me with stories about courage and sacrifice so that when I hit my own Thermopylae somehow I can stand fast. And don't lie to me. The slave South was not "Gone with the wind" and the frontier was not "Dances with Wolves". Tell me the story with integrity like Solomon Northup's "Twelve Years a Slave", as with Michael Shaara's depiction of Gettysburg in "The Killer Angels" or with Joanna Stratton's "Pioneer Women", on the hardships faced by families on the Kansas frontier. Ken Burns, with his Civil War epic, and Steven Spielberg's version of "Schindler's List" both capture a riveting story with honesty and clarity.

We can all share in the glory and disasters that are our own. Refusing to share in either risks the loss of our own humanity, for the lens to our individual soul becomes unfocused. Kenneth Clark said that we need to learn from history because it is ourselves. But without a leap of the imagination and a willingness to be part of the collective human race, there is little that history can do for us.

57. The author believes that Clara Barton was extremely _____.
   A) gifted
   C) noble
   B) good
   D) complex in nature

58. The author doesn't think _____ truly represents history.
   A) "Twelve Years a Slave"
   C) "The Killer Angels"
   B) "Dances with Wolves"
   D) "Schindler's List"

59. What is the word "capture"(Line 6, Para. 2) most likely to mean?
   A) Make a prisoner of.
   C) Tell.
   B) Obtain.
   D) Represent successfully.

60. It can be inferred that _____.
   A) the author, as a teacher, believes multiple-choice quizzes are important
   B) history study should not include rational analysis
   C) the author wants to relax, so he reads history as story
   D) the author believes we should share in the glory and disaster in history

61. Which of the following is probably the best title for this passage?
   A) To Learn from History
   B) What Should History Be Like?
   C) I Want a Story
   D) Imagination through Honesty and Clarity

Part V   Error Correction   (15 minutes)

Directions: *This part consists of a short passage. In this passage, there are altogether 10 mistakes, one in each numbered line. You may have to change a word, add a word or delete a word. Mark out the mistakes and put the corrections in the blanks provided. If you change a word, cross it out and write the correct word in the corresponding blank. If you add a word, put an insertion mark (∧) in the right place and write the missing word in the blank. If you delete a word, cross it out and put a slash (/) in the blank.*

注意：此部分试题在**答题卡 2** 上；请在**答题卡 2** 上作答。

Part VI   Translation   (5 minutes)

Directions： *Complete the following sentences on **Answer Sheet 2** by translating into English the Chinese given in brackets.*

注意：此部分试题请在**答题卡**2上作答，只需写出译文部分。

72. _____
    （关于妇女取得平等权利的问题），many people stated their own opinion.

73. In fact，there are many approaches to solve the problem，_____
    _____（他却倔强地坚持错误的想法）.

74. The increasing price _____
    （使得许多靠微薄养老金生活的老年人感到了压力）.

75. _____
    （据我所知），they broke up for almost a year.

76. _____
    （如今很多年轻人沉溺于电脑游戏），which makes their parents worry a lot.

答题卡 1 (Answer Sheet 1)

学校：
姓名：
划线要求	

准			考			证			号					
[0]	[0]	[0]	[0]	[0]	[0]	[0]	[0]	[0]	[0]	[0]	[0]	[0]	[0]	[0]
[1]	[1]	[1]	[1]	[1]	[1]	[1]	[1]	[1]	[1]	[1]	[1]	[1]	[1]	[1]
[2]	[2]	[2]	[2]	[2]	[2]	[2]	[2]	[2]	[2]	[2]	[2]	[2]	[2]	[2]
[3]	[3]	[3]	[3]	[3]	[3]	[3]	[3]	[3]	[3]	[3]	[3]	[3]	[3]	[3]
[4]	[4]	[4]	[4]	[4]	[4]	[4]	[4]	[4]	[4]	[4]	[4]	[4]	[4]	[4]
[5]	[5]	[5]	[5]	[5]	[5]	[5]	[5]	[5]	[5]	[5]	[5]	[5]	[5]	[5]
[6]	[6]	[6]	[6]	[6]	[6]	[6]	[6]	[6]	[6]	[6]	[6]	[6]	[6]	[6]
[7]	[7]	[7]	[7]	[7]	[7]	[7]	[7]	[7]	[7]	[7]	[7]	[7]	[7]	[7]
[8]	[8]	[8]	[8]	[8]	[8]	[8]	[8]	[8]	[8]	[8]	[8]	[8]	[8]	[8]
[9]	[9]	[9]	[9]	[9]	[9]	[9]	[9]	[9]	[9]	[9]	[9]	[9]	[9]	[9]

Part I   **Writing**   **(30 minutes)**

Directions: *For this part, you are allowed 30 minutes to write a short essay entitled Is Credit Card Important to Our Life? You should write at least 150 words following the outline given below.*

1. 有人认为信用卡对我们的生活是必要的
2. 有人认为信用卡没有什么作用
3. 我的看法

Is Credit Card Important to Our Life?

....
....
....
....
....
....
....
....
....
....
....
....
....

答题卡 1 (Answer Sheet 1)

Part II Reading Comprehension (Skimming and Scanning) (15 minutes)

1. [Y] [N] [NG]   5. _____   8. _____

2. [Y] [N] [NG]

3. [Y] [N] [NG]   6. _____   9. _____

4. [Y] [N] [NG]

7. _____   10. _____

答题卡 2 (Answer Sheet 2)

学校:		准 考 证 号

学校:

姓名:

划线要求

准 考 证 号

[0] [0] [0] [0] [0] [0] [0] [0] [0] [0] [0] [0] [0] [0] [0]
[1] [1] [1] [1] [1] [1] [1] [1] [1] [1] [1] [1] [1] [1] [1]
[2] [2] [2] [2] [2] [2] [2] [2] [2] [2] [2] [2] [2] [2] [2]
[3] [3] [3] [3] [3] [3] [3] [3] [3] [3] [3] [3] [3] [3] [3]
[4] [4] [4] [4] [4] [4] [4] [4] [4] [4] [4] [4] [4] [4] [4]
[5] [5] [5] [5] [5] [5] [5] [5] [5] [5] [5] [5] [5] [5] [5]
[6] [6] [6] [6] [6] [6] [6] [6] [6] [6] [6] [6] [6] [6] [6]
[7] [7] [7] [7] [7] [7] [7] [7] [7] [7] [7] [7] [7] [7] [7]
[8] [8] [8] [8] [8] [8] [8] [8] [8] [8] [8] [8] [8] [8] [8]
[9] [9] [9] [9] [9] [9] [9] [9] [9] [9] [9] [9] [9] [9] [9]

Part III   Section A   Section B

11. [A] [B] [C] [D]   16. [A] [B] [C] [D]   21. [A] [B] [C] [D]   26. [A] [B] [C] [D]   31. [A] [B] [C] [D]
12. [A] [B] [C] [D]   17. [A] [B] [C] [D]   22. [A] [B] [C] [D]   27. [A] [B] [C] [D]   32. [A] [B] [C] [D]
13. [A] [B] [C] [D]   18. [A] [B] [C] [D]   23. [A] [B] [C] [D]   28. [A] [B] [C] [D]   33. [A] [B] [C] [D]
14. [A] [B] [C] [D]   19. [A] [B] [C] [D]   24. [A] [B] [C] [D]   29. [A] [B] [C] [D]   34. [A] [B] [C] [D]
15. [A] [B] [C] [D]   20. [A] [B] [C] [D]   25. [A] [B] [C] [D]   30. [A] [B] [C] [D]   35. [A] [B] [C] [D]

Part III   Section C

President Bush says Russia should not feel (36)_____ by NATO enlargement. Speaking in Poland, the fourth stop of a five nation European tour, Mr. Bush (37)_____ a second wave of NATO expansion eastward. Poland was one of three former Warsaw Pact nations, along with Hungary and the Czech Republic, that became NATO members two years ago. At a news conference with his Polish (38)_____, Aleksander Kwasniewski, Mr. Bush praised Poland's (39)_____ to a democracy and a market economy, saying it serves as a fine example for future members of NATO.

The President looked forward to next year's NATO (40)_____ in Prague when the (41)_____ is expected to welcome new members, but he avoided (42)_____ any specific candidates. Nine former communist bloc nations are seeking (43)_____ . "My government believes NATO should expand," he said. "(44)_____

_____. We do not believe any nation should have a veto over who is accepted."(45)_____,

especially to the Baltic states, (46)_____

_____.

答题卡 2 (Answer Sheet 2)

Part IV   Section A   Part V   Error Correction   (15 minutes)

47. _____

48. _____

49. _____

50. _____

51. _____

Part IV   Section B

52. [A][B][C][D]
53. [A][B][C][D]
54. [A][B][C][D]
55. [A][B][C][D]
56. [A][B][C][D]
57. [A][B][C][D]
58. [A][B][C][D]
59. [A][B][C][D]
60. [A][B][C][D]
61. [A][B][C][D]

An international team of scientists are studying the event of pollution and dust in Asia. One hundred and thirty scientists from twelve countries have gathered in the western Pacific area to observe thick dust storms. They will observe the dust storms as they mix some of the world's heaviest pollution. The thickest dust storms in recent years were reported in Beijing, China and another Asian cities last spring. The dust storms came from deserts in China and Mongolia. This year, similar dust storms have begun move east toward large Asian cities and the northwest Pacific Ocean. The dust storms happen in winter over deserts high under sea level. In spring, the storms move east, over large cities in China, Japan and Korea. By summer, rainstorms break up the dust and help with reduce pollution in the air. The scientists plan to observe the dust storms through the middle of May. They are using research ships, airplanes, satellites or instruments on the ground to gather information. Aerosols are very small particles in the air. The scientists are studying aerosols contain sulfate and carbon that are produced by the burning of soft coal, woods and plants. Barry Hubert of the University of Hawaii is the lead investigator for the study. He says developing nations in Asia use a mixture of fuels that are not useful in other areas.

62. _____

63. _____

64. _____

65. _____

66. _____

67. _____

68. _____

69. _____

70. _____

71. _____

Part VI   Translation   (5 minutes)

72. _____

73. _____

74. _____

75. _____

76. _____

PRACTICE TEST 9

Part I   Writing   (30 minutes)

注意：此部分试题在**答题卡** 1 上。

Part II   Reading Comprehension (Skimming and Scanning)
                                                (15 minutes)

Directions: *In this part, you will have 15 minutes to go over the passage quickly and answer the questions on* **Answer Sheet 1**.

   For questions 1 – 4, mark

Y *(for YES)*   *if the statement agrees with the information given in the passage;*

N *(for NO)*   *if the statement contradicts the information given in the passage;*

NG *(for NOT GIVEN)*   *if the information is not given in the passage.*

   For questions 5 – 10, complete the sentences with the information given in the passage.

Learning from a Native Speaker，Without Leaving Home

   The best way to learn a foreign language may be to surround yourself with native speakers. But if you can't manage a trip abroad, the Internet and a broadband computer connection may do the job, too, bringing native speakers within electronic reach for hours of practice.

   Web-based services now on the market let people download a daily lesson in French or Hindi, pop on their headsets, and then use Internet telephone service and the power of social networks to try their conversational skills with tutors or language partners from around the world.

   For those who want to polish their high-school German before a vacation, or to master snippets of well-intoned Mandarin Chinese to charm a future business host in Shanghai，these sites offer alternatives to more traditional tools like textbooks and CD-

ROMs. LiveMocha (livemocha.com), for example, is a free site where members can tackle 160 hours of beginning or intermediate lessons in French, German, Mandarin Chinese, Spanish, Hindi or English. There is no charge for tutoring; instead, members tutor one another, drawing on their expertise in their own native language.

Members chat online by typing messages, by talking or, if they have a Webcam, by video, in exchanges with others who want to tutor or be tutored. English speakers learning Spanish, for example, can write or speak descriptions of a vacation and receive feedback on their grammar and choice of idioms from native Spanish speakers on the network. A Spanish speaker, in turn, may seek advice from the English speaker about English assignments.

LiveMocha introduced its Web site in late September 2007, said Shirish Nadkarni, chief executive of the company, which is based in Bellevue, Wash. Since then, he said, about 200,000 users from more than 200 countries have joined.

"It's a community of like-minded learners who can leverage their native language proficiency to help one another," he said. The name "LiveMocha" is meant to evoke the relaxed atmosphere of a coffee shop.

The site is still in beta, or testing, phase, Mr. Nadkarni said. Advertising will soon be added, as well as charges for some premium content and services.

Paul Aoki, director of the language learning center at the University of Washington, Seattle, signed up at LiveMocha primarily to see if his students might benefit. He says he thinks the site's social networking component makes it useful. "It seems to be a pretty powerful opportunity for people around the world to connect with language partners," he said.

He also likes the chat capability. "Doing voice and text chat simultaneously is very useful," he said. "If you don't understand something your language partner is saying," he said, even when people at the other end speak slowly, "they can type it out and you can read it."

Curtis J. Bonk, a professor of education at Indiana University in Bloomington, is specializing in ways to integrate online technologies into teaching. He says LiveMocha is part of an explosion of educational resources for language learning on the Web.

"You no longer have to learn language as an individual in a silo somewhere, using a canned program on a CD-ROM," he said. "Instead, you have thousands of tutors to pick from — if the first one doesn't work out, you can choose another."

Another electronic-based language learning program takes a different approach: podcasting. Praxis Language, based in Shanghai, offers free lessons in Mandarin Chinese (ChinesePod.com) or Spanish (SpanishPod.com) as podcasts.

Many lessons include business-based vocabulary on topics like how to hire a courier in China, said Ken Carroll, a co-founder of Praxis. While the podcasts are free, transcripts, exercises and other services typically cost $9 to $30 a month, he said. For $200 a month, members can receive daily tutoring from professional, native-speaking teachers by way of Skype, the Internet-based telephone service.

Mr. Carroll says ChinesePod has more than 270,000 visitors a month, several thousand of them paying about $240 a year for a combination of premium services. Most of the paying customers live in the United States, he said.

"They tend to be thirty-somethings, slightly mature, with some kind of business connection to China," he said.

Mike Kuiack, an investment banker in Vancouver, British Columbia, who often travels to China, was an off-and-on student of Chinese for eight and a half years before he signed on to ChinesePod. He has since been studying diligently for a year and a half, paying about $240 a year for premium services.

Since he started using the service, he said, his vocabulary has grown as much as it did in all of the previous years of study combined.

"Speaking and listening skills were what I needed," he said. "The podcasts have been very useful for this. Part of the reason I've made so much progress is that they are so enjoyable."

He works on lessons whenever he has a moment. "I listen when I'm stuck in traffic," he said, "and also at my PC, where I can listen and read at the same time."

The studying is starting to pay off at work.

"I don't try to conduct negotiations in Chinese," he said, "but now at least I can listen to what's going on in meetings."

注意：此部分试题请在**答题卡 1** 上作答。

1. Web-based services permit people to learn foreign languages with native speakers face to face.

2. For those who want to polish their high-school foreign language, these sites offer tools like textbooks and CD-ROMs.

3. LiveMocha is a foreign language training Web site which means to offer a relaxed atmosphere.

4. Curtis regards LiveMocha as an effective and indispensable explosion of educational resources for language learning on the Web.

5. If you can't manage a trip abroad to study a foreign language, you may turn to _____ for help.

6. By LiveMocha, members chat online by _____ or _____
_____.

7. Paul Aoki thinks LiveMocha is useful in that _____.

8. Another electronic-based language learning program, podcasting, offers _____.

9. Mike Kuiack comments that since he started using the service, his Chinese _____.

10. Once choosing an electronic-based learning program, a person can work on lessons when _____.

Part III Listening Comprehension (35 minutes)

Section A

Directions: *In this section, you will hear 8 short conversations and 2 long conversations. At the end of each conversation, one or more questions will be asked about what was said. Both the conversation and the questions will be spoken only once. After each question there will be a pause. During the pause, you must read the four choices marked A), B), C) and D), and decide which is the best answer. Then mark the corresponding letter on Answer Sheet 2 with a single line through the center.*

注意：此部分试题请在**答题卡** 2 上作答。

11. A) The traffic condition is terrible in their city.
    B) The man ran into the rush hour when going to the lecture.
    C) The woman suggests the man take the subway.
    D) Taking the subway is no better than other traffic means in rush hour.

12. A) The woman is glad to travel with the man.
    B) The woman thinks the journey is too long for her to go.
    C) The woman isn't interested in traveling.
    D) The woman isn't interested in Tibet.

13. A) Greek is too difficult for her to pass.
    B) She has to attend the make-up exam for Greek.
    C) French is totally not understandable for her.
    D) She managed to pass the exam at last.

14. A) At the accountant's office.　　　C) At the Customs House.
    B) At a post office.　　　D) At a bank.

15. A) She is not interested in the man's form.
    B) She has had a glance at the man's form.

C) She has submitted the form to the board meeting for discussion.

D) She is too busy to see that.

16. A) The man should do more physical exercise.

B) The man would concentrate better on study after physical exercise.

C) The man needs more sleep to concentrate better.

D) The man has already had too much sleep.

17. A) She doesn't want to postpone the picnic because her husband is wrong so much of the time.

B) She doesn't want to postpone the picnic because she doesn't believe in the weather forecast.

C) She agrees to postpone the picnic because it is going to rain soon.

D) She agrees to postpone the picnic because of the weather forecast.

18. A) The woman has once dropped the English class.

B) It took the woman a long time to get through English.

C) The woman doesn't think it necessary to continue the English class.

D) The woman is going to drop the class soon.

Questions 19 to 21 are based on the conversation you have just heard.

19. A) It is not sure at all, because it depends on the weather.

B) Late Wednesday or early Thursday.

C) Possibly late Thursday or early Friday.

D) Late Friday or early Saturday.

20. A) Yes, they will arrive on Thursday.

B) Yes, they will arrive early on Friday.

C) No, two of them will arrive early on Thursday.

D) No, two of them will arrive early on Friday.

21. A) 346 8900 extension 71.   C) 345 9800 extension 17

B) 345 9800 extension 71.   D) 345 8900 extension 17.

Questions 22 to 25 are based on the conversation you have just heard.

22. A) The quality of the goods isn't the one John's company ordered.

B) The quality of the goods is very poor, so John calls to complain.

C) The quantity of the goods doesn't match the number that John's company ordered.

D) The quantity of the goods exceeds the number John's company ordered.

23. A) John's company.   C) Weather.
    B) Mary's company.   D) Post office.

24. A) John's company threatens to sue Mary's shipping company for the
       carelessness.
    B) Mary's company gives the load a 20% discount and ships them a new required
       load right away.
    C) Mary's company offers 20% cash compensation to John for such an
       inconvenience.
    D) John's company requires a quick re-load.

25. A) Sincere.   C) Doubtful.
    B) Assertive.   D) Arbitrary.

Section B

Directions: *In this section, you will hear 3 short passages. At the end of each passage,
you will hear some questions. Both the passage and the questions will be spoken only
once. After you hear a question, you must choose the best answer from the four
choices marked A), B), C) and D). Then mark the corresponding letter on **Answer
Sheet 2** with a single line through the center.*

注意：此部分试题在**答题卡**2上；请在**答题卡**2上作答。

Passage One

Questions 26 to 28 are based on the passage you have just heard.

26. A) New methods adopted by companies on Wall Street.
    B) The weakness of the market on Wall Street.
    C) Economic depression throughout the whole world.
    D) The stock market on Wall Street.

27. A) 20.   C) 8.
    B) 80.   D) 18.

28. A) The Dow Jones Industrial Average.
    B) The second quarter earnings of U.S. companies.
    C) Nortel Networks of Canada.
    D) The U.S. car factories.

Passage Two

Questions 29 to 31 are based on the passage you have just heard.

29. A) Taking a trip to Florida.
    B) Learning more advanced music techniques.
    C) Running music camps.
    D) Opening their concerts.

30. A) Polio.   C) Harmonicon.
    B) Violin.   D) Brass.

31. A) Help gifted young musicians.
    B) Earn more money.
    C) Practice their music techniques.
    D) Help professional musicians communicate with each other.

Passage Three

Questions 32 to 35 are based on the passage you have just heard.

32. A) The 1960s.   C) The 1980s.
    B) The 1970s.   D) The 1990s.

33. A) "God Bless the USA".   C) "From a Distance".
    B) "Get Together".   D) "Ballad of the Green Berets".

34. A) Political subject matters.
    B) The introspective impulse.
    C) Condemnation of the ambition of Saddam Hussein.
    D) Opposition to the territorial ambitions.

35. A) During the Gulf War period.   C) After 9.11 terrorism.
    B) During Vietnam War.   D) Before World War Ⅱ.

Section C

Directions: *In this section, you will hear a passage three times. When the passage is read for the first time, you should listen carefully for its general idea. When the passage is read for the second time, you are required to fill in the blanks numbered from 36 to 43 with the exact words you have just heard. For blanks numbered from 44 to 46 you are required to fill in the missing information. For these blanks, you can either use the exact words you have just heard or write down the main points in your* own words. *Finally, when the passage is read for the third time, you should check what you have written.*

注意：此部分试题在**答题卡**2 上；请在**答题卡**2 上作答。

Part IV Reading Comprehension (Reading in Depth)
(25 minutes)

Section A

Directions: *In this section, there is a short passage with 5 questions or incomplete statements. Read the passage carefully. Then answer the questions or complete the statements in the fewest possible words on **Answer Sheet 2**.*

Questions 47 to 51 are based on the following passage.

American researchers have discovered new evidence that suggests a huge space rock crashed into Earth 250,000,000 years ago. Luann Becker of the University of Washington led the study.

The researchers believe the changes caused by the crash killed almost all the plants and animals on Earth. They say this mass extinction happened within one hundred thousand years. In their study, the researchers found carbon molecules trapped in rocks dating back to the Permian period. The molecules are called Fullerenes, or buckyballs. They contain gases that are found only in space. Ms. Becker says buckyballs form under extreme pressure, such as when a meteor hits Earth's surface. Based on her research, she says the force of the meteor hitting Earth spread buckyballs around the planet.

Scientists found these molecules in rocks from China and Japan. No huge hole has been found to mark where the meteor crashed. Some scientists think it happened in Western Australia. Ms. Becker disagrees. She says the event happened so long ago that any hole made by a meteor has been smoothed back into Earth's surface. Researchers say the buckyball molecules should ease any disbelief that a mass extinction happened more than two hundred and fifty million years ago.

注意：此部分试题请在**答题卡**2 上作答。

47. What result has such a crash led to?

48. Where is gas in buckyballs from as researchers have recovered?

49. Where are these molecules found?

50. In which point does Ms. Becker disagree with some other scientists?

51. What is the attitude of Ms. Becker about the place of the meteor collision?

Section B

Directions: *There are 2 passages in this section. Each passage is followed by some questions or unfinished statements. For each of them there are four choices marked A), B), C) and D). You should decide on the best choice and mark the corresponding letter on **Answer Sheet 2** with a single line through the center.*

Passage One

Questions 52 to 56 are based on the following passage.

Biological clocks are physiological systems that enable organisms to live in harmony with the rhythms of nature, such as the cycles of day and night and of the seasons. Such biological "timers" exist for almost every kind of periodicity throughout the plant and animal world, but most of what is known about them comes from the study of circadian, or daily, rhythms.

Circadian rhythms cue typical daily behavior patterns even in the absence of external cues such as sunrise, demonstrating that such patterns depend on internal timers for their periodicity. No clock is perfect, however. When organisms are deprived of the hints the world normally provides, they display a characteristic "free-running" period of not quite 24 hours. As a result, free-running animals drift slowly out of phase with the natural world. In experiments in which people are isolated for long periods of time, they continue to eat and sleep on a regular base, but increasingly out of phase. Such drift does not take place under normal circumstances, because external hints reset the clocks each day.

Light, particularly bright light, is believed to be the most powerful synchronizer of circadian rhythms. Recent studies on humans have shown that the amount of artificial indoor light to which people are exposed per day can resynchronize the body's cycle of sleep and wakefulness. People can inadvertently reset their body clocks to an undesired cycle by such activities as shielding morning light with shades and heavy curtains or by reading in bed at night by bright lamp light. Many organisms also make use of rhythmic variations in temperature or other sensory inputs to readjust their interval timers. When a clock's error becomes large, complete resetting sometimes requires days. This phenomenon is well known to long distance air travelers as jet lag.

Apparently, biological clocks can exist in every cell and even in different parts of a cell. Hence, an isolated piece of tissue removed from an organism — for example, the eye of a sea slug — will maintain its own daily rhythm but will quickly adopt that of the whole organism when restored to it. In the brains of most animals, a master clock appears to exist that communicates its timing signals chemically to the rest of the organism. For example, a brain removed from a moth pupa and exposed to an artificial sunrise of one time zone, then implanted into the abdomen of a headless pupa on a different time zone schedule, will cause the second pupa to emerge at the time of day appropriate to the disconnected brain floating in its abdomen.

The clock in the brain triggers the release of a hormone that switches on all the complex behavior involved in pupal emergence. In hamsters, experiments have shown a master biological clock to be located in the hypothalamus. Scientists believe that the biological clock in humans is located in the hypothalamus, the part of the brain that regulates such basic drives as hunger, thirst, and sexual desire. The biological clock itself is believed to be a cluster of nerve cells called the suprachiasmatic nucleus.

52. Biological clocks cannot be found in _____.
   A) stones   C) animals
   B) plants   D) human beings

53. To reset a person's biological clock, the most effective way is the use of _____.
   A) free-running   C) light
   B) rewinding the clock   D) changing the temperature

54. The word "maintain" (Line 3, Para. 4) means _____.
   A) keep   C) adopt
   B) abandon   D) protect

55. _____ is not said to be controlled by the hypothalamus.
   A) Biological clock   C) Thirst
   B) Hunger   D) Reading

56. The phrase "out of phase" (Line 6, Para. 2) means _____.
   A) out of order   C) out of action
   B) out of touch   D) out of operation

Passage Two

Questions 57 to 61 are based on the following passage.

Movies are a billion-dollar industry. Americans pay more than 41.4 billion yearly to see movies. The payroll for workers in the U.S. film industry totals about 6 billion. There are more than 23,000 screens showing movies throughout the United States.

The motion picture industry is divided into three branches — production, distribution, and exhibition. From about 1915 to the late 1940s, large movie studios controlled all three branches of the U.S. movie industry. The studios not only made the films, they distributed them to the theaters, the biggest and most important of which they owned. In 1948, the Supreme Court of the United States ruled that studio control over production, distribution, and exhibition was an illegal monopoly. The court ordered the motion picture studios to give up their role as exhibitors. By 1953, most of the Hollywood studios had sold their movie theaters. Also during the late 1940s, the studios began to curtail their role in the production of movies, partly because of economic competition from television.

The studios discovered that, in most cases, they could earn more money by financing and distributing movies made by independent producers.

The distributor charges the film's producer a fee of 30 to 50 per cent of all the money the film takes in. A new producer may have to pay a larger fee to attract a distributor than does an established producer with a record of profitable films. Distributors also charge for making the copies of the film sent to the theaters. In addition, they charge for advertising and publicizing the film. The costs of copying the film, advertising, and publicity come out of the first money the film takes in. The producer receives money only after these costs and the distribution fees have been deducted. The distributor can thus make a profit on a picture, while the film's producer may earn nothing. After the producers and the distributor arrange a distribution deal, the distributor carefully identifies the film's audience. The distributor generally arranges for sneak previews to judge the film's effectiveness and to identify its main audience.

At a sneak preview, the distributor assembles an audience that may be chosen for such characteristics as age, income level, or occupation. During the screening, the distributor's staff usually watches the audience, observing their reactions and level of enjoyment. Afterward, the audience may be asked to fill out information cards on their reaction to the film. They may also meet with the distributor's staff to discuss their reactions. After reviewing the preview responses, the distributor designs the advertising campaign and decides how to release the film most effectively. Sometimes the audience's responses prompt the distributor to ask the producer to reedit or re-shoot parts of the film.

57. The word "payroll" (Line 2, Para. 1) means _____ .

    A) payment   C) list of plays

B) list of payment   D) cast

58. Movie industry includes all the following branches except _____.
    A) production   C) exhibition
    B) distribution   D) self-regulation

59. In _____, the American Court began to enact a law against studio monopoly.
    A) 1950   C) 1948
    B) 1915   D) 1958

60. In which of the following books is this article likely to be found?
    A) *Movie Industry*.   C) *Creation of Movies*.
    B) *Movies and Televisions*.   D) *Film Producer and Director*.

61. Which of the following statements about the distributor is NOT true according to the text?
    A) To arrange a sneak preview of films.
    B) To observe the audience's reactions to films.
    C) To fill out information cards on reactions to films.
    D) To design the advertising campaign for films.

Part V   Error Correction   (15 minutes)

Directions: *This part consists of a short passage. In this passage, there are altogether 10 mistakes, one in each numbered line. You may have to change a word, add a word or delete a word. Mark out the mistakes and put the corrections in the blanks provided. If you change a word, cross it out and write the correct word in the corresponding blank. If you add a word, put an insertion mark (∧) in the right place and write the missing word in the blank. If you delete a word, cross it out and put a slash (/) in the blank.*

注意：此部分试题在**答题卡2**上；请在**答题卡2**上作答。

Part VI   Translation   (5 minutes)

Directions: *Complete the following sentences on **Answer Sheet 2** by translating into English the Chinese given in brackets.*

注意：此部分试题请在**答题卡 2** 上作答，只需写出译文部分。

72. I'd like to let you know _____
    （我们在任何时候都不会向敌人妥协）.

73. _____
    （尽管他一直声称自己考试没有作弊）, he was more and more upset recently.

74. _____
    （鉴于他一贯诚实的表现）, the company decides to trust this time.

75. The company is weak _____
    （在质量和品牌知名度上）.

76. _____
    （只要你坚持好的生活习惯, 改掉熬夜的坏毛病）, you will be healthier.

答题卡 1 (Answer Sheet 1)

学校:		准 考 证 号

姓名:

划线要求

[0] [0] [0] [0] [0] [0] [0] [0] [0] [0] [0] [0] [0] [0] [0]
[1] [1] [1] [1] [1] [1] [1] [1] [1] [1] [1] [1] [1] [1] [1]
[2] [2] [2] [2] [2] [2] [2] [2] [2] [2] [2] [2] [2] [2] [2]
[3] [3] [3] [3] [3] [3] [3] [3] [3] [3] [3] [3] [3] [3] [3]
[4] [4] [4] [4] [4] [4] [4] [4] [4] [4] [4] [4] [4] [4] [4]
[5] [5] [5] [5] [5] [5] [5] [5] [5] [5] [5] [5] [5] [5] [5]
[6] [6] [6] [6] [6] [6] [6] [6] [6] [6] [6] [6] [6] [6] [6]
[7] [7] [7] [7] [7] [7] [7] [7] [7] [7] [7] [7] [7] [7] [7]
[8] [8] [8] [8] [8] [8] [8] [8] [8] [8] [8] [8] [8] [8] [8]
[9] [9] [9] [9] [9] [9] [9] [9] [9] [9] [9] [9] [9] [9] [9]

Part I   **Writing**   **(30 minutes)**

Directions: *For this part, you are allowed 30 minutes to write a short essay entitled Should Grade Be Important for Students? You should write at least 150 words following the outline given below.*

1. 有些学生认为成绩很重要
2. 有些学生认为成绩并不重要
3. 我的看法

Should Grade Be Important for Students?

....
....
....
....
....
....
....
....
....
....
....
....

答题卡 1 (Answer Sheet 1)

Part II   Reading Comprehension (Skimming and Scanning) (15 minutes)

1. [Y] [N] [NG]   5. _____   8. _____

2. [Y] [N] [NG]

3. [Y] [N] [NG]   6. _____   9. _____

4. [Y] [N] [NG]

                      7. _____   10. _____

答题卡 2 (Answer Sheet 2)

Part III   Section A   Section B

11. [A] [B] [C] [D]   16. [A] [B] [C] [D]   21. [A] [B] [C] [D]   26. [A] [B] [C] [D]   31. [A] [B] [C] [D]

12. [A] [B] [C] [D]   17. [A] [B] [C] [D]   22. [A] [B] [C] [D]   27. [A] [B] [C] [D]   32. [A] [B] [C] [D]

13. [A] [B] [C] [D]   18. [A] [B] [C] [D]   23. [A] [B] [C] [D]   28. [A] [B] [C] [D]   33. [A] [B] [C] [D]

14. [A] [B] [C] [D]   19. [A] [B] [C] [D]   24. [A] [B] [C] [D]   29. [A] [B] [C] [D]   34. [A] [B] [C] [D]

15. [A] [B] [C] [D]   20. [A] [B] [C] [D]   25. [A] [B] [C] [D]   30. [A] [B] [C] [D]   35. [A] [B] [C] [D]

Part III   Section C

In Peru, where (36)_____ charges are mounting against allies of former President Alberto Fujimori, there is a videogame that pokes fun at the (37)_____ and turns computer players into defenders of (38)_____ . But this game is also causing (39)_____ . The hero is called "Nico Justo". He is nine years old and wears a bandanna. He has a toy gun to shoot sponge balls at politicians (40)_____ as dragons, witches or two-headed (41)_____ . The name of the game is "Vladigame", called after Peru's (42)_____ former spy chief Vladimiro Montesinos. He (43)_____ the country last year after a video showed him trying to buy support for former President Alberto Fujimori from an opposition politician. In "Vladigame", Nico the hero has (44)_____

_____

before attempting to put Mr. Montesinos and Mr. Fujimori in jail. One of the game's creators, Sebastian Zileri from the Peruvian political magazine *Caretas*, says Nico is a model for a cleaner Peru. "(45)_____

_____ because Nico represents in some way the normal kid here in Peru (46)_____

_____ ," he says.

答题卡 2 (Answer Sheet 2)

Part IV   Section A   Part V   Error Correction   (15 minutes)

47. _____
_____

48. _____
_____

49. _____
_____

50. _____
_____

51. _____
_____

Part IV   Section B

52. [A][B][C][D]
53. [A][B][C][D]
54. [A][B][C][D]
55. [A][B][C][D]
56. [A][B][C][D]
57. [A][B][C][D]
58. [A][B][C][D]
59. [A][B][C][D]
60. [A][B][C][D]
61. [A][B][C][D]

Scientists say this is a good time to observe the planet
Mars. Mars changes in bright more than any other planet.
In June and July, Mars will shine brighter than Sirius, the
normally brightest star in the sky. Mars is also interested to
watch from week to week because it moves among the stars
more quickly other planets. Mars is known as "the red
planet". On fact, it is bright orange. This month, Mars
will be especially bright mainly for two reasons. About
every two years, Mars reaches a point opposite the sun in
our sky. Usually a planet is told to be at "opposition"
where this happens. Mars reached opposition on June thirteenth.
Mars also has an unusual orbit. The distance from Earth to
the sun changes largely because Earth's orbit is almost a
perfect circle. But Mars orbit is shaped more like an egg
than a circle. But its distance from the sun changes much
more during the Martian year. This year, even a small
telescope will show that Mars is round like a very small full
moon. A larger telescope will show markings that caused by
different qualities of the Martian soil. Some areas reflect
more sunlight than others do. On the Earth, we see these
differences as spots or markings of different colors.

62. _____
63. _____
64. _____
65. _____
66. _____
67. _____
68. _____
69. _____
70. _____
71. _____

Part VI   Translation   (5 minutes)

72. _____

73. _____

74. _____

75. _____

76. _____

PRACTICE TEST 10

Part I Writing

(30 minutes)

注意：此部分试题在**答题卡** 1 上。

Part II Reading Comprehension (Skimming and Scanning)

(15 minutes)

Directions: *In this part, you will have 15 minutes to go over the passage quickly and answer the questions on Answer Sheet 1.*

For questions 1 – 4, mark

Y *(for YES)*   *if the statement agrees with the information given in the passage;*

N *(for NO)*   *if the statement contradicts the information given in the passage;*

NG *(for NOT GIVEN)*   *if the information is not given in the passage.*

For questions 5 – 10, complete the sentences with the information given in the passage.

One Friend Facebook Hasn't Made Yet: Privacy Rights

A co-worker apologized to me recently for being slow on a task. "It's probably just your insomnia from last night," I said. She was confused about how I knew, but I reminded her we were Facebook friends, and that she had posted a "status update" about her sleeplessness.

It's a common phenomenon: people "friending" work colleagues on Facebook and then discovering that — as Seinfeld's George Costanza would melodramatically put it — "worlds collide". I gained all sorts of insights into another young co-worker when her college friends left reminiscence-filled birthday wishes on her Facebook "wall".

Facebook was in the news this month for its disturbing policy of making it all but impossible for users to quit the site and erase their personal information. The issue was presented as one of privacy, which it is, but it is more precisely a matter of what the sociologist Erving Goffman called "identity management", which takes on whole new levels on the Internet.

Goffman argued that people spend much of their lives managing their identity through "presentation of self". Offline, people use clothing, facial expressions, and the revealing and withholding of personal information to convey to the world who they are, or who they want to be taken to be.

The physicality of the offline world provides built-in protections. When people talk to a group of friends, they can look around to see who is listening. When they buy a book or rent a video, if they pay in cash, no record is made connecting them to the transaction.

It's more complicated online. Social networking sites like Facebook and MySpace create identities for people, and disseminate information about them to large numbers of people. I am Facebook friends with Pierre Omidyar, the founder of eBay, who is an avid "twitterer". He uses the Twitter social network to send his friends frequent bulletins, which feed into their Facebook pages, about his whereabouts (Hanoi, the other day) and what he is reading (a lot about telecom immunity).

This sort of sharing is unobjectionable because Mr. Omidyar is deciding what information he wants to put out. More problematic is the amount of unintended sharing going on. There have been countless stories of young people losing job offers when prospective employers find their MySpace pages and read tales of alcohol and drug use.

Most troubling of all is the growing inclination of Web sites to spread personal information without users' consent. Facebook was rightly pilloried last fall when it introduced its Beacon service, which notified users' friends — without the users' consent — about online purchases. (Hey, Mary bought a pregnancy test!) Google Reader crossed a similar line when it began automatically sharing the news stories users read with their instant-messaging contacts.

It's no secret why Web sites like to spread information of this sort: they are looking for more ways to make more money. Users' privacy is giving way to Web sites' desire to market to their friends and family. Technology companies are also stockpiling personal information. Google has fought hard for its right to hold on to users' searches in a personally identifiable way.

What Web sites need to do — and what the government should require them to do — is give users as much control over their identities online as they have offline. Users should be asked if they want information to be viewable by others, and by whom: Their friends? Everyone in the world? Privacy settings, which allow for this kind of screening, should be prominent, clear and easily managed. (I'm not sure I was part of the intended audience for my colleague's college-years anecdotes.)

Before Web sites disseminate information the user did not ask to share, like an online purchase, the user should be notified and should have to affirmatively "opt in". It should be easy for users to disappear from a Web site that they have been part of, or simply to delete some information about themselves.

In a visit to the editorial board not long ago, a top Google lawyer made the often-heard claim that in the Internet age, people — especially young people — do not care about privacy the way they once did. It is a convenient argument for companies that make money compiling and selling personal data, but it's not true. Protests forced Facebook to modify Beacon and to ease its policies on deleting information. Push-back of this sort is becoming more common.

No one should have personal data stored or shared without their informed, active consent. If they still want to tell the world — including job interviewers and employers — about their wild weekends, they're on their own.

注意：此部分试题在**答题卡** 2 上；请在**答题卡** 1 上作答。

1. The author knew that one of his colleague was sleepless the night before by observing carefully the facial expression.
2. Social networking may disseminate information to a large number of people.
3. Sharing information online can be very subjective and can hardly be brought under strict control.
4. If Web sites disseminate information the user did not ask to share, the user can be notified.
5. One disturbing policy of Facebook is that _____.
6. When offline, people convey to the world who they are or who they want to be taken to be by _____.
7. What gives the offline world built-in protections is _____
   _____.
8. The biggest trouble of the growing inclination of Web sites is _____
   _____.
9. Web sites like to spread information of this sort because _____.
10. The Web sites need to _____ to protect users' privacy right.

Part III Listening Comprehension (35 minutes)

Section A

Directions: *In this section, you will hear 8 short conversations and 2 long conversations. At the end of each conversation, one or more questions will be asked about what was said. Both the conversation and the questions will be spoken only once. After each question there will be a pause. During the pause, you must read the four choices marked A), B), C) and D), and decide which is the best answer. Then mark the corresponding letter on* **Answer Sheet 2** *with a single line through the center.*

注意：此部分试题请在**答题卡 2** 上作答。

11. A) Peter is active in the party.
    B) Peter is a Beetle member.
    C) Peter is listening to Beetle music.
    D) Peter impressed Beetle very much.

12. A) He found his watch at last in the haystack.
    B) He looked for a needle in the supermarket.
    C) It is very hard for him to find his watch.
    D) He found the watch as well as the needle.

13. A) Customer and salesperson.   C) Teacher and student.
    B) Boss and employee.   D) Guest and waitress.

14. A) He can't eat well.   C) He has to work late at night.
    B) He has to sit up late.   D) He can't sleep well.

15. A) At a bank.   C) At a hotel.
    B) At the Customs House.   D) At the office.

16. A) She wants to fill in the forms.   C) She wants to get some medicine.
    B) She wants to change money.   D) She wants to ask for directions.

17. A) In May.   C) In December.
    B) In August.   D) In September.

18. A) It will last for three weeks.   C) It will probably continue.
    B) It has come to a halt.   D) It will end before long.

Questions 19 to 21 are based on the conversation you have just heard.

19. A) Four days.   C) A week.
    B) Five nights.   D) Six nights.

20. A) 2,900 francs.   C) 2,200 francs.
    B) 2,600 francs.   D) 1,800 francs.

21. A) Two single rooms and three double rooms on the fifth floor.
    B) Two single rooms and three double rooms on the ground floor.
    C) A single room and two double rooms on the fifth floor.
    D) A single room and two double rooms on the ground floor.

Questions 22 to 25 are based on the conversation you have just heard.

22. A) Boss and receptionist.
    B) Interviewer and interviewee.
    C) Marketing people and client.
    D) Boss and marketing people.

23. A) No, she just graduated from university.
    B) No, but she has been an intern for half a year.
    C) Yes, she has been working as a public relations person in a European country.
    D) Yes, she has worked for Europa Marketing.

24. A) She is good at dealing with public relations.
    B) She is good at dealing with marketing issues.
    C) She is good at speaking French and Italian.
    D) She is good at engineering job.

25. A) She wants something challenging.
    B) She failed to get on well with her colleagues.
    C) Her last company makes her upset.
    D) She can get higher pay in this company.

Section B

Directions: *In this section, you will hear 3 short passages. At the end of each passage, you will hear some questions. Both the passage and the questions will be spoken only once. After you hear a question, you must choose the best answer from the four choices marked A), B), C) and D). Then mark the corresponding letter on **Answer Sheet 2** with a single line through the center.*

注意：此部分试题请在**答题卡**2 上作答。

Passage One

Questions 26 to 29 are based on the passage you have just heard.

26. A) 15.4%.
    B) 14.4%.
    C) 15.5%.
    D) 14.5%.

27. A) Political and religious causes.
    B) Racial and ethnic causes.
    C) Poverty and population causes.
    D) Psychological and economic causes.

28. A) Between capitalist people and socialist people.
    B) Between rich nations and poor nations.
    C) Between the richest people and the poorest people.
    D) Between urban people and rural people.

29. A) American economic problems.
    B) Discrepancy between the rich and the poor.
    C) Urban poverty and homelessness.
    D) Population problems in America.

Passage Two

Questions 30 to 32 are based on the passage you have just heard.

30. A) 5 years after the play's birth.
    B) 15 years after O'Neill's death.
    C) 2 years after O'Neill's death.
    D) 2 years after the play's birth.

31. A) In Sweden.
    B) In Switzerland.
    C) In the U.S.
    D) In England.

32. A) It has no plot, no story and no acts.
    B) It is O'Neill's last drama.
    C) It is an autobiography.
    D) It is a comedy.

Passage Three

Questions 33 to 35 are based on the passage you have just heard.

33. A) She had been seriously ill before entering the hospital.
    B) She died after being injected for wrong.
    C) She died shortly after gulping down the jigger of the medicine given by the nurse.
    D) She died because of the intentional mistake made by the nurse.

34. A) They were indifferent to the accidents.
    B) They felt shocked but claimed no responsibility for them.
    C) They apologized and meant to take actions.
    D) They wanted to make investigations first.

35. A) Those were accidents and the hospital didn't have to shoulder the responsibility.
    B) It was the employee of the pharmacy to blame, not the hospital.
    C) The hospital should take the responsibility since the accidents could have been avoided.
    D) They have no comment on those accidents.

Section C

Directions: *In this section, you will hear a passage three times. When the passage is read for the first time, you should listen carefully for its general idea. When the passage is read for the second time, you are required to fill in the blanks numbered from 36 to 43 with the exact words you have just heard. For blanks numbered from 44 to 46 you are required to fill in the missing information. For these blanks, you can either use the exact words you have just heard or write down the main points in your own words. Finally, when the passage is read for the third time, you should check what you have written.*

注意：此部分试题在**答题卡** 2 上；请在**答题卡** 2 上作答。

Part IV Reading Comprehension (Reading in Depth)

(25 minutes)

Section A

Directions: *In this section, there is a short passage with 5 questions or incomplete statements. Read the passage carefully. Then answer the questions or complete the statements in the fewest possible words on **Answer Sheet 2**.*

Questions 47 to 51 are based on the following passage.

In the years since World War Ⅱ, Americans have awakened, as never before, to the world's art heritage, and have discovered the startling truth that a sizable and important part of that heritage exists in their own backyard. U.S. art, as Americans in general are beginning to realize, is neither a series of blurred engravings out of half forgotten school histories nor a dim reflection of painting abroad. For the past two centuries it has stood on its own feet, comparing favorably with the art of every other nation except France. Drawing depth and drama from history it helps illustrate, it has reflected not European painting but American life — rough and smooth, tumultuous and diverse. And though it is a great river of many sources and many passing moods, its strongest single current throughout is a searching realism. The revered champion of that tradition in America today is Edward Hopper. Less recognized, but equally true, is the fact that, at 74, Edward Hopper, painter extraordinary, expresses the present moment of American life with all the vigor and attachment of youth. One remark of Emerson's applies very well to Hopper's painting: "In every work of genius we recognize our own rejected thoughts: they come back to us with a certain alienated majesty." Hopper is clearly a genius of this kind. He paints not only what Americans have seen from the corners of their eyes, but also what they have dimly thought and felt about.

Hopper has opened a whole new chapter in American realism, painting a new world never before pictured. Where Copley created a whole world of men, Cole a world of nature, and Homer a world of struggle between the two, Hopper paints the raw, uneasy world that Americans have built on this land.

注意：此部分试题请在**答题卡**2上作答。

47. What truth did Americans discover in art field?

48. What is the major characteristic of Americans' paintings?

49. What does the statement "it is a great river of many sources" (Line 9, Para. 1) imply?

50. What is Hopper famous for?

51. In which aspects can Hopper's painting be regarded as genius work?

Section B

Directions: *There are 2 passages in this section. Each passage is followed by some questions or unfinished statements. For each of them there are four choices marked A), B), C) and D). You should decide on the best choice and mark the corresponding letter on **Answer Sheet 2** with a single line through the center.*

Passage One

Questions 52 to 56 are based on the following passage.

American rules for assigning racial status can be arbitrary. In some states, anyone known to have any black ancestor, no matter how remote, is classified as a member of the black race. This is a rule of descent (it assigns social identity on the basis of ancestry), but of a sort that is rare outside the contemporary United States. It is called hypo-descent (hypo means "lower") because it automatically places the children of a union or mating between members of different groups in the minority groups that have been unequally treated in their access to wealth, power, and prestige.

The following case from Louisiana is an excellent illustration of the arbitrariness of the hypo-descent rule and of the role that governments (federal, or state in this case) play in legalizing, inventing, or eradicating "race" and ethnicity. Susie Guillory Phipps, a light-skinned woman with Asian features and straight black hair, discovered as an adult that she was "black". When Phipps ordered a copy of her birth certificate, she found her race listed as "colored". Since she had been "brought up white and married white twice", Phipps challenged a 1970 Louisiana law declaring anyone with at least 1/32 "Negro blood" to be legally black. Although the state's lawyer admitted that Phipps "looks like a white person", the state of Louisiana insisted that her racial classification was proper. Cases like Phipps' are rare because "racial" identity is usually ascribed at birth and doesn't change. The rule of hypo-descent affects blacks, Asians and Native Americans. The ascription rule isn't as definite, and the assumption of a biological basis isn't as strong.

52. According to the passage, American rules for assigning racial status _____.
   A) are made cautiously and put to strict effect
   B) obey the convention that race is determined by biology or simple ancestry
   C) are made imprudently without justifiable reasons
   D) show strong prejudice against black people

53. Hypo-descent is a rule which _____.
   A) determines people's race in reference to their nearest ancestor
   B) ascribes people's race to their minority ancestor
   C) ascribes people's race to different groups
   D) determines people's race by biological genes

54. As to the state of Louisiana, Phipps should be labeled "black", because _____.
   A) she was brought up by black parents
   B) she had got a remote black ancestor

C) her birth certificate showed she was black

D) she married a black

55. The author cites Phipps' example to show that _____.

    A) hypo-descent leads to inequality among different groups

    B) race can be changed by resorting to the law

    C) colored people can change their race by marrying the white

    D) governments have no sound reason when determining race

56. We can infer from the passage that _____.

    A) Phipps challenged the 1972 Louisiana law and won the case

    B) Phipps lost the case because she didn't look like a white

    C) Phipps won the case by persuading the lawyer of her white originality

    D) Phipps was still labeled "colored" after the case

Passage Two

Questions 57 to 61 are based on the following passage.

Anthropologists agree that cultural learning is uniquely elaborated among human beings, that culture is the major reason for human adaptability, and that all humans share the capacity for culture. Anthropologists also unanimously accept a doctrine originally proposed in the nineteenth century: "the psychic unity of man." Anthropology assumes bio-psychological equality among human groups. This means that although individuals differ in emotional and intellectual tendencies and capacities, all human populations have equivalent capacities for culture. Regardless of physical appearance and genetic composition, humans can learn any cultural tradition.

To understand this point, consider that contemporary Americans and Canadians are the genetically mixed descendants of people from all over the world. Our ancestors were biologically varied, lived in different countries and continents, and participated in hundreds of cultural traditions. However, the earliest colonists, later immigrants, and their descendants have all become active participants in American and Canadian life. All now share a common national culture. To recognize bio-psychological equality is not to deny differences between populations. In studying human diversity in time and space, anthropologists distinguish between the universal, the generalized, and the particular. Certain biological, psychological, social, and cultural features are universal, shared by all human populations in every culture. Others are merely generalities, common to several but not all human groups. Still other traits are particularities, unique to certain cultural traditions.

57. What is the meaning of "unanimously"(Line 3, Para. 1)?
    A) Culturally.   C) Without exception.
    B) Simultaneously.   D) Reluctantly.

58. What does "the psychic unity of man" mean?
    A) Psychologically speaking, people are the same.
    B) Individuals have unity in emotion, culture and intellect.
    C) People have equal capacity to accept culture.
    D) People have unity of genetic composition.

59. Which of the following best illustrates "capacity for culture" in the first paragraph?
    A) People's ability to adapt themselves to culture.
    B) People's ability to create new culture.
    C) People's ability to understand different cultures.
    D) People's ability to imitate another culture.

60. What can we get from the example of "American and Canadian life" in the second paragraph?
    A) Different people may live harmoniously together owing to the same cultural tradition.
    B) Different people are hard to mix together due to different biological and cultural backgrounds.
    C) Different people may live well together due to the cultural capacity.
    D) Different people who mix together cannot be a whole.

61. According to the passage, which group of cultural features does "Women Must Wear Veils" belong to?
    A) Universal features.   C) Particular features.
    B) American features.   D) General features.

Part V Error Correction   (15 minutes)

Directions: *This part consists of a short passage. In this passage, there are altogether 10 mistakes, one in each numbered line. You may have to change a word, add a word or delete a word. Mark out the mistakes and put the corrections in the blanks provided. If you change a word, cross it out and write the correct word in the corresponding blank. If you add a word, put an insertion mark (∧) in the right place and write the missing word in the blank. If you delete a word, cross it out and put a slash (/) in the* *blank.*

注意：此部分试题在**答题卡**2上；请在**答题卡**2上作答。

Part VI Translation   (5 minutes)

Directions: *Complete the following sentences on **Answer Sheet** 2 by translating into English the Chinese given in brackets.*

注意：此部分试题请在**答题卡**2上作答，只需写出译文部分。

72. I would rather go out for a walk _____
    （也不愿意呆在教室里两个小时不动）.

73. I am afraid _____
    （没有人能受得了这样突如其来的打击）.

74. The influence of advertisement _____
    （在很大程度上取决于消费者的性格和环境）.

75. Our university encourages students _____
    （独立思考，不要受到老师观点的束缚）.

76. He will be sentenced to death _____
    （一旦找到他犯罪的确凿证据）.

答题卡 1 (Answer Sheet 1)

	准 考 证 号														
学校:	[0]	[0]	[0]	[0]	[0]	[0]	[0]	[0]	[0]	[0]	[0]	[0]	[0]	[0]	[0]
	[1]	[1]	[1]	[1]	[1]	[1]	[1]	[1]	[1]	[1]	[1]	[1]	[1]	[1]	[1]
姓名:	[2]	[2]	[2]	[2]	[2]	[2]	[2]	[2]	[2]	[2]	[2]	[2]	[2]	[2]	[2]
	[3]	[3]	[3]	[3]	[3]	[3]	[3]	[3]	[3]	[3]	[3]	[3]	[3]	[3]	[3]
划	[4]	[4]	[4]	[4]	[4]	[4]	[4]	[4]	[4]	[4]	[4]	[4]	[4]	[4]	[4]
线	[5]	[5]	[5]	[5]	[5]	[5]	[5]	[5]	[5]	[5]	[5]	[5]	[5]	[5]	[5]
要	[6]	[6]	[6]	[6]	[6]	[6]	[6]	[6]	[6]	[6]	[6]	[6]	[6]	[6]	[6]
求	[7]	[7]	[7]	[7]	[7]	[7]	[7]	[7]	[7]	[7]	[7]	[7]	[7]	[7]	[7]
	[8]	[8]	[8]	[8]	[8]	[8]	[8]	[8]	[8]	[8]	[8]	[8]	[8]	[8]	[8]
	[9]	[9]	[9]	[9]	[9]	[9]	[9]	[9]	[9]	[9]	[9]	[9]	[9]	[9]	[9]

Part I **Writing** **(30 minutes)**

Directions: *For this part, you are allowed 30 minutes to write a short essay entitled **Is Victory Everything to the Sports Game?** You should write at least **150** words following the outline given below.*

1. 有人认为对于体育比赛来说, 胜利是一切
2. 有人认为体育比赛有很多重要的意义, 胜利并不是一切
3. 我的观点

Is Victory Everything to the Sports Game?

....
....
....
....
....
....
....
....
....
....
....
....
....

答题卡 1 (Answer Sheet 1)

_____
....
....
....
....
....
....
....
....
....
....
....
....
....
....
....
....
....
....
....
....
....
....
....
....

Part II   Reading Comprehension (Skimming and Scanning) (15 minutes)

1. [Y] [N] [NG]   5. _____   8. _____
2. [Y] [N] [NG]
3. [Y] [N] [NG]   6. _____   9. _____
4. [Y] [N] [NG]
                         7. _____   10. _____

答题卡 2 (Answer Sheet 2)

Part III Section A　　　　　　　　　　Section B

11. [A] [B] [C] [D]　16. [A] [B] [C] [D]　21. [A] [B] [C] [D]　26. [A] [B] [C] [D]　31. [A] [B] [C] [D]
12. [A] [B] [C] [D]　17. [A] [B] [C] [D]　22. [A] [B] [C] [D]　27. [A] [B] [C] [D]　32. [A] [B] [C] [D]
13. [A] [B] [C] [D]　18. [A] [B] [C] [D]　23. [A] [B] [C] [D]　28. [A] [B] [C] [D]　33. [A] [B] [C] [D]
14. [A] [B] [C] [D]　19. [A] [B] [C] [D]　24. [A] [B] [C] [D]　29. [A] [B] [C] [D]　34. [A] [B] [C] [D]
15. [A] [B] [C] [D]　20. [A] [B] [C] [D]　25. [A] [B] [C] [D]　30. [A] [B] [C] [D]　35. [A] [B] [C] [D]

Part III Section C

The nuclear family is one kind of (36)_____ group that is widespread in human societies. Other kin groups include (37)_____ families (families consisting of three generations and/or of (38)_____ adult (39)_____ and their children) and descent groups — lineages and clans. Descent groups, which are composed of people claiming (40)_____ ancestry, are basic units in the social organization of (41)_____ food producers. There are important differences between nuclear families and descent groups. A descent group is (42)_____; a nuclear family lasts only (43)_____ the parents and children remain together. (44)_____

_____ (by a rule of patrilineal or matrilineal descent) and is lifelong. In contrast, most people belong to at least two nuclear families at different times in their lives. (45)_____

_____. When they reach adulthood, they may marry and establish a nuclear family that includes the spouse and eventually the children. (46)_____

_____.

答题卡 2 (Answer Sheet 2)

Part IV   Section A   Part V   Error Correction   (15 minutes)

47. _____

48. _____

49. _____

50. _____

51. _____

Part IV   Section B

52. [A][B][C][D]
53. [A][B][C][D]
54. [A][B][C][D]
55. [A][B][C][D]
56. [A][B][C][D]
57. [A][B][C][D]
58. [A][B][C][D]
59. [A][B][C][D]
60. [A][B][C][D]
61. [A][B][C][D]

Sometimes opponents of capital punishment horrify about tales of lingering death on the gallows, of faculty electric chairs, or of agony in the gas chamber. Partly in reaction to such protests, several states such as North Carolina and Texas switched to execution by lethal injection. The condemn person is put to death painlessly, without ropes, voltage, bullets, or gas. Did this answer the objections of death penalty opponents? Of course not. On June 22, 1984, the New York Times published an editorial that sarcastical attacked the new hygienic method of death by injection, and stated that "execution can never be made humane through science." So it is not the method·which really trouble opponents. It's the death itself which they consider barbaric. Admittedly, capital punishment is not a pleasant topic. However, one does not have to like the death penalty in order to support it anymore as one must like radical surgery, radiation or chemotherapy (化学疗法) in order to find it necessary these attempts at curing cancer. Ultimately we may learn how to cure cancer by a simple pill. Unfortunately, the day has not yet arrived. Today we are faced with the choice of let the cancer spread or trying to cure it with the methods available, methods that one day will almost certainly be considered barbaric. But to give up and do nothing would be far more kind and would certainly delay the discovery of an eventual cure.

62. _____

63. _____

64. _____

65. _____

66. _____

67. _____

68. _____
69. _____

70. _____

71. _____

Part VI   Translation   (5 minutes)

72. _____

73. _____

74. _____

75. _____

76. _____

PART TWO

KEY AND NOTES

Practice Test 1

Part I　Writing

Should China OK Euthanasia?

(Student's sample)

Euthanasia, or doctor-assisted suicide, is a matter of great controversy for a long time. A majority of doctors have seen the continous and unbearable sufferings of the patients. They think that it is humane to allow doctors to help patients, who are afflicted by incurable diseases, part with the living in a peaceful and respectful way as long as they make a voluntary, well-considered and lasting request to die.

However, many others hold strong views of opposite. They, including some lawyers and government officials, argue from a more practical perspective that euthanasia is infeasible in the present China, where there is no mature system of medical care. How can we make sure that the patients in the grip of fatal diseases can't make a medical wonder? Who can guarantee that doctors won't withdraw treatment from people who can't afford the medical fee or whom they don't like?

Furthermore, as the public health service is given to only a small proportion of the large population in China, euthanasia will make it easy for people to give up a burden of the family, especially in the underdeveloped regions.

As for me, I completely support the latter view that euthanasia shouldn't be initiated in China presently. As we've entered the new millennium, we should make more efforts to alleviate the pain of patients, to develop better cures for the traditionally incurable diseases and to prolong people's life rather than to encourage the helpless to give up the hope of life.

(Improved sample)

Euthanasia, or doctor-assisted suicide, **has long been of great controversy**. A majority of doctors, **having witnessed the continuous and unbearable sufferings of the terminally**

ill，hold that it is humane to allow doctors to **help patients afflicted by incurable diseases part with** the living in a peaceful and respectful way as long as they make a voluntary，well-considered and lasting request to die.

However，the opposition is also strong. Others，including some lawyers and government officials，argue from a more practical perspective that euthanasia is infeasible in the present China **in the absence of a sophisticated system** of medical care. How can we make sure that the patients in the grip of fatal diseases can't **work** a medical wonder? Who can guarantee that doctors won't withdraw treatment from people who can't afford the medical fee or whom they don't like?

Furthermore，as the public health service **covers** only a small proportion of the large population in China，euthanasia will make it easy for people to give up a burden **to** the family，especially in the underdeveloped regions.

As for me，I completely support the latter view that euthanasia shouldn't be initiated in China presently. As we've entered the new millennium，**more efforts should be directed towards** alleviating the pain of patients，**developing** better cures for the traditionally incurable diseases and **prolonging** people's life rather than **encouraging** the helpless to give up the hope of life.

Part II   Reading Comprehension (Skimming and Scanning)

1. N   为了让他们双方知道更多的细节，安修改了他们的信。
          细节题。文章里提到母亲和儿子通过安来通信，安会把信编辑一下，把泄露情况的细节涂黑删掉。从他们通信中的许多省略号也能看出，一些地名和人名被删掉了而不是添加。

2. N   21 年来母亲的工作是演员，在舞台上演出同样的戏。
          语义理解题。当母亲第一次见到儿子时她说 21 年来的每一天她脑海里都闪动着这一幕。此处的 play this scene 不是指在舞台上表演。

3. Y   当母亲第一次见到她失去的儿子，她既高兴又伤心。
          细节题。当母亲第一次见到儿子时她既高兴又悲伤，因为儿子已经长大成人了，她自己将近 40 岁，那些岁月都失去了。

4. Y   第一次见面后过了一年，母亲和她失去的儿子才适应了新生活和新家庭。
          细节题。文中提到，然后又是一个 10 月 18 日，我们的第一个周年纪念日。我们的日子找到了节奏。高涨的情绪正在平静。这说明他们至少用了一年时间才适应了新生活。

5.   the days when they were only allowed to write to each other through Ann 作者认为"我们那鬼魂似的日子"是指那些他们通过安的转达互相通信的日子。
          词义理解题。文章开头提到母亲和儿子通过安通信，后来"我们那鬼魂似的日子"慢慢地变得看得见摸得着了，五个月后安安排他们见面了。所以这段日子是指他们互相写信的日子。

6. blurted out every thought that came as they tried to reconstruct the lost years 当母亲第一次见到她失去的儿子时，他们出去散步并且絮絮叨叨地想到哪里说哪里，因为他们想要重温那些遗失的岁月。

    细节题。本题明显是要提问他们第一次见面后干了些什么，可以很快找到文章中部关于他们见面的叙述。他们见面后沿着河边的泥路散步，想到什么就说什么，他们的谈话是跳跃式的，因为他们要找回失去的岁月。

7. for her younger sons to pay the price for her history 母亲因内疚而难受，她的一些朋友也觉得要让她的小儿子们为她的过去付出代价不公平。

    细节题。第一次见面后 Ron 提出要见见他的两个弟弟。母亲觉得对两个小儿子很内疚，她知道她是在要求他们从容地接受她的过去。后来母亲和朋友们讨论这件事时，有人认为让她的小儿子们为她的过去付出代价不公平，应该再次离开 Ron。

8. tried hard to accept the information; struggled to integrate this information into his 21-year-old identity 当母亲对失去的儿子讲他父亲的事情时，他努力地去接受这一信息，拼命地要把这些事情和自己的身份联系起来。

    细节题。母亲和儿子第一次见面时谈起过他的生身父亲，当时他拼命地要把这些事情和自己的身份联系起来。

9. was astonished and felt guilty as if she had stolen their son 露丝和汉克高兴地欢迎她，然而她感到又震惊又内疚，好像她偷走了他们的儿子。

    细节题。露丝和汉克是儿子的养父母，应该定位在 Ron 带生母去他家时的情景。令人吃惊的是，露丝和汉克向母亲表示欢迎，好像他们因为她已经是 Ron 的生活的一部分而感到高兴。而母亲感觉好像自己偷了他们的儿子。

10. they knew they were a family and they loved and needed each other 经过了漫长的分离之后，他们有信心将来会一直在一起再也不分开，因为他们知道他们是一家人，他们彼此需要、彼此热爱。

    细节题。文章的最后提到，并没有一种模式来做这样的事情，我们不能设计未来，但是我们有指引未来的地图，那就是我们是一家人，我们彼此需要、相亲相爱。

Part III   Listening Comprehension

Section A

11. C	12. C	13. B	14. A	15. D
16. B	17. B	18. A	19. B	20. D
21. C	22. D	23. A	24. C	25. B

Section B

26. D	27. A	28. C	29. B	30. C
31. C	32. D	33. C	34. B	35. A

Section C

36. witnessed	37. decade	38. growth	39. emerge
40. collapse	41. equivalent	42. sank	43. commodities

44. Growth rates have also been reduced from an expected 5 percent to about 3 percent this year.

45. Leading banks in Latin America entered into partnership with major foreign banks and acquired a sense of confidence they didn't have before.

46. Finance ministers and central bankers from developing countries are warned to be cautious with economic policies and strengthen their financial systems.

Part IV　Reading Comprehension (Reading in Depth)

Section A

47. People aesthetically reject fox as food. 在审美上，人们拒绝把狐狸当作食物。
本题答案可以从文中第二段找到。第二段的第三句讲有时我们得承认我们强烈地拒绝吃某种肉并不是因为生理机能而是出于审美观。因此可知狐狸肉从来也不会出现在餐桌上也是由于审美原因。

48. Diets vary greatly in different cultural backgrounds./Diets are heavily influenced by cultures. 饮食因不同的文化背景而发生变化。/饮食受到文化的巨大影响。
本题答案可以从文中第三段找到。第三段中提到假设生物学是选择人类食物的基础，那么世界各地的饮食将相当类似。但是，事实上人类选择食物的活动既是身体本质的一部分，也同样是一个社会事务。由此可知人类选择食物并不能用生物学来解释。

49. Spatial layout and chronological layout. 空间和时间的安排。
本题答案可以从文中第四段找到。第四段的第一句告诉我们许多文化中一餐饭要包括特定的一贯固有的安排。然后在下文中作者举出两个例子，一种是印度饮食，它根据空间安排，另一种是英国或美国饮食，它们是根据时间顺序来安排。所以，吃饭的两种固有的安排就是根据时间和空间做出的。

50. They might miss their accustomed stop signals. 他们可能失去了原来所熟悉的停止信号。
本题答案可以从文中第四段找到。第四段的第四句告诉我们当英国人看到茶或者美国人看到咖啡，他们知道进餐结束了。但是当他们在其他的文化中吃饭时他们可能失去了原来所熟悉的停止的信号，结果不是感到吃不饱就是觉得吃得太多。

51. Nothing signals them the end of the meal. 没有信号让他们知道这餐饭结束了。
本题答案可以从文中第四段找到。第四段的后半部分告诉我们在美国中餐的口味可能已经改良过，适应了美国人的口味，然而中餐的形式没有改变。美国人习惯了在吃饭时有清楚划分的不同阶段，在不同的阶段吃肉或蔬菜等等，当他们吃中餐时就没有了高潮感，也没有信号告诉他们这餐饭结束了，所以他们吃完中餐一小时后就感到饿了。

Section B

Passage One

52. D 细节题。见第三段,可知小孩六岁时常发出一些尖锐的声音,因为盲人往往用回声来确定方向,这一点使孩子成为电子回声装置理想的实验者。

53. D 语义理解题。见第四段,可知装在特制帽子上的发射器发射出的超声波形成一个 6 英尺长的 80 度的圆锥区域,只有由这个范围的物体产生的回声才能被接收器转化为声音信号,因此 Dennis 听不见后面的声音,也听不见 80 度圆锥体以外的 6 英尺以内的物体的声音。

54. B 推断题。见最后一段,是测试这一装置的目的。其他几项都包含错误的信息。

55. C 细节题。见第五段第一句,可知小的物体声音轻。

56. B 细节题。见第五段第一句,可知近的物体音调低。

Passage Two

57. B 细节题。见第二段,可知 Allen 认为经济问题是学生今后在婚姻生活中面临的最大问题。

58. C 词义理解题。见第一段,由于这仅是模拟婚礼,不是真正的婚礼,所以主持婚礼的牧师也是模仿的,因此使学生发出阵阵笑声。

59. D 细节题。见最后一段第一句,可知这一课程受到学生的赞同,使他们认识到了婚姻生活中可能遇到的问题。

60. A 语义理解题。文中并没有提到一些学生在这一课程后放弃了结婚的打算,只是暴露了恋人之间存在的分歧和婚姻生活中可能遇到的问题。B,D 两项在文中均提到,C 项在第四段中有所暗示。

61. C 主旨题。此句为本文的主旨,也是这一课程的目的所在。其余三项均与文章内容不符。

Part V　Error Correction

62. high→higher　高等教育: higher education,不是 high education。

63. careers ∧ which→for　本句中 careers 的定语从句中缺少介词 for,原来的结构是 their education has prepared them for careers,因此 which 前加上 for。

64. this→it　本句中只有 it 才能充当形式主语,真正的主语是 that 引导的主语从句。

65. useless→useful　根据句意,即使不从事一般人所认为的工作,上过大学对她们也颇有益处,因此 useless 应该为 useful。

66. only ∧ minority→a　小部分: a minority of。

67. position→positions　担任其他高级职务,不止一个,所以 other senior positions。

68. such→so　本题考 such 和 so 的用法。such + a + adj. + n., so + adj. + a + n.,因此,必须用 so great a proportion;如用 such,应为 such a great proportion。

69. no→/　根据上下文,有迹象表明,一个人即使大学肄业也比根本未上大学有更好的就业前景,因此删除 no。

70. disturbing→disturbingly 学了一两年后退学的人数也多得惊人。副词 disturbingly 修饰形容词 large。

71. of ∧ who→those/people 本句中定语从句缺少先行词,所以加上 those 或 people。

Part VI Translation

72. I was defeated in the table tennis match **partly due to the tight clothing, which, to some extent, impeded my movement**.(我在乒乓球比赛中失败了,部分原因应该归咎于紧身的衣服,在某种程度上,它阻碍了我的行动。)

本题测试了 partly due to 的用法,此处用该词组非常贴切,简洁紧凑。另外插入语 to some extent 在定语从句中的用法和位置也值得注意。

73. In spite of the lack of the scientists' support, many local residents **assert that what they saw is an authentic UFO**, not their imagination.(尽管缺乏科学家的支持,许多当地居民声称他们所看见的是个真正的不明飞行物,而不是他们的想象。)

本题中应当注意单词 assert 和 authentic 的用法,这个句子中使用这两个单词比较合适,另外 what 从句的用法也值得注意。

74. The migratory habits of some fish **make it very difficult for scientists to pinpoint where they lay their eggs**.(一些鱼的迁徙习惯使科学家很难精确定位它们产卵的地方。)

本题中动词 pinpoint 的使用非常生动准确,另外,it 可作为形式宾语,结构 make it + 形容词 + for somebody to do something 也很重要。

75. **Based on the premise that everyone is created equal**, the constitution forbids the rich to challenge the right of the impoverished.(基于人人生来平等的前提,宪法禁止富人们对穷人们的权利表示异议。)

本题中应当注意整个句子的主语是 constitution,所以"基于……"应该翻译成 based on。另外名词 premise 作为先行词引出的是同位语从句,that 要保留。

76. Money was to be provided for the playground **as long as the town councillors approved the project unanimously**.(只要镇政务会委员一致同意,该方案会有钱造操场的。)

本题中应当注意 approve something unanimously 的用法。

Practice Test 2

Part I Writing

On Cloning

(Student's sample)

There is no doubt that cloning is a milestone breakthrough in reproductive technology for it makes a lot of exciting things possible. The greatest benefit of the cloning technology to human beings is that replacement organs, such as hearts and eyes, can be cloned from a cell for transplant patients so that they don't have to wait for organ donors or live on life-supporting machines and medicines. Besides, by using the cloning technology, many endangered species can be saved from extinction and agricultural production can be increased dramatically.

However, cloning, like many other modern technologies, is a double-edged sword. Scientists are mostly worried about the application of the technology to human beings. If human beings can be cloned, the universal truth that life is the supreme value will be threatened. In addition to the breaking of the ethical principle, cloning is a very inefficient procedure. The incidence of death among offspring produced by cloning is much higher than it is through natural production.

In my opinion, the cloning technology should be restricted to the medical treatment and any form of artificial reproduction of life must be absolutely banned worldwide. For although cloning can be suggested as a means of bringing back a relative killed tragically, life is no longer unique and sacred and its value will be devastated.

(Improved sample)

There is no doubt that cloning is a milestone breakthrough in reproductive technology for **it opens up many exciting possibilities**. The greatest benefit of the cloning technology to human beings is that replacement organs, such as hearts and eyes, can be cloned from a cell for transplant patients so that they don't have to wait for organ donors or live on life-supporting machines and medicines. Besides, by using the cloning technology, many endangered species can be saved from extinction and agricultural production can be increased dramatically.

However, cloning, like many other modern technologies, is a double-edged sword. **The biggest concern among scientists is** the application of the technology to human beings. **If so**, the universal truth that life is the supreme value will be threatened. **Apart from the violation of the intrinsic ethical principle**, cloning is a very inefficient procedure. **The incidence of death among offsprings produced by cloning occupies a much higher proportion than it does through natural production.**

In my opinion, the cloning technology should be restricted to the medical treatment and any form of artificial reproduction of life must be absolutely banned worldwide. **Anyway**, although cloning can be suggested as a means of bringing back a relative killed tragically, life is no longer unique and sacred and its value will be devastated.

Part II　Reading Comprehension (Skimming and Scanning)

1. N　卢克戴着一副又小又圆的无框眼镜,因为他认为其他眼镜都不够好。
   细节题。文章第一段的最后一句说因为他的视力不好,他才戴眼镜,那副眼镜又小又圆,没有框。

2. N　卢克的儿子,胡安·曼纽尔只听从他母亲的意见,对卢克的看法毫不理会。
   细节题。文章第四段提到了卢克的家庭,告诉我们要说他儿子只听从他母亲的意见的话,那并不完全是事实。

3. Y　由于老板给卢克大量的工作,他只好一直加班,但是得到的工资却少得可怜。
   细节题。文章的第五段提到了卢克的工作情况。他的薪水低得出奇,但他仍然每天在办公室里多呆3-4小时,因为老板给他的工作太多了,他根本不可能在正常的工作时间里完成。

4. N　卢克得了慢性咳嗽,而且他痛恨抽烟,所以他从不抽烟。
   细节题。文章第二部分的第四段告诉我们卢克的肺不好又痛恨抽烟,但是尽管如此,一旦在公车里他就抵挡不住诱惑,点上一支又便宜又大的雪茄。

5. 　stopped buying his newspaper and the *Reader's Digest*,(his two favourite publications)当他妻子决定送他们的儿子去一所昂贵的学院读书后,卢克就不再买报纸和《读者文摘》(他最喜欢的两种出版物)。
   细节题。文章第五段提到卢克的工资又一次减少了,他妻子决定让他们的儿子上一所昂贵的学院,这样卢克就不再买报纸和《读者文摘》(他最喜欢的两种出版物)。

6. 　turning the volume of his portable radio up full (to listen to boxing match and football match)周六晚上和周日,卢克把他的便携式收音机的音量开到最响(来收听拳击比赛和足球比赛),这样他把公共汽车上的其他乘客们折磨一番。
   细节题。文章第二部分的第五段说卢克对体育并不感兴趣,但是周六晚上和周日,卢克把他的便携式收音机的音量开到最响,来收听拳击比赛和足球比赛,这样他把公共汽车上的其他乘客们折磨一番。

7. 　putting his hands in his pockets and his elbows embedding in his neighbours'

ribs 如果已经有四名乘客坐在后排座位上,卢克会坐下,把双手插在口袋里,他的双肘直刺相邻的人的肋骨,这样他就占有了更多的空间。

细节题。文章第二部分的第六段说公车的最后一排可以坐五个人,尽管卢克人很瘦小,但是他坐着的话就只有四个人或者甚至只有三个人的位置了。他能够做到这点就是因为当他坐下,他就把双手插在口袋里,他的双肘直刺相邻的人的肋骨,这样他就占有了更多的空间。

8. watches him or her closely and throws a shadow of his head on the victim's book 当卢克发现有人在公车上看书,他就凑得很近去看他或她,并且把自己脑袋的影子投射在受害者的书上。

细节题。文章第二部分的第九段说如果有人在阅读,那他们很容易就成为卢克的猎物,他会凑得很近去看他们,并且把自己的脑袋靠近灯光,这样那影子就会投射在受害者的书上。

9. consume/eat a salami sandwich and a glass of red wine 如果公车非常拥挤,卢克就吃下一个蒜味三明治和一杯红酒,然后把嘴凑到其他人的鼻子边上,并大声叫喊"对不起,请让一让。"

细节题。文章第二部分的第十段说卢克知道什么时候公车会非常拥挤,在那种情况下卢克就吃下一个蒜味三明治和一杯红酒,带着嘴边的面包屑和牙齿缝里的大蒜,他把嘴凑到其他人的鼻子边上,从车头走到车尾,并大声叫喊"对不起,请让一让。"

10. he finds himself in one of the last rows 当卢克发现自己坐在车尾的几排位子上,他就大声叫喊来让出自己的位子。

细节题。文章的倒数第二段提到卢克让座的情景,他如果坐在前排就从不让座。但当他坐在后面的几排位置,他就大声叫喊来让出自己的位子。

Part III Listening Comprehension

Section A

11. B	12. C	13. D	14. B	15. B
16. B	17. A	18. D	19. D	20. C
21. A	22. B	23. C	24. D	25. A

Section B

| 26. B | 27. D | 28. C | 29. D | 30. A |
| 31. C | 32. A | 33. A | 34. C | 35. B |

Section C

36. moral   37. strength   38. thrifty   39. authority

40. sacrifices   41. narrow   42. distressing   43. scorned

44. who accused them of being too concerned with money and too anxious to impress the neighbors

45. They themselves had been brought up to respect traditional values and respect money because it was scarce during their teenage years

46. And self-fulfillment consists of reaching one's goals and achieving happiness in one's own way without paying attention to rules, duties or the opinion of others

Part IV   Reading Comprehension (Reading in Depth)
Section A

47. Because they hope to gain approval from their peers. 因为他们希望从同龄人那里得到认可。
    本题答案可以从文中第一段找到。第一段的最后一句告诉我们年轻人渴望追逐时尚并非借口,而是一种想要得到同龄人的认可的愿望。

48. running naked. 裸奔
    本题答案可以从文中第三段找到。第三段的第四和第五句告诉我们社会对于 streaking 的容忍源于 20 世纪 60 年代的性解放,而在 50 年代任何一个敢于在校园里裸奔的学生都可能被认为有伤风化而马上被制止。据此推断,streaking 是指裸奔。

49. Because students took to swallowing goldfish. 因为学生们开始吞金鱼。
    本题答案可以从文中第四段找到。第四段的最后两句告诉我们家长们失去了胃口,因为学生们开始吞金鱼。

50. social climate / social environment. 社会的大气候/社会环境
    本题答案可以从文中第四段找到。第四段的第一句告诉我们,如果有适当的社会大气候,甚至最荒唐的行径也可能成为青少年时尚的基础,所以可以推断出在很大程度上青少年的时尚受到社会环境的影响。

51. They are not good for them. 它们对于青少年没有好处。
    本题答案可以从文中第五段找到。第五段的最后一句告诉我们总体上讲,青少年们看起来正在做一些对他们没啥好处的事,这就是作者对于 90 年代青少年时尚的看法。

Section B

Passage One

52. B 细节题。见第一段第三句,可知处于不断变化的社会中的人们更会相互之间产生妒忌和偏见。

53. D 词义理解题。见第二段第三句,群体之间都把对方想象得最坏,因此相互之间会产生冲突。

54. A 细节题。见第二段第一句,可知当一个群体对未来没有把握时,尤其倾向于把自己与外界隔绝起来。

55. B 细节题。显然,群体采取中立的立场不会导致相互之间关系的恶化。

56. B 主旨题。综观全文,主要是阐述了社会偏见产生的原因。

Passage Two

57. C 推断题。见第一段第二句,可知在 1962 年的修正条例增加了对药物有效性的要求,在此前是不必在临床上证实其疗效的。

58. C 语义理解题。见第二段最后一句,可知 drug lag 也可指每年进入其他发达国家市场(introduced)的新药数量和每年进入美国市场的新药数量的差距,而不是发明新药的数量。其他三项在第二段都有相关表述。

59. D 词义理解题。见第三段第六句,可知每年批准的新药的数量大大下降了,但称得上是重要的新药数量保持在五六种。因此可推测 entity 指的是 drugs。

60. A 语义理解题。见最后一句,always present 和 that 同位语从句都是修饰 possibility 的。considering ... 说明这样一个 assessment 为什么是重要的。

61. A 推断题。从最后一句可看出,作者对药品有效性的要求持肯定态度。

Part V   Error Correction

62. that ∧ English→the   英语:English 或 the English language,可数名词的单数形式前加定冠词 the,表示种类。

63. anything→something   根据句意,对于语言的堕落能做一些事,所以 do something about it,而不是任何事 anything。

64. for→against   根据句意,struggle against,为反对滥用语言而努力,for 表示赞成。

65. lie→lies   本句为全部倒装,主语为 the sub-conscious belief,单数形式。

66. instrument ∧ which→with   本句中 instrument 的定语从句中缺少介词 with,原来的结构是 we shape our own purposes with an instrument,因此 which 前加上 with。

67. had→/   此处无需用完成式,不是猜测过去发生过的事情,而是对一般事实进行猜测。

68. on→of   根据句意,语言的堕落有社会根源,并不仅仅是某个作家(对语言)造成的坏影响。因此句子结构是 bad influence 来自作家,而不是施加在作家身上。

69. makes ∧ easier→it   本句缺少了形式宾语 it,真正的宾语是不定式。

70. not→/   根据上下文,这一过程是可以逆转的,所以删除 not。

71. less→more   根据上下文,去掉语言中的坏习惯可以使思维更清晰。

Part VI   Translation

72. **It was clear from the audience's boredom** that his lengthy explanations were superfluous.(从听众的厌烦状态中就能明白他那冗长的解释是多余的。)
本题的关键是 it 可以当形式主语,给出部分的 that 从句是真正的主语。另外值得注意的是名词 boredom 的用法。

73. The information we have received has **confirmed our suspicion that he is in collaboration with the enemy**.(我们收到的信息确认了我们对他勾结敌方的怀疑。)
本题测试词组 be in collaboration with 和 that 引导的同位语从句的用法。

74. If you **use too many big words where simpler ones would do**, you may sound

pretentious as if you're showing off.（如果你在适合用较简单的单词的地方使用了太多的大字眼，你就会听上去矫揉造作好像在炫耀。）

本题主要测试 where 状语从句的用法。

75. The criminal was told **he would be immune from punishment if he said what he knew of the murder**.（罪犯被告知如果他说出他知道的关于谋杀案的一切，他将被免除惩罚。）

本题测试词组 be immune from... 和 what 从句的用法。

76. My dog seems to have **some intuition that tells him whom to trust**.（我的狗好像有一种直觉，告诉它去相信谁。）

本题测试定语从句的用法。

Practice Test 3

Part I Writing

DINK Family

(Student's sample)

Nowadays a new family pattern appears and is getting more and more in big cities. That is, the DINK family — Double Income No Kids. Statistics show that an increasing number of young couples, especially well-educated and high-income white collars decide to choose a childless life. Why are they not interested in giving birth to a child?

Perhaps the main reason for the appearance of the DINK family is the intense competition in modern society. In order to make a good living, people devote the best and the most productive time to establishing the career and therefore have no more time and energy for raising a child. If they bear a child and raise him by themselves, they should take more responsibilities of taking care of him not only physically but mentally as well. What's more, young people increasingly adopt a more liberal attitude toward life. Their philosophy is to enjoy life and freedom rather than living under burdens and making endless sacrifices.

As far as I am concerned, I would like to have a child if I get married. A child is always the source of happiness to the family life. All the obligations and sacrifices for a child are part of a meaningful life. And with the birth of a child, the couple's love can be enhanced and their lives can be continued by means of having a child. I also regard bearing a child as everyone's duty to carry on the human society, but not just a personal thing.

(Improved sample)

Nowadays a new family pattern **has gradually emerged and spread** in big cities. That is, the DINK family — Double Income No Kids. Statistics show that an increasing number of young couples, especially well-educated and high-income white collars decide to choose a childless life. **Why is childbearing losing its appeal to them?**

Perhaps the main reason for the appearance of the DINK family is the intense competition in modern society. In order to **survive and succeed**, people devote the best and the most productive **years of life** to establishing the career and therefore have no more time and energy for raising a child. **Bringing a child into the world creates the responsibility of taking care of him not only physically but mentally as well. What's more，young people increasingly adopt a more liberal attitude toward life. Their philosophy is to enjoy life and freedom rather than living under obligations** and making endless sacrifices.

As far as I am concerned，I would like to have a child if I get married. A child is always the source of happiness to the family life. All the obligations **to** and sacrifices for a child are part of a meaningful life. And with the birth of a child, the couple's love can be enhanced and **their lives will be carried on through the child's blood. Besides, bearing a child is not merely a personal matter since everybody is committed to the duty of perpetuating the human species.**

Part II　Reading Comprehension (Skimming and Scanning)

1. Y　在某些研究中游戏里的言语和非言语因素都很重要。
细节题。第二段的最后一句告诉我们在这种研究中,游戏的非言语因素和言语因素一样重要。

2. N　Newell 和 Brewster 的专著建议把游戏划分为歌唱型的和非歌唱型的,这种区分比其他人提出的系统要糟糕。
语义理解题。第三段第二句中的"is no better than"是指和其他的一样,都不理想,不能和"is not better than"混淆起来。

3. N　如果两个人一起荡秋千,一个坐着,一个站着推,这也可以被认为是游戏。
细节题。文章的第四段着重强调了游戏和消遣之间的区别,其一就是游戏引入了竞争,而消遣则没有。该段中的最后一句告诉我们两个人一起荡秋千,一个坐着,一个站着推,这仍然是消遣。

4. N　如果我们向自己保证完成一项令人不快的或让人吃力的任务后就给自己回报,那么这项任务就变成了游戏。
语义理解题。第五段的最后一句中有词组"making a game of it",意味着把某事看做是游戏,有苦中作乐的意思,而这项任务或工作本身并没有变成一场游戏。

5. 　Grouping games according to anthropologists' requirements by either physical skill, strategy, or chance 根据人类学家的要求把游戏按照身体技能、策略或机会来分组,这被证明对于研究游戏对文化和环境因素的关系是有意义的。
细节题。文章第三段说进一步研究的基础是给游戏分类,但这个问题还没有完全解决。该段中的第四和第五句告诉我们要研究游戏对文化和环境因素的关系的话,根据人类学家的要求把游戏按照身体技能、策略或机会来分组被证明是有意义的。

6. 　the primary kind of play activity involved 如果是出于民俗收集归档的目的,所涉及的游戏的基本种类就可以作为基础来进行更加可行的分类。

细节题。同样是讲游戏分类问题,所以还是定位在第三段。该段中的最后一句说出于民俗收集归档的目的,所涉及的游戏的基本种类就可以作为基础来进行更加可行的分类。

7. having healthy competitions in strength and skill between individuals or teams 有些游戏,比如"Leap Frog","Tag","King on the Hill"满足了个人或团队间就力量和技巧进行健康竞争的需求。

细节题。第六段的最后两句,这些游戏满足了这些需求,这些需求指的是提供了机会让个人或团队间就力量和技巧进行健康竞争。

8. a certain amount of mimicry of life situations 有些游戏,例如"Jampile","Fox Hunt","Arrow Chase",包含了对于真实生活情景的一定程度的模仿。

细节题。可以从这些游戏的名称入手定位到第七段,该段的第一句就告诉我们大部分游戏包含了对于真实生活情景的一定程度的模仿。

9. "Charades" and "Twenty Questions" 在电视游戏节目中我们可以发现两个民俗游戏,它们是"Charades" 和 "Twenty Questions"。

细节题。最后一段的第三句告诉我们"Charades" 和 "Twenty Questions"是两个最后能进入电视"game shows"的民俗游戏。

10. "yes or no" 当人们玩民俗游戏"Botticelli"时应该向领队提出回答"是或否"的问题。

细节题。文章的最后一句告诉我们,每次领队都不能说出其他游戏者想到的人名,他必须实事求是地直接回答"是"或"否"。

Part III   Listening Comprehension

Section A

11. A	12. C	13. D	14. B	15. B
16. B	17. A	18. D	19. D	20. B
21. C	22. D	23. D	24. B	25. A

Section B

26. C	27. B	28. D	29. A	30. B
31. C	32. A	33. C	34. D	35. D

Section C

36. maintained   37. intellectual   38. contemporary   39. sophisticated

40. enrich   41. beginner's   42. flexible   43. specialty

44. they are not getting too much useful knowledge and not enough practical, updated information in their chosen field.

45. the world has become increasingly complex and education should adapt itself to the realities of modern society.

46. not only did the students ask for changes in the list of required subjects, but they

also demanded the right to choose their courses according to their own tastes and future needs.

Part IV   Reading Comprehension (Reading in Depth)

Section A

47. Because they have fewer opportunities to hurt innocent people. 因为他们伤害无辜人们的机会更加少了。

    本题答案可以从文中第一段找到。第一段的第二句告诉我们在监狱里罪犯们伤害无辜人们的机会更加少了，所以将罪犯关入监狱是合理的惩罚手段。

48. Because it doesn't do anyone any good. 因为这对于任何人都没有任何好处。

    本题答案可以从文中第二和第三段找到。第二和第三段告诉我们将一名罪犯投入监狱对于社会、对于受害者、对于受害者家庭有什么好处呢？让罪犯弥补他的过错才会有帮助。另外罪犯被投入监狱后不可避免地和其他狱友有联系，他们进一步"学习"犯罪，走向犯罪的深渊，结果被判更多的刑期。由此可见，法官们质疑把罪犯投入监狱这一做法的原因是它对于任何人都没有好处。

49. having them help their victims or work for their communities 让他们帮助受害者或者为社区服务

    本题答案可以从文中第四段找到。第四段的第二句告诉我们他们通过帮助受害者，为社区无偿劳动，或者用工资赔偿受害者这些方式来赎罪。所以法官惩罚犯罪较轻的罪犯的手段是让他们帮助受害者或者为社区服务。

50. They are not exposed to dangerous company. 他们不会受到危险团伙的影响。

    本题答案可以从文中第四段找到。第四段的第一句告诉我们这些新的惩罚形式对于犯罪较轻的罪犯是安全的，因为他们不会受到危险团伙的影响，所以这对于他们有好处。

51. He has to be thrown in jail. 他必须被关进监狱。

    本题答案可以从文中第四段找到。第四段的最后一句告诉我们如果被宣判的罪犯更愿意接受监狱里的刑期，他们有权力拒绝这种新的惩罚方式，那么他必须被关进监狱。

Section B

Passage One

52. B 词义理解题。见第一段，可知科学界的沟通合作使信息普及化，取得巨大进展。因此 wiring 是 cooperation 之意。

53. C 归纳题。第二段中所举的例子都说明了学术研究创造了新技术。

54. A 细节题。作者在第二段中引用了许多学术研究运用于实践创造新技术的例子，这是其中之一。

55. C 推断题。见最后一句，说明由于国会与总统在首要问题的认识上存在分歧，科学界人士要共同努力确保政府的投入。

56. C 归纳题。综观全文，主要讲了把学术成果运用于科技实践中，推动社会进步。

Passage Two

57. D 归纳题。综观全文，对美国人对死亡的态度最确切的表述应为"厌恶"（disgust）。

58. D 细节题。见第一段第三句，可知在这些伟大作品中，人们可以发现美国人对死亡态度的根基。

59. C 词义理解题。见第二段：surrounding it with word avoidance，pass away 作为委婉语，体现了美国人在语言中回避死亡的态度。

60. B 语义理解题。见第二段倒数第二句，对 Margaret Mead 话的正确理解是：当新的生命降临时，或在婚礼上，人们尽情快乐，但却让死者没有任何仪式地匆匆退场，人们没有意识到死亡和出生一样是生命的一部分。

61. D 细节题。见最后一句，可知对美国人而言，死亡与这一生命的最后一个阶段和其他阶段的相似之处在于很标准（standardized）。

Part V Error Correction

62. for→against　defense 与 against 搭配，表示抵御。

63. infecting→infected　受感染的地区：infected area。

64. In→By　介词 by 跟动名词，表示通过什么方式。

65. in→to　把……投入使用：put sth. to use。

66. being→/　根据句意，表示原因，并不强调动作正在进行，因此无需用现在分词。

67. has→had　时态不一致，by 跟一个过去时间点表示到那时为止，动词用过去完成式。

68. arrived→reached 或 arrived ∧ ，→at　达成协议：reach an agreement 或 arrive at an agreement。

69. and→/ 或 which→them　句子结构错误。and 连接并列句，可把从属连词 which 改为代词 them，或删去 and，形成定语从句。

70. that→what　这是一句主语从句，连接词 what 在从句中充当主语：一旦得知是什么造成了疾病流行。而 that 不能充当任何成分。

71. it→them　句中第二个 it 指代上文中的 outbreaks，所以用表示复数的代词 them。

Part VI Translation

72. The government was corrupt because of **incidents of bribery and greed among its officials**.（由于一些受贿事件和官员们的贪婪，该政府腐败了。）
本题中应注意到已给出部分的结尾是 because of，其后应给出名词性结构，另外翻译部分中的介词也值得注意。

73. They have pledged that they will **keep it a strict secret under whatever circumstances**.（他们发过誓，在任何情况下严格保守这个秘密。）
本题测试两个词组：keep something a secret 和 under... circumstances；特别要注意两个词组中可以有修饰成分。

74. At least one newspaper contended that **the disaster could have been avoided if the number of guards had not been reduced**.（至少有一家报纸坚持认为如果保安的数量没有减少的话，这场灾难是可以避免的。）

本题测试的是 contend 后面的虚拟语气，这里的虚拟语气均为与过去的事实相反的情况。

75. The reason why the Hiltons are having problems with their son is that they were **too lenient with him when he was small，giving him everything he wanted**.（希尔顿夫妇与他们的儿子有矛盾的原因是在他小的时候对他太宽容，他要什么给什么。）

本题测试点有两个：其一，词组 be lenient with somebody；其二，"他要什么给什么"完全可以处理成现在分词作独立结构的情况，这样紧凑简练。

76. The government will **deport the five people who were suspected of being spies**.（政府将把那五个被怀疑是间谍的人驱逐出境。）

本题测试定语从句和词组 be suspected of 的用法。

Practice Test 4

Part I Writing

Should the Exam System Be Abolished?

(Student's sample)

In recent years, many people support that the exam system should be abolished. Many students, teachers and even some education experts complain that students are forced to pay all of their attention to what is to be tested and fill their brain up with it before the exam. But after the exam they forget everything, because they think nothing is more important than the exam score, the unique measurement of their academic performance. This encourages memorizing mechanically rather than thinking creatively. Secondly, exam scores usually give a false image of a person's ability. Some really talented people, if not good at taking exams, may lose their opportunity of success. And with the intensified competition in society, the exam system places greater pressure onto students. The number of students committing suicide for failure in exams is on the increase. Besides, the exam system also lowers the standard of teaching. Since teachers themselves are often judged by exam results, they degrade their teaching level to training their students in exam techniques instead of helping them learn subjects.

However, although the exam system contributes so little to learning as well as teaching, it is highly infeasible to abolish it in China for the time being. Presently in China there are very limited educational resources but very fierce competition for college education. What is more effective and authoritative than exams to give all the students a fair chance to compete and achieve success? So despite the harmful effects on both students and teachers, the exam system should be preserved.

(Improved sample)

In recent years, there have been strong appeals to abolish the exam system. Many students, teachers and even some education experts complain that **as the exam scores are the only measurement of one's academic performance, students are driven to concentrate on the contents to be tested only and cram them into memory before the exam.** This encourages memorizing mechanically rather than thinking creatively. **Moreover, exam scores often give a distorted idea of a person's ability and aptitude.** Some really talented people, if not good at taking exams, may lose their opportunity of success. And with the intensified competition in society, the exam system **induces greater pressure on students**. The number of students committing suicide for failure in exams is on the increase. Besides, the exam system also lowers the standard of teaching. Since teachers themselves are often judged by exam results, **they are reduced to** training their students in exam techniques instead of helping them **master** subjects.

However, although the exam system contributes so little to learning as well as teaching, it is highly infeasible to abolish it in China for the time being. **When the educational resources are still very limited and the competition for college education very fierce, what else** is more effective and authoritative than exams to give all the students a fair chance to compete **for** and achieve success? So despite the harmful effects on both students and teachers, the exam system should be preserved.

Part II Reading Comprehension (Skimming and Scanning)

1. Y 机械革命和工业革命是两个共同发展的过程,它们互相影响,但在根源上和实质上是不同的。
   细节题。第一段的第二句表明了机械革命和工业革命之间的关系,这两个过程一起进行还经常互相影响,但它们的根源和实质是不同的。

2. N 对于被称为机械革命的社会的和经济的发展在历史上已经有一个先例了。
   语义理解题。文章的第一句是个长句,对长句的理解很重要。这句指出历史上有一种趋势,往往把机械革命和工业革命混为一谈,机械革命是史无前例的,但是工业革命早就已经有历史先例了。

3. Y 工厂是劳动分工的结果,在有电力和机械之前就有工厂了。
   细节题。第一段的第五和第六句告诉我们,工厂在发明电力和机械之前就有了,工厂不是机械的产物而是劳动分工的产物。

4. Y 早在18世纪中叶以后,信奉能量的人们就非常愿意把目光转向机械力量和机器。
   细节题。第二段的最后一句表明那些人渴望发财,把想法从奴隶和劳动力团队上转移到机械力量和机器上了。

5. the idea of factory/the idea of herding poor people into establishments to work collectively for their living 早在17世纪末,工厂(把穷人赶入厂房,集中在一起为糊口而工作的这个想法)就已经在英国盛行。
   细节题。第一段的倒数第三句告诉我们在17世纪末之前的英国就盛行了一种做法,就是把穷人赶入厂房,集中在一起为糊口而工作。

6. the difference in the character of labour that the mechanical revolution was bringing about 18和19世纪的资本集中和以前的任何情况都不相同,其根本区别在于机械革命带来的劳动力特性的差别。
   细节题。第三段的中间告诉我们在罗马共和国的晚期出现了财富的聚集,小农场主、小商贩消失,但这与18和19世纪的资本集中不同,其根源在于机械革命带来的劳动力特性的差别。

7. human beings with intelligence and the ability to make right choices 在"旧世界"需要连头脑都多余的服从者,然而在19世纪需要的是能够做出正确选择的聪明人。

细节题。第三段的最后三句告诉我们,只有在需要做出选择和运用智慧的地方才用得到人,人被当作人而被需要,那些听话到连头脑都多余的做苦工的人就不被需要了。

8. men's labour...machinery 在机械革命前人的劳动力比机械便宜。

语义理解题。第四段的最后一句表明,如果说几十年以来机械不得不等着轮到它来挖矿,那原因仅仅是因为有一段时期人比机械便宜。

9. The second half of the 19th century 19世纪的下半叶是整个西方社会普及教育得到迅速发展的一个阶段。

细节题。第五段告诉我们,那些聪明人意识到人必须受教育,受过教育的普通人比只会干苦力的人更有用。该段的后半部分里可以找到这样的信息:在整个西方社会普及教育得到迅速发展的一个阶段是19世纪的下半叶。

10. read, discuss, communicate and go here and there to see things 受到工业革命影响的普通人也能够清楚地把工业革命看作是一个整体过程,因为他们能够阅读、讨论、相互交流、走到各地去观察。

细节题。文章的结尾出告诉我们工业革命持续进行到19世纪末,就连受到它影响的普通人也越来越清晰地看到它是一个完整的过程,因为他们识字,能够讨论交流,走到各地去观察,这些在以前都是非常罕见的。

Part III Listening Comprehension

Section A

11. B	12. C	13. D	14. C	15. C
16. A	17. D	18. C	19. B	20. C
21. D	22. B	23. A	24. D	25. C

Section B

26. B	27. C	28. D	29. B	30. B
31. B	32. D	33. C	34. C	35. B

Section C

36. demonstrates 37. progress   38. feeds   39. Nutrition

40. rural   41. eliminate   42. ignorance 43. compulsory

44. The state has put strict controls on industrial pollution in an effort to improve the overall urban environment.

45. China is taking measures to keep its labour force fully employed so that the urban

employment rate has remained between 2 and 3 percent.

46. There have been reforms in the social security system which aim to provide necessary facilities and services for homeless children, senior citizens, unemployed and disabled people.

Part IV Reading Comprehension (Reading in Depth)

Section A

47. Because they want to escape from isolation and loneliness. 因为他们想逃离孤独和寂寞。

本题答案可以从文中第二段找到。第二段的第一句告诉我们许多学生把结婚当作他们个人问题的解脱,所以年轻人很早就结婚的原因是他们想逃离孤独和寂寞。

48. They believe they have found the true center of life's meaning. 他们相信他们找到了生活的意义的真正中心。

本题答案可以从文中第二段找到。第二段的第五句告诉我们年轻人的家长们认为成功就是最好的结局,但年轻人认为家长们的这个观点是错的,这本身是正确的,但是他们却错误地认为他们已经找到了生活的意义的真正中心。

49. utopian / unrealistic 乌托邦式的/不现实的

本题答案可以从文中第二段找到。第二段的第六句告诉我们年轻人对于婚姻的期望实质上是乌托邦式的或不现实的,所以是不能实现的。

50. (Tragic) Disillusionment. (可悲的)幻想破灭。

本题答案可以从文中第二段找到。第二段的第七句告诉我们他们要求太高,结果必定是悲剧式的幻想破灭。

51. Emotional maturity of both partners. 双方在情感方面的成熟度。

本题答案可以从文中第三段找到。第三段的第三句告诉我们令人满意的婚姻不是由实际年龄决定的,而是由双方的情感成熟度决定的。所以幸福婚姻中的决定性因素是双方在情感方面的成熟度。

Section B

Passage One

52. B 细节题。见第二段最后一句,可见孩子不能区分的是暴力行为的动机。

53. B 细节题。见第二段,暴力行为的三种背景是:cartoon violence, make-believe violence, realistic (acted) violence,都是虚构的(fictional)。

54. B 词义理解题。见第三段第四句,可知 cold imitation 即是 direct association between television violence and aggressive behavior,不受任何刺激,对电视上暴力行为的直接模仿。

55. C 细节题。见第三段第三句,可知刺激会导致暴力行为。

56. B 归纳题。见第四段最后一句,可知我们的文化崇尚暴力,对孩子造成了影响,而非电视中的暴力。

Passage Two

57. C 细节题。见第一段最后一句,可知造成艾滋病发病率下降的原因是高危人群已经被感染,而不是人们对自身行为的调整。

58. B 语义理解题。见第二段最后一句,可知这些药物能延缓疾病在相对健康的病人身上的发展,而不能对健康人起预防作用。

59. B 词义理解题。根据上下文,主要是关于 antiretroviral therapy 的疗效。

60. D 细节题。见第四段,可知 antiretroviral therapy 的问题之一是复杂的服药方案,要考虑到饮食,而不是复杂的饮食方案。

61. C 推断题。见全文最后一句,可见停止治疗不到三周,HIV 的浓度就会反弹。

Part V   Error Correction

62. at→by 根据句意,在美国,孩子长到十几岁时,已经看约 18,000 个广告了。介词 by 跟一个时间点表示到那时为止,符合主句的完成式,而 at 表示在某一时刻。

63. influence→influences 动词 influence 的主语为 the number,单数形式。

64. way ∧ which→in 或 which→that 或/ 修饰 way(方法)的定语从句用关系词 that 或 in which 引导,也可省去关系词。

65. which→what 根据句意,孩子们无法理解广告的目的是为什么。原句结构为:they (advertisements) are for what。

66. had→have 本句应用现在完成式,说明我一直思考至今。

67. are→do 主句中用的是行为动词:they don't see things carefully,因此从句中须用助动词 do 构成省略。如果主句中是 be 动词,则从句中用 be 动词构成省略。

68. that→how 根据句意,我感到疑惑的是广告商如何能控制孩子的世界观,所以用 how 作连词。

69. with→/ 伴随某人(做某事):join sb. (in sth. /doing sth.)。

70. she→it 固定词组 when it comes to …:当谈到,涉及,it 无具体实指意义。

71. it→/ 固定词组 make sure:确信。

Part VI   Translation

72. As they entered the village, the old lady behind the counter **extended her welcome by beaming at them kindly**. (当他们进村时,站在柜台后的老妇人向他们亲切微笑以示欢迎。)
本题测试了 extend one's welcome 的词组搭配,以及 by doing something 的用法。

73. My fingernails are so brittle that **they break off before they get long enough to polish**. (我的指甲很脆弱,它们还没长到足够去抛光的长度就断裂了。)
本题的关键在于考生对于 before 从句的理解和应用,before 从句里出现的情况往往是被否定的,而它前面的主句表示结果,正好和给出部分中的 so … that …结构应和。

74. **The President's failure to denounce the neighboring country's policy** alienated his

supporters and jeopardized his position.（总统没有公开指责邻国的政策，这使他和支持者疏远了并危及他的职位。）

本题的关键是考生应当注意要求翻译的部分和已给出部分的结构关系。此句中缺少的是主语，因此考生应该灵活地把"没有公开指责"处理成名词性成分，使整个句子完整正确。

75. **Threatening a scandal，he blackmailed the firm into paying** him a large sum of money for keeping quiet.（以丑闻为威胁，他胁迫该公司支付给他一大笔钱来让他守口如瓶。）

本题有两点值得注意：其一，"以丑闻为威胁"应该译为"threatening a scandal"，这是分词作独立结构，应当注意其逻辑主语和句子语法主语是一致的；其二，"胁迫某人做某事"是用"blackmail somebody into doing something"的结构。

76. A dialogue **that caters to the students' curiosity** has an inherent interest for him.（他对于迎合学生们的好奇心的对话有着与生俱来的兴趣。）

本题测试定语从句以及词组"cater to"的用法。

Practice Test 5

Part I   Writing

Should High School Students Study Abroad?

(Student's sample)

Since the late 1990s, more and more high school students have gone abroad for education and recently the trend has got stronger and stronger. Many people believe that attending a foreign school has many distinct advantages. Students can acquire more advanced knowledge from excellent professors and with first-rate facilities. And years of life and study abroad can help them study a foreign language. More important, without parents' staying aside, the youngsters have to rely on themselves. This can develop their independence and interpersonal skills.

However, some education experts are strongly against sending high school students abroad. Firstly, the family will have to bear a heavy economic burden. Secondly and most importantly, the experts are afraid that once drowned in the western culture, the immature teenagers will follow western styles blindly and as a result lose their identity and even reject Chinese culture. Besides, many students feel extremely lonely and miserable in completely strange background and social customs. This might affect their studies.

In my opinion, the student himself should decide if he is going abroad to have further study. If the education in China can't meet the need of a top and capable student, it is quite helpful for him to experience the western culture so that he can absorb its essence to fully develop his potentials. On the contrary, if a student can't do well even in China, it will be the parents' empty dream that their child can make a miracle in a foreign country.

(Improved sample)

Since the late 1990s, more and more high school students have gone abroad for education **and the trend intensifies recently**. Many people believe that attending **a school abroad** has many distinct advantages. Students can acquire more advanced knowledge from excellent professors and with first-rate facilities. And years of life and study abroad can help them **master** a foreign language. More important, without parents'

taking care, the youngsters have to rely on themselves. This can develop their independence and interpersonal skills.

However, some education experts are strongly against sending high school students abroad. **Apart from the heavy economic burden on the family, their biggest concern is that** once **immersed in** the western culture, the immature teenagers will follow western styles blindly and **consequently** lose their identity and even reject Chinese culture. Besides, many students feel extremely lonely and miserable in completely strange background and social customs. This might affect their studies.

In my opinion, **whether to pursue education abroad depends on the student himself.** If **domestic** education can't meet the need of a top and capable student, it is quite helpful for him to experience the western culture so that he can absorb its essence to **broaden his outlook** and fully develop his potentials. On the contrary, if a student can't do well even in China, **parents' expectation of his miraculous academic achievement abroad will definitely fail.**

Part II Reading Comprehension (Skimming and Scanning)

1. **NG** 我不喜欢 Fear Factor 节目,它以让参与者面对最大的恐惧著称。
    细节题。可根据 Fear Factor 节目名称快速定位在第一段,但内容中没有提到作者对于该节目是否喜欢。

2. **Y** 因为我非常喜欢吃,所以我是食品购物狂。
    细节题。从第四段的最后一句可以知道作者认为他对于吃的热爱融化在热爱食品中。

3. **N** 我朋友 Nick 在白人文化中长大,几周前他和我站在黄色海洋里。
    细节题。文章第六段告诉我们作者带朋友 Nick 去亚洲超市,而第七段的第一句是说在黄皮肤的顾客人群中他的白皮肤非常惹眼。

4. **Y** 亚洲超市的最里面是卖生鲜食品的地方,美国人往往对那里的鲜血和产品感到震惊,好像他们进入了另外一个空间。
    细节题。第十段第一句提到了肉类、家禽和海鲜柜台在超市的里面,这些都是生鲜食品,同时这一段里作者告诉我们,当他带美国人到这种地方,他们总是非常震惊。

5. **an Asian supermarket** 我和父母经常去亚洲超市买食品。
    细节题。第二段第二句告诉我们作者和他父母习惯于看那些奇怪的东西,因为他们经常去亚洲超市买吃的。

6. **eaten for dinner** 那只青蟹弄伤了我,然后成了桌上的菜肴被吃了。
    细节题。第三段讲作者小时候有个爱好,喜欢逗弄青蟹,一次他右手的食指差点被夹掉,但是不久以后那只蟹被当作晚餐吃了。

7. **considered exotic** 我对亚洲超市的一切都很熟悉,但是对于外国人来说,这里被认为有异国情调。

归纳题。文章倒数第四段的第二句说亚洲超市的一切都让人熟悉,至少对于我如此。该段的倒数第三句讲对于外国人来说,那被认为有异国情调。

8.   The European supermarket 欧洲超市干净、花哨、档次高又昂贵。

    细节题。文章的倒数第三段第五句提到欧洲超市一尘不染,非常花哨,档次高而昂贵。

9.   the trademark of the goods 在欧洲超市顾客按照货物的品牌买东西。

    细节题。文章的倒数第三段告诉我们,踏入 a Jonathans or a Ralphs or a Trader Joes(欧洲超市的名称)就像踏入一个高级的中产阶级家庭,顾客买的是品牌而不是货物。

10.   we all enjoy the comfort of food and the comfort of family 尽管亚洲超市和欧洲超市有区别,但总有相似的地方,那就是我们都喜欢食物和家庭带来的舒适。

    细节题。文章的最后一句告诉我们,不管我们喜欢的是牛舌头还是哥伦比亚咖啡,我们都喜欢食物和家庭带来的舒适。

Part III   Listening Comprehension

Section A

11. D	12. A	13. D	14. B	15. A
16. B	17. B	18. D	19. A	20. D
21. C	22. D	23. C	24. B	25. A

Section B

26. D	27. A	28. A	29. C	30. C
31. D	32. A	33. C	34. B	35. D

Section C

36. inability	37. prosperity	38. impartial	39. Impressive
40. societies	41. superior	42. stability	43. combined

44. success for Asian societies is dependent on their adoption of Western values and institutions.

45. They appear to overlook the fact that their societies frequently demonstrate features which are far from desirable.

46. The time has surely come for Western leaders to consider what might be learned from Asian examples and to reflect on the fact that Asian models have never claimed the sort of universal authority which Western models claim for themselves.

Part IV   Reading Comprehension (Reading in Depth)

Section A

47. It falls into the category of social science. 它属于社会科学类。

本题答案可以从文中第一段找到。第一段的第一句告诉我们很少有社会科学类的现代作品能比 David Riesman 的《孤独的云》更能引起广泛的兴趣，所以这本书属于社会科学类。

48. ambitious and competitive 雄心勃勃又争强好胜

本题答案可以从文中第二段找到。第二段的最后一句告诉我们通常来说，从自我中心向顺从他人的转变意味着雄心勃勃又争强好胜的个性在美国文化中变得越来越不典型，所以可以推断出由内心驱动的人是雄心勃勃又争强好胜。

49. Other direction. 顺从他人。

本题答案可以从文中第二段找到。第二段的第二和第三句告诉我们这种变化可以被描述为从"自我中心"向"顺从他人"的转变，通常来说，这种转变意味着雄心勃勃又争强好胜的个性在美国文化中变得越来越不典型，那么如今更能代表美国人的性格的是"顺从他人"。

50. An increase of cooperativeness and friendliness. 加强合作，更加友善。

本题答案可以从文中第三段找到。第三段的最后一句告诉我们他也同样意识到更多地顺从他人就意味着加强合作，更加友善，这是美国人性格变化的好处。

51. A lessening of individualism and energy. 个性和精力的减少。

本题答案可以从文中第三段找到。第三段的倒数第二句告诉我们他看到自我中心的减少意味着个性和精力的减少。这是美国人性格变化的不利之处。

Section B

Passage One

52. C 细节题。见第二段，可知文化相对主义使人们对非洲文化进行客观现实的审视。

53. D 细节题。见第四段第一句，可知欧洲人对非洲艺术的热情是出于对西方文化的古典主义和自然主义根源的一种反抗。

54. C 词义理解题。见第四段：对非洲艺术的不加评论的热情是基于上一句中的 an excess of romantic rebellion ... against the Classical and Naturalist roots of Western art，扫除了对其理性的思考。

55. C 语义理解题。见第一句，可知非洲艺术在 15 世纪传入欧洲，但未引起关注。其他三项都在文中提到。

56. A 推断题。见最后一段第一句，可知西方近代艺术在定位上不是积极的。

Passage Two

57. C 语义理解题。见第一段第二句，可知科技日趋复杂化、科学无穷的技术潜能以及解决基本问题的过程中带来的飞跃都是科技发展无止境的原因，而对科技发展缺乏有理性的预见与此无关。

58. B 细节题。见第一段，作者同意 Altdorfer 画像的解释，Babel 塔施工无法继续的原因是所有的人力都被用于维修上，因此没有人继续施工了。

59. D 语义理解题。见第一段倒数第三句，可知由于所有的人力都被用于对我们所生活的高科技世界的重建维修（reconstruction），因此进一步的发展（enlargement）

将不可能实现。这正是作者用 Babel 塔作类比的目的。

60. A 归纳题。见第二段倒数第三句,可知作者尽管认为科技的发展增强了人类破坏自然的能力,对科技的发展对人类的进步表示了怀疑,但并没有否认增强了人类对自然的控制。

61. A 推断题。综观全文,不难判断作者对科技的发展持否定的态度。

Part V Error Correction

62. not→no 固定词组 no longer 表示"不再"。

63. How→However 本句为让步状语从句,由 however 引导,意为"无论这些变化多么巨大"。

64. men→men's 变化发生在男性的角色和女性的角色之间,而不是两者共同的角色,所以 men 要用所有格形式,省略了 roles。

65. and ∧ building→are 或 building→build building 缺少助动词 are。

66. for→/ 准备晚餐:prepare the dinner。

67. When→While/Although 根据句意,主从句之间应为让步关系,而不是时间关系。

68. has→is 本句结构为倒装,被动语态,正常语序为:it is written nowhere that ...

69. ,∧ a→being 根据句意,做全职家长是一项工作,全职家长本人不是工作。

70. this→these 上文提到了许多变化,所以应用复数指示词。

71. and→or 根据句意,这些变化不是在一夜之间或在几年的时间里发生的。所以 overnight 和 even in a few years 之间是选择关系,应用 or。

Part VI Translation

72. **It is imperative that you submit to the principal a report** on the meeting because your expenses were paid by the school.(你必须在开会时向校长递交一份报告,因为你的费用是由学校支付的。)

本题测试 it is imperative that... 这个句子结构,考生首先要知道 imperative 这个词在这里最恰当,而且在 that 从句中应该用到(should)+ 动词原形的虚拟语气,此处的 should 往往省略。

73. **When the more moderate measures failed to produce any alteration** in the rules, the students resorted to violence.(当比较温和的措施没有产生任何规则上的改变时,学生们采取了暴力。)

本题有两个引起注意的考点。"比较温和的措施"是特指,必须用定冠词。更重要的是有关否定的表达不仅仅是 no 或 not,这里更确切的是用 fail to。

74. This material was exposed to the sunshine too often, **as a result it faded from dark blue to grey in no more than half a year.**(这面料过于频繁地暴露在阳光下,结果仅仅半年时间里它就褪色了,从深蓝色变成灰色。)

本题主要测试两点。"从深蓝色变成灰色"中的"变成"应从汉语的动词改译成介词词组 from... to...,加上英语动词 fade 就比较紧凑。另外,"仅仅半年时间"应该译为

"no more than half a year"。"less than half a year"表示不到半年时间,而"not more than half a year"表示不超过半年,有两种可能,正好半年或半年不到,两者都不确切。

75. Father says **it is necessary to save some money to fall back on** in emergency.(父亲说必须省出一些钱以备急用。)

本题测试两点:其一是 it is necessary to do something 的结构;其二是 to fall back on 这个词组。

76. My husband tried to **smooth over his argument with me by making me laugh**,but I didn't buy it.(丈夫试图逗我笑来缓和他同我的争论,但我还是不依不饶。)

本题测试两点:其一"缓和争论"应该用"smooth over an argument"来表达,其二"逗我笑"是手段,用 by doing something 结构更好,而 try to do 是表达目的,此处的不定式应该是 to smooth over。

Practice Test 6

Part I Writing

My View on Choosing the Right Career

(Student's sample)

Choosing the right career is very important. Only with interest can we put all our passion and willingness to do something well. In addition, most of us will spend a great part of our lives at our jobs. A career which we do not like will make such a long time hard to do with. For these reasons we should try to find out what our talents are and how we use them. Therefore, the most important thing is to find out what kind of career suits us most.

There are several ways which can help us during the career choice. First, we should know where our interest lies in. Then we can do some aptitude tests, interview with experts and study books in our field of interest. Once we find something fit for us, we should try to do it whole-heartedly. As for me, I am interested in dealing with people and I want to find a place in personnel management or public relations. I am studying courses in these aspects now and I think I can fulfill my dream one day.

(Improved sample)

Choosing the right career is very important. **Only when dealing a career with interest can we devote all our passion and willingness.** In addition, most of us will spend a great part of our lives at our jobs. A career which we do not like will make such a long time **hard to endure.** For these reasons we should try to find out what our talents are and **how we can put them to full use.** Therefore, the most important thing **is to choose a right career.**

There are several ways for us to make the right choice. First, we should **make clear** where our interest lies in. Then we can do some aptitude tests, interview with experts and study books in our field of interest. Once we find something fit for us, we should try to do it whole-heartedly. As for me, I am interested in dealing with people and I want to find a place in personnel management or public relations. I am studying courses in these aspects now and I think I can fulfill my dream one day.

Part II　Reading Comprehension (Skimming and Scanning)

1. N　讲座的听众一致认为，玩耍是孩子的特权，人们一旦长大，这项特权就被剥夺了。

　　　细节题。文章第一段即是本题提要所在。讲座指出，玩耍包括各个年龄层次。

2. NG　玩耍时间太长将会导致孩子肥胖。

　　　判断题。文章第二段第五句起讨论了玩耍和肥胖的关系。但是没有提到玩耍时间过长会导致孩子肥胖与否。当我们根据文章内容不能回答"是"，但也不能回答"不是"的时候，命题没有提到。

3. N　布朗认为电子游戏纯属垃圾。

　　　细节题。文章第三段第三句，布朗告诉那位妇女，电子游戏确实有一些玩耍的价值。

4. Y　科学家开始从进化论的角度更多地了解了玩耍。

　　　理解题。文章最后一句表明了科学家从进化论的角度研究了玩耍。这道题目考查学生对长句子的理解。

5. play, sleep, dreams 学习、记忆力和健康至少与玩耍、睡眠和做梦有关。

　　　细节题。答案在第一段的最后一句。学习、记忆力、健康和玩耍、睡眠和梦有关。

6. idle, creative and unstructured play 心理学家心目中童年的真谛是什么。

　　　细节题。第二段第四句说明了心理学家认为童年的真谛就是：悠闲、有创造性而无组织性的自由玩耍。

7. kids don't play the way they themselves did — or think they did 家长们抱怨孩子们不像他们当年那样或他们想象的那样玩耍。

　　　细节题。第二段第六句说明家长抱怨孩子们没有像他们当年那样或他们想象的那样玩耍。

8. a child is engaging all five senses by playing in the three-dimensional world 布朗认为人与人之间的差异只有当孩子全身心地投入在三维世界的玩耍的时候才能展现。

　　　细节题。第三段的最后一句表明了布朗的看法。

9. promote a scientific argument for play 科学家借助生物学中进化理论的研究来推进对玩耍科学性的争辩。

　　　细节题。最后一段第七句。

10. they can't be addressed by a single field of study 科学家讨论的话题如此之大，这些话题不能在一个学科范围内得到解答。

　　　总结题。答案在最后一段第五句。

Part III　Listening Comprehension

Section A

11. B　　　　12. D　　　　13. C　　　　14. D　　　　15. B

16. B   17. A   18. C   19. B   20. D
21. C   22. D   23. A   24. C   25. B

Section B

26. B   27. D   28. BC   29. C   30. A
31. D   32. A   33. D   34. A   35. C

Section C

36. fragile   37. upholding   38. chiefs   39. implement
40. differentiate   41. clashes   42. comply   43. respond

44. We are strong enough to say and to declare we don't want to solve the problem through military means.

45. and the army has eased restrictions on Palestinian commercial traffic

46. The military has also reopened crossings connecting

Part IV   Reading Comprehension (Reading in Depth)

Section A

47. Community broadcast radio with computers and the Internet. 教科文组织通过计算机和网络进行的社区广播帮助人们。

    见第二段第七句,提到教科文组织用到的具体技术是社区广播。第三段首句具体解释了该技术。

48. They do not know how to read or write. 使用信息科技的弱势群体是不会读和写的人们。

    第二段的第二句提到了使用计算机的前提是人们需要会读和写。

49. The radio station has powerful transmitters around the world. 遥远地区的人们依然能够收听到广播,这归功于无线电站强大的信号。

    "遥远地区的人们"没有明确提出,但文章第二段第八句,表明了世界各地均能收到广播,这句话暗示了远近地区。

50. Go to ask workers there for broadcast of the answer. 人们可以去问那里的工作人员。

    这道题目相对简单。文章第三段首句提到题眼"multi-media community center"。答案在下一句。

51. Learn what makes Kothmale a success and how to help illiterates to use Internet. 人们去 Kothmale 的目的在于学习成功经验并帮助不会读和写的人使用网络。

    文章第三段的结尾处清晰地点明了目的。

Section B

Passage One

52. B   词汇考核题。根据上下文可推测出所要考核词组的大意。文章第一句话即为题眼,根据下句得知,feel under the weather 意思是"不舒服",B正确。

53. D 细节题。文章第二段介绍了英国的天气状况,段中不止一次提及英国天气特点 "highs"和"lows"的交替存在,D 为正确答案。

54. D 细节题。关于传统预测天气状况的方式文章第三段详细的进行了介绍。第三段 第五句提到了利用松果进行预测的方法,D 正确。

55. C 词汇考核题。这类题目一般都要求学生揣测上下文并联系整篇文章的主题对单 词或词组作出推测。这里由第四段最后一句及其上下文推测出,chaotic 是"无 法预料"的意思。

56. D 判断题。本题 D 选项与文章最后一段最后一句内容一致,因此为正确答案。

Passage Two

57. B 词义理解题。根据第一段上下文意思可以推断出在这里 temper with 的意思为 "改变"。B 符合题意。

58. C 细节题。见文中第二段第三句:苏格兰警察早在 20 世纪 50 年代就用一种扁平 的帽子取代了圆锥形头盔。由此可知,C 为正确选项。

59. C 细节题。首先判断文章中那一部分在描述种种优点,在通过排除法锁定没有提 到的那一个。答案在文章第四段,该段提到了 A、B、D 项,C 项未提到。

60. B 细节题。伦敦传统的旅游景点包括哪些?首先寻找讨论伦敦旅游特色的段落, 在第一段最后一句和第二段第一句,这两句中包括了 A、C、D 项,只有 B 未提 及。答案为 B。

61. C 细节题。赞成抛弃传统头盔的看法包括哪些?文章中第三段列举了大多数警察 认为传统头盔不实用的几种论点,包括选项 A、B、D 的内容,只有 C 未提及。

Part V   Error Correction

62. worse→worst   the 修饰最高级,而且根据上下文这里应该是"最差"的环境问题。

63. Which→It   原文 which 前面的标点符号是句号,代表另一个主题开始,而 which 是 从句的标志,无法引导一个单独的句子。

64. increases→reduces   首先根据文中的 also,上下文应该一致,再者根据题意,污染应 该是减少了农作物的收成。因此将 increases 改为 reduces。

65. tells→says   tell 为及物动词,后面要求跟"某人",而 say 后可以直接跟说话的具体 内容,不需要加间接宾语"某人"。

66. dangerous→dangerously   副词才能修饰形容词,这里是副词"危险的"修饰 high。

67. within→among   在一段时间内可以用 within,而在一群人中间用 among。这里题 目的意思是"在孩子群体中间",因此将 within 改为 among。

68. also ∧ linked→been   现在完成时的被动态,肾病是被和庄稼中的金属联系在一起 的,因此用被动式。

69. observe→observable   首先两个动词原形 cause 和 observe 不能连用,而后面的"损 害"是名词,根据形容词修饰名词的规则,observe 改为形容词态。

70. crop ∧ harvested→is   "庄稼"是被收割的,所以加上 is,将原文改为被动式。

71. more→longer 这是道固定词组搭配的考题；no longer 与 no more 都可以表示"不再"，但 no longer 强调时间上的不再延续，而 no more 强调数量，次数上的不再。根据题意，庄稼应该是在时间上不再新鲜了，因此改为 no longer。

Part VI Translation

72. He won the first prize in spoken English contest, **which was largely owing to his diligence and hard-working, because he almost spent all his spare time keeping practicing**.（他在英语口语竞赛中得了一等奖，这在很大程度上归功于他的勤奋和努力，因为他几乎将所有的空余时间都用在了坚持练习上。）

本题测试"归功于"这个词组的说法，要求学生弄清楚 contribute to 和 attribute to 的区别。并且要求学生掌握"花"时间，"花"钱的说法，即 spend time/money (in) doing something，或者 spend time/ money on something。例如：He spends a whole million buying that villa.

73. It is a common phenomenon that **old people find it difficult to hold back changes among the young**.（老年人发现很难阻止年轻人的改变，这是正常现象。）

本题测试"阻止某人做某事"这个词组，除了 prevent somebody from doing something 或者 keep somebody from doing something 之外，六级要求掌握更多的变通说法，如：hold back something; restrain from doing something; refrain from doing something 等。例如：Though I am very angry, I refrain from bursting into his office.

74. Some parents fail to know that **it is wrong to impose their own opinion upon their kids**.（一些父母没能意识到把自己的观点强加在孩子身上是错误的。）

本题测试 impose something on somebody 即"将某事强加在某人身上"这个词组的运用。

75. **I would rather he hadn't gone abroad to further his study** though it is too late now.（我宁愿他当初没有出国留学，尽管现在已经太迟了。）

本题测试虚拟语气。虚拟语气一直是英语考试侧重的语法点，这个考点十分繁琐，需要考生记住特殊词所引发的各种特殊虚拟方式。对 would rather 来说，后面可以直接跟动词原形，若要跟句子，则要用过去时对现在虚拟，过去完成时对过去虚拟。例如：I would rather he told me the truth instead of hiding the fact as he always does.

76. **Harmonious society requires that everybody should obey moral doctrines** which is known to all.（和谐社会要求每个人都遵守道德准则，这一点众所周知。）

本题测试虚拟语气。"坚持"、"建议"、"要求"、"命令"等动词后要求宾语从句使用虚拟语气：should＋动词原形。例如：She suggests that everybody should arrive here on time. 本题的另外一个答案是：Harmonious society requires everybody to obey moral doctrines.

Practice Test 7

Part I Writing

The Importance of Environmental Protection

(Student's sample)

Our environment faces a big problem nowadays. We are constantly warned of water pollution, air pollution, dangers of greenhouse effect, etc. It seems that we, human beings, have turned the earth into a mess.

If such a situation is not changed, things will be worse. The result might be temperature rises to the degree until every species on the earth dies. It may result in bad water system which can never provide enough fresh water for us to live on. Or perhaps we can not find enough resources to keep our civilization going on. No matter which situation happens, the result can be disastrous.

As a member living on earth, we can do a lot to help the environment. For example, walk or ride a bicycle whenever we can to save the use of fossil fuels; recycle plastic bags and bottles; we should use wooden or nature ones instead of plastics for better environment. If each of us makes just one small effort like this every day, we can make a substantial difference.

(Improved sample)

Our environment is facing a big problem. We are constantly warned of water pollution, air pollution, dangers of greenhouse effect, etc. It seems that we, human beings, have turned the earth into a mess.

If such a situation is not changed, **the consequences will be terribly severe. The result might be the steady rise in temperature until every species on the earth dies. It may also result in the destroyed water system which can never provide sufficient fresh water for us to live on.** Or perhaps we can not find enough resources to keep our civilization going on. No matter which situation happens, the result can be disastrous.

As a member living on earth, we can do a lot to help the environment. For example, walk or ride a bicycle whenever we can to save the use of fossil fuels; recycle plastic bags and bottles; **if we have a choice, buy glass, wood or other natural materials instead of plastic ones.** If each of us makes just one small effort like this every day, we can make a substantial difference.

Part II   Reading Comprehension (Skimming and Scanning)

1. NG 根据文章得知,"美国偶像"中金发碧眼的美女通常缺乏地理知识。

判断题。文章第一段的第一句和最后一句提到了某位选手,但不能扩大到整个美国偶像节目的选手。文章没有提及选手对地理知识了解的整体状况,因此,本题没有提到。

2. Y Siegel 先生被"新共和"停职了,因为他为私利用了假信息。

细节题。文章第四段的第二句提到了 Siegel 先生的具体情况,原文与题意相符,因此本题正确。

3. N Ms. Jacoby 的梦想是革新全国教育系统并抵制像"美国偶像"之类的垃圾电视节目。

细节题。这道题目主要考学生"scan"知识点的能力。带着问题"Jacoby 对教育的方法",迅速浏览全文,在文章第十一段的第一句,我们看到了她的看法,和题目正好相反。答案为 N。

4. N Ms. Jacoby 自称为文化激进人士,因为她想做些什么来改变现状。

细节题。同样考查学生快速浏览的能力。答案在倒数第二段,Jacoby 把自己定位为"文化保守者",而不是"文化激进者",这与题目不同,因此题目错误。

5. Such lack of global awareness 驱使 Jacoby 写这本书的目的是有些美国人对世界的无知。

细节题。答案在第二段的第一句,文章明确指出了 Jacoby 创作的目的。

6. what she feels is a generalized hostility to knowledge 她的书并不是为了体现某个具体的技术,而是集中表达她对仇视知识这种普遍心态的感觉。

细节题。读者带着问题浏览文章,在第五段的第一句,文章提到了这本书的目的。

7. anti-intellectualism and anti-rationalism have fused in a particularly insidious way 对 Jacoby 来说,发生了一件不同寻常的事情:反知识与反理性以一种有害的方式联系在了一起。

细节题。答案见第七段。

8. a failing educational system Jacoby 认为应当受到责难的是失败的教育体系。

细节题。读者带着 Jacoby 认为谁应当受责备这个问题浏览文章,寻找题眼:blame 或者其同义词 criticize 等,读至第十二段时看到了提示语 blame。因此答案为 a failing education system。

9. critical 作者对正统基督教反科学的态度是不赞同的。

细节题。首先找题眼 religious fundamentalism,答案一目了然,就在第十三段第一句,文章用的是 blame,因此作者的态度是批判性的。

10. creationism to be taught along with evolution 三分之二的美国人想要进化论和上帝造人的宗教观同时教学。

细节题。既然问到三分之二美国人的看法,当然到文章先找到这些人,答案依旧在第十三段,这道题目相对简单。

Part III Listening Comprehension

Section A

11. C	12. A	13. D	14. D	15. C
16. C	17. B	18. C	19. D	20. C
21. A	22. B	23. C	24. D	25. A

Section B

| 26. B | 27. D | 28. C | 29. D | 30. C |
| 31. B | 32. A | 33. B | 34. A | 35. B |

Section C

| 36. droughts | 37. threatening | 38. livestock | 39. impoverished |
| 40. peninsula | 41. relief | 42. decades | 43. worst-hit |

44. help desperate farmers pour water into

45. Aid organizations say the communist country is facing the worst food crisis since floods and droughts three years ago helped the poverty-stricken nation plunge into famine.

46. experts believe that the harvest of these crops will only be about 50 percent. If it doesn't rain, all will be lost.

Part IV Reading Comprehension (Reading in Depth)

Section A

47. For safety reasons. 比萨斜塔关闭主要是为了安全考虑。
本题答案就在第二句,作者提到了 leaning tower,然后提到了关闭以及原因。

48. Its foundation is soil which cannot support its weight. 斜塔之所以斜,因为它的地基是土壤,承受不了塔的重量。
答案在第四句,介绍了斜塔的近况后,作者开始介绍塔斜的原因,答案明显。

49. In 1173. 斜塔最初建立在 1173 年。
时间概念的题目比较容易掌握,主要要求学生仔细看清问的是什么时间。答案在第七句。

50. By using special drills. 工程师凭借特殊的钻头移除塔底的土壤。
文章后几行提到了工程师们的种种努力,其中倒数第三句提到移除土壤的方法。

51. Move the tower back to where it was. 修缮工作取得的成果就是将塔移回至几百年前它矗立的老地方。
答案在全文最后两句,提到了这次修缮取得的成果。

Section B

Passage One

52. B 细节题。文章第一段最后两句清楚地说明了在拉丁美洲山茶花的状况：传统上在许多南美洲国家中茶花是用在葬礼上的。因此，B 选项完全符合。

53. C 词义推测题。这类题目要求学生根据上下文的暗示猜出词或词组的意思；根据前半句的 superior learning 这样褒义的形容词词组，再加上上下文，我们猜出后半句中 pick up 也是褒义，结合语境和四个候选项，我们推测出 pick up 意思是"得到提高、进步"的意思。

54. C 细节题。这种是典型的排除法。即根据四个选项的描述，浏览全文，挨个排除。这道题目中，C 项的描述与第二段后半部分中所举的宝洁公司的例子正好相反，因此 C 不对。

55. A 主旨题。按照英文写作的习惯，多数的中心思想被放在全文第一段或者最后一段，而这两段的首尾两句又是段落的核心所在。因此主旨题主要是仔细揣摩这几句的意思。本文开始就指出了研究和了解文化差异的价值，因此选 A。

56. A 主旨题。文章最后一段道出忽视文化的后果可能是灾难性的，答案选 A。

Passage Two

57. C 细节题。本文从第二段的第二句和第三段的第二句来看，A、B、D 三项都已包括，唯独 C 没有提到，答案选 C。

58. D 词义推测题。通过上下句构成的语境，尤其是下句当中的 stress（精神压力），推测出 hectic 这里的意思为"繁忙"。

59. A 细节题。答案在第六段第二句，文章提到 2－5 岁，那么最早的开始年龄是 2 岁，答案应为 A。

60. B 细节题。第四段第一句符合 B 的内容，本题选 B。

61. B 细节题。同样通过排除法，第五段的最后一句说："偶尔会有一些转瞬即逝的奇思异想打乱我们更有条理的思维，我们可以通过关注这些来学到点东西。"这与 B 说法不一，因此 B 不对。

Part V Error Correction

62. protect→protected protect 为动词原形不能修饰名词 area，需要将其变化成动名词或过去分词，动名词表示主动，过去分词表示被动，熊猫是被保护的，因此将 protect 变为 protected 修饰地区。

63. that ∧ not→are 被动式缺少谓语，"没有被保护的地区"，从句也必须是完整的句子。

64. panda→pandas panda 是可数名词，应用复数，并且和后面的谓语复数形式 live 呼应。

65. that→where 这里是地点状语从句，用 where 引导，或者用介词＋which 引导，但改错只能改一个地方，所以将 that 改为 where 即可。

66. with→and compare...with 虽然是固定搭配，但在这句话中不妥，这里缺的是比较的两个宾语,第一比较开放前后卧龙森林的变化率,第二比较开放前后的环境,两个宾语同样隶属 compare,用 and 表示并列。

67. not→/ 本题是语义判断题,根据上下文应该是"已经控制",而不是"没有",所以将 not 去掉。

68. said→says 根据主从句时态一致的规则,这里不用过去时,改成 says 后可以与后半句的 have grown 的时态相呼应。

69. for→because for 是表示目的为主的连词;这里用 because 引出原因。

70. to→by to 后跟数字或百分率表示"增长到",而 by 后跟数字或百分比表示"增长了"。这里根据上下文应该是增长的幅度,因此将 to 改为 by。

71. Which→This 这里是一个单独的句子,which 只能引导从句,而从句不能单独成句。

Part VI Translation

72. According to the report, **police are trying to stop the crimes caused by drug-taking**. (据报道,警察正在试图阻止因吸毒而引起的犯罪。)
本题测试几个动词的连用。一句话只能有一个谓语,如果要表示几个动词连用,谓语后出现的动词要用非谓语形式或者用从句。例如:Wherever you go, you will see the product advertised.

73. Only when there is a certain need, **can there possibly be a certain invention**. (只有当有了某种需求,才可能有某种发明。)
本题测试 only + 状语置于句首引起的倒装句。副词 only 置于句首强调时间状语、地点状语、条件状语、方式状语等,主句需要倒装。例如:Only in this way can we avoid the trouble. 但是放于句首的 only 所修饰的不是状语时,句子用正常语序。例如:Only confession can help him.

74. Having dinner at such a fancy hotel **is beyond our means**. (在如此豪华的饭店就餐超出了我们的承受能力。)
本题测试介词 beyond 的用法。beyond 表示"超越,为……所不能及",例如:Understanding this article is beyond my capacity.

75. He took it for granted that **his boss will give him a pay rise according to his real talents**. (他想当然的认为老板会根据他的实际能力给他加工资。)
本题测试英语在实际生活中的用法,如"加工资"(get a pay rise)、"谈判"(negotiate)、"加班"(work overtime)、"跳槽"(job-hopping)等实用英语词汇。

76. **However hard he has tried, he can't get out of current trouble** which makes him quite upset. (无论他如何努力,他都无法摆脱目前的困境,这使得他颇为沮丧。)
本题测试特殊疑问词的用法,特殊疑问词 + ever 相当于 no matter + 特殊疑问词。例如:Whatever she does, the boss is not satisfied. 相当于 No matter what she does, the boss is not satisfied.

Practice Test 8

Part I   Writing

Is Credit Card Important to Our Lives?

(Student's sample)

Credit card steps into people's lives gradually. Some people find that it makes our lives much more convenient than ever before. We don't have to carry a large sum of cash around, worried about being robbed all the time. And it can also free us from the direct contact with the dirty notes.

However, other people think entirely differently. They think credit card deprives people of the joy of counting notes, which is a much more direct way to prove how good you are. Moreover, together with other cards, credit card contributes to making our world more machine-like. It acts as if people worked all the time just for numbers.

As for me, I think despite its disadvantages, credit card does make our lives much safer and easier. Even losing them won't cause heavy financial loss. One call to the bank will still make our money safe. It indeed provides an alternative way for us to enjoy life.

(Improved sample)

Credit card steps into people's lives gradually. Some people find that it makes our lives much more convenient than ever before. We don't have to carry a large sum of cash around; **we don't have to be worried about being robbed all the time.** And it **also frees us** from the direct contact with the dirty notes.

However, **other people hold completely different idea.** They think credit card deprives people of the joy of counting notes, which is a much more direct way **to evaluate one's performance.** Moreover, together with other cards, credit card contributes to making our world more **mechanized. It acts as if people worked all day long just to be judged by indifferent numbers.**

As for me, I think despite its disadvantages, credit card does make our lives much safer and easier. Even losing them won't cause heavy financial loss. One call to the bank will still make our money safe. It indeed provides an alternative way for us to enjoy life.

Part II   Reading Comprehension (Skimming and Scanning)

1. N   据说在美国 20% 的孩子生活在贫困线之下，这比起 1969 年多出了很多，作者认为这夸大了事实。

细节题。文章第四段比较了 1969 和 2006，该段最后一句话说这个统计有可能低估了贫困现状。这句话与题目相反，故题目的说法是错误的。

2. Y   根据文章，现在的贫富差距比起 40 年前要大得多。

比较题。关于现在贫富差距和 40 年前的比较，出现在文章第五段的第二句话。

3. Y   大脑发展的最新研究得出结论：贫困家庭出身的孩子读完大学的机会较少。

细节题。文章第十段提到了这个话题，描述与题目相符。故判断为正确。

4. NG   奥巴马针对贫困问题提出了很多新的设想，这些设想取得了很大成功。

细节题。文章倒数第二段的最后一句话提到了 Barack Obama 的设想，但只是说这些想法规模不大，也不是竞选的核心计划。至于这些想法有没有取得很多成就，文章未作评论。故该题没有提到。

5.   unhealthy levels of stress hormones; neural development 神经科学家发现：在贫困家庭长大的很多社会地位低的孩子处在不健康的荷尔蒙压力之下，这会损伤神经发展。

细节题。neuroscientists 是神经科学家。神经科学家对贫困的看法在文章第二段，他们认为贫困家庭的孩子会处在不健康的荷尔蒙压力之下，这会损伤神经发展。

6.   the suffering of the poor; the alleged abuses of welfare queens 1969 年之后注意力从穷人受苦转移到了滥用福利上。

细节题。abuse 是"滥用"的意思。文章第三段第三句表明：1969 年之后注意力从穷人受苦转移到了滥用福利上。

7.   the cruel fact that to be poor in America today is to be an outcast in your own country 神经学家认为毒害孩子大脑的是这样一个残酷的事实：在美国贫穷就意味着在自己的国度被放逐。

细节题。再次提到神经学家的看法是在第五段最后两句。

8.   great creativity in making excuses 美国未能减少贫困激发出的不是反思，而是其在这方面找各种借口的创造力。

细节题。文章第六段叙述了美国对贫困问题的现状以及不停找借口的怪现象。

9.   government programs that help the poor and unlucky 美国的贫困率比欧洲的低，这要归功于政府帮助穷人和不幸人们的项目。

细节题。文章倒数第四段比较了美国和欧洲并列出了原因。

10.   ending the poverty that still poisons so many American lives 作者让我们回到

我们抛弃已久的任务上去,这个任务就是结束那仍然毒害许多美国人生活的贫困。

细节题。文章最后一句清晰地表明了作者的观点:我们要回到我们的任务上来,那就是结束贫困。

Part III   Listening Comprehension

Section A

11. C	12. A	13. C	14. C	15. C
16. B	17. B	18. C	19. D	20. B
21. C	22. D	23. D	24. B	25. A

Section B

26. B	27. D	28. C	29. A	30. A
31. B	32. C	33. A	34. C	35. A

Section C

36. threatened	37. endorsed	38. counterpart	39. transformation
40. summit	41. alliance	42. endorsing	43. entry

44. We believe no one should be excluded because of history or location or geography

45. His last point is a reference to Russian objections to extending the NATO defense umbrella

46. which were once annexed by the Soviet Union

Part IV   Reading Comprehension (Reading in Depth)

Section A

47. A group of engineers and scientists. 一群工程师和科学家启动了VITA项目。
本题答案在第三段的第一句。这一句告诉了我们VITA启动的时间和创始人。

48. People with important skills and experience. VITA雇用的是掌握重要技能和有经验的人士。
本题答案在第三段的第四句,它告诉我们VITA雇用的是诸如工程师、商人和农场主等有技能有经验的人士。

49. Solve technical problems in developing countries. VITA志愿者要做的是解决发展中国家的技术问题。
本题答案在第三段的第五句,VITA志愿者主要解决亚非拉等发展中国家的技术问题。

50. On weekends or evenings. 志愿者通常在周末或晚上工作。
本题答案在全文倒数第四句,文章解释了志愿者的工作时间——他们在空余时间工作,也就是周末或者晚上。

51. Sending mails or e-mails and reading publications from VITA. 通过发电子邮件、寄

信或阅读 VITA 期刊来获取帮助。

本题答案在文章最后几句,这几句介绍了和 VITA 联系的种种方式。

Section B

Passage One

52. B 词义理解题。根据下一句"如何把价格标签贴上去"推测出这是个"实际的"问题,pragmatic 的意思最有可能是"实际的"。答案选 B。

53. A 理解题。欧元给联合利华带来了更大的问题。这道题要去找题眼:"欧元"和"问题",答案在第四、五段,那些没有自己定价的公司遇到的问题更大。而联合利华的产品由各地零售商自己定价,所以联合利华遇到了更大的麻烦,答案选 A。

54. D 计算题。第四段第三句说:1.50 的价格差价中仅有一半是由于税收、分销和劳动力成本等因素造成的,那么剩下的 0.75 就是法国商人多赚的利润了,所以 D 为正确选项。

55. C 推断题。最后一段前两句提到了两大巨头对"欧元"和"价格差异"之间关系的看法。联合利华认为要花上几年时间才能解决好"价格差异问题",因为大多数人用"现金"买日常用品,第二句紧接着说麦当劳也认为它不会纠正差价,除非人们使用"欧元"。这两句话合在一起告诉我们:第一句话中的"现金"指的是本国货币,不是欧元;而且人们在近几年内不会使用"欧元"买日常用品,因此 C 为正确答案。

56. C 理解题。文章第三段在讨论同一商品不同价格的话题,第三句尤其指出:这种对产品的态度是变化的。C 最为接近。

Passage Two

57. C 细节题。作者认为 Clara Barton 是位尊贵的人。本题答案在第一段第三、四句,作者列举了一系列尊贵的人,Clara Barton 是其中之一,故答案选 C。

58. B 细节题。第二段后半部分列举了几部出名的文学作品与历史的关系。"南方的奴隶制不像《乱世佳人》,而拓展前线也不像《与狼共舞》",我们得知答案应为 B,《与狼共舞》与历史不符。

59. D 词汇理解题。根据所在这一句的意思"辛德勒名单忠实而清晰地_____了历史",这里 capture 的含义应为褒义,represent successfully 意为"成功反映"。D 正确。

60. D 推断题。见文章第三段的第一句,作者相信我们应该分享历史上的荣誉与灾难。D 正确。

61. A 总结题。本文的中心思想或者是本文的标题,问的都是文章的主要内容概括。根据英文写作的习惯,中心思想一般会被概括在第一段或最后一段的首尾句。从最后一段的最后两句得知,"我们从历史中学习。"答案选 A。

Part V Error Correction

62. event→issue 或 problem　event 指发生的重大事件(如庆祝游行、国家领导人出访等),用在此处不合适;一般话题用 issue 或 problem 即可。

63. mix ∧ some→with　mix 表示"与……混合为一体"时为不及物动词,后不能直接跟宾语,应该加 with 构成词组方能使用。

64. another→other　another 是"另外一个",而 other 表示"其他的",该句中修饰的是复数 cities,题意应为"其他一些国家",而非"另一个国家",因此将 another 改为 other,后接复数。

65. move→moving　begin doing sth. 或者在 begin 后加 to, begin to do sth. 开始干某事。两个动词原形 move 和 begin 不能连用。

66. under→above　above 指"在……上方",暴风雪来自海面上方,而非下方,故根据题意应将 under 改为 above。

67. with→\,或者 with→to　help with 后跟名词,与后面动词原形 reduce 不能搭配,所以只能改为 help to do sth. 帮助做某事。

68. or→and　这里应为并列关系,列出各种采集信息的工具。

69. aerosols ∧ contain→that　应加 that,将后面变成定语从句,否则一句话有了两个谓语,语法上不成立。想要将两个动词原形并列于一句话中,要么用连词并列,要么使用从句。

70. woods→wood　woods 表示森林,wood 表示树木。

71. useful→used　根据上下文,这里应该是"被使用",而不是"有用的",动词过去分词表示被动,因此将 useful 变为 used。

Part VI　Translation

72. **Upon the issue about how women get equal rights**, many people stated their own opinion.（关于妇女取得平等权利的问题,许多人说出了自己的看法。）
本题测试从句使用技巧。关于特殊疑问句引导的从句合并在介宾结构中作宾语的用法,很多学生不是很熟悉。首先应该确定信息主体,再通过关系副词将一句话粘在主体后构成从句。例如：It is surprising he succeeds where other more experienced experts fail.

73. In fact，there are many approaches to solve the problem，**but he stuck to the wrong one stubbornly**.（实际上解决这个问题有很多方式,他却倔强地坚持错误的想法。）
本题测试词组和单词量的掌握。一些常见词组如 stick to, attach importance to, deprive of, accuse of 等均应熟练掌握。

74. The increasing price **makes many old people who live on petty pensions feel pressure.**（上涨的物价使得许多靠微薄养老金生活的老年人感到了压力。）
本题首先考查了 make sb. do sth. 这词组,make 后接不带 to 的不定式 feel。其次考查在 make 的宾语 many old people 后面插入了一个 who 引导的定语从句。

75. **As far as I know**, they broke up for almost a year.（据我所知,他们分手已经差不多一年了。）

本题测试学生的固定连词和词组的运用能力；类似的考点包括 nevertheless，whereas，as far as I am concerned，as long as 等。

76. **Now many young people are indulged in video games**，which makes their parents worry a lot.（如今很多年轻人沉溺于电脑游戏,这使得他们的父母十分担心。）

本题主要考查"沉溺于"这个词组的使用；"沉迷于"、"专心致志于"可以用以下意思相近的词组表达：be indulged in；addict to；be engaged to；plunge in；devote to 等。例如：Addicting to drugs will not only hurt oneself but also hurt people around him/her.

Practice Test 9

Part I Writing

Should Grades Be Important for Students?

(Student's sample)

Some students think grades are important and they should get a better one during college study. They think they have to be careful about it because grade is an important criterion to judge their performance at school. Whenever they want to further their study, find a job or even get a part-time job, they would be required to show their grade. In this case, they have to make it.

However, other students seem not to so careful towards grade. In their eyes, grade is no more than one of the means to evaluate their performance. There are many other more important things waiting for them to acquire, for example, the ability to adapt to society, the skills in interpersonal communication, etc.

As for me, grade is certainly important, but we should not be distracted by it. Grade may make the first step to success easier, but there are still a lot of other things we must do. If we want to further our success in society, we should learn more things and keep them balanced.

(Improved sample)

Some students regard grades as the most important thing they strive for during college study. They think **they have to be grade-conscious** because grade is an important criterion to judge their performance at school. Whenever they want to further their study, find a job or even get a part-time job, they would be required to show their grade. **In this case, what can they do except trying to get a better one?**

However, other students **seem to be more liberally-minded towards grade.** In their eyes, grade is no more than one of the means to evaluate their performance. There are many other more important things waiting for them to acquire, for example, the ability to adapt to society, the skills in interpersonal communication, etc.

As for me, grade is certainly important, but we should not be distracted by it. Grade may make the first step to success easier, but there are still a lot of other things we must do. If we want to further our success in society, **we need to prepare ourselves in**

a more balanced way.

Part II   Reading Comprehension (Skimming and Scanning)

1. **N**   以网络为基础的服务能够让人们跟着本国人面对面地学习外语。
细节题。第二段详细地介绍了以网络为基础的服务模式,提到了跟外国人学外语,但不是面对面,而是通过网络。所以这道题目是错的。

2. **N**   对于那些想要改进他们在中学所学的外语的人来说,这些网站提供了诸如教科书和光盘之类的工具。
细节题。第三段第一句指出网站走的不是传统的老路,而是给学生提供替代传统工具的帮助。

3. **Y**   LiveMocha 是一个训练外语的网站,它想要提供一个让人轻松的氛围。
细节题。第六段第一句说明 LiveMocha 是一个大家可以相互提高外语水平的网站;第二句说 LiveMocha 的含义是"创造像咖啡馆一样人人放松的气氛"。

4. **NG**   Curtis 把 LiveMocha 看作网络上关于语言学习的教育资源的有效且必要的迸发。
细节题。第十段的最后一句以及第十一段的开始说明 Curtis 对网络教育的态度是肯定的,但是没有提到 indispensable（必不可少）的意思。所以这道题没有提到。

5.   the Internet and a broadband computer connection   如果你没有办法通过出国来学习外语,你可以借助因特网和宽带计算机互联来学习。
细节题。答案在第一段第二句。

6.   typing messages; talking   借助 LiveMocha,会员们通过打字或说话聊天。
细节题。文章第四段指出会员们通过键入短信息或说话进行网上聊天。

7.   the site's social networking component helps learners a lot   Paul Aoki 认为 LiveMocha 的用处在于网站的社会网络构成给学习者提供了很大帮助。
细节题。in that 后跟从句,表示具体解释、说明。第八段提到了 Paul Aoki 对网络学习的看法。第二行后半句指出 Paul 认为网站的社会网络组成对学生十分有用。

8.   free lessons in Mandarin Chinese（ChinesePod. com）or Spanish（Spanish-Pod. com）   另外一个被称为 podcasts 的电子学习系统提供了免费学习汉语和西班牙语的机会。
细节题。另外一个以电子为基础的语言学习项目 podcast 的情况在文章第十二段进行了详细的介绍,它的特征之一就是提供学习汉语和西班牙语的免费课程。

9.   vocabulary has grown as much as it did in all of the previous years of study combined   Mike Kuiack 评论道:自从他开始使用这种服务,他新掌握的汉语词汇数量是前几年学习的总和。
细节题。文章第十六段第一次提到 Mike,第十七段提到了他的体会。他认为他新掌握的汉语词汇数量是前几年学习的总和。

10. he is free/it is convenient for him 一旦选择了电子教学方式,学习者可以机动掌握学习时间。

细节题。答案在倒数第三段。

Part III Listening Comprehension

Section A

11. C	12. A	13. C	14. D	15. D
16. B	17. B	18. B	19. C	20. C
21. B	22. A	23. B	24. B	25. A

Section B

26. B	27. C	28. D	29. C	30. B
31. A	32. A	33. C	34. B	35. B

Section C

36. corruption	37. scandals	38. justice	39. controversy
40. depicted	41. monsters	42. fugitive	43. fled

44. to pass several levels avoiding monsters who throw bundles of cash in bribes

45. We're happy to have done something to create some sort of conscience on kids

46. who sees his interests as a boy being affected by the situation how these people left the country

Part IV Reading Comprehension (Reading in Depth)

Section A

47. Mass life extinction on Earth. 这样的大爆炸导致了地球上大量生命的灭绝。

    本题答案在第二段的第一、二句可以找到。文章指出爆炸引起的变化杀死了地球上几乎所有的动植物。

48. From outer space. buckyball 当中的气体来自外太空。

    本题的答案在第二段的第四、五句,它们所含的气体只有太空才有。

49. In rocks from China and Japan. 这些分子来自中国和日本的岩石。

    本题的答案在第三段的第一句:科学家在中国和日本的岩石中发现了这样的分子。

50. Where the meteor crashed. Beck 与其他科学家意见分歧的地方是:流星爆炸的地点。

    本题关于 Beck 的观点在第三段第三、四句。其他科学家认为爆炸发生在澳大利亚西部,但 Beck 不同意。

51. It is hard to identify the place where it crashed. Beck 认为已经过去很长时间,很难给出确切答案。

    本题的答案在第三段第五句。

Section B

Passage One

52．A 细节题。第一段的第二句讨论了生物钟存在的地点：生物定时器存在于各种动物和植物之中。石头没有生命，因此没有生物钟。

53．C 细节题。关于重设生物钟的话题，见第三段第三句。根据这一句和上下句，我们得知：光被认为是最能使生物钟同步的装置。因此答案为C。

54．A 词义理解题。第四段的第二句出现 maintain。maintain 有"保持"、"维护"的意思，这里根据语境和候选项，答案是"保持"，选 A。

55．D 细节题。哪一个不属于视丘下部的控制。文章最后一段的倒数第二句讨论了这个话题，在这一行中，只有阅读没有提到，答案选 D。

56．C 词义理解题。文章第二段提到了 out of phase，相当于 not working，停止起作用。下文说他们继续吃和睡，转折连词 but 暗示后半句是停止起作用的意思。

Passage Two

57．B 词义理解题。payroll 是个常见词，从上下文看，首先和钱有关，排除 C 和 D，其次不是指个人报酬，而是工人薪水的总和，因此选 B。

58．D 细节题。文章第二段第一句介绍了电影业的概况，第一句就说电影业包括制作、发行和放映，没有提到 D，因此选 D。

59．C 细节题。关于美国法庭通过制定法律插手电影业见文章第二段，特别是第四句；根据这一句的描述，法律的制定时间应该是 1948 年，选 C。

60．A 主旨题。这道题目考查的是学生对文章主旨的掌握，通过文章首尾两段和前三道题目给我们的内容提示，我们较容易得出结论：本文主要涉及关于电影院的介绍，因此 A 正确。

61．C 细节题。最后一段第二句讨论了发行方做的种种事情，第三句明确指出被请求填写信息卡的是观众，而非发行人员。因此选 C。

Part V Error Correction

62．bright→brightness 根据介宾结构的语法规则，介词 in 后面要加名词或动名词，因此将 bright 改为名词形式 brightness。

63．interested→interesting interested 表示人对某件事情或东西的评价或态度：感兴趣的；而 interesting 表示事物本身的性质：有趣的。这句话想说的是火星的性质，因此用 interesting。

64．quickly∧other→than 典型的比较级结构，more … than …句型前后呼应。

65．On→In in fact 表示"实际上"。固定词组搭配，要求考生细心记住词组中的不同介词。

66．told→said "据称"用 said。tell 后面跟某人，可以跟双宾语，而 say 后面不直接跟某人。"据说"的英文表达是：it is said…

67．where→when 语法上看 where 引导了从句，补全了句子结构，但是根据后半句的语境,6 月 13 号是日期,when 引导日期,因此将 where 换成 when。

68. largely→little 根据后半句的意思,地球是个几近完美的球体,那么前半句当中地球不同部位距离太阳的距离变化应该很小。

69. But→So 上半句提到火星轨道像个鸡蛋,因此它的各个部分距离太阳的距离是不等的,后半句应为因果转折。

70. that∧caused→are 这些记号是由不同质量的火星土壤引起的,因此用被动式。

71. On the Earth→On Earth 这里是固定搭配,中间不加 the,指"在地球上"。

Part VI Translation

72. I'd like to let you know **that we will never compromise to enemies at any time**.(我想让你们知道,我们在任何时候都不会向敌人妥协。)

本题测试"妥协"的英文表达方式;"妥协"的表达方式有以下几个较常使用的:compromise to sb.; yielded to sb.; give way to sb. 等。例如:After long-time argument,I yielded to my customer.

73. **Though he kept claiming that he didn't cheat in the exam**,he was more and more upset recently.(尽管他一直声称自己考试没有作弊,他最近越来越不安。)

本题测试"声称"的表达方式,要求学生掌握 claim,declare,announce 和 state 在用法上的区别。claim 带有些许贬义,应慎用。

74. **With regard to his usual honest behavior**,the company decides to trust this time.(鉴于他一贯诚实的表现,公司这次决定相信他。)

本题测试"鉴于"的表达方式,相近的表达方法包括:as far as … is / are concerned,with regard to,taking sth. into consideration 等。

75. The company is weak **in terms of quality and brand fame**.(在质量和品牌知名度上,这个公司不够强。)

本题测试"具体在哪方面"的表达,in terms of 后接名词,in that 后接从句。例如:He is a clever person in that he knows how to grasp chance.

76. **So long as you keep your good living habit and stop staying up late**,you will be healthier.(只要你坚持好的生活习惯,改掉熬夜的坏毛病,你就会更健康。)

本题测试"坚持"、"改掉"和"熬夜"的表达方式。"坚持"常用的说法有:keep doing,insist on,persist in,stick to,"改掉"常用词组是 get rid of,eliminate;"熬夜"的常见说法是 stay up late。

Practice Test 10

Part I Writing

Is Victory Everything to the Sports Game?

(Student's sample)

Some hold that victory is everything to a game. People can't enjoy a sport if they don't work hard with it. And if players don't play to win, what do they do?

However, others argue that people who are too serious make the game look not funny any longer, and victory is not everything. We have got many things that matter more in sports, for example, participation, friendship and thrill feeling.

I agree with the second opinion. Thinking only of the game will make it uninteresting, and it's no game any longer. Take football for example, mere emphasis on victory will distort the basic spirit of the game. Friendship will be overcast by furious competition. Remember football hooliganism? It is one of the most notorious results. It doesn't matter whether you win or lose in the game. The point is that you participate and do your best. Victory is not everything.

(Improved sample)

Some hold that victory is everything to a game. People can't enjoy a sport **if they don't put a hundred percent in it.** And if players don't play to win, **why do they join the game?**

However, **others argue that people who are too competitive take the fun out of the sport**, and victory is not everything. We have got many things that matter more in sports, for example, participation, friendship and thrill feeling.

I agree with the second opinion. **Only victory in mind during a game will spoil the fun,** and it's no game any longer. Take football for example, mere emphasis on victory will distort the basic spirit of the game. Friendship will be overcast by furious competition. Remember football hooliganism? It is one of the most notorious results. It doesn't matter whether you win or lose in the game. The point is that you participate and do your best. Victory is not everything.

Part II　Reading Comprehension (Skimming and Scanning)

1. **N**　作者通过仔细观察同事的面部表情得知同事头天晚上失眠。

　　细节题。答案在第一段。在 Facebook 的"最近状态"一栏里,同事给自己打上了失眠的标签。

2. **Y**　社会网络系统有可能将信息传播给很多人。

　　细节题。第六段的第二句明确指出社会网络体系不仅能够创造个人身份,也能将个人信息传播给很多人。

3. **Y**　网络传播个人信息可以是随心所欲的,很难对其进行控制。

　　推测题。根据文章第八段的第一句话,网站有了一个愈演愈烈的倾向:不经过当事人的同意就散发他的信息。这句话说明个人信息的传播是随心所欲的。

4. **N**　当网站传播用户不想被分享的私人信息时,网站会通知用户。

　　推测题,根据第三道题目所在部分即知道用户的私人信息会被泄漏;文章倒数第三段的第一、二句告诉我们用户应该享有被告知的权力。但是现在还未实现。

5. 　it is impossible for users to quit the site and erase their personal information Facebook 的一个令人不快的规定是用户无法中途退出网站,无法清除个人信息。

　　细节题。文章第三段第一句就提到了 Facebook 的这个规定。

6. 　clothing, facial expressions, and the revealing and withholding of personal information 一旦下了线,人们通过衣着、面部表情和透露或保留个人信息来向世界传递他们是谁,他们想要被看做是谁的信息。

　　细节题。文章第四段的第二句提到了没有上网时人们传达自己身份和透露个人信息的方式。

7. 　the physicality of the offline world 当下线时,脱机世界的物质性给了用户内在保障。

　　细节题。见文章第五段第一句。

8. 　its spread of personal information without users' consent

　　细节题。文章第八段的第一句提到了最大的麻烦就是未征得用户同意就散播用户的个人信息。

9. 　they are looking for more ways to make more money

　　细节题。网络为什么要散播这类信息？答案在第九段的第一句:网络为了寻找赚钱的更多方式。

10. 　give users as much control over their identities online as they have offline 网站需要在用户上网和脱机时都能严格保护用户的身份,这样才能保证用户的隐私权。

　　细节题。文章第十段的第一、二句给出了网站保护用户私人权利的方式:给网上用户犹如网下那样掌管自己身份的权利。

Part III   Listening Comprehension

Section A

11. A	12. C	13. B	14. D	15. A
16. C	17. D	18. D	19. B	20. A
21. D	22. B	23. D	24. C	25. A

Section B

| 26. D | 27. D | 28. C | 29. D | 30. C |
| 31. A | 32. B | 33. C | 34. D | 35. D |

Section C

36. kin   37. extended   38. multiple   39. siblings
40. common   41. non-industrial 42. permanent   43. as long as

44. Descent group membership is often ascribed at birth

45. They are born into a family consisting of their parents and siblings

46. Since most societies permit divorce, some people establish more than one family through marriage

Part IV   Reading Comprehension (Reading in Depth)

Section A

47. They found that they had their own valuable art heritage. 美国人发现他们有着属于他们自己的珍贵的艺术遗产。

   本题答案在第一段第一句。

48. Their paintings reflected true American life. 美国绘画的主要特征是他们的画反映了真实的美国生活。

   本题答案在第一段第四句。美国的绘画并不是欧洲绘画的影子,而是美国生活的真实再现。

49. American paintings are diverse in the ways of artistic expressing. "拥有很多源头的河流"意思是美国绘画在艺术表达上兼容并蓄,采纳百家之长。

   本题题目在第一段第五句,这是一个类比,将艺术比作河流,将河流的源头比作艺术的起源。

50. For being a representative champion painter who searched realism. 画家 Hopper 出名在于他是现实主义画派的大师。

   本文第一次提到 Hopper 是在文章第一段第六句,根据上文可知:"受人尊敬的追求现实主义的大师是 Hopper。"

51. His paintings can reveal the thought and feeling of Americans. Hopper 的作品被认为是天才之作,因为他的作品反映的是美国人的思维和感情。

   本题答案在第一段的最后一句,该句阐述了 Hopper 作品的意义所在。

Section B

Passage One

52. C 词义理解题。文章第一段第一句话"American rules for assigning racial status can be arbitrary."就清楚地表明了美国的规则。这道题目主要依赖对 arbitrary 一词的理解："任意的，武断的"，故应选 C。

53. B 细节题。文章第一段第二、三句详细解释了 hypodescent 的涵义：在某些州，只要得知你有黑人祖先，不管血缘关系多远，你都被定义为黑人，这条规定根据祖先来划定一个人的社会身份，第四句总结，这就叫做 hypodescent.

54. B 推测题。文章第二段介绍了 Phipps 的情况，根据文章第一段 hypo-descent 的含义，可知 Phipps 被定义为黑人是因为她的远祖有黑人。答案选 B。

55. D 概括题。参见文章第二段，叙述完 Phipps 的例子后，作者作了评论，这与第一段中文章的中心思想相呼应："政府在确定种族时并没有充分的理由。"

56. D 推测题。可以通过排除法做。答案在文章第二段的第五句：虽然州律师承认 Phipps"看起来像白人"，但路易斯安那州仍坚持对她的种族划分是合理的，那么我们推测出 Phipps 在官司过后依然被划分为"黑人。"答案为 D。

Passage Two

57. C 词义推测题。文章第一段第二句出现了 unanimously，同句中，还出现了 also。also 给了我们暗示前后是并列结构，上一句说 all humans ...那么这一句也应该是 all 的意思。据此推测，unanimously 的意思是"毫无例外"。答案选 C。

58. C 信息理解题。题目出在第一段的第二句，答案在下面两句，解释得十分清楚："人们接受文化的能力是平等的。"答案选 C。

59. A 细节题。文章第一段的第一句就提出了这个问题，该句第二个分句指出文化是解释人类适应力的根源，所有人类都享有"文化能力"。这句话也是全文中心思想所在，指出了人类的适应力和文化的关系选项 A 合乎原文思想。

60. C 信息理解题。文章第二段以美国和加拿大的文化为例说明了，虽然起源不同，但由于文化的包容力，不同的种族可以很好地生活在一起。答案选 C。

61. C 推测题。根据第二段后半部分对各种文化的分析和说明，"妇女必须戴面纱"只存在于少数阿拉伯民族，并不常见，根据第二段对各种文化的定义，这应说列为 C：个别特征。

Part V Error Correction

62. about→\ horrify 是及物动词，直接跟宾语；horrify 的形容词形式 horrified，表示人的态度时用 be horrified about sth.

63. reaction→response reaction 与 response 虽然是近义词，但 in response to 为固定搭配，不可随意更改。正如 keep in mind 不可以说成 keep in head 一样。

64. condemn→condemned 动词原形 condemn 不能修饰名词 people，因此要变成非谓语动词，动名词 condemning 表示主动，过去分词 condemned 表示被动，这里是"被判刑的人"，因此改为 condemned。

65. sarcastical→sarcastically 副词修饰动词 attacked。形容词修饰名词，副词修饰动词或形容词。

66. trouble→troubles trouble 的主语是 method，主语是单数，谓语要加"s"。

67. as→than 比较句型用 anymore ... than。

68. it→\it 去掉后，attempts 是 find 的宾语，而 necessary 是补足语。

69. by→with by 是 by means of 的缩写，一般指凭借某个动作，而 with 后加名词表示凭借某种工具、物品等。

70. let→letting 介词后要求跟名词或动名词，因此要用动名词 letting。

71. kind→cruel 根据这句话中的 and，前后都应该是表示"不好"的形容词。根据语境，这里要将 kind 改为反义词 cruel。

Part VI　Translation

72. I would rather go out for a walk **than stay still in classroom for two hours**.（我宁愿出去散步也不愿意呆在教室里两个小时不动。）
  本题测试 rather than 后接的动词形式。这里要提醒的是 than 后接的动词没有固定语法形式，关键是看 than 后面的动词和前面已有的哪个动词并列，两个动词的语态一致即可。

73. I am afraid **nobody can bear such a sudden blow**.（恐怕没有人能受得了这样突如其来的打击。）
  本题测试"忍受"的英文表达。常见的表达包括 put up with，bear，stand 和 endure。

74. The influence of advertisement **depends largely upon consumers' character and environment to a big degree**.（广告的影响在很大程度上取决于消费者的性格和环境。）
  本题测试"取决于"的表达方法。depend on 和 rely on 都有"依靠"的意思，但只有 depend on 可以表示"取决于"。例如：Whether we go or not depends on weather.

75. Our university encourages students **to think independently and not to be restricted by teachers' idea**.（我们大学鼓励学生独立思考，不要受到老师观点的束缚。）
  本题测试"束缚"的英文表达和动词不定式的否定式。"束缚"经常表达为 be confined to，be limited to，be restricted by。动词不定式表达否定时，否定词 not 一定要放在 to 的前面。

76. He will be sentenced to death **once solid evidence of his crime is found**.（一旦找到他犯罪的确凿证据，他将被判处死刑。）
  本题测试"确凿"一词的用法。solid 除了在本题中表示"确凿"外，还可以表示"扎实的"。例如：I admire your solid command of English.

PART THREE

TAPESCRIPTS

Practice Test 1

11. M: How could you beat Mary in the tennis match? She is the top player in our department.

    W: Yes. But she couldn't stand playing in rain. And what is worse, she was too conscious of her new boyfriend who kept giving her pieces of advice.

    Q: What was the main reason for the woman beating Mary?

12. W: Dear, I miss you so much. What have you been engaged in these two months?

    M: Well, sorry. I would have written to you if I hadn't been so occupied.

    Q: What can we learn from the conversation?

13. M: When will you be going on holiday with me?

    W: I'm not sure. I won't be able to go now because I have my hands full with the report. My boss wants it for the conference next month.

    Q: Why can't the woman go on holiday with the man?

14. W: I've heard you've had a new boss in the company. What do you think of her?

    M: Oh! There is no one of us but like her.

    Q: What does the man mean?

15. M: Do you have anything to declare?

    W: Well, sir, I've got some fashionable clothes and several books in my case and this is my passport.

    Q: Where does the conversation most probably take place?

16. M: How much is the microwave oven you bought last month?

W: Well, it's a good bargain. I thought it would cost 200 dollars, but it turned out to be only a quarter of the price. Finally, I even got a 10 percent discount.

Q: How much did the woman pay for the microwave oven?

17. M: I've been working at the math problem for two days. And I'm tired to death.

W: You can't be too careful with it!

Q: What does the woman mean?

18. M: I waited one hour for you at the library until 5 o'clock. But you didn't appear.

W: Sorry, I stayed in the office for the whole day and hurried back by bus without dinner. It took me one hour and a half and I arrived at 6 o'clock.

Q: Where was the woman when the man came to the library?

Now you'll hear two long conversations.

Conversation One

M: It's so great to finally meet you. I've heard a lot about you. Bob tells me you're a stock analyst.

W: Yeah, and what is it that you do exactly?

M: I'm a lawyer. I specialize in international law.

W: That must be so fascinating.

M: It really is. One of the best things is that I get to travel so much. Just a couple of weeks ago I met with a group of international lawyers about extradition law. There was a big conference in New York. Have you ever been to New York?

W: Well, as a matter of fact, I was there for a weekend last month. I stopped over on my way to meet a client in Paris.

M: Paris, hmmm. Actually, my firm is planning to send me to Europe next month.

W: That's wonderful. I think it is so important to travel and see the world. Last summer I spent my vacation in Tibet, and it was one of the most important learning experiences of my life.

M: Oh, you've actually been to Tibet. I guess there must be good money in stock analysis. I just got a raise myself. That should just about put me in the six-figure range. That should show them I've made it.

W: Hmmm, I don't really look at it that way. I just want to have enough to provide for the things I care about.

M: Not for me. I think the best part of success is having other people know you're successful.

Questions 19 to 21 are based on the conversation you have just heard.

19. Where has the man been?

20. Which of the following points will the woman probably agree on?
21. Which of the following statements is true?

Conversation Two

M: Yes, madam? Can I help you?

W: Oh yes, please, but you're just closing, aren't you?

M: Well, yes, we are, madam. The shop shuts in five minutes.

W: I shan't keep you long then. It was about some saucepans you had in your window last week.

M: Last week, madam? I really can't remember which ones you mean. What were they like?

W: Oh, they were sort of imitation wood, dark brown color, country-style you know, and the lids, if I remember rightly, had a sort of leaf pattern, or was it flowers?

M: That's strange. I don't recognize any of the ones we had from that description. Are you sure they were in this shop?

W: Oh, you must know the ones I mean. They were in a sale. A real bargain. Reduced to a quarter of the original price. I couldn't believe my eyes when I saw them.

M: I'm afraid the sales are over now, madam.

W: I don't think you did, you know. At least, my neighbor, Mrs Cliffe, told me she saw some here only yesterday.

M: Er, well, madam, as you know, we were just closing.

W: Yes, yes, I'm sorry I won't keep you. It must get on your nerves when customers come in right on closing-time. But they were such beautiful saucepans! I'd have bought them then if only I'd made up my mind on the spot.

M: Perhaps, madam, if you came back tomorrow, I could show you all we have in our range of kitchen ware. And there are still one or two things at sale price.

W: Oh look! That one there! That's the sort of thing I was looking for! But it's not quite the right color.

M: That might be the artificial lighting, madam. Of course, if you came back in daylight, you might find it's exactly what you're looking for.

W: There it is! That's the pattern! Thank goodness they haven't been sold out! And thank you so much for being so patient with me. Yes, those are the ones!

Questions 22 to 25 are based on the conversation you have just heard.

22. When did the conversation most probably take place?
23. What might be the relationship between the two speakers?
24. According to the man, why is the saucepan not quite the right color?

25. Which of the following statements is NOT true?

Section B

Directions: *In this section, you will hear 3 short passages. At the end of each passage, you will hear some questions. Both the passage and the questions will be spoken only once. After you hear a question, you must choose the best answer from the four choices marked A), B), C) and D). Then mark the corresponding letter on* **Answer Sheet 2** *with a single line through the center.*

Passage One

Microsoft, probably the largest software developer in the U. S. , is being sued for the violation of the law for unfairly trying to crush its competitors. It nearly dominates the software market. Some 8 out of 10 computers run the Microsoft software. It required computer makers to pay a sum of money for each machine sold that could run Microsoft software, whether or not it actually contained that software. It also manipulated design decisions and used aggressive pricing to drive competitors off the road. Last summer, Bill Gates, Microsoft CEO, finally agreed to settle the issue with the government. Both sides agreed on a deal. But the agreement has to be reviewed by a federal judge, who never learns the meaning of the words "It's none of my business." He does not like the settlement that has been worked out and insists on the role that he ought to perform. This case will prove to be a difficult one. He probably will not let the computer giant off too easily.

It is widely held that if the market is cornered by one corporation, there will be no competition, without which market economy will have no driving force. However, in some industries, like iron and steel, or power, it is difficult to have many competitors. Therefore, government has the responsibility to interfere and regulate.

Questions 26 to 29 are based on the passage you have just heard.

26. For what did Microsoft company ask computer makers to pay a sum of money?
27. Why is Microsoft company being sued?
28. What does the federal judge think of the agreement reached by Bill Gates and the government?
29. According to the talk, which of the following industries is NOT mentioned as having few competitors?

Passage Two

American scientists have created the world's first genetically engineered monkey. They took a gene from a kind of a sea animal, for it produces a protein that looks green under blue light, an effect that can be seen. They put the gene into a special virus that does not cause infection and then put the virus into more than two hundred eggs from monkeys. Only forty of the eggs were successfully fertilized and began to develop. The scientists placed the fertilized eggs into twenty female monkeys. Three baby monkeys were born and survived. One monkey carried the particular gene. However, no part of the monkey shows the change of colour. The scientists say the genes are in the cells of the monkey. The method used to place genes from one kind of animal into another is not new. The process has been used to genetically engineer fruit, flies, cows, pigs, and other animals. However, this is the first time scientists have genetically changed a member of the group of animals that includes monkeys, apes and humans. The goal of the experiment is to create monkeys that have been genetically engineered to develop human diseases so that scientists could then use the animals to study new treatments for humans with the disease. However, other scientists rather doubt the effectiveness of the research, for this method only creates animals with added genes while most human genetic diseases are caused by a missing or abnormal gene.

Questions 30 to 32 are based on the passage you have just heard.

30. Why did the scientists use a gene from a kind of a sea animal?
31. Why was a virus used in the experiment?
32. What can we learn from the passage?

Passage Three

Americans love pets. And it's not just puppy love. Many pet owners treat their pets as part of the family. At least 43 percent of U.S. homes have pets of some sort. Exotic creatures, such as monkeys, snakes and even wolves, find a home with some Americans. More common pets include fish, mice and birds. But the all time favorites are cats and dogs, even at the White House.

Beneath the luxuries there lies a basic American belief: Pets have a right to be treated well. At least 75 animal welfare organizations exist in America. These provide care and adoption services for homeless and abused animals. Pet doctors can give animals an incredible level of medical care for an incredible price. To pay for the high-tech health care, people can buy health insurance for their pets. And when it's time to say good-bye, owners can bury their pets in a respectable pet cemetery.

The average American enjoys having pets around, and for good reasons. Researchers have discovered that interacting with animals lowers a person's blood pressure. Dogs can offer protection from burglars and unwelcome visitors. Cats can help rid the home of unwanted pests. Little creatures of all shapes and sizes can provide companionship and love. In many cases, having a pet prepares a young couple for the responsibilities of parenthood. Pets even encourage social relationships: they give their owners an appearance of friendliness and they provide a good topic of conversation.

Questions 33 to 35 are based on the passage you have just heard.

33. Which of the following animals is NOT mentioned as Americans' pets?
34. What do animal welfare organizations do for animals?
35. According to the speaker, which of the following is NOT the reason to have pets home?

Section C

Directions: *In this section, you will hear a passage three times. When the passage is read for the first time, you should listen carefully for its general idea. When the passage is read for the second time, you are required to fill in the blanks numbered from 36 to 43 with the exact words you have just heard. For blanks numbered from 44 to 46 you are required to fill in the missing information. For these blanks, you can either use the exact words you have just heard or write down the main points in your own words. Finally, when the passage is read for the third time, you should check what you have written.*

Latin America has witnessed sheer economic troubles. The debt crisis of the 1980s led to what many observers called the lost decade, a period when most countries in the region experienced little economic growth. Just as many countries were beginning to emerge from the lost period, they faced a second major crisis, brought on by the collapse of the Mexico Peso (比索) in 1994. By last year, most countries in Latin America were experiencing growth rates nearly equivalent to growth rates in Asia before the region sank into its current crisis. As a result, prices for some commodities, such as copper and oil, dropped dramatically, forcing government to cut spending. Growth rates have also been reduced from an expected 5 percent to about 3 percent this year. But Latin bankers are expected to be in better shape than their colleagues in Asia. Leading banks in Latin America entered into partnership with major foreign banks and acquired a sense of confidence they didn't have before. So there is little chance that Latin America's economy will suffer the same type of problems that Asian economies went through. Finance ministers and central bankers from developing countries are warned to be cautious with economic policies and strengthen their financial systems.

Practice Test 2

Section A

Directions: *In this section, you will hear 8 short conversations and 2 long conversations. At the end of each conversation, one or more questions will be asked about what was said. Both the conversation and the questions will be spoken only once. After each question there will be a pause. During the pause, you must read the four choices marked A), B), C) and D), and decide which is the best answer. Then mark the corresponding letter on **Answer Sheet 2** with a single line through the center.*

11. M: I had to fly to Chicago to prepare for a conference for my boss last night. Did you have a good time?
    W: I almost fell asleep for I didn't have a good view from the balcony.
    Q: Where was the woman last night?

12. W: I was absent from class today. Could you tell me what our homework assignment is?
    M: Well, I am at the tennis club meeting. Can you make an appointment?
    Q: What does the man mean?

13. M: Your new model seems to be of the latest fashion. It must be very expensive, isn't it?
    W: Not at all. For another 75 dollars, I could have bought a newer model.
    Q: What does the woman mean?

14. W: Mr. Brown, Bill and his brother John are learning at your school. Can you tell me something about them?
    M: Oh, they are both nice boys. But John outdoes Bill in math.
    Q: What does the man mean?

15. M: I need your help, Miss. How can I cash the check?
    W: You must show a valid driver's license with your photograph on it.
    Q: What does the man want to do?

16. W: Professor, what do you think of my suggestion to the subject? I've been working on it for three days.
    M: It's out of the question. You need to do experiments to get first-hand data.
    Q: What does the man mean?

17. W: The dishwasher went on the blink this morning. Should I call the service center across the street?

M: They will rob us blind. Come on and help me with the dishes.

Q: What will the man do?

18. M: The weather forecast says it's going to rain. Why aren't you using the dryer for the wet clothes?

W: I just don't want the electric company to get rich.

Q: What does the woman mean?

Now you'll hear two long conversations.

Conversation One

M: What's on the telly this evening? I feel like relaxing.

W: Why ask me that? You know I never watch it.

M: Too busy with the latest hobby, are you? What is it this time, knitting socks for your nephews? Or collecting buttons? I wish I had as much free time as you do.

W: Man! As a matter of fact, you probably have more than I do. But you waste it all watching your telly.

M: That's not a waste of time. I've got to rest sometimes.

W: Sometimes, maybe, but not all the time. And anyway, I relax with my hobbies. A change is as good as a rest.

M: Well, the telly's my hobby, and I learn a lot from it.

W: But it doesn't teach you to do anything, does it? You just sit there and stare at it. That's not learning.

M: But I do learn. There are lots of educational programmes.

W: But you don't watch them, do you? Whenever an educational programme comes on, you either switch over to the other channel or go to sleep.

M: When I come home from work, I need to put my feet up, at least for a while. Life's not all work, you know.

W: Hobbies aren't work, Jeff. I like putting my feet up, too, at the end of the day, but I like doing things while I rest. Life's too short for us to waste time.

M: Mary dear, as I've said many times, we're just different.

W: That's right.

M: So now we agree. Live and let live. You can go peacefully back to your button collection, and I can watch TV.

W: But I'm not collecting buttons.

M: What are you doing then? Making sculptures from potatoes?

W: No, I'm learning how to make Turkish cakes, and the first ones came out very well. Of course, if you're too tired, I won't insist on you trying them.

Question 19 to 21 are based on the conversation you have just heard.

19. What is the woman's latest hobby?
20. What does relaxation mean to the man?
21. Where did the conversation most probably take place?

Conversation Two

W: Yeah, when did you start smoking?

M: Well, I started when I was about sixteen, and I really started because I ... well, my family smoked and that really made me want to. Somehow it was like growing up.

W: Yeah.

M: My friends around me were smoking and when we left school we'd go over the park and have a quick cigarette. I do remember when I first started that I didn't really draw cigarettes because I didn't really know how to do it and I didn't think it was very pleasant; and it's only as time goes by you get more and more involved in that ... in that process until finally you realise that you can't give up.

W: I've smoked since I was eighteen and I started as you did, sort of socially. I was a freshman at university. Everybody else smoked. But it wasn't a lot of fun to start with.

M: Yeah. You really get smoke in your eyes and your eyes would water. But it was quite embarrassing to give up when you only just started.

W: Right. In fact, when I first started I used to pretend that I was so hooked that I couldn't give up, because it was like being a child. I wanted to be a grown-up. You know, grown-ups say they can't give up smoking and they wish they couldn't smoke. I used to pretend to say that. Of course, by the time it really happens it's too late. I actually want to give up but I can't.

M: Yeah. I started smoking a long time ago before anything was known about cancer and it was just the thing to do. As you said, it was being grown-up. It was drawing that line, you know: I am, now grown up.

W: You are right. But it seems to me that it was an awful waste of time and money.

Questions 22 to 25 are based on the conversation you have just heard.

22. When did the man begin to smoke?
23. Why did the woman started to smoke?
24. What does the woman think about smoking now?
25. What is NOT in common between the man and the woman?

Section B

Directions: *In this section, you will hear 3 short passages. At the end of each passage,* *you will hear some questions. Both the passage and the questions will be spoken only once. After you hear a question, you must choose the best answer from the four choices marked A), B), C) and D). Then mark the corresponding letter on **Answer Sheet 2** with a single line through the center.*

Passage One

After rising steadily for almost a century, standards of education in the public schools of Europe and North America have leveled off and, in the opinion of many parents and employers, are actually falling. More and more children are leaving school with little more than a basic knowledge of reading, writing and arithmetic, and illiteracy is becoming a social problem once again. With dropout rates of twenty-seven percent in high schools and fifty percent in colleges, the American education system is clearly in trouble; European dropout rates, though lower than those of the U.S., are rising too.

Various factors have been blamed for the apparent decline in educational standards. Some people say that overcrowding and lack of discipline are major factors.

Others maintain that subjects like art and drama have been overemphasized at the expense of more practical subjects. The negative influence of television is frequently mentioned as a reason for growing illiteracy. Many teachers and principals, however, insist that the problem is not of falling standards but of rising expectations on the part of parents and employers.

Whether or not standards in public schools are actually falling, many parents feel that the only way to secure a good education for their children is to send them to private schools, which generally have smaller classes and stricter discipline. The popularity of such schools is growing steadily, despite the high tuition fees. In the United States, for example, thirteen percent of all school children attend private schools; in France, over sixteen percent do so.

Questions 26 to 29 are based on the passage you have just heard.

26. What leads to the growing illiteracy?
27. What is the main cause of the problem?
28. What are the advantages of private schools?
29. What is the dropout rate in U.S. colleges each year?

Passage Two

Half of the hundreds of thousands crowded into 32 refugee camps in the desert are believed to be children. Such is the tragedy of Somalia today. They are totally dependent on outside help — and that includes our help. Until very recently serious drought threatened their lives. Water was so short, people had to dig in dried out river beds to get a little extra. Then heavy storms caused flash flooding. Rather than solving the refugees' problem this adds to them.

Food supplies have been damaged, trucks broke down, and roads washed away. The shallow wells have got some days' extra water, but with so many refugees, water supplies are desperately short. We have a medical team in the North and have now agreed to spend thousands of pounds on a major new water scheme. But money is still very short and our funds will soon run out. The refugees are desperately waiting for your help. Please send a donation today. Every penny will be used for the refugees. 5, 25 or whatever you can afford will help.

Questions 30 to 32 are based on the passage you have just heard.

30. What is the refugees' biggest problem?
31. Which of the following is not mentioned as problems arising as a result of heavy storms?
32. What is the purpose of this passage?

Passage Three

The sea is the largest unknown part of our world. Some oceanographers are studying ways of bringing the ocean's huge supply of water to the deserts of the world. Others hope to control the weather by learning more about the exchange of heat and moisture between the ocean and the air. Others are studying the ways in which sound travels and is affected by water and heat. What happens when sea water touches different elements is another subject of study.

One of the most interesting projects in oceanography is the work of mapping the ocean floor. And it can mean the difference between life and death to men in submarines. Long ago there was only one way to find out how deep the ocean was. A seaman could throw a weighted rope over the side of his ship. Then he pulled the rope up after it had reached the bottom. In the twentieth century a better way was found. Sound was used to measure the ocean. Seamen dropped a number of devices that would burst with a loud noise when they hit the bottom and measured the time it took for the sound to reach the ship. Underwater photography is also important in mapping parts of the ocean floor.

If the waters of the ocean could be moved away, the sea floor would be an unbelievable sight. Around the edges of the continents the ocean floor is flat and the water does not become much deeper for about thirty miles.

Questions 33 to 35 are based on the passage you have just heard.

大学英语六级水平测试试题集 *710*分

33. Which of the following is not the research of oceanographers?
34. Which of the following is not mentioned as ways to map the ocean floor?
35. Where is the ocean floor flat?

Section C

Directions: *In this section, you will hear a passage three times. When the passage is read for the first time, you should listen carefully for its general idea. When the passage is read for the second time, you are required to fill in the blanks numbered from 36 to 43 with the exact words you have just heard. For blanks numbered from 44 to 46 you are required to fill in the missing information. For these blanks, you can either use the exact words you have just heard or write down the main points in your own words. Finally, when the passage is read for the third time, you should check what you have written.*

For many young people, the late 1960s was a period of revolt against the moral values that had been the strength and pride of the past generation. They didn't want to be hardworking and thrifty, as their ancestors had been. They rejected all forms of authority and the idea that individuals must make sacrifices when it is necessary for the good of their children or of their community. All these narrow ideas, they declared, were things of the past and had always been wrong anyway. It was a distressing time for their elders. Previously happy parents found themselves scorned by the young, who accused them of being too concerned with money and too anxious to impress the neighbors. More parents found it hard to accept their children's attitude. They themselves had been brought up to respect traditional values and respect money because it was scarce during their teenage years. However, the young people claimed that true success is not a matter of money or position. It's a matter of self-fulfillment. And self-fulfillment consists of reaching one's goals and achieving happiness in one's own way without paying attention to rules, duties or the opinion of others.

Practice Test 3

Section A

Directions: *In this section, you will hear 8 short conversations and 2 long conversations. At the end of each conversation, one or more questions will be asked about what was said. Both the conversation and the questions will be spoken only once. After each question there will be a pause. During the pause, you must read the four choices marked A), B), C) and D), and decide which is the best answer. Then mark the corresponding letter on **Answer Sheet 2** with a single line through the center.*

11. M: I'd like to send the parcel and three registered letters to New York. How much will they cost?

    W: Five 25-cent stamps and three 20-cent air letter envelopes.

    Q: How much should the man pay in total?

12. W: Can you explain the three insurance plans in detail?

    M: Yes. The coverage of plan A is not as complete as that of plan B, but is more comprehensive than plan C.

    Q: What conclusion can be drawn from the conversation?

13. M: What about the lecture yesterday? The speaker was supposed to be a Nobel Prize winner.

    W: If only I had known it wasn't at all boring!

    Q: What does the woman mean?

14. W: What's the matter? The flash isn't working right.

    M: I think you've got the batteries in upside down since they are not in the camera for long.

    Q: What does the man mean?

15. M: I wasted two hours waiting for the engineer repairing the computer last week. But this time the data ought to be available.

    W: Unless the computer breaks down again.

    Q: What can we learn from the conversation?

16. W: Do you know Professor Smith? I hear he has been pretty successful in his studies.

    M: Pretty successful? That's the understatement of the year.

    Q: What does the man mean?

17. W: I'd love to come to your party on Saturday, but my brother is arriving from New York that day.

    M: Oh! The more, the merrier.

    Q: What does the man mean?

18. W: I haven't seen John for a long time. Do you know what he has been doing these days?

    M: You'd better ask someone else. He is the last person I want to see.

    Q: What does the man mean?

Now you'll hear two long conversations.

Conversation One

M: Now that grandma has a broken hip she's going to need extra care, even after she recovers.

W: Yeah, I don't really think she should live alone and I don't know if we have the time or resources to take care of her properly.

M: Maybe we should consider putting her into a home.

W: That seems so heartless. She's our mother! She took care of us and I think we should take care of her!

M: Do you realize that that involves coming home after working a full day and caring not only for your own family but for an elderly woman who needs special things, like being bathed and having special meals?

W: I know that, but maybe we could spend the money we would otherwise spend on a home to hire a home health care worker to do some of that.

M: So then you'll have her in the house plus having the health care worker there a lot of the time. Don't you think that would be difficult for your family? They have rights too.

W: But even if we put her in a home, how do we know that she'll get the care she needs? Not to mention the fact that she'll be extremely lonely.

M: Yes, but sometimes it's better for the elderly to be around people their own age, and those places have a lot of interesting activities designed for their patients.

W: I just think family should take care of family.

Question 19 to 21 are based on the conversation you have just heard.

19. What is the probable relationship between the man and the woman?

20. According to the man, what is the best way to take care of grandma?

21. According to the woman, what is the disadvantage of putting grandma into a home?

Conversation Two

W: Good morning. How are you?

M: I'm very worried, doctor.

W: Oh? What are you worried about?

M: I'm afraid that I'm very ill.

W: I'm sorry to hear that. Why do you think so?

M: Because I feel tired all the time, even when I wake up in the morning. I find it very difficult to do any work. I have no appetite. My wife cooks me delicious meals but I can only eat a little.

W: How do you sleep?

M: Very badly, doctor.

W: Do you find it difficult to get to sleep, or do you wake up early?

M: Both, doctor. I never get to sleep until 2 o'clock and I always wake at 5.

W: Are you worried about anything?

M: Well, yes, I am. I'm worried about my work. I've just taken a new job. I earn a lot of money but it's difficult work. I'm always afraid of making a mistake.

W: I see. Please take off your shirt and lie down on the couch.

M: Yes, doctor.

W: Well, there's nothing very much wrong with you, I'm glad to say. You're working too hard and worrying too much. Do you take much exercise?

M: No, doctor. I never have enough time for exercise. I start work very early in the morning and finish late in the evening. Then I can't get to sleep. Can you give me some medicine to help me to sleep?

W: I am the doctor. I know what to do. I'm not going to give you any medicine, because you don't need any. You need advice. Don't work so hard. Too much work is bad for you. Don't worry about your work. It's silly to worry. Take regular exercise.

M: But I may lose my job, doctor! It's hard to get a job like mine.

W: Then get an easier one, even if you earn less money. Which would you rather have, health or wealth?

M: You're right, doctor. It's more important to be healthy than wealthy. I'll change my job. I'm grateful for your advice.

W: Come and see me again in a month's time. I think you'll be a different man!

Questions 22 to 25 are based on the conversation you have just heard.

22. What is the patient's key problem?

23. How long can the man sleep at night?

24. What does the doctor do to the man?

25. What will the man do next?

Section B

Directions: *In this section, you will hear 3 short passages. At the end of each passage, you will hear some questions. Both the passage and the questions will be spoken only once. After you hear a question, you must choose the best answer from the four choices marked A), B), C) and D). Then mark the corresponding letter on **Answer Sheet 2** with a single line through the center.*

Passage One

Britain spends about 15% of its GNP on welfare, less than other European countries such as Sweden and the Netherlands, but sufficient to ensure that none of its citizens die of starvation.

In return for weekly contributions made during periods of regular employment, the National Insurance scheme provides weekly cash benefits during periods of sickness and unemployment and after retirement.

Sickness benefits are paid for an unlimited period but unemployment benefits are only paid for periods of unemployment of up to one year. The social security system provides an income for people who are jobless for more than one year.

Weekly pensions are paid to those who retire at the minimum pension age (65 for a man and 60 for a woman) and to those who continue to work for more than five years after the minimum pension age.

In addition to sickness and unemployment benefits and pensions, all British citizens are entitled to receive free medical treatment under the National Health Service.

A generous welfare state must be financed by high taxes. In Britain, taxation amounts to 37% of the national income. Most British taxpayers agree, however, that paying high taxes is preferred to letting fellow citizens starve.

Questions 26 to 29 are based on the passage you have just heard.

26. How long can unemployed people have financial help?
27. Which of the following does the National Insurance scheme not provide?
28. Who is entitled to a weekly pension?
29. How do taxpayers feel about the taxation?

Passage Two

An opinion poll was conducted last month about the cultural attitudes of people of 5 countries in western Europe, Britain, France, Italy, Spain and Germany.

The results of the poll show interesting differences between the participating nations in terms of which components of culture they regard as the most important. For the French and Italians, literature comes well at the top of the list. Economics is given priority by the Germans. History, which occupies the first place for the Spanish and the second place for the Italians and French, is given low priority by the British, who place high value on mathematics.

France has the distinction, according to the results of the poll, of being the country which provokes most interest from its British, Italian and German neighbors. Spanish interviewees indicate more interest in Italy than in France. It would seem that the literary nations of France and Italy are more culturally exciting than the scientific British and the practical Germans.

The people of the 5 countries of the survey share the view that books are the best way of broadening knowledge. The French, Germans and Italians identify radio and television as the second best means of improving knowledge but for the British and Spanish, travel is in the second place.

Questions 30 to 32 are based on the passage you have just heard.

30. People of which country regard history as the most important component of culture?
31. Which of the following best describes the British according to the speaker?
32. Which of the following is not mentioned as a means of expanding knowledge?

Passage Three

British Prime Minister Tony Blair and his wife Cherie are to make an unprecedented protest over a story in last weekend's newspaper about their 10-year-old daughter Kathryn's school.

In the story, the paper said parents whose children had been rejected by the Sacred Heart school, west London, had accused the Blairs, who live 6 miles away in another education authority area, of receiving preferential treatment. Kathryn Blair has been granted a place at the school, even though 11 children at the local primary schools have been refused places.

But a spokesman for the Prime Minister said, "As the school head and the local education authority have made clear, all the normal procedures were followed, in line with the school's admission policy and the Prime Minister's daughter received no special treatment."

The Blairs would also be asking for protection for the children of prominent public figures, the spokesman said.

The Prime Minister and Mrs. Blair tolerate a great deal of media attacks and invasion in their privacy without complaint. But they see no reason why the life of their children should be exposed to the outside, Mr. Blair's spokesman said.

The spokesman also said, the Blairs wanted to send Kathryn to a comprehensive girls school of which there are none nearby.

Questions 33 to 35 are based on the passage you have just heard.

33. What are the Blairs accused of?
34. What do the Blairs complain of?
35. Why do the Blairs send their daughter to the Sacred Heart school?

Section C

Directions: *In this section, you will hear a passage three times. When the passage is read for the first time, you should listen carefully for its general idea. When the passage is read for the second time, you are required to fill in the blanks numbered from 36 to 43 with the exact words you have just heard. For blanks numbered from 44 to 46 you are required to fill in the missing information. For these blanks, you can either use the exact words you have just heard or write down the main points in your own words. Finally, when the passage is read for the third time, you should check what you have written.*

The supporters of traditional education have always maintained that maturity of thought could only be gained by the study of past thinkers and past events. In their view only a thorough intellectual training can give a person the ability to look at contemporary problems from above in a sophisticated way. They remind the students that the purpose of a college education is to enrich the mind; it has never been to help graduates get a beginner's job. And, they add, this broad education was flexible because it was never limited to a narrow specialty. However, a majority of students complain that they are not getting too much useful knowledge and not enough practical, updated information in their chosen field. Since sciences and techniques have changed a great deal in the latter half of the century, they think, the world has become increasingly complex and education should adapt itself to the realities of modern society. There is much more to know in every field to get prepared for a career, a job. Moreover, not only did the students ask for changes in the list of required subjects, but they also demanded the right to choose their courses according to their own tastes and future needs.

Practice Test 4

Section A

Directions: *In this section, you will hear 8 short conversations and 2 long conversations. At the end of each conversation, one or more questions will be asked about what was said. Both the conversation and the questions will be spoken only once. After each question there will be a pause. During the pause, you must read the four choices marked A), B), C) and D), and decide which is the best answer. Then mark the corresponding letter on* **Answer Sheet 2** *with a single line through the center.*

11. M: Congratulations. You certainly did quite well and I must say you deserve that grade.
 W: You must have made a mistake. I have to take a make-up.
 Q: What does the woman mean?

12. W: I was told the tennis match yesterday was very tense and lasted nearly three hours. Did Tom win the championship in the end?
 M: If only he had scored one more point!
 Q: What does the man mean?

13. W: What else needs to be done apart from mailing the form and the fee?
 M: You ought to have your high school transcript and recommendations sent as soon as possible.
 Q: What is the woman doing?

14. W: It's said the new movie was on last night. Did you go to see it?
 M: Half of our crowd went to the cinema, but only three of us could afford the ticket, so four went home disappointed.
 Q: How many people of the crowd didn't see the movie last night?

15. W: The show begins an hour earlier tonight. So if it takes two hours, it will finish at 9:30.
 M: I will be waiting for you. Have a good time!
 Q: When does the show usually begin?

16. W: Do you think the bus is still available this time? It's much better to walk home than wait. Don't you agree?
 M: I couldn't agree more.
 Q: What does the man mean?

17. W: How are you, Mike? I heard you were sick.

M: You must be thinking of someone else. I've never felt better.

Q: What does the man mean?

18. W: Frank looked so unhappy. Do you know what happened?

    M: He let Louise use his car, but she loaned it to me without his permission.

    Q: Why was Frank unhappy?

Now you'll hear two long conversations.

Conversation One

M: Mrs. Weaver, I have been with this company now for five years. And I've always been very loyal to the company. And I feel that I've worked quite hard here. And I've never been promoted. It's getting to the point now in my life where, you know, I need more money. I would like to buy a car. I'd like to start a family, and maybe buy a house, all of which is impossible with the current salary you're paying me.

W: Bob, I know you've been with the company for a while, but raises here are based on merit, not on length of employment. Now, you do your job adequately, but you don't do it well enough to deserve a raise at this time. Now, I've told you before, to earn a raise you need to take more initiative and show more enthusiasm for the job. Uh, for instance, maybe find a way to make the office run more efficiently.

M: All right. Maybe I could show a little more enthusiasm. I still think that I work hard here. But a company does have at least an obligation to pay its employees enough to live on. And the salary I'm getting here isn't enough. I can barely cover my expenses.

W: Bob, again, I pay people what they're worth to the company, now, not what they think they need to live on comfortably. If you did that the company would go out of business.

M: Yes, but I have ... I have been here for five years and I have been very loyal. And it's absolutely necessary for me to have a raise or I cannot justify keeping this job any more.

W: Well, that's a decision you'll have to make for yourself, Bob.

Question 19 to 21 are based on the conversation you have just heard.

19. Where does the conversation most probably take place?

20. What might Bob do if he can't have a raise?

21. Why didn't Mrs. Weaver agree to give Bob a raise?

Conversation Two

M: What'd you do last night?

W: I watched TV. There was a really good movie called *Soylent Green*.

M: *Soylent Green*?

W: Yeah. Charlton Heston was in it.

M: What's it about?

W: Oh, it's about life in New York in the year 2022.

M: I wonder if New York will still be here in 2022.

W: In this movie, in 2022 New York has forty million people.

M: Ouch!

W: And twenty million of them are unemployed.

M: How many people live in New York now? About seven or eight million?

W: Yeah, I think that's right.

M: Mm-hmm. You know, if it's hard enough to find an apartment now in New York City, what's it going to be like in 2022?

W: Well, in this movie most people have no apartment. So thousands sleep on the steps of buildings. And there are shortage of everything. The soil is so polluted that nothing will grow. And the air is so polluted that they never see the sun. It's really awful.

M: I think I'm going to avoid going to New York City in the year 2022.

W: And there was this scene where the star, Charlton Heston, goes into a house where some very rich people live. They have tomatoes and lettuce and beef. He almost cries because he's never seen real food in his life, you know.

M: Well, if most people have no real food, what do they eat?

W: They eat something called *soylent*.

M: Soylent?

W: Yeah. There's soylent red and soylent yellow and soylent green. The people eat it like crackers. That's all they have to eat.

M: That sounds disgusting.

W: Well, you know, it really isn't that far from reality.

M: No?

W: Yeah. Because, you know the greenhouse effect that's beginning now and heating up the earth ...

M: Oh, yeah, I've heard about that.

W: I mean, in this movie New York has ninety degree weather all year long. And it could really happen.

M: You know something? I don't think that movie is a true prediction of the future.

W: I don't know. It scares me. I think it might be.

Questions 22 to 25 are based on the conversation you have just heard.

22. In that movie, how many people are unemployed in 2022 in New York?
23. Why did the star, Charlton Heston, almost cry in one scene where he goes into very rich people's house?
24. According to that movie, which of the following is NOT true in 2022 in New York?
25. What did the man think about the movie?

Section B

Directions: *In this section, you will hear 3 short passages. At the end of each passage, you will hear some questions. Both the passage and the questions will be spoken only once. After you hear a question, you must choose the best answer from the four choices marked A), B), C) and D). Then mark the corresponding letter on **Answer Sheet 2** with a single line through the center.*

Passage One

The overall crime rate is continuing to rise and there has been a sharp increase in violent crimes, according to a report issued by the F. B. I. yesterday. The report shows that the overall crime rate for the U.S. has risen by nearly five percent over last night. The authorities are particularly concerned about the sharp increases in the number of murders and armed robberies in large cities such as New York, Chicago and Los Angeles. It is said that black males living in New York have a one in twenty chance of being murdered, which doubles the chance of death for U.S. soldiers during the Second World War. Another source of anxiety is the sharp increase in juvenile crime rates.

Larry Hicks, a 24-year-old unemployed mechanic from New York, was arrested yesterday and charged with the murder of a gas station owner. According to a police statement, Hicks tried to rob the victim as he was closing up the station for the day and when the victim resisted, he shot and killed him. He was arrested for a traffic violation a few hours later and identified as the killer from a description given by several witnesses. The murder weapon was found in his car and, after being questioned by police for some time, Hicks confessed to the crime. He is expected to plead for death penalty.

Questions 26 to 29 are based on the passage you have just heard.

26. Which of the following has not aroused serious concern?
27. Which of the following cities is not mentioned as having sharp increases in crimes?

28. What is the chance of death for U.S. soldiers during the Second World War?

29. Why was Larry Hicks arrested?

Passage Two

Our broadcasting day will begin at 6:00 a.m. with New Morning, two hours of big band music. The show features big bands from the 1930s. Tomorrow's show includes the music of Duke Ellington and Count Basie.

Next it is The Jazzway from 8:00 until 10:30. Tomorrow you will be hearing some of our latest jazz albums.

Tune in at 10:30 for Modern Talk. Female poet Ellen Bass says that women have different ideas which they are only now learning how to express. At 10:30 she will discuss the writing of women poets.

At 11:00 Voice of America will be broadcasting the first in a series of programs about American foreign policy. The show will cover such topics as the problems of world energy and the United States' relationship with Canada and Mexico. And we will have an outlook of the recent conflicts in the Middle East. Be sure to listen to Great Decisions every Thursday at 11:00 a.m. starting this week.

Following Great Decisions there will be a half-hour play, American Modern by Joanna Glass. American Modern is about a married couple trying to deal with middle age. Noontime news will be on the air from 12:30 to 1:00. The news will be followed by an hour program, Third World Affairs, which examines different aspects of third world politics and cultures.

Questions 30 to 32 are based on the passage you have just heard.

30. Which of the following will not be covered in Great Decisions?

31. What is the program American Modern about?

32. When should you tune in for news?

Passage Three

There have been a number of studies on smoking among the young. In general, it has been found that many of the children living in an environment in which adults or other children smoke begin smoking at an early age. And there is a fairly rapid progression through three stages. These three stages are: the first, occasional smoking on relatively infrequent special occasions; the second, fairly frequent smoking as the social and other occasions for smoking increase; and finally, regular smoking, usually characterized by carrying cigarettes. Regular smokers among the young are far from heavy smokers by adult standards. The age at which each stage takes place and the progression from one stage to the next can vary from one culture to another.

Studies on the characteristics that distinguish smokers from non-smokers have found four patterns. First, smoking is more common in children whose parents smoke and in children who have older brothers or sisters who smoke. Second is a pattern of low achievement; smoking is more common among children who do less well at school and set themselves lower goals than among children who do well in school and set themselves higher goals. Third is a pattern of peer group influence; smokers tend to associate with other smokers. Finally, there is some misconception that smoking for some children is a symbol of independence.

Questions 33 to 35 are based on the passage you have just heard.

33. Which of the following statements is true about young smokers?
34. In which stage do young smokers have cigarettes on them?
35. According to the studies on smokers and non-smokers, which of the following statements is NOT true?

Section C

Directions: *In this section, you will hear a passage three times. When the passage is read for the first time, you should listen carefully for its general idea. When the passage is read for the second time, you are required to fill in the blanks numbered from 36 to 43 with the exact words you have just heard. For blanks numbered from 44 to 46 you are required to fill in the missing information. For these blanks, you can either use the exact words you have just heard or write down the main points in your own words. Finally, when the passage is read for the third time, you should check what you have written.*

A study of facts and figures on development demonstrates that China has made remarkable social progress in a range of significant areas. China feeds 22 percent of the world's population with only 7 percent of the world's farmland. Nutrition has improved greatly for both urban and rural residents. The Chinese government has taken a series of measures to eliminate or reduce poverty. Educational developments have liberated millions of Chinese people from ignorance and illiteracy. In 1986, China instituted 9 years of compulsory schooling with the result that by 1993, school enrolment had reached 97.7 percent. The state has put strict controls on industrial pollution in an effort to improve the overall urban environment. Ecological methods of farming are promoted and forest coverage has increased. China is taking measures to keep its labour force fully employed so that the urban employment rate has remained between 2 and 3 percent. China is also working toward the goal of health care for everyone. There have been reforms in the social security system which aim to provide necessary facilities and services for homeless children, senior citizens, unemployed and disabled people.

Practice Test 5

Section A

Directions: *In this section, you will hear 8 short conversations and 2 long conversations. At the end of each conversation, one or more questions will be asked about what was said. Both the conversation and the questions will be spoken only once. After each question there will be a pause. During the pause, you must read the four choices marked A), B), C) and D), and decide which is the best answer. Then mark the corresponding letter on* **Answer Sheet 2** *with a single line through the center.*

11. M: Do you know that professor? I heard once he was so lost in thought that he missed his stop.

    W: Do you mean that one? It didn't happen to him for the first time.

    Q: What can we learn from the conversation?

12. W: You are 15 minutes late for the meeting. Why didn't you drive your car but take a bus?

    M: The driveway was blocked by an illegally parked car.

    Q: What can we learn from the conversation?

13. M: If these treatments don't help you by Friday, come in and we'll try something else.

    W: I hope I needn't come. But if so, I will. A million thanks.

    Q: Where does the conversation most probably take place?

14. W: So many people were absent from yesterday's conference. It was held at weekend in a distant city. What about Mary?

    M: She couldn't have gone had her boss not paid her way.

    Q: What does the man mean?

15. M: What about Jeff after getting out of prison?

    W: He was able to prove that he was innocent of the crime of which he was convicted.

    Q: What can we learn from the conversation?

16. W: I've stayed up for several nights. But I don't see how I could possibly pass the history exam.

    M: Are you serious?

    Q: What does the man imply?

17. M: I found myself out of coins when I picked up the receiver. Do you have any?

W: I don't have any either. I put several in the slot machine for a cup of coffee.

Q: What is the man going to do?

18. M: My friend has told me you offer first-class service at a reasonable price. Can you tell me when the shop is open?

W: We stay open from 10 till 8 on Sundays, from 8 till 12 on weekdays, and from 8 till 6 on Saturdays.

Q: When does the shop close on Tuesday?

Now you'll hear two long conversations.

Conversation One

M: Phyllis, it's so nice to have you here with us today. I know our studio audience is as excited as I am. So I understand you have a new film out. What can you tell us about that?

W: That's right, and I'm just thrilled about it. I think it's some of my best work yet. The film is a political thriller about the attempts of a young journalist to expose corruption in the federal government. I play a congressional aide torn between loyalty to my boss, the senator, and my ideals, which of course leads me to want to expose all the wrongdoings that he's involved in.

M: Wow! And I heard you had a very close relationship with your costar, Grant Chase, who plays the journalist in this film.

W: Grant and I had a wonderful working relationship. I think anyone would be privileged to costar with him in a film. He's a very talented actor.

M: Oh, come on, Phyllis, rumor has it that there's much more to your relationship than just the professional. Isn't it a fact that your marriage broke up during filming?

W: My husband and I are working through a difficult time right now. I'm not sure that the film had anything to do with it. And to get back to the film, I'm particularly excited about the final courtroom scene. I think it has some of the most suspenseful moments we've had on the screen in recent years.

M: Speaking of suspenseful moments, can you comment on the recent police interview with your son, Jarrad, who was allegedly caught selling drugs to other boys at his prep school?

W: Jarrad is a very sensitive boy, and it's not easy being the son of a celebrity. I'm sure you feel as strongly as I do that Jarrad's well-being should be protected at this delicate time.

Question 19 to 21 are based on the conversation you have just heard.

19. What did Phyllis play in the new film?

20. What did Phyllis say about her and her husband?

21. Which of the following statement is NOT true?

Conversation Two

M: Good morning. Robert Potter speaking.

W: Good morning. My name's Julian Harris and I have a friend in Spain who's interested in applying for a place at one of the colleges. There are one or two questions which she'd like me to ask you.

M: Go ahead, please.

W: Thanks. The first one is: What language is used for normal lessons?

M: Well, the main language of instruction in all the colleges is English. But at Pacific College in Canada some subjects are taught in French, and at the College of the Adriatic some may be taught in Italian.

W: Right. Her next question is about fees. Is it expensive to go to one of the colleges?

M: Students' parents don't have to be rich, if that's what you mean. There are scholarships for all colleges, but we do ask parents to help by paying what they can afford.

W: Good. She'll be glad to hear that. Now she wants to know something about getting into a college. Does she have to get high marks in her examinations?

M: Ah, yes, well, she will have to do well, but academic ability is not the only thing that's important. We also look at personal qualities.

W: What sort of things do you mean?

M: Maturity, the ability to get on well with people from different countries, that sort of things.

W: Of course. I understand what you mean. Her last question is about her other interests. Can she do painting and modern dancing, for example?

M: Yes, probably. It depends on the staff at the college she enters. Each college has its own special activities, such as theatre studies or environmental work, in which students can take part.

W: Good. I think that's all. Thank you very much for your help.

M: You're welcome. I hope your friend sends in an application.

W: I'm sure she will. Thanks again, Goodbye.

M: Goodbye.

Questions 22 to 25 are based on the conversation you have just heard.

22. Which of the following statements is true?

23. What should students' parents do?

24. What will NOT be considered by a college when it makes decision of whether or

not to admit a student?

25. What do the special activities of each college depend on?

Section B

Directions: *In this section, you will hear 3 short passages. At the end of each passage, you will hear some questions. Both the passage and the questions will be spoken only once. After you hear a question, you must choose the best answer from the four choices marked A), B), C) and D). Then mark the corresponding letter on **Answer Sheet 2** with a single line through the center.*

Passage One

Possession and use of guns are far more limited, and regulation far more strict, in major industrial societies other than the United States, according to a survey by *Washington Post* journalists.

In Japan, a buyer would have to get permission to own the weapon, and this is granted only after a strict background check. In Spain, where controls are even more severe, the licenses must be renewed each year. In Britain, almost no licenses can be given for private possession of a gun. The licenses that are given generally are limited to the protection of property. In Germany, a person seeking to purchase a weapon not only must prove a specific need, but also must prove experience or training in the use of guns and take a special examination in the presence of a police officer. The Japanese go one step further: they also control possession of swords with blades longer than 15 centimeters.

The Canadian experience of vastly lower figures for violent crimes and for crimes involving guns is reflected elsewhere in the industrialized world, although sociologists rather doubt drawing a direct relationship between lower figures for violent crimes and laws controlling guns.

In almost every country surveyed, illegal possession of guns is punishable by a one-to-three-year sentence and in some cases up to six years. Illegal sales of guns also carry strict penalties, ranging up to five years' imprisonment.

Questions 26 to 29 are based on the passage you have just heard.

26. In which country must the licenses be renewed each year?
27. Which of the following is NOT necessary for people seeking to purchase a weapon in Germany?
28. According to the speaker, which of the following statements is NOT true?
29. What is the maximum sentence for illegal sales of guns?

Passage Two

A new study conducted among 110,000 American adults has once again shown several factors that are associated with a greatly increased risk of death and disability from heart disease.

The study reported that men and women who smoke cigarettes face twice the risk of suffering a first heart attack as do non-smokers.

Men who are classified as "most active" showed no advantage in terms of heart attack rate over men considered "moderately active". Men who are "least active", both on and off the job, are twice as likely as "moderately active" men to suffer a first heart attack. The study didn't show that other differences between active and inactive men, such as the amount they smoke, could account for their different heart attack rates.

The heavier men in the study had a 50 percent greater risk of suffering a first heart attack than the lighter-weight men. An increased risk was also found among women who had gained a lot of weight since age 25. None of the differences in risk could be explained on the basis of variations in exercise habits.

The incidence of heart attacks was also found to be higher among white men than among non-whites and among Jewish men than among Christians. But the heart attack rate among Jewish women was not markedly different from that among non-Jewish women.

Questions 30 to 32 are based on the passage you have just heard.

30. Who is most likely to have a heart attack?
31. Which of the following statements is NOT true?
32. Which of the following does not affect the incidence of a heart attack?

Passage Three

Good afternoon and thank you for your kind introduction. I should like to begin by stating that I first became interested in domestic violence for very practical reasons. I was married for 3 years to a man who regularly beat me up. I couldn't believe it was happening to me and I was shocked to realize that my immediate response was to pretend everything was fine. My close friends slowly began to realize that something was dreadfully wrong when I started appearing with black eyes and bruises so often that they knew I was lying when I said I'd fallen down or knocked my head against something. With their help, I realized I had to stop feeling that the violence was my fault and I should do something about it. Ending my marriage was very difficult but I learned a lot from the whole experience.

The problems experienced within a marriage are by no means restricted to husbands and wives. According to a recent survey in Britain, children may suffer long term trauma as a result of exposure to domestic violence. Children who grow up in violent households are likely to develop sleeping problems, become anxious or withdrawn. Consequently, many will find it very difficult to form close, trusting relationships.

3 out of 4 women who responded to the survey said their children witnessed violent incidents at home. 60% of the children had actually seen their mothers being beaten and a disturbing 13% of children had been present while their mothers were raped. It's hardly surprising that these children develop bed-wetting problems and behave violently.

Questions 33 to 35 are based on the passage you have just heard.

33. What's the speaker's first response to the violent attacks by her husband?

34. Which of the following is NOT mentioned as problems of children growing in violent households?

35. According to the survey, how many children see their mothers being raped?

Section C

Directions: *In this section, you will hear a passage three times. When the passage is read for the first time, you should listen carefully for its general idea. When the passage is read for the second time, you are required to fill in the blanks numbered from 36 to 43 with the exact words you have just heard. For blanks numbered from 44 to 46 you are required to fill in the missing information. For these blanks, you can either use the exact words you have just heard or write down the main points in your own words. Finally, when the passage is read for the third time, you should check what you have written.*

Western attitudes towards the societies of East Asia are a sad reflection of an inability to appreciate the economic achievements and prosperity of Japan, South Korea, Singapore, and, more recently, China. No impartial observer can deny that Asian models of economic and political development are proving successful. Impressive rates of economic growth have been achieved in at least some East Asian societies. The resulting standard of health care and education is superior to that of many western countries. In addition, social stability is frequently combined with these East Asian economic success stories. Asian models of political and economic development draw on their cultural tradition. However, there is still a widespread belief that success for Asian societies is dependent on their adoption of Western values and institutions. For many people in the West, their Western ideals and practices have universal authority.

They appear to overlook the fact that their societies frequently demonstrate features which are far from desirable. Crimes against poverty in Britain are very common. Over 1 million U.S. citizens are currently being kept in prison. The time has surely come for Western leaders to consider what might be learned from Asian examples and to reflect on the fact that Asian models have never claimed the sort of universal authority which Western models claim for themselves.

Practice Test 6

Section A

Directions: *In this section, you will hear 8 short conversations and 2 long conversations. At the end of each conversation, one or more questions will be asked about what was said. Both the conversation and the questions will be spoken only once. After each question there will be a pause. During the pause, you must read the four choices marked A), B), C) and D), and decide which is the best answer. Then mark the corresponding letter on **Answer Sheet 2** with a single line through the center.*

11. W: I'm tired of Paul's radical comments. He is always exaggerating the worsening of the situation.

    M: If I were you, I would take what he said with a grain of salt.

    Q: What does the man suggest?

12. W: Tom, you see, I am busy with my project, and the deadline is coming. Don't you have to turn the radio so loudly?

    M: Oh, I am sorry. I didn't realize you are busy.

    Q: What will the man do?

13. W: Have you run into any objection during the trial of the new project?

    M: I haven't started it yet.

    Q: What can we know from the conversation?

14. W: I am trying to find out how the washing machine works. The manual is in Japanese.

    M: Maybe you can send the clothes to the laundry.

    Q: What does the man suggest?

15. W: Have you had your holiday to Australia with your wife yet?

    M: Oh, she wasn't able to get time off.

    Q: What does the man mean?

16. W: I hear you got lost on the way to the stadium.

    M: I don't know how I did it. I have been there a thousand times.

    Q: What does the man mean?

17. W: I'd better tell Jane the speech contest is put off till next week.

    M: Why bother? You will see her at lunch.

    Q: What does the man suggest?

18. W: Don't forget to bring your dictionary.

M: Oh, the reading course is cancelled.

Q: What does the man imply?

Now you'll hear two long conversations.

Conversation One

M: Er ... good morning. I bought this box of computer paper last week but it's not the right size — it should be A4.

W: Oh, sorry about that. Um ... it says A4 on the box.

M: Oh, yes I know, but ... here ... if look inside you'll see: it's a smaller size.

W: Oh, yeah so it is. I'm very sorry. I'll get you another box.

M: All right. Thanks.

W: I am very sorry but we haven't got another box in stock.

M: Oh, no!

W: I am sorry about that. If you like, I will call our other branch to see if they have any.

M: oh, no, don't bother. Um ... I'd prefer a refund.

W: Of course. That's 11.95 ... Here you are. Sorry about that.

M: That's all right. Thank you all the same.

Question 19 to 21 are based on the conversation you have just heard.

19. What happened to the man?
20. Which of the following statements is true?
21. What is true about the price mentioned in the conversation?

Conversation Two

M: What do you think of this advertisement?

W: Mm, I quite like it.

M: So do I. It makes the product seem sort of likable, doesn't it?

W: Mm, it's an advertisement of three products really: hotel and restaurant guides, guidebooks of places to see and maps.

M: I like the way the nice pale colors catch your attention — and the smiling Michelin man looking straight at you makes you want to step into the countryside — even thought it's only a drawing. It has a nostalgic, old-fashioned look and that makes you interested in reading the text.

W: That's right. And when you read the text you find the selling points of each of the three products. It makes them all seem very desirable.

M: What kind of people is this message directed at, do you think?

W: Well, I suppose motorists and tourists, people who stay in hotels or eat in restaurants.

M: Yes, and what seems to be the Unique Selling Proposition of products, according to the ad?

W: It's actually different for each product. The red guides list more hotels and restaurants than their competitors. The green guides use a star system to rate places of interest.

M: Yes. It also says the three products are cross-referenced, which means they can be used together easily.

W: You are right.

Questions 22 to 25 are based on the conversation you have just heard.

22. What do the man and woman think of the advertisement mentioned above?
23. What does this advertisement speak for?
24. What kind of people is this advertisement directed at?
25. What seems to be the Unique Selling Proposition of the products, according to the ad?

Section B

Directions: *In this section, you will hear 3 short passages. At the end of each passage, you will hear some questions. Both the passage and the questions will be spoken only once. After you hear a question, you must choose the best answer from the four choices marked A), B), C) and D). Then mark the corresponding letter on Answer Sheet 2 with a single line through the center.*

Passage One

A United Nations report says significant progress in global child welfare has been achieved in the last 10 years but 10 million of the world's children still die each year from easily preventable causes. Some of the positive achievements include a 99 percent reduction in reported polio cases compared to a decade ago. More of the world's children are now attending school than ever before and there has been a 5 percent reduction in the rate of childhood malnutrition. However, the report says that about 10 million children die each year, most of them from easily preventable causes. It also takes note of the increasing number of ethnic conflicts and civil wars in the last decade, conflicts in which children are either direct targets or collateral victims.

Then, the devastation of HIV-AIDS, especially in sub-Saharan Africa, has taken a terrible toll on children. Just last year, 600,000 young people under 15 were infected with HIV and there are now an estimated 13 million AIDS orphans. But Carol Bellamy, Director of UNICEF, the United Nations Children's Fund, says as bad as the situation looks, there is now some reason for hope. "If there is good news in sub-Saharan Africa, it is what I would call the 'conspiracy of silence' has been broken and at least there is now a much broader mobilization of efforts to confront HIV-AIDS," she says. However, Ms. Bellamy cautioned that HIV-AIDS should not be viewed as an "African issue". She said there are still other parts of the world where HIV infection is considered shameful, hampering efforts to deal with it realistically. The problems relating to HIV-AIDS and children will be one of the major topics later this month when the U.N. General Assembly holds a special session on the disease.

Questions 26 to 28 are based on the passage you have just heard.

26. What is the main idea of this passage?
27. In which aspect have some achievements been made for children's welfare according to this passage?
28. Which of the following statements is NOT true according to the passage?

Passage Two

North Korea's famine, poverty and other problems have brought the nation's health care system near collapse and sharply boosted the mortality rates. The U.N.'s top health official talked with reporters in Beijing about her trip to North Korea in the last week. The head of the World Health Organization, Gro-Harlem-Brundtland, says malaria has infected up to 300,000 North Koreans, with tuberculosis striking tens of thousands more. And North Korean medical facilities do not have the means to treat many of the infected. Dr. Brundtland brought a delivery of medication to North Korea that will make it possible to treat thousands of victims. Malaria was once nearly eliminated in North Korea, but years of famine, natural disaster, and economic mismanagement have allowed the scourge to reappear along border areas with China and South Korea. Dr. Brundtland says the diseases are one reason the death rate for North Koreans has risen about 35 percent in recent years. The U.N. health chief urged North Korea's foreign and health ministers to spend more money on health care, but acknowledged the international community will have to step in with millions of dollars to make a difference. "These are not overdone appeals and it is no way more than needed, so that is a challenge," she said during her trip to North Korea, Dr. Brundtland opened the U.N. World Health Organization's first permanent office in Pyongyang.

Questions 29 to 31 are based on the passage you have just heard.

29. What kind of disease has reappeared in North Korea?
30. Which has NOT been mentioned in this passage as having a bad effect on North

Korea's health care system?

31. Which of the following statements is NOT true according to the passage?

Passage Three

U. S. astronauts are installing a new exterior passageway on the International Space Station, giving the outpost a door for spacewalkers. The task requires two shuttle crewmen outside in the vacuum of space.

Today's installation of a pressurized vestibule is the main event of this weeklong joint mission. Two spacewalkers and the robot arms of both spacecrafts are involved in the maneuver to transport it from the visiting U. S. shuttle Atlantis and mount it on the station. The new station arm then will go to work for the first time, lifting the passage way out of the shuttle's cargo bay and moving it to the outpost. Astronauts Mike Gernhardt and Jim Reilly are riding the Atlantis crane to disconnect and reconnect cables and other hardware on the unit. The job will be completed after two more space walks later this week when the two crewmen attach the oxygen and nitrogen canisters that will pressurize the chamber.

The work will give the station a portal to space from which future spacewalkers will take place, to continue assembling and maintaining the outpost.

Questions 32 to 35 are based on the passage you have just heard.

32. What is the main idea of this passage?
33. Which is NOT mentioned as an advantage that this job can bring after completed?
34. What will the two astronauts do in this job?
35. When will this job be completed as planned?

Section C

Directions: *In this section, you will hear a passage three times. When the passage is read for the first time, you should listen carefully for its general idea. When the passage is read for the second time, you are required to fill in the blanks numbered from 36 to 43 with the exact words you have just heard. For blanks numbered from 44 to 46 you are required to fill in the missing information. For these blanks, you can either use the exact words you have just heard or write down the main points in your own words. Finally, when the passage is read for the third time, you should check what you have written.*

Israeli and Palestinian security officials met Friday to discuss a fragile U. S. brokered cease-fire. Both sides are accusing each other of not upholding the terms of truce.

The chiefs of the Israeli and Palestinian security services met to discuss the first 48 hours of the cease-fire, and plans to implement requirements of the agreement.

In a statement, Israeli Prime Minister Ariel Sharon said violence and acts of terrorism have not stopped, and he accused the Palestinians of failing to arrest Islamic militants. Mr. Sharon said Israel will continue to uphold the cease-fire, but adds it will "differentiate between quiet areas and those where violence is continuing."

The prime minister added if clashes continue, Israel will have no alternative but to "foil the attacks and strike at the attackers." Israeli Defense Minister Binyamin Ben Eliezer, speaking during a trip to Paris, said Israel will comply with the terms of the agreement. "We will increase the support and we will see," he said. "We have enough time to respond in a different way. We don't want to use that. We are strong enough to say and to declare we don't want to solve the problem through military means."

Israeli tanks have pulled back in several parts of the occupied territories, and the army has eased restrictions on Palestinian commercial traffic and the use of coastal waters off the Gaza Strip. The military has also reopened crossings connecting the Palestinian territories with Egypt and Jordan.

Practice Test 7

Section A

Directions: *In this section, you will hear 8 short conversations and 2 long conversations. At the end of each conversation, one or more questions will be asked about what was said. Both the conversation and the questions will be spoken only once. After each question there will be a pause. During the pause, you must read the four choices marked A), B), C) and D), and decide which is the best answer. Then mark the corresponding letter on **Answer Sheet 2** with a single line through the center.*

11. W: So what is your opinion of modern education, Bill?
    M: If you ask me, I should say it is not so satisfactory; children are sent to school when the fish are still biting.
    Q: What is the man's opinion of modern education?

12. W: What if the sports game is postponed because of rain? Does it mean I waste my money on the ticket?
    M: In that case, you will get a rain-ticket which can be used at a later date.
    Q: What does the man mean?

13. W: I used to collect rare volumes, but I hardly have time to group them.
    M: That's a pity. I always reclassify my stamps.
    Q: What can we infer from the conversation?

14. W: Would you turn down the radio? I could hardly hear what Mary is saying on the phone.
    M: Sure. I didn't realize that it had disturbed you.
    Q: What does the woman mean?

15. W: The lecture given by that famous linguistic expert sounds awful.
    M: You could have expected that. Don't you know that someone called him a quack?
    Q: What do we learn from the conversation?

16. W: 500 *yuan* for this bag? You must have got robbed.
    M: It can't be; I was told it was a real bargain.
    Q: What are they talking about?

17. W: Having been driving for 20 years, will you still be nervous sometimes during driving?
    M: In some cases, I will. Nevertheless, a driver can't be too careful.

Q: What does the man mean?

18. W: How are you getting on with your advertisement recently?

M: Oh, it is awful. Some clients think free lance means free.

Q: What does the man mean?

Now you'll hear two long conversations.

Conversation One

M: Good morning, Ms. Ross, do come in.

W: Hello, Mr. Fisher. Nice to see you.

M: Nice to see you face to face instead of on the phone. How are you?

W: Fine, thanks, very well.

M: We are just about to open a branch in New Zealand.

W: Will you be going there on your travels?

M: Oh, I am hoping to, if I can justify it to the marketing director! How is your little boy, has he started school yet?

W: He is in the second year now.

M: What, already? Doesn't time fly! Is he enjoying it?

W: Very much. It's much more fun than being at home!

M: That's great.

Question 19 to 21 are based on the conversation you have just heard.

19. What is probably the relationship between the two speakers?
20. Will the man fly to New Zealand on business?
21. What is the style of this conversation?

Conversation Two

W: David, thanks for coming.

M: You are welcome.

W: OK, I've sketched out a rough agenda, here.

M: Fine, yes, that looks as if it covers everything. And I agree that we've simply got to sort out a procedure for preventing this kind of thing happening again. We do need some guidelines.

W: I think the basic problem is one of communication. None of the things that went wrong are really any single person's fault.

M: Right, now let's talk about J. L.'s report on the trip to Germany. As you know, J. L.'s self-employed. He isn't a member of our staff. But he was traveling on our behalf and we were supposed to make all the arrangements.

W: The first problem is about finance. He complained that he'd had to pay his expenses out of his own pocket.

M: I wonder, should he have a company credit card as our salesman do?

W: Oh, that's not necessary. But we need to estimate how much he needs, say, 100 dollars, in advance for emergencies.

M: I'd say 200 dollars would be more realistic.

W: And we'll be responsible for booking and paying for the air tickets.

M: That's right. I will talk to J.L. tomorrow.

Questions 22 to 25 are based on the conversation you have just heard.

22. What might be the man's profession?
23. According to the woman, what is the root cause for last unhappy thing happening?
24. What do you know about J.L. according to the conversation?
25. What is the woman's suggestion to solve the problem?

Section B

Directions: *In this section, you will hear 3 short passages. At the end of each passage, you will hear some questions. Both the passage and the questions will be spoken only once. After you hear a question, you must choose the best answer from the four choices marked A), B), C) and D). Then mark the corresponding letter on Answer Sheet 2 with a single line through the center.*

Passage One

Not long ago, many people believed that babies only wanted food and to be kept warm and dry. Some people thought babies were not able to learn things until they were five or six months old. But doctors in the United States say babies begin learning on their first day of life. The National Institute of Child Health and Development is an American government agency. Its goal is to discover which experiences can influence healthy development in humans. Researchers at the Institute note that babies are strongly influenced by their environment. They say a baby will smile if his mother says or does something the baby likes. A baby learns to get the best care possible by smiling to please his mother or other caregivers. This is how babies learn to connect and communicate with other humans. The American researchers say this ability to learn exists in a baby even before birth. They say newborn babies can recognize and understand sounds they heard while they were still developing inside their mothers.

One study shows that babies can learn before they are born. The researchers placed a tape recorder on the stomach of a pregnant woman. Then, they played a recording of a short story. On the day the baby was born, the scientists tested to find out if the baby knew the sounds of the story he had heard while inside his mother. The researchers did this by placing a device in the mouth of the newborn baby. The baby would hear the story if he moved his mouth one way. If the baby moved his mouth the other way, he would hear a different story. The researchers say the baby clearly liked the story he heard before he was born. They say the baby would move his mouth so he could hear the story again and again. A few years ago, researchers in Britain showed one way a mother may influence the intelligence of her baby. They found that babies who are fed milk produced by their mothers might develop greater intelligence than those who are fed other kinds of milk. The British study involved 300 babies born early, before the end of the normal nine-month development period. 210 babies were fed breast milk produced by their mothers. The other 90 babies were given a liquid called formula. Formula is commonly used in place of mother's milk. The babies were too small to take the milk directly from their mother's breasts or from bottles. So, they were fed through tubes. That means the way the babies were fed did not affect the study. The babies involved in the study were given intelligence tests when they were eight years old. Those who were given breast milk did better on the tests than those who received formula. The British researchers said their study should not be considered final proof that children who are breast-fed are more intelligent. But they said the study did produce strong evidence that human milk contains fats and hormones needed for development.

Questions 26 to 28 are based on the passage you have just heard.

26. What is the major factor that will influence babies?
27. Why does the passage mention the experiment that researchers placed a device in the newborn baby's mouth?
28. Which of the following statements is true according to the passage?

Passage Two

Kenya's parliament has passed a bill to make AIDS drugs cheaper and more easily available.. The Industrial Properties Bill will allow Kenya's government to declare AIDS a national emergency and suspend the patents on essential drugs. This will allow the manufacture and importation of cheaper generic versions of AIDS medication from countries like India and Brazil. More than 2 million Kenyans are infected with the HIV virus that causes AIDS. More than 500 Kenyans die from AIDS every day. Antiretroviral drugs allow those with HIV to live longer and healthier lives by delaying the onset of full-blown AIDS. But major pharmaceutical companies hold the patents to the drugs and the prices often are well beyond the reach of those most infected, especially people in developing countries. In Kenya, the AIDS medications sell for at least 1,300 per patient per year. Most Kenyans earn less than 1 a day. The pharmaceutical companies have come under increasing international pressure to relax drug patents in the developing world so that local companies can produce them more cheaply.

On Monday, British pharmaceutical giant Glaxo Smith Kline announced it would cut prices of AIDS-fighting drugs in 63 developing countries, including all of sub-Saharan Africa. Bertha Gachui of the Kenya Coalition on Access to Essential Medicine says this is still not good enough. "They may bring down the prices, but to what level? That is the question," she said. "They still have the monopoly. Why we are fighting for this bill is because if this bill is passed there will be parallel importation. Kenya can shop around the world for the best, cheapest drug anywhere in the world. Like from Brazil, from India. That is the freedom we are looking for." Kenya is the second African country to move to change its laws to help prolong the lives of people living with HIV/AIDS. In April, international outcry forced 39 of the world's biggest drug companies to drop legal action in South Africa aimed at preventing the production and importation of generic drugs.

Questions 29 to 31 are based on the passage you have just heard.

29. Which of the following statements is NOT true about this bill according to the passage?
30. Where does Kenya intend to shop for the cheaper AIDS drug?
31. Which of the following statements is NOT true according to the passage?

Passage Three

Most people have probably never heard that opening part of Irving Berlin's "God Bless America". It speaks of gathering storm clouds and raising voices to a land that's fair. And most people who have heard it probably assume that was written just prior to World War II, since that's when it became popular. But according to Ed Jablonski, Irving Berlin's friend and colleague, "God Bless America" was written at the end of World War I for a revue called *Yip Yip Yaphank*. Yaphank was a small town close to where Irving Berlin was stationed in the Army. But "God Bless America" never made it into that revue. Mr. Jablonski said, "In 1939, the war began in Europe, and he sort of felt that it could hit us. So he dug out this song from 1918, revised the lyrics a bit, and gave the song to Kate Smith, who was a very popular singer at the time." Berlin's friend Ed Jablonski was glued to his radio for that first performance. "I remember I heard it on November 11, 1939," he said. "I was a kid in high school then. And I really loved it. It's simple. It's to the point. It's not war-mongering."

Today many actors, singers, sports figures and just ordinary people are giving generously in support of the victims of the recent terror attacks. But Mr. Jablonski recalled that this kind of generosity has a long tradition. Take, for example, Irving Berlin's royalties for "God Bless America". The Boy Scouts received support from "God Bless America" royalties. "All the royalties that came in from that song, which became one of the most popular songs in the country for years, all the income from that song went to the Boy Scouts and Girl Scouts, and people never forgot it. This guy was one of the really true patriotic Americans that I have met." Mr. Jablonski explained why he thought there was such a renewed interest in "God Bless America" at this specific time. "Of course," he said, "now it's even more memorable than before because of what happened. When something horrible happened, it's amazing how people worked together and helped each other. I've heard some wonderful things about what people are doing now. It happened after Pearl Harbor here. It happened in the Battle of Britain. And, it happened after the madmen ran into those towers." Mr. Jablonski lives in New York City and witnessed the crumbling of the towers of the World Trade Center. He added, "My daughter said she was walking along the street somewhere in Brooklyn. She was closer to the thing that I was. And, she was breathing smoke and ash. She said the whole text of the song was written on a window." Irving Berlin's "God Bless America" — a hymn to freedom, once again inspiring a nation.

Questions 32 to 35 are based on the passage you have just heard.

32. What is the main idea of the passage about the song "God Bless America"?
33. When was the song written?
34. As to the talk of Mr. Jablonski, why is there a renewed interest in this song after 9.11?
35. Which of the following statements is NOT true according to the passage?

Section C

Directions: *In this section, you will hear a passage three times. When the passage is read for the first time, you should listen carefully for its general idea. When the passage is read for the second time, you are required to fill in the blanks numbered from 36 to 43 with the exact words you have just heard. For blanks numbered from 44 to 46 you are re-quired to fill in the missing information. For these blanks, you can either use the exact words you have just heard or write down the main points in your own words. Finally, when the passage is read for the third time, you should check what you have written.*

In northern Asia, one of the worst droughts in recent memory is threatening crops, livestock and economies. A severe drought in North Korea is raising fresh fears of a serious food crisis in the already impoverished communist country.

A vast area from northwestern China, across Mongolia to the Korean peninsula has had little or no rain for the past three months with little relief in sight. In South

Korea, the current drought is the worst in almost nine decades. Serious water shortages have shut down some factories in several cities and rice farmers in the worst-hit areas say they may not be able to plant any crops at all. Earlier this week, the government sent more than 110,000 soldiers to the countryside to help desperate farmers pour water into their parched rice paddies. The situation is even more dire in North Korea. Aid organizations say the communist country is facing the worst food crisis since floods and droughts three years ago helped the poverty-stricken nation plunge into famine. Kathy Zellweger is an aid worker for Caritas in Hong Kong. "The winter wheat, barley, and early potatoes have been badly affected," she said. "Even if it rains within the next few days, experts believe that the harvest of these crops will only be about 50 percent. If it doesn't rain, all will be lost."

Practice Test 8

Section A

Directions: *In this section, you will hear 8 short conversations and 2 long conversations. At the end of each conversation, one or more questions will be asked about what was said. Both the conversation and the questions will be spoken only once. After each question there will be a pause. During the pause, you must read the four choices marked A), B), C) and D), and decide which is the best answer. Then mark the corresponding letter on **Answer Sheet 2** with a single line through the center.*

11. W: Please hold the line, Mr. Smith. Mr. White is downstairs; and he will talk to you in a minute.
    M: I am afraid I have to hang up. I don't have enough coins.
    Q: Where is the man?

12. W: A good professor should be both learned and passionate. Most of all, he should know how to communicate with students.
    M: That is too demanding. Such professors would be very rare.
    Q: What does the man mean?

13. W: Well, Mr. Smith. I want to know what I will do for the new job.
    M: You will take phone calls, arrange tickets and handle hotel reservations for our clients.
    Q: Where will the woman work?

14. W: I heard your daughter won the international chess championship this time. She is very smart, I must say.
    M: Thank you. But I don't know where she gets it.
    Q: What does the man mean?

15. W: John is the funniest person in our company. We all like him.
    M: I think I still have to get used to his sense of humor.
    Q: What does the man mean?

16. W: I want all these caps. How much should I pay you?
    M: It is 40 for each cap. And four caps make a total of 160. But today we offer a 10 percent discount.
    Q: How much should the woman pay for those caps?

17. W: Have you heard that? John's scholarship for next semester is cancelled.
    M: He deserves it. I have advised him to work harder.

Q：What is the man's attitude toward John?

18. W：Have you got the latest news? You don't have to be laid off after all.

M：Well, sometimes I think I am tired of working here.

Q：What is the man's reaction to what the woman has said?

Now you'll hear two long conversations.

Conversation One

W：Hello, can I help you?

M：Hello, this is Wong calling from Singapore. May I speak to Mrs. Cox please?

W：Oh, I am afraid Mrs. Cox is away. She has the flu and she may not be back in the office till Monday. I expect her assistant Mr. Box can help. I will see if he is in his office. Hold on a moment please ... Hello, Mr. Wong?

M：Yes.

W：I am sorry he is out just now. Can I take a message for him?

M：Yes, please. Will you tell him I won't be arriving in Melbourne until quite late this Saturday? And will Mrs. Cox still be able to meet me?

W：Right.

M：And informing Royal Hotel that I will be arriving very very late.

W：Sure.

M：Wonderful! Thank you very much.

W：You are welcome.

Questions 19 to 21 are based on the conversation you have just heard.

19. Who is Mr. Box?

20. Why does this man make this call?

21. What is the profession of the woman?

Conversation Two

W：Today we are talking to Philip Knight about the structure of Biopaints International. Philip's the general manager of the Perth factory. Philip, do you think you could tell us something about the way Biopaints is actually organized?

M：Yes, certainly. We employ about two thousand people in all in two different locations. Most people work here at our headquarters plant. And this is where we have the administrative departments, of course.

W：Well, perhaps you could say something about the departmental structure.

M：Yes, certainly, first of all we've got two factories, one here in Perth, Australia, and the other in Singapore. Lee Boon Eng is the other general manager in Singapore.

W: And you are completely independent of each other, is that right?

M: Yes, our two plants are fairly independent. I mean, I am responsible to George Harris, and we have to cooperate closely with Rosemary Broom, the Marketing Manager.

W: Mm, yeah.

M: But otherwise, as far as day-to-day running is concerned, we are pretty much left alone to get on with the job.

W: Yes, and what about the board of directors and chairman?

M: Yes, well, they are at the top, aren't they, of course? I mean, a couple of executives are directors themselves.

W: Thank you for your introduction.

M: You are welcome.

Questions 22 to 25 are based on the conversation you have just heard.

22. Who is Philip Knight?
23. Where are the two factories located respectively?
24. How do the two factories work together usually?
25. How does Philip comment the board of directors?

Section B

Directions: *In this section, you will hear 3 short passages. At the end of each passage, you will hear some questions. Both the passage and the questions will be spoken only once. After you hear a question, you must choose the best answer from the four choices marked A), B), C) and D). Then mark the corresponding letter on Answer Sheet 2 with a single line through the center.*

Passage One

The Pentagon has temporarily blocked public access to some military Internet websites following an apparent attack by a new computer virus. Pentagon computer security remains at a heightened level following detection of a new threat known as the "Code Red" worm, a type of computer virus that harms Internet servers and has the ability to spread to other systems. Pentagon spokesman, Rear Admiral Craig Quigley, says computer experts have been installing a so-called "patch" or repair program to make military systems impenetrable. Admiral Quigley says no serious harm has been done. But he describes the apparent attack as inconvenient. "We were able to catch it in the very early going," he said, "and we have no operational impact — I should say in that context of tactical military operations around the world. We have no detectable impact there. Certainly none of our classified systems were affected. But it is inconvenient."

The spokesman says the inconvenience stems from the shutdown of some military business and information-sharing links accessible to the public. Last week it was reported to have infected computers which were, in turn, instructed to flood the White House website, apparently in an effort to shut it down. Admiral Quigley says Pentagon experts have no information on the source of the threat. He also says he cannot predict how long Defense Department websites will remain closed. The National Infrastructure Protection Center operated by the Federal Bureau of Investigation (FBI) has issued a warning calling the "Code Red" bug a significant threat.

Questions 26 to 28 are based on the passage you have just heard.

26. What is the main idea of this passage?
27. What is true about this new virus according to what the Pentagon spokesman has said?
28. According to the passage, what is NOT one of the effects of the virus?

Passage Two

The Bush administration is looking at ways to grant legal status to millions of Mexicans living illegally in the United States. This is a politically explosive issue in Washington. White House spokesman Ari Fleischer says no decision is imminent. But he acknowledges a high-level administration panel is looking at the possibility of some sort of amnesty for illegal Mexican immigrants.

Mr. Fleischer says it is one of many options under review. He says for the moment the focus is on revamping a program that provides legal status for temporary workers. The White House spokesman says the notion of a review of immigration policy grew out of a meeting in February between President Bush and Mexican President Vicente Fox. He says the review panel is ready to deliver an interim report, which lists options but makes no firm recommendations. Any administration proposal to help illegal immigrants is likely to have a tough time winning Congressional support. Many conservatives in Congress, who usually ally themselves with President Bush, have vowed to fight any amnesty plan.

Questions 29 to 31 are based on the passage you have just heard.

29. Where does the notion of a review of immigration policy come from?
30. According to the White House spokesman, what is true about this proposal?
31. According to this passage, what difficult problems will such a proposal probably meet?

Passage Three

The Group of Eight summit is wrapping up in Genoa, Italy. The leaders of the world's richest industrialized nations and Russia ended their formal talks with a summit communiqué. The communiqué says all participants in the summit agree on the need to curb emissions of greenhouse gases. But they are unable to bridge the gap on the Kyoto treaty on global warming. Europeans still support it. President Bush remains firmly opposed. On other issues, however, the members of the Group of Eight stand as one. They include support for a new round of world trade talks. But as they prepare to leave Genoa, the eight heads of state and government know only too well that this summit will not be remembered for words on paper, but for the bloodshed that occurred in the streets of this Italian port city.

Tens of thousands of demonstrators massed throughout the weekend to protest the economic policies supported by the G8. A young Italian protester was killed, and hundreds of demonstrators and police were injured. As a result, there will be some changes at next year's summit. It is expected to be a relatively small affair at a mountain resort in Alberta, Canada — a remote spot where access can be easily controlled.

Questions 32 to 35 are based on the passage you have just heard.

32. In which issue has an agreement not been reached?
33. Where has this communiqué taken place?
34. What accident has happened during the period of this meeting?
35. According to this passage, what is a reason for the selection of Alberta as the place for next year's meeting?

Section C

Directions: *In this section, you will hear a passage three times. When the passage is read for the first time, you should listen carefully for its general idea. When the passage is read for the second time, you are required to fill in the blanks numbered from 36 to 43 with the exact words you have just heard. For blanks numbered from 44 to 46 you are required to fill in the missing information. For these blanks, you can either use the exact words you have just heard or write down the main points in your own words. Finally, when the passage is read for the third time, you should check what you have written.*

President Bush says Russia should not feel threatened by NATO enlargement. Speaking in Poland, the fourth stop of a five nation European tour, Mr. Bush endorsed a second wave of NATO expansion eastward. Poland was one of three former Warsaw Pact nations, along with Hungary and the Czech Republic that became NATO members two years ago. At a news conference with his Polish counterpart, Aleksander Kwasniewski, Mr. Bush praised Poland's transformation to a democracy and a market economy, saying it serves as a fine example for future members of NATO.

The President looked forward to next year's NATO summit in Prague when the alliance is expected to welcome new members, but he avoided endorsing any specific candidates. Nine former communist bloc nations are seeking entry. "My government believes NATO should expand," he said. "We believe no one should be excluded because of history or location or geography. We do not believe any nation should have a veto over who is accepted." His last point is a reference to Russian objections to extending the NATO defense umbrella, especially to the Baltic states, which were once annexed by the Soviet Union.

Practice Test 9

Section A

Directions: *In this section, you will hear 8 short conversations and 2 long conversations. At the end of each conversation, one or more questions will be asked about what was said. Both the conversation and the questions will be spoken only once. After each question there will be a pause. During the pause, you must read the four choices marked A), B), C) and D), and decide which is the best answer. Then mark the corresponding letter on **Answer Sheet 2** with a single line through the center.*

11. M: I need to attend the lecture at 11 o'clock, but I am afraid it is rush hour now.
    W: When you take the subway, you don't have to deal with the traffic.
    Q: What are they talking about?

12. M: I've planned to manage a trip to Tibet this summer and I don't want to go alone.
    W: Be sure to count me in, but I am afraid I haven't been so far away from home.
    Q: What does the woman mean?

13. M: You attended French class last term, right? What do you think of it?
    W: Well, it is completely Greek to me. I had to do the make-up exam at last.
    Q: What does the woman mean?

14. M: I would like to have a current savings account.
    W: Sure. First, fill in the form and make a small deposit.
    Q: Where does the conversation take place?

15. M: Mrs. Smith, have you seen my application form yet?
    W: To be frank, I am fully occupied by the board meeting recently before I have time to have a glance at your form.
    Q: What does the woman mean?

16. M: I can't concentrate on the study yet. Maybe I'd better take a nap first.
    W: You said a little physical exercise would help you to be more alert.
    Q: What does the woman imply?

17. M: We'd better postpone our picnic, sweetheart. The weather forecast said it is going to rain hard this afternoon.
    W: But there isn't a cloud in the sky and sometimes you can take what he said with a grain of salt.

Q: What does the woman mean?

18. M: I'm thinking about dropping my English class. I'm just not catching on.

   W: Stick with it. I did and I got through it eventually.

   Q: What can we infer from the conversation?

Now you'll hear two long conversations.

Conversation One

M: Hi, I am John.

W: Hello, this is Kate.

M: At last! When can we expect the next consignment in our warehouse?

W: Late Thursday or early Friday, depends on the traffic and the weather. When will you accept deliveries?

M: Up to 4 pm and from 7:30 am. Whose trucks are delivering the goods?

W: Two of ours, and the others are on hire from Alpha airport.

M: How many trucks will be coming?

W: Five.

M: Will they arrive all on the same day?

W: Two will set off half a day early, so they should arrive Thursday.

M: How long will it take to unload each truck?

W: About an hour. We can't unload more than two at a time.

M: What is the name of the manager who is in charge of this?

W: Mr. Ferrari.

M: What is his number?

W: 345 9800 extension 71.

M: Thank you very much.

W: You are welcome!

Questions 19 to 21 are based on the conversation you have just heard.

19. According to the conversation, when will the next consignment arrive in the warehouse?

20. Will the trucks arrive on the same day?

21. What is Mr. Ferrari's phone number?

Conversation Two

W: Good morning, Carpenter and Sons, can I help you?

M: Hello, this is John of Schreiner International.

W: Hello, John. This is Mary. What can I do for you?

M: Well, I think there may have been some ... misunderstanding about our last order.

W: Oh dear, what seems to be the problem?

M: We've just started unloading the truck and the quality of the goods doesn't appear to be Class A1, which is what we ordered.

W: Oh, dear, I'm very sorry. Let me just check this on the computer ... Er ... oh dear, yes, there has been a slip-up in our shipping department. I am very sorry, it's certainly our fault. Wh ... what would you like us to do about it?

M: Well, we can keep the goods and use them for another order of ours, if you will charge us 20% less for the load and ship us a load of Class A1 right away.

W: That sounds fair enough. Let me just check the stock position ... Yes, we can ship tomorrow morning, if that's all right.

M: Oh, yes, that will be fine.

W: Thank you very much, John. I am very sorry that happened.

Questions 22 to 25 are based on the conversation you have just heard.

22. Why does John call Mary?
23. Who should be blamed of this accident?
24. How is the problem solved?
25. What's Mary's attitude to this accident?

Section B

Directions: *In this section, you will hear 3 short passages. At the end of each passage, you will hear some questions. Both the passage and the questions will be spoken only once. After you hear a question, you must choose the best answer from the four choices marked A), B), C) and D). Then mark the corresponding letter on **Answer Sheet 2** with a single line through the center.*

Passage One

Wall Street is anticipating a weak stock market at least for the next week or two, as investors grapple with negative corporate news. The market is in a so-called "confession" period, when companies let Wall Street know if they think they will miss their profit targets for the quarter. The Dow Jones Industrial Average will start the week at 10,623, having dropped 3 percent last week. The tech-weighted NASDAQ composite will start more than 8 percent lower. The list of U.S. companies announcing lower second quarter earnings keeps getting longer. Some heavyweights are included among the corporate victims of a slower U.S. economy, and it goes beyond U.S. borders. On Friday, Nortel Networks of Canada, the world's leading supplier of telecommunications equipment, said it would take a big loss and plans to cut more jobs. Meanwhile,

U.S. manufacturing slumped in May for an eighth consecutive month. And businesses are cutting prices in the face of slower demand. Analysts say all this weight is proving too heavy for the average investor to bear.

Questions 26 to 28 are based on the passage you have just heard.

26. What is the main idea of this passage?
27. How many percent has NASDAQ composite dropped since last week?
28. According to the passage, what is not mentioned as being in depression?

Passage Two

Violinist Itzhak Perlman is among the world's most recorded and admired classical musicians. He also serves as an inspiring role model for disabled persons. When Mr. Perlman was three, he asked his parents for a violin. The next year, he contracted polio and ever since, he has had to wear braces on his legs and walk with crutches. A native of Israel, Itzhak Perlman performs about 90 concerts a year and continues to thrill audiences around the world with his intensity. "What I try to do is have a total commitment to the music and transform it for the audience," he says. "In other words, to show the audience what I feel about the music." During summer months in North America, Itzhak Perlman and his wife Toby devote their time to running a music camp for young people in Long Island, New York. Now in its sixth season, the Perlman Music Program invites 35 students from around the world.

Toby Perlman, who directs the program, says the music camp tries to provide a relaxed atmosphere for gifted, young musicians. "What happens to the early bloomer is that often the parents push, and they push [them] into the professional world," she says. "Children need to be in school and they need play dates for their friends. They need a 'normal' upbringing because later on, they will have to survive in the real world." Toby Perlman who is along with her husband teaching musicians said at some music camps in New York state.

Questions 29 to 31 are based on the passage you have just heard.

29. What are Itzhak Perlman and his wife doing in summer according to this passage?
30. Which music instrument did Itzhak Perlman first touch?
31. What does the Perlman Music Program aim for?

Passage Three

The dust has yet to settle from the ruins of New York's World Trade Center, and recovery efforts continue at the Pentagon. But, already the music world is mobilizing. Record companies have pledged donations totaling millions of dollars. Michael Jackson is assembling an all-star cast to record a benefit song. Rock acts first came to terms with war in the 1960s, when artists such as The Youngbloods spoke out against the Vietnam conflict with their 1967 hit, "Get Together". The Vietnam conflict exposed deep philosophical divisions within the United States. While many individuals expressed their opposition to U.S. involvement, others declared their unequivocal support for U.S. policies. Staff Sergeant Barry Sadler reached number one on the national charts with his 1966 hit, "From a Distance". As America entered the post-Vietnam years, it largely looked within. Pop artists of the 1970s and 1980s reflected this introspective impulse, with little focus on political subject matter. In 1991, the U.S. rallied an international coalition against the territorial ambitions of Iraqi ruler Saddam Hussein. This volatile time produced one of the modern era's most widely-heard prayers for peace: Bette Midler's rendition of "From a Distance". Written by Julie Gold, and performed by Bette Midler, "From a Distance" became perhaps the best-known song to emerge from the Gulf War era. Although written and recorded prior to the actual conflict, it was quickly adopted by listeners the world over. As Americans attempt to fathom terrorism's impact, they rally around their leaders, their families, and friends. The present sense of national resolve is perhaps best expressed in Lee Greenwood's patriotic hit from 1984, "God Bless the USA".

Questions 32 to 35 are based on the passage you have just heard.

32. When did Rock acts first relate to war?
33. Which of the following is popular for peace during the Gulf War?
34. What did pop artists of the 1970s and 1980s focus on?
35. When was "Get Together" made?

Section C

Directions: *In this section, you will hear a passage three times. When the passage is read for the first time, you should listen carefully for its general idea. When the passage is read for the second time, you are required to fill in the blanks numbered from 36 to 43 with the exact words you have just heard. For blanks numbered from 44 to 46 you are required to fill in the missing information. For these blanks, you can either use the exact words you have just heard or write down the main points in your own words. Finally, when the passage is read for the third time, you should check what you have written.*

In Peru, where corruption charges are mounting against allies of former President Alberto Fujimori, there is a videogame that pokes fun at the scandals and turns computer players into defenders of justice. But this game is also causing controversy. The hero is called "Nico Justo". He is nine years old and wears a bandanna. He has a toy gun to shoot sponge balls at politicians depicted as dragons, witches or two-headed monsters. The name of the game is "Vladigame", called after Peru's fugitive former spy chief Vladimiro Montesinos. He fled the country last year after a video showed him trying to buy support for former President Alberto Fujimori from an opposition politician. In "Vladigame", Nico the hero has to pass several levels avoiding monsters who throw bundles of cash in bribes before attempting to put Mr. Montesinos and Mr. Fujimori in jail. One of the game's creators, Sebastian Zileri from the Peruvian political magazine *Caretas*, says Nico is a model for a cleaner Peru. "We're happy to have done something to create some sort of conscience on kids because Nico represents in some way the normal kid here in Peru who sees his interests as a boy being affected by the situation how these people left the country," he says.

Practice Test 10

Section A

Directions: *In this section, you will hear 8 short conversations and 2 long conversations. At the end of each conversation, one or more questions will be asked about what was said. Both the conversation and the questions will be spoken only once. After each question there will be a pause. During the pause, you must read the four choices marked A), B), C) and D), and decide which is the best answer. Then mark the corresponding letter on **Answer Sheet 2** with a single line through the center.*

11. W: Who is the guy doing the Beetle impression?
    M: Oh, that's Peter. He is the life of the party.
    Q: What do we know from the man's answer?

12. W: I heard you lost your watch in the supermarket. Did you try to find it?
    M: Yeah, I did, but it is like looking for a needle in a haystack.
    Q: What does the man imply?

13. W: I am exhausted. I have been working on the schedule day and night.
    M: I know. I will give you three days off as a reward after you finish.
    Q: What is the probable relationship between the two speakers?

14. W: You look pale recently. What's the matter with you?
    M: It's a number of things. One is that I toss about all night.
    Q: What is one of the man's problems?

15. W: Fill out these forms and I will get you a passbook. How much do you wish to deposit?
    M: One thousand dollars. Can I withdraw them at any time?
    Q: Where do you think the conversation takes place?

16. W: I'd like to have these prescriptions filled, please.
    M: Certainly, if you will wait a few minutes.
    Q: What does the woman want to do?

17. W: I am going to South Korea in September, that's for sure. Where do you intend to go this year?
    M: My wife keeps urging me to take her to Norway. We are going there in August.
    Q: When will the woman go to South Korea?

18. W: The strike of taxi drivers has lasted for three weeks. Do you think it will end soon?

   M: So far as I know, the talks between the management side and the union representatives have made progress.

   Q: What does the man think of the strike?

Now you'll hear two long conversations.

Conversation One

M: Hotel Concorde.

W: Good morning. My name is Vera. I'd like to book some accommodation for tomorrow for five nights.

M: April 1st to 5th. Just one moment, madam. We are rather full at the moment, because of the trade fair. What kind of rooms would you like?

W: I'd like three single rooms, all on the same floor.

M: I have three double rooms but not three single rooms available, sorry.

W: What's the difference in price?

M: Single rooms are 400 francs, doubles are 700 francs.

W: I see. Now, one of the guests is in a wheelchair. Are these rooms accessible by wheelchair?

M: Ah, no, madam. The lift goes to the fifth floor only. In this case you could have three rooms on the ground floor, one single and two doubles. No view of the city, but close to the garden.

W: That's fine.

M: Can I have your telephone number please.

W: Yes, it's 41223489.

Questions 19 to 21 are based on the conversation you have just heard.

19. How long will the woman stay in the hotel?

20. How much will the woman pay if she books two singles and three doubles?

21. What rooms does the woman most probably have at last?

Conversation Two

M: Good morning, miss ...

W: Miss Jones. Good morning.

M: Miss Jones, yes, right. Hi, now, you'd like to join our team, I guess.

W: Yes, I would.

M: That's very good. I'd like to know a little bit about you. Perhaps you could tell me a bit about your education.

W: Oh yes, right. I left school at 18 and for the first two years I went to Gibsons, you might know them, they are an engineering firm.

M: Ah, yes, right. That's very interesting, Miss Jones. I'd like to know, do you have any specialties besides your major?

W: Er, I am quite fluent in French and Italian.

M: Italian? That might be very useful. Now tell me a little bit about the work you are doing at present.

W: Well, I've been working in Europa Marketing since my graduation. It is a marketing and public relations company.

M: Yes, I've heard of it. Er, I am curious why you leave Europa and join our company.

W: I know Europa is a great company. I feel I would have more scope and opportunity in your company and the work would be more challenging to me.

M: Yes, good, nice to have talked with you. Thanks for coming here.

W: Thank you very much.

Questions 22 to 25 are based on the conversation you have just heard.

22. What is the relationship between the two speakers?
23. Does the woman have any working experience before?
24. What is the woman's specialty besides her major?
25. According to the woman, why does she want to work here?

Section B

Directions: *In this section, you will hear 3 short passages. At the end of each passage, you will hear some questions. Both the passage and the questions will be spoken only once. After you hear a question, you must choose the best answer from the four choices marked A), B), C) and D). Then mark the corresponding letter on **Answer Sheet 2** with a single line through the center.*

Passage One

In 1992, 14.5% of the American population lived below the official poverty line. Poverty and homelessness are obvious on the streets of big cities in North America and worldwide. For example, millions of rural Brazilians have migrated to urban towns. Abandoned children camp in the streets, bathe in fountains, beg, rob, and scavenge like their homeless counterparts in North America. Homelessness in North America is an extreme form of downward mobility, which may follow job loss, layoffs, or situations in which women and children suffer from domestic abuse. The causes of homelessness are varied — psychological, economic, and social. They include inability to pay rent, sale of urban real estate to developers, and mental illness. The homeless are poorly clad urban nomads, shaggy men and bag ladies who carry their meager possessions with them as they move.

Today's most extreme socioeconomic contrasts within the world capitalist economy are between the richest people in core nations and the poorest people on the periphery.

Questions 26 to 29 are based on the passage you have just heard.

26. How many people lived below the official poverty line, according to the passage?
27. What are the causes for homelessness mentioned in the passage?
28. What are the most extreme socioeconomic contrasts within the capitalist economy?
29. What is the main topic of the passage?

Passage Two

When Playwright Eugene O'Neill in 1941 inscribed the work to his wife Carlotta, he called it "this play of old sorrow, written in tears and blood". So personal and painful were its harsh, acid scenes that O'Neill withheld publication or performance until after his death. As he lay dying, he asked that the first performance of his last play be given in Sweden, where his popularity was always greater than it was in the U.S. Last week, two years after his death and 15 years after the play's birth, O'Neill's wish was fulfilled. *Long Day's Journey into Night* had its world premiere at Stockholm's Royal Dramatic Theatre. A dazzling audience of Sweden's artistic, social and political celebrities packed the theatre. They sat down to witness a trying spectacle, as demanding on the audience as on the cast. *Long Day's* is less a drama than a dramatized autobiography. Its four long acts take four and a half hours to perform. There is no plot, no story, no anecdote, nothing to relieve the dark, brooding atmosphere of tragedy.

As the curtain fell, the audience rose and applauded for almost half an hour. Critical reaction ranged from "One of the most powerful realistic dramas written in this century" to "The most gripping picture of hell that has ever been seen in the theatre."

Questions 30 to 32 are based on the passage you have just heard.

30. When was *Long Day's Journey into Night* first performed on stage?
31. Where was *Long Day's* first performed?
32. What is true about *Long Day's* according to what you hear?

Passage Three

Mrs. Marion duMont, 55, was not seriously ill when she checked into Newton Wellesley hospital of Newton, Mass. one day last week. She was to be X-rayed for backache the next day, so it seemed convenient to check in and get a good rest the night before. Mrs. duMont and her husband had hardly settled down for a chat when a nurse came in, started to give Mrs. duMont an injection, then discovered that she had the wrong patient. Another nurse entered with a jigger of medicine and a glass of water. "How do you know this is right?" Robert duMont asked. "You've got to trust someone," said his wife, and gulped it down. An instant later Mrs. duMont blanched, tried to speak but could not. Her lips turned blue. Minutes later she was dead. A few doors away, at almost the same time, Gordon M. McMullin, 53, died in the same way. Quick autopsies showed that both patients had been dosed with sodium nitrite, a powerful poison used as a hospital cleansing agent, instead of sodium phosphate, a mild cathartic. Shocked hospital authorities refused to explain the matter until they had made an investigation, but the district attorney's office, opening a full-scale inquiry, indicated that an employee of the hospital pharmacy had been temporarily transferred to other work. He apparently had reached for the wrong container.

Questions 33 to 35 are based on the passage you have just heard.

33. How did Mrs. duMont die?
34. What was the attitude of the hospital authorities towards those accidents?
35. What was implied about the attitude of the district attorney's office according to the passage?

Section C

Directions: *In this section, you will hear a passage three times. When the passage is read for the first time, you should listen carefully for its general idea. When the passage is read for the second time, you are required to fill in the blanks numbered from 36 to 43 with the exact words you have just heard. For blanks numbered from 44 to 46 you are required to fill in the missing information. For these blanks, you can either use the exact words you have just heard or write down the main points in your own words. Finally, when the passage is read for the third time, you should check what you have written.*

The nuclear family is one kind of kin group that is widespread in human societies. Other kin groups include extended families (families consisting of three generations and/or of multiple adult siblings and their children) and descent groups — lineages and clans. Descent groups, which are composed of people claiming common ancestry, are basic units in the social organization of non-industrial food producers. There are important differences between nuclear families and descent groups. A descent group is permanent; a nuclear family lasts only as long as the parents and children remain together. Descent group membership is often ascribed at birth (by a rule of patrilineal or matrilineal descent) and is lifelong. In contrast, most people belong to at least two nuclear families at different times in their lives. They are born into a family consisting of their parents and siblings. When they reach adulthood, they may marry and establish a nuclear family that includes the spouse and eventually the children. Since most societies permit divorce, some people establish more than one family through marriage.